Secrets of the Last Castle

Visit us at www.boldstrokesbooks.com

By the Author

Sins of Our Fathers

Secrets of the Last Castle

SECRETS OF THE LAST CASTLE

by

A. Rose Mathieu

2018

SECRETS OF THE LAST CASTLE

ISBN 13: 978-1-63555-240-9

This Trade Paperback Original Is Published By
Bold Strokes Books, Inc.
P.O. Box 249
Valley Falls, NY 12185

First Edition: August 2018

CREDITS
EDITOR: CINDY CRESAP
PRODUCTION DESIGN: SUSAN RAMUNDO
COVER DESIGN BY MELODY POND

Acknowledgments

Always thankful to my loving family for allowing me the time to write and read my stories aloud as my characters and their dialogue make their way to the page. I am also thankful to my editor, Cindy Cresap, for being a reliable guide through the writing process.

Dedication

In loving memory of Ann Elizabeth Mathieu for the faith, love, and joy that she brought into this world.

PROLOGUE

Samuel hummed a soft tune as he hunched over the worn wooden stairs that led to the small porch and drove a final nail into the loose step in hopes of securing its wobbling state. He inspected his work and moved up and down the stairs a few times, testing their strength, and was reasonably certain that they would withstand another decade or more of use, not that he was expecting any guests for the dilapidated wooden shack.

With the late afternoon sun at his back, he wiped the sweat from his brow with the sleeve of his shirt and stepped back to look around the expansive property, planning his next project. He had given his life to this land, and it was all he really knew.

"Samuel."

He knew she was coming, but hearing her smooth, Southern inflection made him shiver; time had not diminished her effect on him. He turned and could only stare at her soft oval face, features that he had memorized. She was still as beautiful as the day they met.

"I've been waiting for you," he whispered as he closed the space between them and reached out to stroke her cheek.

She leaned into his touch and closed her eyes, before returning the loving stare. "You work too hard," she said, caressing his calloused hands.

He shrugged and looked past her. "This place just needs some extra attention. She's getting old."

"I know, but tomorrow is another day. Come on home. I'll cook your favorite supper."

Answering for him, his stomach grumbled, and he could already savor her gravy and cornbread. It had been a long time since he enjoyed his favorite meal.

CHAPTER ONE

The stars were not aligned for Elizabeth Campbell, as she cursed the blinking yellow light that advised drivers of construction ahead. A small oversight of failing to set her alarm had her running late already, plus she'd snagged her pantyhose on her car door in her haste. She resigned herself to the will of the traffic god and sank back into her leather seat, enjoying the moment of solitude. It seemed that her life had been thrown into a whirlwind the last few months. She had only been living back in her own home for a day, after spending two challenging months in her parents' home and under her mother's reign; however, that seemed to be the least of the sharp turns that her life had taken. A little over a week ago, she was unemployed, essentially fired from the Southern Indigent Legal Center, but was now returning as the supervising attorney. This was only after being hunted by a psychopathic priest. Yet, that was the least of it: she kissed Detective Grace Donovan.

As the traffic began to move, she was pulled from her thoughts and maneuvered her car with a sudden sense of urgency into spaces most people would assume too small for a vehicle and continued to weave her way through, until she finally arrived at her usual parking spot for her coveted Roadster. After raising the collar of her jacket in an attempt to fight off the brisk morning air, Elizabeth rushed to SILC as fast as her impractical shoes would permit. However, her pace in combination with her shoe choice was a decision she soon regretted. When her heel met with a crevice in the uneven sidewalk, the crevice won and she found herself stuck. Part of her felt like leaving the damn shoe behind, but knowing that wasn't practical, she bent and tugged on the trapped shoe until the crevice gave up its hold. As she leaned her hand on the stucco wall for extra support to return the shoe to her foot, she felt a sticky substance. She pulled back from the offending wall and looked at the new graffiti art that was on display that included a caricature of a man with a larger than life penis protruding from his pants. When she realized which body part her hand had been resting on, she shuddered at the foreign substance that was still stuck to her.

She reached her good hand into her leather messenger bag that managed to remain perched on her shoulder through the ordeal and searched for a tissue, expelling expletives in the process, but was interrupted when a small solid object was thrust into her back.

"Give me your wallet."

"What?" She wheeled around and was surprised to find a young man with his hand stuck in his pocket, holding a hidden object. His brown eyes darted wildly as he searched for witnesses. She assessed his scruffy, sandy blond hair that looked unwashed and wrinkled clothes that showed evidence of several days' wear and were wholly inappropriate for the onset of winter. After weighing her options, she allowed her bag to slip off her shoulder and drop to the ground. She reached inside and moved items about as though looking for the proverbial needle in a haystack of files, loose documents, pens, stray paper clips, and half a bag of Cheetos.

When she realized that her search was taking longer than her companion liked, she raised her index finger in a gesture, silently requesting his patience. He shifted from foot to foot, eager to be done with his task as he watched Elizabeth continue her exploration of what could only be compared to Mary Poppins's endless bag of trinkets.

"Come on, lady!" he demanded as he nervously turned his head to the sound of distant voices.

"Here it is," Elizabeth said as she reached for him and snapped a handcuff around his free hand.

"What the f—"

Before he could finish his cursing tirade, she encased her wrist with the other side of the handcuff.

"You're crazy, bitch!"

"Many would agree with you," she said as she bent to collect her bag and yanked on his arm to follow.

"I'm not going with you."

"Okay then, where should we go? Perhaps we can wander around the city, see the sights. We might attract a bit of attention being like this and all." She lifted their cuffed hands for emphasis.

"Where's the key?"

"For that, we will need to go to my office."

He sighed deeply and dropped a thick stick that he had been holding, resigning himself that he was trapped.

"So how did you know I didn't have a gun?" he asked as Elizabeth led him down the street toward SILC.

"It's a good thing for your sake that you didn't. Given how my morning is going, I might have kicked your ass and then shot you."

She remembered where her hand had been just before their encounter and shuddered, then rubbed it on his shirtsleeve in a feeble attempt to wipe off the unmentionable foreign substance.

"What are you doing?" he asked, trying to pull away and create as much space as possible between them.

"I'm just a touchy-feely person." She pulled on him to speed him along when she saw the entrance to SILC. "Come on, I'm already late."

She stopped in front of the glass door and turned to him. "Okay, let me do the talking."

He looked at her in bewilderment before she yanked him through the door.

"Morning, Amy," she said as nonchalantly as she could to SILC's receptionist who sat at the front desk. Elizabeth and Amy had become friends over the last four and a half years, so Elizabeth figured Amy would only be half surprised to see her handcuffed to a strange man.

"Ummm, should I ask?" Amy asked with a skeptical look.

"Probably best not to." Elizabeth reached into her bag and handed over her phone. "Would you do me a favor and call Detective Donovan and ask if she can bring the key to these cuffs?" She held their joined hands up in case there was any doubt as to which cuffs she meant.

"What? You said you had the key!"

"Nooo, I said we would have to go to my office. I never said I had the key."

With the misunderstanding cleared up, she strode through SILC and stopped in the kitchen to grab some sustenance for her new friend before she proceeded to her office in the back corner. Elizabeth sat in the worn black leather guest chair across from her desk and motioned for her companion to sit in the mismatched chair next to her. He resisted at first, until she set a leftover roast beef sandwich and carton of milk on the desk in front of his intended seat. As though drawn to the food, he plopped down and eagerly grabbed at it, pulling on Elizabeth's arm as he used two hands to unwrap the sandwich and shove it into his mouth. Elizabeth watched as he devoured every bit of his food and milk in a matter of moments, which told her everything she needed to know about him.

"I'm Elizabeth Campbell. What's your name?"

"Danny Johnson," he mumbled as he wiped at his mouth.

"How old are you, Danny?"

"Eighteen," he answered while staring at a candy bowl that sat at the side of her desk.

"Go ahead, help yourself."

Not needing to be told twice, he grabbed a handful of Skittles and popped them in his mouth. She was amazed at how fast he could eat.

"When was the last time you ate, Danny?"

He offered a shrug in response.

"Do you have a place to live?"

Refusing to make eye contact, he shook his head.

"You want to tell me your story?"

She could sense his mistrust, and she guessed it was a learned response.

"Maybe I can help," she said. "That's what I do. I try to help people."

"I've never done that before."

"Done what?"

"Tried to rob someone. I was just…" he choked out. "I was just hungry."

"Where are your parents?" she asked softly.

Certain that her question was going to be his undoing, she squeezed his hand and held it, and she could feel his breath quicken.

"They hate me."

"Why would you say that?"

"Because that's what they said."

Elizabeth sat quietly and tightened her grip on his hand.

"I told them I'm gay," he whispered as his lip quivered, and he began nervously playing with a small key that was intertwined into a braided rainbow-colored bracelet on his wrist.

She moved away a lock of hair that dangled in his eyes so she could get a better look at him. "I'm sorry. Your parents were wrong."

Danny lifted his head unsure if she was mocking him.

Elizabeth couldn't imagine how an eighteen-year-old could face such rejection. A moment of panic passed through her as she thought of her own parents and how they would react if she told them about Grace. However, that was a dilemma for another day, and she refocused on the hurt teenager who sat beside her and looked at her with hope that he might have found a friend.

"I'll tell you what. I could use some help around here. How about a job?" She knew the clinic's budget couldn't afford another employee after she brought on Rosa Sanchez, her last client who found herself in need of a job, but she didn't care. She would pay him out of her own salary if she had to.

He nodded in acceptance, but she could sense the weight still resting on his shoulders at his immediate predicament.

"And here." She reached into the side pocket of her bag at her feet and pulled out her wallet.

"Here is…" She counted out the cash. "Two hundred and forty dollars."

He eyed the money but hesitated. She suspected that he wasn't accustomed to being treated so nicely, especially from a woman he nearly robbed.

"Consider it an advance. It is enough to get a good meal, a motel nearby, and a new set of clothes. Oh, and a jacket," she said in an afterthought. "Be here tomorrow at nine a.m. and we'll work out the employment details and find you a more permanent place to stay. Sound like a deal?"

He offered a watery smile and graciously accepted the money, shoving it into his pocket. Elizabeth was unsure if she would ever see him again, but if not, she still thought it was money well spent.

She bent to replace the wallet in her bag, and it stuck to her hand. "Oh, this is just gross." She turned to him. "Let's go. I need to go to the bathroom."

Danny hesitated, but she gave him no choice but to follow as she dragged him out of her office behind her. Elizabeth pushed open the ladies' room door, but it swung closed on him before he could make it through, and a thud could be heard as his body made contact with the wooden surface and Elizabeth was yanked backward. She pulled open the door and eyed him. "Come on, keep up."

She turned the water on full force and rubbed vigorously, yanking Danny back and forth with each movement. Satisfied that she had removed all the slimy disgustingness, she took the opportunity to stare at her reflection in the scarred mirror and ran her hands through the front of her hair, but the cuff on their joined hands snagged her dangling earring.

"Shit," she exclaimed, as the earring catapulted through the air followed by a delicate splash sound. "No, no, no."

She dashed into the stall and dropped to her knees, bringing Danny down with her, but she was too late to rescue her earring that slid down the porcelain tunnel. After hastily pushing up her sleeve, she jammed her free hand in the toilet, and Danny looked away in disgust. As she searched for the lost artifact, the bathroom door swung open.

"Elizabeth," Amy called out. "Are you in here?"

Elizabeth held her breath and hoped she would go away, this not being a position she wanted to be caught in, but Danny's snicker gave them away. Amy rounded the corner of the stall and stood over them.

"Is there something I should know?" Amy asked accusingly with her hands on her hips.

"My earring fell in and I tried to get it out, but now I'm stuck."

"Stuck you say...interesting," Amy said as she scratched her head in fake consternation.

"Would you stop enjoying this so much and help me get out."

"Well, I was watching this nature show, and when an animal gets its leg stuck in a trap, it chews it off."

Elizabeth offered a growl in response, but Danny was rather enjoying the exchange and ineffectively hid a snicker.

"I'm not saying you should chew off your arm."

"Thank you."

"I have a nail file. I might take a while, but—"

Amy's thoughtful suggestion was interrupted by Rosa's entrance, who was followed by Grace.

Unsure of what to make of the sight, Rosa backed out of the room, still trying to adjust to the unusual American customs, leaving Grace to gawk at them.

"What the hell?" Grace asked as she tried to decipher Elizabeth's situation with one hand cuffed to a male stranger and the other stuck in a toilet. "I can't even imagine how this happened," she laughed.

Thoroughly humiliated, Elizabeth tried to use her cuffed hand to cover her face, but Danny was not willing to cooperate.

"Would you just uncuff us?" Elizabeth pleaded as Amy backed up to give Grace room and decided it was a good time to make her exit.

"Please?"

"Please," Elizabeth barked.

With a smirk firmly in place, Grace reached down and grabbed the chain between the cuffs and used the key to release its hold on them.

"Thank God," Danny murmured as he rubbed at the red mark around his wrist.

But before Danny could make his escape, Grace towered over him. "Who are you?"

"Let him be, Grace, and help me out of here."

Danny took the opportunity to scurry out of the bathroom, and Elizabeth was convinced that she would never see him again. *And who would blame him?*

Now that they were alone, Grace bent down by her ear and whispered, "If you're going to steal my cuffs, there are far more fun things to do with them."

"I didn't steal your cuffs! You left them in my office the other day." Elizabeth glared at Grace and realized that she was being played. "Are you going to help me?"

Without a word of warning, Grace reached down and yanked on her arm, freeing her captive hand.

"Ouch!" Elizabeth said in indignation at Grace's rough treatment as she examined her hand to make sure all fingers were present.

After being helped to her feet, Elizabeth walked to the sink and began washing her hands. Grace stood behind her, watching her through the mirror. Even stuck in a public toilet, she was beautiful, and an ache of longing began to grow inside. They hadn't seen each other since their kiss a few days ago. They had spoken, but Elizabeth seemed distracted, and the kiss was never mentioned, and that worried her.

With her task complete, Elizabeth regained her composure and turned to Grace, offering a soft smile. "Hi," Elizabeth whispered, and that simple word was nearly Grace's undoing. There were so many responses she had in her head, including "So about those cuffs," but instead she just stared, speechless. She wanted to reach out and push a stray strand of hair behind Elizabeth's ear, but instead she just stood frozen, uncertain.

After a moment of silence, Elizabeth turned to the door. "So, um…"

"Right, I guess you probably have to get back to work," Grace interjected, embarrassed by her behavior. She watched Elizabeth peel off her jacket with a soggy sleeve, as she exited the bathroom, and an overwhelming loss filled her. She knew she wasn't ready to let her go and followed to catch up. "So you want to tell me what this was all about?"

Elizabeth let out a quick laugh and seemed happy to have her company for a few more moments. As she went through her morning drama starting from the top with her failed alarm clock, Grace smiled at the story, but was more interested in the run in her pantyhose.

When they reached Elizabeth's office, Elizabeth settled into her chair and completed her tale as to how she came to be stuck in a toilet. The easy banter loosened Grace up, and feeling emboldened, she perched herself on Elizabeth's side of the desk, her leg brushing against Elizabeth's arm as she settled herself. Elizabeth offered a coy smile and placed her hand on Grace's knee, causing her breath to quicken as the warmth of Elizabeth's touch sent electric currents up her leg and then some.

Leaning forward, Grace whispered, "So, about those—"

"Elizabeth, Mrs. Francis is here."

Amy stood in the doorway, and Elizabeth stared at her dumbfounded, as though Amy spoke an indigenous language, and Grace winced in pain at the death grip Elizabeth now had on her knee.

"What?"

"Mrs. Francis, your ten o'clock appointment. She's been here for about fifteen minutes, but you were, uh, indisposed." Amy smirked.

"Right, will you bring her in?" Elizabeth asked with a distracted looked.

As Amy left, Grace stood and moved to the other side of the desk and leaned on the back of her guest chair.

"Sorry," Elizabeth said with a look of true regret, which warmed Grace.

"So, how about din—" Grace was interrupted by the entrance of an elderly African-American woman. *Seriously!*

"Mrs. Francis, it's good to see you again." Elizabeth stood to greet her as a younger woman entered behind her.

After accepting her offered hand, Mrs. Francis turned. "This is my granddaughter, Camille."

A fashionably dressed woman stepped forward. "Thank you for seeing us." The woman, who Grace guessed to be in her mid twenties, stood with confidence and gripped Elizabeth's hand, her caramel colored eyes never breaking contact. Camille loosened a brightly colored scarf that complemented her mocha skin, and looked around the modest office before landing her eyes on Grace and offering a small smile and nod in acknowledgement.

Grace returned a strained smile, already knowing the purpose of their visit. Although they didn't know her, she knew them, as the lead detective on the newly opened Francis case. If this meeting went as she expected, the forecast on their fledgling relationship looked gloomy, at least in the short term. Lost in thought and not noticing Elizabeth's approach, she flinched when Elizabeth placed her hand on her arm. "This is Grace Donovan."

Grace went through the perfunctory greeting process before turning to Elizabeth with a guarded look. "I have to get going. I'll call you later."

Elizabeth tried to offer her a reassuring smile, but wasn't sure that it reached her as she watched Grace walk out. *What was that about?*

She decided to save that thought for another time and turned to her guests. "Please have a seat." She rounded her desk to return to her worn black chair, lovingly named Black Devil or BD for short, and stroked its top before sitting. "So tell me what's going on?"

"It's my grandson, Jackson. He's been arrested. They say he killed a woman, but they're wrong. I know that boy; I've raised him since he was five. He wouldn't hurt anyone." Elizabeth watched Mrs. Francis as she twisted the end of her sweater as she spoke. "My son Robert, he found a lot of trouble when he was young, and it finally got him killed. Their mama was nowhere to be found. That's when they came to live with me." She gingerly patted her granddaughter's hand. "Camille was only eleven."

Mrs. Francis fell silent for a moment as she seemed to gather her thoughts. "Jackson is a good boy. He wasn't like his father.

He wants to be somebody. He graduated high school, and he was learning to be an electrician."

After waiting a respectable amount of time in silence to see if Mrs. Francis had completed her story, Elizabeth finally spoke. "So tell me about the arrest."

Mrs. Francis took a deep, fortifying breath before she continued. "He was just walking to the store. A woman was killed, but he didn't do it. He was only trying to help her." Tears filled her eyes, and Camille wrapped a comforting arm around her before reaching into Mrs. Francis's purse and extracting a manila envelope.

"This is the police report." Mrs. Francis took the envelope from Camille and held it out.

Elizabeth reached forward and accepted the envelope, and Mrs. Francis made eye contact. "You have to help him."

Elizabeth was conflicted. Although she knew little about the story, she suspected that the facts wouldn't bode well for Mrs. Francis's grandson. "I will talk to him," was all she could offer, but it seemed enough for Mrs. Francis, who nodded in appreciation.

"Thank you." Mrs. Francis stood and gathered her purse, and Camille silently followed her, but stopped before walking out the door and turned, her eyes filled with hope. "Thank you."

Elizabeth sat staring at the envelope in her hands. "This isn't going to be good."

CHAPTER TWO

Elizabeth sat quietly in the windowless room trying to ignore the incessant ticking of the clock on the bare gray wall of the detention center. Time almost seemed irrelevant in a place like this. The thick glass that separated her from "them" was deeply scratched with gang insignias and obscenities. A bang that reverberated through the confined space caused her to jerk her head to the origin of the sound. Jackson Francis stood on the inside of a heavy metal door, his head bowed, frozen in place. He tightly gripped the material of his orange pants that hung loosely on him. He remained still, and she sensed that he needed a moment to gather himself.

She rested her hands on the envelope containing the police report, which detailed how the nineteen-year-old was spotted standing at the entrance of an alley, acting suspiciously, and appeared to be holding a purse. When the police approached, he discarded the purse and ran. After apprehending him, the police returned to the alley to find an elderly woman dead with her throat cut.

When the young man finally lifted his head to acknowledge her, she offered him a small, reassuring smile, which she guessed might have been the first kind act that he had experienced since his confinement. He seemed to size her up to determine if she was friend or foe before he pushed himself forward and plopped down on the metal stool across from her. He crossed his arms in front of him, and she could see the tight grip he had on himself, as though he was afraid to let go. Elizabeth sat patiently until he lifted his head and faced her. Red streaks marred the whites of his eyes and dark rings were prominently displayed below. No words were needed to understand the toll that incarceration was having on the young man.

She grasped the phone on her left and gestured her head toward the receiver on his side. As he seemed to contemplate her request, Elizabeth glanced at the phone in her hand and wondered how many other hands had held that same phone before her. After remembering that it wasn't that long ago that she had her hand in a toilet, she shrugged it off.

When he finally lifted the receiver, she spoke first and introduced herself. "Your grandmother asked that I talk to you." He stared at her with no emotion. "I hoped we could talk about what happened."

"What do you want to know?" he said barely above a whisper.

"Why don't you tell me what happened from the beginning."

He tapped the phone against his forehead, as though considering her request.

"Please, I am only here to help." She wasn't sure why she was encouraging him. She could simply pick up her things, walk out of this dreary place, and tell Mrs. Francis that she tried, but she didn't. Instead, she sat and watched this helpless man, who appeared to be drowning in front of her. How could she walk away?

After bowing his head, he finally spoke. "I was going to the store. My grandma needed her prescription. My sister was supposed to pick it up, but she had to work late."

He paused to look at her, and she smiled, hoping to encourage him to continue.

"I was walking past this alley when there was this woman. She was standing inside the alley, next to the wall, and she stopped me— said she needed help. She was old, you know, so I thought maybe she was lost...you know, that memory thing?"

"Dementia," Elizabeth said.

"Yeah, that. So, I stepped in the alley and asked if she needed help, and she gave me her purse."

"She handed you her purse?" she asked as though she hadn't heard him correctly.

"Yes," Jackson said defensively. "She shoved it at me and told me to take it and keep it safe. She said…" He paused momentarily and looked down as though replaying the conversation in his mind. "She said it's the key to the castle and to be careful of the knights." He tightly clasped his hands in front of him. "I didn't want to take it, and it dropped to the ground. I bent to pick it up for her, but then she was just gone."

"What do you mean, gone?"

"I don't know. I looked back up, and she wasn't standing there anymore. I looked out on the street to see if she went that way and that's when the police came by."

"Then you ran?"

"Hell yeah, I ran."

"Why? If she gave you the purse, why did you run?"

"Because I'm a black man holding a white woman's purse." Jackson looked as though he was going to cry and swiped at his eyes.

Elizabeth looked away in an attempt to give him some privacy and pondered his story. She was conflicted. He told a convincing tale, yet it seemed implausible, and to clarify, she asked, "She told you to keep the purse safe and that it had a key?"

"Yes, she said it was a key to the castle and something about watch out for the knights."

"What does that mean?"

"I don't know. I assumed she was not operating on all cylinders."

"Do you remember anything else about what she said?"

"No, that was pretty much it, but…"

"But what?"

"There was something written on the outside of the purse in like a red marker."

"What was written?"

"I don't know…I just noticed it when I bent to pick it up. I didn't have time to read it," he said with a bit of sarcasm.

Elizabeth wrote down some notes and returned her attention to him. "The police went into that alley after they arrested you, and they found the woman dead with her throat cut. Do you know how that happened?"

"No. Just like I told the police, I didn't do it. She was alive when I saw her. I was just going to the store." He hung his head. "You're just like the rest of them. You think I did it."

"I didn't say that—"

"You don't have to," he interrupted. "Your face says it all. You can go tell my grandma that you did your job and you talked to me."

Without waiting for a reply, Jackson hung up the phone, pushed himself up with considerable effort, and walked back to the metal door without looking back.

Burdened by her meeting with Jackson, Elizabeth stared at the ground as she approached the front entrance of SILC. She used her shoulder to push open the glass door and nearly fell forward as Raymond Miller yanked open the door from the inside.

"Elizabeth!" he exclaimed, grabbing her in a hug, unable to contain his excitement.

She wrapped her arms around him and squeezed until he squealed in delight. She was truly happy to see him; she missed him. He had become a permanent resident of her parents' home, along with Charlie, her cat that her mother claimed to detest. When it came time to move back to her own home, she was forbidden to take the pampered gray cat.

Finally released from Raymond's grip, Elizabeth turned to her mother and offered a more dignified hug. "What brings you here?" Which was a fair question because in all her years of working at SILC, her mother had never come to visit. It seemed that there was a line that her Mercedes wouldn't cross, and SILC's side of town seemed to be on the wrong side of that line.

"We were running errands and thought we'd swing by and say hello."

Elizabeth found it unlikely that her mother was running errands anywhere near this neighborhood. "I missed you too, Mom. How about a tour?"

Her mother offered a weak smile and looked around the poor excuse of a waiting room dubiously. Nonetheless, she obediently followed Elizabeth to the heart of SILC where dutiful staff bustled about. Raymond trailed behind and touched everything in his path, and anything not bolted down was picked up for inspection.

"This is…" Her mother was at a loss for words because she was trying her best to be polite, but clearly, nothing polite came to mind. Suddenly, she brightened and walked ahead of Elizabeth, no longer in need of an escort. She opened doors and cabinets, poked her head in rooms where she didn't belong, and inspected every inch of the legal clinic, including rolling a chair away from a desk, with the chair's occupant still seated, to get a better perspective of the space. "Yes, that will work, uh-huh, tsk-tsk" were some of the phrases she muttered as she explored. Elizabeth didn't dare stop her as the SILC staff tried not to stare at the nosy lady.

When she was reasonably certain that her mother had completed poking and prodding her staff, Elizabeth approached. "What are you doing?"

"I'm going to redesign this place and make it look like a real law firm."

"Uh, no, Mom, I don't think that's such a good idea." Elizabeth could only envision her mother taking over the space.

"Don't be silly, of course it is."

"Mom, the clinic doesn't have a budget for this."

"Pshaw." She waved her off. "It's my treat."

Elizabeth knew that she should be grateful for the generous offer, but instead a pit sat in her stomach. She was sure nothing good would come of having her mother at the clinic on a regular basis. It would be only a matter of time before she started giving out legal advice.

"Excuse me, Ms. Campbell."

Elizabeth turned to find Danny standing a safe distance from her and her mother. Elizabeth was pleasantly surprised when he showed up for work the day after the bathroom adventure and equally thrilled that he proved to be a dedicated worker and valuable asset to the clinic. "Ms. Francis is in your office. I hope it's okay that I put her there. She has been waiting awhile."

"Thank you, Danny. I appreciate it." Although she was not expecting Mrs. Francis, she was not surprised by her visit either. She had informed her the day before that she planned to visit Jackson. She turned to her mom. "I have a client."

"Oh, don't worry about us. We'll see ourselves out," her mother said as she pulled Raymond along with a bounce in her step and a mission in mind.

Elizabeth closed her eyes and offered a small prayer, *Lord, give me strength*, before she strode to her office. "Mrs. Francis, it is good to see you again." She stopped abruptly inside her doorway as Camille stood and turned to face her. "I'm sorry. When they told me Ms. Francis was in my office, I assumed it was your grandmother."

"Sorry, my grandmother couldn't come. She's in the hospital."

Elizabeth approached her. "I'm sorry to hear that. Will she be all right?"

"It's her diabetes. Her blood sugar goes out of sync when she's stressed, and she hasn't been taking care of herself since, well...you know."

Elizabeth moved to BD and stroked it before she sank into the seat, guilt weighing her down. On her drive back from the detention center, she worked it out in her head how she would tell Mrs. Francis that she didn't see how she could help and would recommend a public defender.

"Did you see my brother?"

"Yes," was all Elizabeth said, still grappling with herself.

"Will you help him?"

"Ms. Francis—"

"Camille," she said.

Elizabeth looked up in to beseeching caramel-colored eyes. "Camille, I—"

She sensed the impending rejection and broke the professional demeanor and pleaded, "He didn't do it. I know my brother. I practically raised him. He wouldn't hurt anyone." Tears filled Camille's eyes as she spoke. "Please, will you help him?"

Elizabeth hesitated for a moment and knew she could give no other answer. "I will do my best."

CHAPTER THREE

It had been five years since Elizabeth had stepped foot inside a classroom, and as she watched the students settle, she was filled with a warm feeling of remembrance. *Law school wasn't so bad.* The rustling of books and papers accentuated by the students' amiable conversations made her nostalgic. There were spirited conversations; professors who liked to challenge, such as Professor Schmidt, (for inexplicable reasons, a name that Elizabeth kept forgetting to pronounce with the "m"), who got right in a student's face with his spit flying insulting every answer. She remembered when it was her turn, she took the Fifth; it was a criminal procedure class after all. Unfortunately, Professor Schmidt failed to see the humor and demanded that she leave the class, forcing her to scrounge for the remainder of the lecture notes from fellow classmates, who proved stingy. *Okay, maybe law school wasn't so great.*

"Good morning, class. I would like to introduce you to our guest, Elizabeth Campbell, Supervising Attorney at the Southern Indigent Legal Center," Professor Elena Dixon announced as she gestured toward Elizabeth, and she straightened, a bundle of nerves finding its way into her stomach. Why was she nervous? It wasn't like her entire life was staked on the grade in this class. *Okay, maybe I'm channeling too much of my law school days.*

She took a deep breath and strode toward the front of the class and stood next to the petite, middle-aged woman, who clearly had the respect of the entire class because no sound, not a paper rustle nor hushed whisper, was made the moment Professor Dixon entered the room. Elizabeth agreed to guest lecture the afternoon class on a moment's notice when she received a call from Professor Dixon, who had by chance seen her in court and thought she would make an interesting addition to her current lecture series. She wasn't sure if it was the six oranges gifted to her by her migrant worker client that gracefully spilled out of her bag and rolled across the well of the courtroom or her sneezing fit in response to opposing counsel's cologne that caught the professor's attention, but she gladly accepted the offer. SILC was running low on legal interns, and as the newly installed supervising attorney, it was her job to generate new (and free) labor. If it meant standing in front of a classroom reliving her law school days, then so be it.

Her anxieties were put at ease as the professor opened a discussion on the US Constitution. "The Founding Fathers gave us a constitution of checks and balances because they realized the inescapable lesson of history that no man or group of men can be safely entrusted with unlimited powers." Professor Dixon then posed the question whether the courts should use strict construction in interpreting the meaning of the Constitution, so that the words were taken as written with no extraneous considerations, as the late Justice Scalia argued, or loose construction, a more liberal approach that consults the current norms and ideals.

A student boldly replied that the courts had to take into consideration the events and moral beliefs of current society for it to be relevant.

"Then what value does the document have if it's subject to the whims and interpretation of a judge?" another student shot back.

"That's the question. Though there has been no constitutional amendment or act of Congress, the Supreme Court can exercise their naked judicial power and substitute their personal political and social ideals for the established law of the land." The professor paused and allowed her words to resonate before she continued. "Or is strict construction of the words suffocating the document that was written in an era that could never have conceived the world we now live in?" Professor Dixon asked.

After several minutes of polite discourse, Elizabeth felt comfortable taking the reins. She followed the professor's easy style and didn't lecture, but threw out questions and allowed an equal conversation to flow between professor and student. The students hung on her words, some of them even writing them down, a boost for her ego. When the topic turned to the current state Supreme Court that was left one justice short after the passing of its chief justice, Elizabeth sat back and let the professor take the lead. She was equally interested in hearing her take on the current state of the court, as without its seventh member, it currently stood equally divided, with three conservatives and three liberals. The late chief justice was the moderate voice and could swing either way depending on the issue.

Judge Davis Powers, the governor's nominee for the open seat, was meeting resistance by several on the left. A twenty-year veteran of the state court of appeals, he was anything but moderate. There had been several attempts to discredit the man and have him removed from the bench, but the "good ol' (white) boys club" was alive and well, and no action or comment, no matter how offensive or unethical, managed to stick. Hence, the state senate was in its second month of deliberating the appointment of Judge Powers. It didn't help that several senators were facing tough reelections as a result of redistricting, making self-preservation their primary concern. As the discussion evolved, the topic shifted to the fate of the prominent cases on the court's docket, ranging from a proposition passed by the voters that allowed businesses to deny services based on religious grounds to the Defense and Rezoning Act, better known as DARA, that was approved in a special session called by the governor. The students debated the Constitution, private liberties, and the "compelling government interest" standard, as the professor watched, nodding thoughtfully at some of the statements.

Elizabeth and many of the students were disappointed when Professor Dixon signaled that the class had come to an end. After she confirmed the reading assignments for the next class, the students filed out, several stopping on their way to collect Elizabeth's business card in hopes of interning. Mission accomplished.

❖

Grace stood with her arms crossed as she deliberately scanned the asphalt for anything that might have been missed. She crouched by the wall and peered behind a trash dumpster certain that the forensic team overlooked a piece of evidence, but was deflated to find only empty space.

"Looking for leftovers?"

Grace jumped at the voice and stood and turned. "Elizabeth, what are you doing here?"

"Oh, I don't know, I saw the alley and was in the mood for a little dumpster diving."

She ignored the quip and trailed her eyes down Elizabeth's navy suit before turning back to the dumpster. "What are you doing here?" she repeated.

"I was driving past, and I saw your car. What are you doing here?"

"My job." Grace didn't really need an answer as to why Elizabeth was here. She already knew when Mrs. Francis walked into her office that they would once again find themselves in this position.

"What are you looking for? Maybe I can help."

"You can't help; we aren't a team. Remember, I put them in jail and you get them out."

"Grace, why are you so upset?"

She couldn't answer the question because she didn't really understand it herself. How could there be a relationship if they couldn't even be on the same side?

"Grace, please, look at me." Reluctantly, she turned to face her and made eye contact. "Remember when we first met, you told me that I should spend my time representing someone who says he's innocent. Well, Jackson claims he's innocent. He needs help."

"Well, then have at it," Grace said, pointing to the dumpster. "Happy diving. I have to get to an appointment." As she started to walk away, she turned and softened. "Don't stay too long; it's getting late."

❖

Grace strode through the family restaurant with her father, arms linked, which he believed was chivalrous, but she held on for extra security in case he stumbled. As much as he physically improved after the stroke, she felt better having a hold on him. The restaurant was a place they knew well, as it was their favorite when she was a child, and he led them to their usual booth. The menu was simple and there were better places where they could dine, but memories kept them coming back.

"So, Pop, what are you having?" she asked as she lifted the plastic menus from a metal holder at the end of the table and handed one to him. The question was not a real question, as he always ate the same thing, meatloaf, but she asked more out of tradition.

Once the orders were placed, her father leaned in. "So what's going on with you?" She suspected something was on his mind because their usual restaurant visit wasn't due for another week.

"The usual, Pop. Just working a new case."

He eyed her as though knowing that there was more going on than a new case. "You want to talk about it?"

Growing up, it had only been the two of them, and they knew each other well, so she wasn't surprised that he sensed her turmoil; however, she wasn't ready to talk. As much as she loved her father, she never told him that she was gay. She never saw the reason because there was never anyone in her life worth it—until maybe now. A headache began to grow in her forehead, and she sipped at her ice water.

"You want to talk about him?" he asked.

Grace choked and nearly spit her water on him. "Him?"

"I know that look, Gracie. This is a matter of the heart."

She could only stare until the server interrupted to bring their food. As they settled in carving up their meat, she hoped the topic passed, but it didn't.

"Well?"

She treaded lightly. "Well, it's complicated."

"It always is when it's worth it."

His one-liners were about to do her in. She didn't know whether to laugh or run. She pushed forward, knowing that she wouldn't be permitted to escape. "We work together, sort of, and that makes it complicated." *Among other things.*

"Do you get along?"

She pondered that question. *Do we?* "We bicker, she…he is stubborn."

"Ah, your mother was stubborn," he reminisced. "When she had her mind set, there was no changing it." Pride was evident in his voice. As his mind returned to the present, he asked, "How do you feel when you're together?"

It's hard to breathe when we're in the same room. "Not sure."

"All right, I drilled you enough. Just know I'm here for you."

"Thanks, Pop."

CHAPTER FOUR

A nd how does the defendant plead?" the judge asked in a manner indicating that he had asked the same question countless times before.

"Not guilty." Jackson spoke loud enough so only those closest to him could hear, causing the judge to order him to repeat it. Elizabeth gave him a reassuring smile, and with his pleading complete, finished with the court formalities before Jackson was led away again out of the court.

Elizabeth approached the assistant district attorney and asked the question that had been bothering her since she received the charging document before she headed out of the court. Camille, who had been sitting in the front row, followed directly behind her.

"He looks too thin. What are they feeding him?"

Elizabeth understood her concern and offered the only response she could. "It will get easier." Although she wasn't sure that was true. She sank down onto a bench outside the courtroom and thumbed through the charging document.

"What's wrong?"

She shook her head. "It's nothing…It's just curious that the victim's name is not identified in his charging document."

"Is that unusual?"

"I honestly don't know."

Camille sat next to her and leaned in to view the court document. "It says Jane Doe." Elizabeth nodded in acknowledgement.

"I'll call someone who may know." Elizabeth reached into her bag for her phone and pushed her speed dial.

Grace stepped off the elevator in time to see Camille lean into Elizabeth. A sense of uneasiness filled her, and she jammed her hand into the closing elevator door and stepped back in. She wasn't sure why she came. She had no reason to be there. Her presence wasn't needed for the hearing, but she wanted to see Elizabeth, if only for a moment, but now she wished she had stayed at the station. Grace's phone began to ring, and she unclipped it from her belt to view the caller. Elizabeth's name appeared on her screen, and she hovered her finger over the button. Before she could decide, the call went to voice mail.

She waited until she found a quieter spot outside the courthouse before she listened to the message. "Hi, Grace, it's me. I have a question, and I know I probably shouldn't be calling you, but I don't know who else to ask." A moment of silence passed, before the message continued. "I miss you." Grace allowed her tense grip on the phone to lessen, finding a bit of comfort in the last three words.

Grace leaned back in the driver's seat with her eyes closed and relaxed her breathing. A gentle sound of crickets filled the still night air, and the peace nearly lulled her to sleep. She hadn't been sleeping well, her mind refusing to shut down. She blamed it on work, but knew that there were other thoughts that kept her awake at night.

Oncoming headlights forced her eyes open, and she pulled herself up, transitioning to full alert. She watched the car slow and pull into the paved driveway. She narrowed her eyes and peered through her passenger window in an attempt to get a better view of Elizabeth, who exited the car with plastic bags dangling from her arms. Realizing disaster was close at hand as a small tear on the bottom of a bag began to widen, Grace dashed out of her car in a heroic effort and snatched up the bag before the contents broke through and spilled.

"God, you scared me! Where did you come from?" Elizabeth asked.

Without answering the question, Grace scooped up another bag to equal out their load and headed for the front door. Elizabeth followed and juggled her remaining bags as she freed her keys from a side pocket of her messenger bag and opened the door, then allowed Grace to enter first.

Grace had only been in her home once before, but she remembered it well and headed for the kitchen.

"Where do you want these?" Grace asked, lifting the bags in a gesture. These were the first words she spoke.

"Just put them on the counter, thanks."

Elizabeth busied herself putting the groceries away as Grace leaned against the counter to watch, running her hand against the cool, smooth marble. She smiled to herself at the site of Elizabeth doing a simple domestic task. She had seen her defend the rights of the less privileged, take on the system when no one else believed, and all around kick ass when those close to her were threatened, but this was different. It was ordinary and simple, and yet it was equally wonderful. Grace shook her head. *Oh God, I'm losing it.*

With her mission complete, Elizabeth pulled down two glasses for wine and poured. "Let's go in the living room." She handed a glass over, and Grace accepted.

Elizabeth settled on her overstuffed couch, crisscrossing her legs and resting her arm on the back. Grace sat at the far end, facing forward, gripping the wine glass. She felt Elizabeth assessing her, making her even more uneasy.

"I'm glad you're here," she said, the glass perched at her lips and her eyes fixed on Grace.

"I got your message," Grace replied as though that sufficiently explained her unexpected visit and tried to keep her eyes trained on the table in front of her, instead of unabashedly staring.

Elizabeth kept her position, quietly sipping her wine and watching.

After a few moments of silence passed, Grace finally spoke. "We don't know who the victim is."

"Huh?" Elizabeth seemed as though her mind was engaged in another internal discussion.

"That's why you called me, right?" Grace turned to her. "You want to know why the name of the victim is not listed in the criminal complaint." Elizabeth nodded, and Grace continued. "I know I shouldn't be telling you this, but you'll get it all during the discovery phase anyway. The victim had no identification on her. Her prints don't match anything in our system, and no one has reported her missing."

"What about her purse?"

"It was nearly empty. There was just a hairbrush, a tube of lipstick, and a compact mirror. No wallet, no ID."

"Could it have spilled out?"

"I checked the alley myself to see if anything was missed, but nothing. How about you? Did you find anything?"

"No, but I didn't even know what I was looking for."

Having said what she came for, Grace set the full glass of wine on the table and pushed herself up with considerable effort.

"Grace, wait." Elizabeth hastily set her glass down and grabbed her arm. Grace offered little resistance and allowed herself to be guided back to the couch. No longer willing to see how things would play out on Grace's terms, Elizabeth leaned into her and brushed against her lips. A delicious shiver traveled from her mouth downward as Elizabeth's lips lingered and taunted.

Grace reached out and caressed Elizabeth's neck. She weaved her fingers into her hair and pulled her closer to deepen the kiss. Elizabeth groaned, and she desperately grasped at the back of Grace's shirt trying to find a hold.

Grace moved her mouth lower below her ear, and Elizabeth turned her head to allow her better access. Resting her hand on Elizabeth's side, she caressed her breast with her thumb. "God, Grace, I've been waiting for this."

Grace pulled back. "Wait, we can't." She stood, putting distance between them.

"What's wrong?" Elizabeth asked.

"We can't do this," Grace said, gesturing her hand back and forth between them.

Elizabeth sank back into the corner of the couch and pulled her knees to her chest, forming a protective barrier.

Grace knelt in front of her. "Honey, I'm the detective on the Francis case, and you're defending him."

"So it's my fault?" Elizabeth snapped.

"No, it's just…"

"Just what?"

"I don't have a choice what case I investigate."

"Oh, and I have a choice who I defend." Elizabeth's hurt was quickly replaced by anger.

There was truth to that statement, but Grace didn't respond because it would have made things between them even worse. Silence was her best option.

Elizabeth rose and walked to the door. "I'll show you out."

Propped up against the couch, Grace remained on her knees, rubbing her hand across her eyes and silently praying that this night would end differently. She chastised herself for coming, warning herself that nothing good would come of it, but she couldn't help it. She just wanted to see her. Realizing her mistake, she pushed herself up with great effort and walked to the door. She stopped in front of Elizabeth. "I'm sorry." Grace heard the door close behind her, but she didn't look back.

CHAPTER FIVE

G race sat at her desk, staring at the words on a crisp white paper, unable to form their meaning as the letters seemed to dance around the page. She pinched the bridge of her nose in an attempt to thwart a nagging headache. She was exhausted, but sleep eluded her. By morning, she had come up with two choices— resign or complete the Francis case. The first was not a true option because her father depended on her, so that left choice number two. By the time she reached the office, Grace convinced herself that she needed to find the identity of the old woman. She wasn't sure why because this wouldn't have been the first case where an unidentified person was killed, but this wasn't a murder in a homeless camp, and somehow finding the woman's identity seemed important; or perhaps, it was just a desperately needed distraction.

The coroner estimated the woman's age to be between seventy to seventy-five years old, which gave Grace the idea to search the archive records. Over the last year, the county had been making efforts to integrate the paper records created before the county went digital into the database, but as the efforts were still underway, Grace knew there was a significant number of records that were still not included. As such, Grace began making inquiries into the records department, archive unit, cold case unit, and any other unit that might be remotely connected to her search for any information. She realized that it was a ghost of a chance, but it was something to do.

The paper silently sitting in front of her, seemingly mocking her, offered no clue. It gave the description of a woman's white leather handbag, with gold-plated clasps at the top, and a small handle allowing it to rest on a woman's arm as she strolled. It was quietly refined and spoke of a different era. Lettering in red lipstick covered much of the outside, and based on the prints, Grace knew to be the woman's doing, but only a few of the words were legible and none of them made sense. Much of it was smeared by both the suspect's and the police's handling of the bag. If there was a message, and she wasn't convinced that there was given the impulsive nature of the murder, it was indiscernible now.

The contents were equally telling, yet had nothing to say. There was a silver hairbrush with a wide face and a quaint scene filled with trees and flowers that reminded her of the countryside etched into the back and down the slender handle. The fine hair trapped between the bristles was identified to be the old woman's. A matching silver compact mirror and lipstick tube, used to mark the outside of the purse, completed the set. That was all Grace had—no name, no identifying marks, nothing but a leather handbag and a trio of trinkets, beautiful and useless.

After the murder, police units scoured the alley and the surrounding blocks for a wallet or any other identifying piece of evidence that might have been discarded, but came up empty. Either the woman intentionally traveled light and with no identity, or someone found the wallet before the police did. Although the latter was the most plausible explanation, Grace began to believe the possibility of the first and wanted to know why.

❖

Elizabeth stared up at the ceiling, leaning back in BD as far as she dared. She began to notice images of a squirrel formed by the small holes in the yellowing, industrial ceiling tile. The more she stared at it, the more it began to look as though the squirrel was walking an alligator. It seemed that the ceiling provided as much insight into the Francis case as the notes she had in front of her. Why did she agree to take this case? By all accounts, Jackson Francis murdered a poor, elderly woman who seemed to have no family, but as terrible as that sounded, the toll this case was taking on her fledgling relationship with Grace troubled her more.

With the preliminary hearing only a day away, she spread across her desk several note cards with pertinent facts of the case, like puzzle pieces. She moved them around as if a new position would provide a new perspective, but the pieces just didn't fit—no wallet or identity, no known family, the phrases "key to the castle" and "beware of the knights," Jackson's statement that she gave him the purse, and a handful of red words written in lipstick on the outside of the purse. She resigned herself to the futility of the effort and began stacking the cards in a pile, when she froze. She grabbed at the file that was pushed to the side and began riffling through the papers, scanning her notes and police report. "It's not here."

CHAPTER SIX

"People versus Francis," the court clerk announced, and Elizabeth rose as the remainder of the case number was recited. Camille, who sat patiently through the morning court calendar, nervously gripped the wooden seat of the bench as Elizabeth squeezed past her to approach the defendant's table. Jackson emerged from a holding room behind a fortified wooden door and was guided to the seat next to her.

Elizabeth knew that preliminary hearings were more formality than substance, as the government only needed to establish that there was sufficient evidence to bring the case to trial, not establish the defendant's guilt beyond a reasonable doubt. There was no jury, only the judge who would decide based on a single witness—the arresting officer. Absent another person bursting through the courtroom door proclaiming his guilt, the preliminary hearing was a foregone conclusion, but she wasn't giving up without a fight.

She patiently watched as Officer Christopher Barron was sworn in and diligently went through his employment record with the force, only taking notes once the officer began recounting the arrest of Jackson.

"My partner and I were driving north on Warren Avenue when I saw the defendant standing at the entrance of an alley. He was holding a white purse," Officer Barron stated in a professional tone.

"What happened next?" the prosecutor asked.

"I instructed my partner to stop the vehicle and I exited and approached the defendant. As soon as he saw me, he threw the purse and began to run. I gave chase and apprehended him."

The officer detailed the recovery of the woman's purse and climaxed with the discovery of the woman's body in the alley. Inwardly sighing, Elizabeth knew he would make a good prosecution witness at trial. As the prosecutor completed his questioning, the judge looked to Elizabeth, silently gesturing for her to begin.

"Officer Barron, you stated that you saw my client standing at the entrance of the alley. What was he holding?"

"A white purse," he answered cordially, not the least annoyed that he was repeating the same answer.

"Where did you recover the purse?"

"Near the entrance of the alley."

"Was the purse open or closed?" Elizabeth asked that question for her own curiosity to explore whether the wallet could have spilled out during the turmoil.

"It was snapped shut."

"Was there an exit to the alley on the other end?" She already knew the answer, but wanted to hear him say it.

"Yes, there is an egress on Green Street."

"You stated that it appeared as though the victim had her throat cut."

"Yes, ma'am."

"Was there any blood on my client?"

"No, but if it was a quick attack and done from behind, that wouldn't be unusual."

"And where is the knife?"

"Excuse me?" the officer asked.

"You stated that when you found the victim her throat was cut, but neither your testimony nor the police report mentions the recovery of a weapon. Did you recover the knife?"

"No."

"If I understand correctly, you did not see my client holding a knife, you did not find the knife on my client when you arrested him, and you did not discover a knife at the scene? Then how did my client kill the victim if he did not have a knife?" Elizabeth chastised herself for not seeing that fact from the beginning. She was too distracted by the quirks in the case to not see the obvious.

"I assume—"

"This man's life is at stake and you assume?"

"What I meant to say is that it is possible that before we returned to the alley, the knife was removed by a third person."

"Isn't it equally possible that someone else killed the victim and left the alley through the other 'egress' to Green Street?"

"The defendant had the woman's purse," was his feeble attempt at an answer.

"Couldn't the true murderer have killed the woman, removed the wallet from her purse, and discarded it? My client simply found the purse lying at the entrance of the alley and picked it up?" Now Elizabeth was having fun.

"Objection, speculation," the prosecutor interjected in an attempt to save his witness.

"I thought that was what we were doing here—speculating," she said, sarcasm evident in her voice.

Clearly done with the proceedings and eager to move along his court calendar, the judge asked, "Ms. Campbell, do you have any other questions?"

"No, Your Honor."

"The court finds that there is sufficient evidence to hold the defendant over for trial. Bailiff please remand him into custody."

Elizabeth shook her head in disappointment. She knew to expect nothing less, but hoped that she would pull off the Hail Mary of preliminary hearings; however, her heart felt lighter when Jackson touched her hand and whispered, "Thank you."

Elizabeth exited with Camille at her heels, almost mumbling to herself, as her feathers were still a bit ruffled by the judge's greater concern over his schedule than justice. Once they cleared the courtroom doors, Camille wrapped her arms around her, startling Elizabeth. "Thank you." Tears welled in her eyes.

"I didn't win in there," Elizabeth said, in case there was any misunderstanding.

"But you believe him."

"Yes, I believe him."

As though being pulled, Camille sank to the seat behind her, and Elizabeth helped guide her down with concern. Caught up in her own struggles with the case, she didn't think of the toll that it was taking on Camille. She guessed Camille was the source of strength in her family, but with her younger brother in prison and her grandmother's health failing, her strength was faltering.

Elizabeth knelt beside her and spoke softly. "I'm sorry. I know this isn't easy on you."

"I'm fine. It's just hard not being able to do anything. It's like I am watching him drown, and I can't swim to jump in and save him."

"Camille, did the police return any of your brother's belongings after they arrested him?"

"They kept his clothes and his shoes, but they gave us his wallet."

"If you think of it, can you let me take a look at it?" She really had no interest in the wallet because if the police returned it, there was no evidentiary value in it. However, it had emotional value because it gave Camille a purpose; even if it was small and short-lived, it gave her something to do instead of standing by, helplessly watching.

Grace hung up the phone after a terse conversation with an unhappy prosecutor and knew she should be upset, but she wasn't upset or even mildly annoyed; she was proud. She didn't tell Elizabeth about the missing knife, a detail that was conveniently left out of the police report and follow-up investigation report. With the state's only obligation to turn over possible exculpatory evidence in the government's possession, not the absence of it, the prosecution saw no need to assist the defense in its case. By the tone of the prosecutor's voice, Elizabeth did well. *Who am I kidding? She kicked ass.*

However, for Grace, this resulted in an unpleasant telephone conversation where the prosecutor demanded to know why no progress had been made in locating the knife. In the most diplomatic manner possible, she advised him that she couldn't simply manufacturer a murder weapon that wasn't located at the scene.

Grace deemed the conversation civil because the terms "asshole," "jackass," and "dipshit" were only muttered in her head during the course of their discussion.

"Detective Donovan."

She jumped at the sound of her name and looked up to find a middle-aged man in an ill-fitting suit standing next to her desk.

"Hey, John, what's up?"

"Hear you were looking for some info. You're going to want to see this." The older detective from the cold case unit dropped a file on her desk as he spoke.

❖

"Come on, Princess, you've pampered and preened long enough." Elizabeth chastised her best friend, Michael Chan, as he stared at his reflection in the side mirror before climbing into the passenger seat of her Roadster.

"Girl, you only gave me thirty minutes' notice. I don't do rushed. My hair takes twenty minutes alone." She knew his grooming routine all too well and didn't need to be reminded. He settled himself in before asking, "So, where are we going?"

"It's a surprise."

After returning from Jackson's preliminary hearing, she wasn't so quick to dismiss the woman's statements to Jackson and the lipstick writing on the outside of the purse, believing the woman may have known her killer and made a futile attempt to pass along a message before her death. She trolled the internet for references to "key to the castle" and "beware of the knights" and found nothing of use, unless she was in search of Sir Lancelot and the knights of the Round Table or other folklore.

She fared slightly better when she combined it with the lipstick writing, which she spent nearly an hour deciphering from the photos. On one side of the purse, she pieced together the words "for" and "Power," at least she believed it was meant to be that word as the last letter had been nearly erased. The smudged words "horse plant" were below, although it looked to be part of a larger sentence. On the other side, she could only discern the last three words near the bottom, which were left untouched, "call WHITE DEMON," the last two words written in all caps. Combining all the words, her search led her to one source, and it happened to be a thirty-minute drive outside the city. Not wanting to go alone, she solicited the company of her BFF, being less than honest as to her plans. It wasn't her fault that he interpreted, "We may be going to hell for this," as a euphemism for "it's going to be a major hang over, call in sick the next day kind of good time."

Michael pulled down the vanity mirror and checked his artistically gelled hair once again in case there had been movement while transporting his body inside the car. "So tell me, what's going on with the lady detective?" he asked to his mirror image. Michael was the only one to whom she confided about "the kiss." He was elated, calling the relationship long before she could unwrap her own feelings about Grace.

"Nothing," was all Elizabeth felt like offering on the matter.

"Come on, come on, come on," he chanted, bouncing in his seat.

"Michael, nothing is going on and nothing will."

"Why? I thought things were going well."

"They were, until she came over and said that she never wanted to see me again." She knew she was being dramatic, but it felt good.

"She said that?"

"Well, sort of."

"Sort of what?"

"She's the detective on the case I'm defending. She said we can't see each other."

"This feels familiar," he muttered. He flipped up the mirror and turned his body toward her. "Honey, I've known you a long time. I've seen you date many people."

"Hey!"

"Shush, don't interrupt. Where was I? Oh yeah, I've seen you date many people."

"Do you have this scripted?"

"Seriously, this is the first time that I've seen you like this."

"Like this?"

"In love."

She had no comeback, no easy banter. She was silenced. After several moments, she finally spoke. "I'm scared."

Michael placed a hand on her arm. "I know, but just give it time."

With nothing more needing to be said, the remainder of the drive passed with only soft jazz filling the car. Michael paid little attention to where they were going, until they pulled off the main road onto a partially paved road. It was probably fully paved at one time, but neglect left it in a state of chunks of pavement with dirt filled in between, making for a rough ride, much to Michael's displeasure. The movement was not good for the hair. As the road transitioned to full dirt, the ride relatively smoothed out, and they pulled up to what she could only describe as an old barn with a dozen or so vehicles surrounding it.

"What is this, an underground club?" he asked.

"Underground may be partially right," she said as she stepped out of the car and headed for a wooden door on the side that was partially propped open.

Michael ran to catch up to her and inspected the area that was surrounded by overgrown brush and trees. He looked at the handful of pickup trucks dispersed throughout the dirt lot. "Is this a hoedown?"

Elizabeth ignored the question and continued to the wooden building that was larger than the average barn. She guessed it was more likely used as a commercial storage facility for processed hay and probably once doubled as a community meeting hall. The faded paint did little to hide the weathered and warped wood.

When they approached the side door, Michael stopped and allowed her to step in front of him to enter. She rolled her eyes because she knew it wasn't chivalry. He was avoiding touching the rusted door handle.

Once inside, she was forced to blink several times in an attempt to help her eyes adjust to the dimness. A limited number of single lights bulbs strategically placed throughout the space provided the only illumination. Several metal folding chairs were lined up in front of a rectangular table where a poster board sat on display with ten neatly numbered and scribed statements, but the print was too small to read from a distance. If that was all she had to go by, she would have assumed that they wandered into an Alcoholics Anonymous or other community group meeting, but for a large red and white flag that hung on the back wall. It depicted a man atop a large white horse holding a cross over his head.

"Is that man wearing a white hood with a pentagram and a horned skull?" he asked, pointing.

Elizabeth lowered his arm. "Yes, Michael, I believe he is."

"What is this place?"

"Welcome to the local chapter of the Order of the White Knights."

"What the hell?"

"Exactly," she said before she moved forward and took a seat in the back row.

He followed and sat next to her, sitting as close as he could, so that they were practically sharing a seat.

In her internet research, she learned that the Order of the White Knights, with its ideology a cross between white supremacy and Paganism, had a well-organized website clearly designed to increase its membership with information on the group and printable application forms. It also featured the online ability to pay monthly dues and purchase merchandise including T-shirts, buttons, and bumper stickers, but what Elizabeth found most helpful was the listing of current events, including the bimonthly meeting for the local chapter.

She looked about the group of people who were conversing in small circles, and she noted that they all had a similar look. They were predominantly male, most with shaved or cropped hair, black boots with jeans, and multiple tattoos. The few women that were mixed in shared a similar style minus the short hair. She recognized some insignias on the T-shirts that ranged from insensitive to hateful and wondered where these people lived in the outside world. During the day, were they her neighbors, people she would encounter in the coffee shop, or pass on the street and think nothing of them?

Distracted by her thoughts, she didn't notice the cloaked man who stepped in front of the table.

"Okay, everyone, take your seats."

The group followed his command and moved to their seats, none sitting in the back near them, for which she was grateful. As the man bowed his head, the members joined him and recited a prayer in unison, and she wondered who they were praying to. Not wanting to be conspicuous, she lowered her head and pushed Michael's down when he continued to stare at the cloaked man.

When the group prayer abruptly stopped, the leader began reciting the ten edicts that she guessed were listed on the poster board, which promoted individual liberty, a natural order in the universe (which not surprisingly put them at the top), and a healthy mix of the Second Amendment, and the assembly followed in harmony. When the recitation was complete, the man tipped his head back and stretched his arms up with the assembly mimicking the action. Elizabeth thought it odd because the little she knew about the group, looking down would seem more appropriate.

"If I am sacrificed tonight, I will never speak to you again," Michael whispered harshly.

"If they sacrifice you, then you will probably be dead, so I wouldn't expect you to speak to me."

"In that case, I will come back and haunt you and throw out all those ridiculous turtleneck sweaters and those god-awful flannel pajamas."

Elizabeth raised her head and stared at him. "What's wrong with my pajamas?"

"Don't think you'll be getting any action with the lady detective wearing little pink flower pajamas with bunny slippers to match."

Elizabeth thumped him in the back of his head.

"Ouch! You messed up my hair!"

"There won't be much to worry about after they remove your head!"

When the room became painfully quiet, Elizabeth realized the congregation had stopped chanting and now openly stared at them. "Sorry, my friend here just gets a little excited by the whole satanic supremacy thing," Michael said, waving his hands in front of him for emphasis.

The cloaked man approached them. "Perhaps you're a little lost? The Abercrombie and Fitch meet and greet is down the block."

"I'm so sorry," Elizabeth said. "We didn't mean to disturb you. I was just looking for someone." She hadn't really planned on what she would do or say once she found the meeting location; winging it seemed like a good idea at the time.

The man remained in front of them, arms crossed, exposing several tattoos, including an 88 on one hand and a horned skull on the other. "Who?"

"White Demon," Elizabeth said, and even Michael seemed to be at a loss for words.

"Who is White Demon?" the man asked, his irritation clearly evident.

"I was hoping you would know. Maybe your leader?"

"I don't know what the hell you're talking about." The hands of his crossed arms gripped tighter.

She knew she was on borrowed time and tried again. "How about the key to the castle? Do you know where that is? Or maybe you know where I can find the horse plant?"

The little patience the cloaked man had expired. "I would appreciate it if you would both leave and allow us to practice our free expression, as guaranteed by the First Amendment, in peace." She could barely see the man's face with the heavy hood draping down, but guessed he wasn't smiling.

A rumbling of agreement came from the crowd, and Michael stood, yanked up Elizabeth, and dragged her out, not stopping until they reached her car.

"Well, that was a good time. We've been exiled from Satan's den. Didn't see that coming tonight."

CHAPTER SEVEN

Elizabeth passed the empty reception desk and found Amy orchestrating a group of men wearing matching red T-shirts with a company logo on the back.

"What's going on?" she managed to ask Amy in between orders.

"Your mom's here."

"Of course." She should have known that when she walked in and found the place thrown into chaos. She hoped to avoid her for as long as possible and maneuvered her way to her office, having to climb over a small cabinet in the process, and closed her door.

After throwing her bag to the ground, she swung her door back open. "Mom, where's my furniture!"

Her mom emerged from behind a very large man holding a desk above his head. "Hello, dear," she calmly said.

Elizabeth took a deep, fortifying breath and asked, "Mom, where is my furniture?" She pointed to her office.

Her mother waved her hand in disgust. "Oh, that flea bitten stuff is in the alley."

"What!"

Elizabeth stormed out the front door and marched around the building to the alley, where she found BD sitting next to an overflowing metal trash can, dejected. "I'm so sorry," she said as she rubbed its top. She spoke sweet nothings to her chair as she rolled it back into SILC and stopped in front of her mother. "The rest you can do with as you like, but BD is off limits."

"Dear God, she needs a date," her mother said as she escorted BD back into her office.

Elizabeth sat on her floor, hunched over a small stack of papers in her lap, with the intent of catching up on other matters that she had neglected the last few days. Given that her prior evening went rather poorly, she decided to move past the Order of the White Knights, chalking it up as a colorful experience. Nothing about the organization seemed to fit the few clues she had, like where to find the key to the castle, or better yet, what castle?

As penance for her evening's faux pas, she took Michael to his favorite French restaurant where he collected big, ordering the most expensive meal. After topping off the best bottle of wine they had, he was feeling no pain, and she was once again in his good graces. Given the feel-good state she left him in the night before, she imagined that he got the hangover he was looking for too.

In line with her pledge to be more productive that morning, Elizabeth sat with a cumbersome legal brief in hand and tried to decipher the author's arguments that used many words, yet had nothing to say. It was talking in circles at its best. To humor herself, she turned the paper upside down. *Ah, that's better.*

She went in search of pen and paper to write down a citation for later reference. The sound of her phone ringing caused her to jump, and she abandoned her search for writing utensils and turned her attention to the missing phone. Crawling on her hands and knees in her skirt, she scurried to the other side of the room, unable to precisely pin down the location of the muffled sound.

"Should I come back?"

Elizabeth turned her head to the voice in her doorway and realized that all she needed was a leash to complete the image. She knew there was no dignified way out of the situation. "No, come on in. Playing leapfrog alone just isn't as much fun."

Camille stepped inside and didn't hold back her chuckle. "I love what you've done with the place. It's so minimalistic."

"You think so? I thought who needs material things, chairs, desk? Anyone can work in that environment, but this..." She gestured around her empty office. "This is the real deal."

Elizabeth's phone rang again, and she lunged to her left and pulled open a box. "Hello? Yes, this is Ms. Campbell. No, I didn't order a water fountain. I am afraid it's a misunderstanding." She hung up the phone and yelled toward her door. "Mom, no fountain."

She turned back to Camille. "So, where were we?"

"I just finished my shift and thought I would swing by and bring you Jackson's wallet. I tried calling, but, well, you know." She gestured toward the phone that Elizabeth placed back in the box.

Her mother walked in the room. "Did you say something, dear?"

Elizabeth rubbed the tension in her forehead. "Mom, we can't put a fountain in the clinic."

"Of course not, it's for the lobby."

"Mom, there's no room."

"Honey, you just lack imagination."

One of the workers called her name, and her mother left as quickly as she entered. She was in her element.

"Your mom?"

"Yep, Beatrice Campbell. She apparently not only runs my life, she also now runs the clinic."

"You mind if I have a seat?"

"Please," Elizabeth said, gesturing to the floor.

Camille sat crossed-legged, not dressed in her usual stylish outfits, but instead sporting practical light blue hospital scrubs. She looked better than the last time Elizabeth saw her outside the courtroom. She seemed lighter.

Elizabeth leaned back on her hands with her legs stretched out and crossed at the ankles. Her skirt made it impractical to sit any other way.

"So you worked the night shift?" Elizabeth asked.

"I'm a nurse at Saint Vincent's. Being the new kid on the block, I get the shifts no one else wants."

Elizabeth played with a paperclip that seemed to be stuck in the ratted carpet. "Nightshift is looking kind of good right now." Elizabeth didn't want to rush Camille, but she was curious about her visit. "So, what's on your mind?"

"I was just coming by to drop off the wallet." She paused and thumped the palm of her hand against her forehead. "Which is sitting in the glove compartment of my car."

"Glad I'm not the only one. I'll walk out with you to get it. I could use the break." As though to emphasize her point, a loud whining noise from a drill sounded from the room next door.

They dodged planks of wood being carried by sweaty men and made their way out the clinic door. On the walk to the car, Elizabeth explained her exploits in trying to find the meaning of WHITE DEMON and the other cryptic words, and she sensed that Camille was disappointed that she was giving up on that angle. To appease her, they ran through various possibilities, but were no closer to an answer by the time they reached the parked car. As Elizabeth had already done, Camille resigned herself that they might never know, and they decided the better strategy was to focus on the missing wallet and knife and prepping Jackson to take the stand. Although Elizabeth didn't favor putting a defendant on the stand and subjecting him to cross-examination, she had to prepare that it might be a possibility.

As they reached the car, Camille searched the glove compartment, while Elizabeth peered inside a metal newspaper dispenser that was stationed nearby to catch the daily headlines in the community paper.

"Anything of interest?" Camille asked as she came up behind her and handed over the wallet.

"Let's see, you can get your dog washed half off this Saturday, there's a gun expo at the convention center, and next door, Bounty Ministries is having a revival. There's a possibility. Oh wait, and here." Elizabeth picked up a flyer from the top of the dispenser that advertised implants on a budget with two large breasts dominating the paper, and she admired the absurdity of it for a moment.

Camille picked up a flyer of her own. "Thinking of a new look?"

"They offer a payment plan."

"The number's easy enough. Just call DD NEW BOOBS for a new you."

"Thanks, like that won't be stuck in my head for the next week." She returned the flyer to the top of the dispenser, thanked Camille, and gave her a quick wave before shoving the wallet into her coat pocket. After a few steps in the direction of the clinic, she stopped and returned to the flyer and picked it up again. Below the letters DD NEW BOOBS were the corresponding digits for the telephone number, she guessed in case a person had trouble spelling.

Camille stood at her open car door and called over. "Really, you don't need it."

Without taking her eyes off the paper, Elizabeth said, "White Demon is a phone number. Call White Demon. Turning the numbers into letters was probably the easiest way for her to remember the telephone number. The other words might have been the address or directions." Elizabeth knew in her gut she was right. "Do you have your phone?"

Camille dialed the letters WHITE DEMON and put her phone on speaker. Elizabeth rushed to her and huddled over it, and they listened to it ring.

After the fourth ring, a breathless voice came on and muttered a name that neither could understand and they both hesitated, unsure what to say, and the person on the other end hung up. Elizabeth took the phone from Camille's hand and hit redial, and a cranky voice answered, "This not funny. I call police."

"I apologize, sir. I was trying to get the name of your establishment."

The irritated voice repeated a nearly indiscernible name, and Elizabeth only caught the word "market." She cringed because she hesitated to ask him to repeat it and decided on another approach. She asked for the address while motioning to Camille to write it down. With impressive speed, Camille dove into her car and reemerged with a pen and small pad of paper. Elizabeth had to give it to her; the woman was organized.

The annoyed voice on the phone recited an address and hung up, clearly not willing to entertain any additional questions. Camille wrote down the address, and they both stood staring at it.

Elizabeth spoke first. "Guess I'll be taking an unscheduled trip to South Heights this fine morning."

"You're not going there alone?"

Clearly, this woman has no idea the places I have found myself in recent history. "Yes."

"I'll go with you."

"You just came off a shift. I can handle this."

"Let's put this into perspective. You are driving to South Heights, where the only white people are the police, in your four-hundred-dollar suit, in your fancy car, to ask the locals about White Demon."

Okay, when she puts it that way, it doesn't sound so good. "You have a suggestion?"

"You find something else to wear, and we drive in my Honda Civic, and you let me do the talking."

Camille pulled into a vacant spot on the street in front of a liquor store, where several heavily tattooed men loitered. Elizabeth stepped out wearing black workout pants and a T-shirt that she found in her gym bag in the trunk of her car. She ignored the remarks about her physical features and what services they could provide and deposited several coins in the meter before rounding the car to join Camille. "Gee, they sure know how to make a girl feel loved."

"Regular Romeos. Okay, Juliet, let's go." Camille led the way down the block, clearly having a better sense of the neighborhood than Elizabeth. She kept up with Camille's quick pace, dodging broken bottles, refuse, feces, and an occasional sleeping person on the way, and stopped once they reached the desired block.

"Ready?" Camille asked as she gestured to a store on the other side of the street that matched the address. A faded sign hung above it with washed out lettering that was as indiscernible as the man on the phone. Elizabeth moved forward past a small tent and several cardboard boxes that were strewn on the sidewalk. Above them, spray paint littered the walls, most of which Elizabeth couldn't decipher, but she did recognize a large penis. *Why is it that painted penises seem to be a theme in my life lately?*

They stopped in front of the store and peered through the window that offered an eclectic display of laundry detergent, colorful candles, and packages of noodles that looked to be at least a decade old. Elizabeth entered first pushing in a glass door covered with advertisements and a small bell at the top rang to alert the storekeeper of their presence. They each walked to separate sides of the store browsing the shelves, one side catering to low quality clothing items including T-shirts, socks, and shorts; and the other side had staple items, cereal, canned goods, and toiletries. Elizabeth riffled through some of the items, but found nothing unusual or demonic. It seemed to be a one-stop shop for local households. They met at the back counter, where cigarettes, lottery tickets, and over-the-counter medicines were out of reach for the customer.

Despite the bell warning their arrival, they stood alone in the store, and Elizabeth continued riffling through an array of items that crowded the counter. An elderly Asian man finally emerged from the back room with a television blasting.

"You going to buy that?" the man asked curtly, pointing to a small box in Elizabeth's hand.

She looked at her hand and found that she was holding a box of tampons. "Uh, sure, yes, I want to buy this, but we're still shopping." She showed faux interest in a T-shirt that read "Homie" across the chest.

"It'd look good on you. You could wear it to work," Camille said with a straight face.

"Only if you promise to wear this." Elizabeth handed her a black baseball cap that said "BITCH."

"You touch, you buy," the cranky man snapped at them.

"Wow, customer service at its best," Elizabeth said as she gathered the T-shirt, baseball cap, and box of tampons and set them on the counter.

"That will be forty-five dollars."

"And a discount too," she said, pulling out three twenties. The man's surly disposition was wearing thin, and Elizabeth decided to cut to the chase. "Do you own this store?"

"Who wants to know?"

"Given that I asked the question, that would be me. I want to know."

"Why?"

"An elderly woman who..." Elizabeth hesitated to choose her words. "Recently passed away, gave out the phone number to your store as a contact. I was hoping you could tell us who the woman was—a customer maybe?"

The man stared at her and shrugged. "Don't know the woman."

"Well, I haven't even described her."

The man puffed, but otherwise remained silent.

"She was in her seventies, Caucasian."

"Don't know the woman."

"Are you sure?"

"No white women come here, except you."

"Does the name White Demon have any meaning to you?"

"No. Now you go," the man said in staccato.

"I think he likes you," Camille whispered as she passed her heading for the door.

Elizabeth realized that she wasn't going to find any answers in the cramped, overpriced mini market and followed behind Camille.

"Somehow, I don't think that was what we were looking for," Elizabeth said as they headed back to the car.

"What are you looking for, bitches?"

They stopped and turned to see three teenagers step out from a recessed doorway, tattoos heavily marking their arms and necks, which resembled those on Elizabeth's friends back at the car. She assumed they were affiliated. Their pants sagged well below any level that could be deemed appropriate, leaving their underwear vividly on display. She didn't consider herself a prude, but underwear, penises, and breasts all in one day, *oh my*.

"Hi there, we are art curators at the Metropolitan Museum, and we're looking for some new pieces for display that depict the modern urban life and political strife of the inner-city male adolescent." Even Elizabeth didn't know what the hell she just said.

The three gang members stared at her. She realized that she still had the floor and continued. "We are particularly interested in that piece of work." She pointed to the painted penis. "The upward brush stroke emphasizes the bold statement." The teens made crude comments about the size of their own body parts.

Elizabeth continued the discussion, pointing out different writings and drawings on the walls and sidewalk as she moved the group toward Camille's car. The teenagers seemed fascinated by her and engaged in a discussion about the artists and purpose of the graffiti. In a different circumstance, Elizabeth would have found the conversation fascinating because there was much more behind what she initially thought was simple scrawling. By the time they reached the vehicle, a camaraderie had been formed, and Elizabeth found that she actually liked the boys.

The teenagers saw them off before they joined the men loitering in front of the store. Had they been dealt a different hand, they would probably have a whole other existence. As much as she liked to curse her privileged upbringing, she was grateful for it.

They drove back reminiscing on their adventure, but Elizabeth felt a bit deflated. She was certain that WHITE DEMON was a phone number, but the cranky man's market, as Elizabeth dubbed it, didn't figure in the puzzle.

"What if it was a phone number?" Camille asked. "What if the number was an old number, got disconnected, and then recycled out again to the cranky man's market?"

"That makes sense! It could have been a phone number from her past."

Elizabeth pushed her foot on the imaginary gas pedal on the passenger floor in hopes of accelerating their return trip; however no matter how hard she pushed, the Civic remained at the speed limit. By the time they reached SILC, her foot was one large muscle cramp, and she gimped out of the car.

She didn't wait for Camille, but left her to catch up. Wrapped in her thoughts, she barely heard the warning "Watch out!" that came from above. She covered her head, and a bucket crashed down to the sidewalk and thick paint splattered across the front of her.

Camille rushed to her side, the concern on her face replaced with a smirk, as blotches of paint dripped off her chin. "Well, at least you have a new T-shirt you can change into."

"Are you okay, ma'am?" a concerned voice came from above.

Elizabeth looked up and gave a thumbs-up. "Doing great." She wasn't surprised to find one of her mother's workmen on the roof.

❖

"Turn right up ahead." Danny leaned forward from the back seat and pointed, knocking the map out of Elizabeth's hand. What they were searching for didn't register on any modern navigation system.

"Danny, would you sit back," she said as though talking to a child.

"That is the turn and your map is upside down," he said.

"It is not."

"Well, either north suddenly faces down or you're holding the map upside down."

"Am not."

"Children, don't make me stop this car," Camille interjected. She had remained wordless through much of their drive, but it was clear that their bickering was getting the better of her.

After the revelation that WHITE DEMON was an old phone number, Elizabeth solicited the services of her old friend Rich Porter, who was the knower of all, at least where public records were concerned. He had access to information well beyond the county recorder's office where he worked through his network of acquaintances and had proven himself indispensable in the Raymond Miller case. He seemed to have a soft spot for her and was always willing to help.

Between Rich's access to information and Danny's prowess on the internet, they were able to obtain the former owner of WHITE DEMON, the phone number anyway. Danny insisted on joining them on their adventure as they drove to the location. He was more like a stubborn dog that insisted on going on a car ride, whether the owner approved or not. As soon as Camille unlocked her car, he dove into the back seat, and there was no pulling him out.

Camille slowed and turned on the unmarked dirt road that Danny indicated, and he sat back with smug self-satisfaction.

"My map was not upside down," Elizabeth said, not willing to admit defeat.

"And Santa's in the South Pole and birds fly north for the winter."

The car bounced as it hit a sizeable dip; one Camille could have possibly navigated around. Elizabeth and Danny peered outside at their surroundings. The rustic road seemed to be swallowed by overgrown trees, and Camille slowed to more carefully plot out their course. "Definitely the road less traveled."

Near the entrance of the private road, two decaying statues of powerful white horses stood guard, time eroding away parts of their faces, limbs, and tails, but what prominently remained were the large testicles that proudly hung. Those were built to last.

The trees above were once an artistically crafted archway, but with the passage of time and lack of care, became a twisted canopy of mangled branches. After crossing through nature's tunnel, they found themselves on the other side of Alice in Wonderland's rabbit hole. There was an expanse of open land with a large estate prominently displayed in the middle. For a moment, it felt as though they had transported back into time, and their vehicle seemed an interloper.

Camille continued their slow pace and directed them to the structure, parking her car in what appeared to have once been a circular drive. In the middle, stood another white horse that was equally well endowed, clearly related to the others.

They exited and stood silently before what was once a dignified antebellum mansion, but time had not proven kind. Its foundation and structure were intact, but its trimmings were broken and faded. It was clear that its architecture meant for it to stand the test of time, and it would have made its creators proud.

"She must have been beautiful at one time," Danny observed as he unfolded himself from the back seat and approached a majestic column. He knocked on it as though verifying its authenticity.

"So what do we know about this place?" Camille asked.

"According to Rich, it was built by Frederick Lawton in 1840 during the height of slavery. The Lawton Plantation, also known as the White Horse Plantation," she said gesturing to the statue, "was a cotton plantation that once housed over fifty slaves." The smeared lipstick words, "horse plant" confirmed in Elizabeth's mind that the woman was trying to provide an address to the estate.

"Who owns it now?"

"Rich is looking into that. It looks like it has been passed down from generation to generation, but seems abandoned now."

"Ya think?" Danny said, and she opted to ignore his sarcasm.

"I'm surprised vandals haven't gotten to it," Camille said.

"I don't think many people know it's here." Elizabeth gestured to the overgrown tree tunnel through which they entered.

Danny had already taken off to explore the property, and Camille began to walk around the side of the massive home. Elizabeth was taken by a set of smaller structures that were efficiently lined up in the distance and decided to head in that direction.

When she reached the buildings, she noted that their construction was nowhere near the craftsmanship of the main house. The buildings were crude wooden structures with sheets of corrugated iron interspersed for extra support where the wood rotted and offered little, if any, insulation from the summer's heat or winter's frost. It was apparent that these desolate structures once housed the slaves that were forced to live on the plantation. She approached the first small home and slowly walked up the two steps that led to the petite, open porch. The wood creaked under her feet, and she treaded lightly. She wasn't sure why she had to look inside, but she knew she just did. She pushed open the wood plank door, and it squealed, clearly not used to such exercise in a long while.

The home consisted of one room with rope lines that ran across the ceiling, which she assumed once held drapes to partition the quarters into smaller areas for privacy. There were no windows to offer light, and it was nothing more than a wooden box. A fine layer of dirt covered the space, and a small dark patch scarred the floor where a cooking fire once sat, but now the room was barren, but for a decrepit chair in the corner that balanced itself on three legs.

Without much thought, she sat in front of the black ring and ran her hand across the coarse floor. She couldn't imagine the lives of the men, women, and children that once called this shack home. A deep sense of sadness blanketed her, and she felt the need to escape, a luxury she knew the prior occupants didn't have. She struggled to gain her footing and lift herself up, but an oppressive weight seemed to be holding her down. A moment of panic coursed through her, an illogical fear that an unseen force was holding her hostage in the confined wooden room. She closed her eyes and took a deep, calming breath, surrendering to the space that seemed to possess a wisdom or perhaps it was only a rich history, and she absorbed it. She pushed herself up again and was able to stand with ease and dismissed the event a moment earlier as an overactive imagination triggered by the repressive setting. She moved to the door and looked once more at the small room before she made her exit and pulled the door closed behind her. She started down the steps and was startled when she nearly ran into someone. Expecting Camille or Danny, she blurted out, "This is so sad, I—" She stopped short when she realized that she was looking into the eyes of a stranger.

"I'm sorry, I didn't mean to startle you, ma'am," a melodic voice washed over her. An African-American man held out his hands as though to catch her if she lost her balance. He was dressed in a red checked flannel shirt, sleeves efficiently rolled up, black suspenders supporting his dark brown trousers, and a straw hat to hide his cropped hair.

"Who are you?" Elizabeth asked, although she knew he should probably be the one asking that question.

"My name is Samuel Harris. I guess you can call me the caretaker of this here place." He possessed a gentle demeanor that put her at ease. "Is there something I can help you with?"

"I'm sorry to intrude. I thought the place was abandoned. I'm Elizabeth Campbell, and my friends and I are doing a little research on this place, and I just wanted to take a look around."

"She sure is abandoned. Has been for fifty-some years."

"How much do you know about this place?"

"My family has been part of this land for the last three generations. I'd say this place has been standing for a good hundred and seventy-five years. Not many places can say that. She started as a cotton plantation. Those there were the slave quarters." He gestured to the structure that Elizabeth just vacated, and she was struck by how at ease he was as he spoke of the history of the place, but she guessed he had long come to peace with the land.

"After the Great War, the plantation didn't survive, with no one to work the land and all." Elizabeth surmised that the Great War was the Civil War. "The place fell into disarray, but some members of the Lawton family continued living on the land and kept it in the family, but many believed her to be haunted, and it seems no one stayed too long. Josiah Webb returned about sixty years ago with thoughts of bringing her back to her grandeur, but that too ended when he died. Now she sits once again alone. Maybe she's best left alone."

She moved down a step, and the board beneath her feet made a loud squeak in protest.

"Ah, you found the lucky stair."

Elizabeth stared at him, trying to decipher where the conversation just went. He pointed to the stair. "My grandmother used to say that a squeaking stair is a lucky stair, and you should make a wish."

She realized that he was serious, so she closed her eyes, and as silly as it seemed, wished for things between Grace and her to improve, before resuming the prior conversation. "And what's down there?" She turned and pointed to a large wooden structure beyond the row of shacks.

"That was the stable. It once housed some of the country's finest horses, but be careful. It's not very safe now. I'm afraid it's been neglected, and the beams have rotted and part of the roof has collapsed. There haven't been horses on this property since the end of the war. Mr. Josiah Webb saw no need to bring any back because he hated them. Said he was allergic." Samuel scoffed.

"Do you think it's haunted?"

Samuel offered a smile. "Perhaps. The walls hold many secrets."

"Secrets?"

"Yes, ma'am."

"What kind of secrets?"

"Oh, if she wants you to know, she'll let you know. There were many souls lost on this land in its day."

Elizabeth wanted to ask many more questions, but she was cut off before she could speak.

"Well, ma'am, I'm afraid I must get going. I have to get home to my Olivia. If I am so much as a split hair late for dinner, she will have my hide. You are welcome to look around." He turned toward the main house. "You'll find her open. The lock doesn't quite work anymore, and I haven't gotten 'round to fixing it. I just ask that you close her up tight before you leave." Samuel removed the hat from his head, revealing his dark curly hair, and offered a slight bow.

"Thank you, Samuel. It was a pleasure meeting you, and I'll be sure to close her up tight." She couldn't help but refer to the property in the feminine after talking with him.

"Just remember to follow the setting sun," he said, looking back again at the home where the sun was beginning to dip, and he once again gave a slight bow and returned his hat to his head before turning and departing toward the fields. She figured that there was a back road offering a shortcut to the main road, and she watched him leave. When he was no longer in sight, she turned and headed back to the main house in search of her friends.

"Where have you been?" Camille asked as she stood on the porch of the main house. Her arms were crossed and she was glaring at Elizabeth as she approached. Danny stood at her side with a look of concern and relief crossing his face. "We were getting worried. You shouldn't wander off like that."

"I'm sorry. I didn't plan to be gone so long," Elizabeth said. "I went to look at the living quarters down there." She pointed to the direction where she met Samuel. "I met the caretaker of this place."

"Caretaker?" Danny asked.

"Yeah, he said he looks after this place."

Danny looked around the overgrown fields and dilapidated trimmings on the home. "Not sure they're getting their money's worth."

"He confirmed that the property is still owned by the same family, but has been abandoned for at least fifty years after one of the last family members to live here died. They thought it might be haunted. He gave us permission to look around as long as we close her up when we leave."

"So, what part of haunted and going inside to look around go together?" Danny asked.

"You can wait out here if you want, but I want to take a look inside while we still have some light left."

Elizabeth held the ornate handle and pushed down the latch, which offered resistance, and she used her other hand for additional pressure, and the door gave way. She wondered why they opted not to fix the lock, but for her sake was grateful that they didn't. She pushed it open and stood just inside the entryway, taking in the expansive dome shaped ceiling where a large crystal chandelier poised motionless before she turned to the artistically carved staircase that went straight up to a landing that divided left and right. She moved inside and the hardwood surface made a slight squeaking sound as it met with her sneakers, as though offended by the disturbance. Undeterred by the ornery floor, she wandered into a sitting room on the left that was still occupied with furniture hidden under protective coverings. She grabbed one of the sheets and lifted it off a shapeless heap to reveal a delicate floral designed couch complemented with hand carved wood trimming, and a heap of dust scattered through the air, causing a violent high-pitched sneeze reaction in Danny.

"You sneeze like a little dog," Elizabeth said as she backed away from him.

"No, I don't."

"Yeah, you kinda do," Camille confirmed.

Elizabeth wandered through the stale, lifeless room, peaking under additional coverings and opening an occasional drawer, only to find it vacant. An archway led to an adjoining room, which boasted a large dining table that could easily seat twenty with high back chairs sitting around its circumference silently waiting to be of use. Empty glass cabinets that were built into the wall sat on opposite ends of the room, their contents probably too valuable to be left behind unprotected. As she wandered through the first floor, she found each room fully furnished, but devoid of life. The rooms were spacious and could easily accommodate a small army of occupants, if necessary.

She imagined the house once hosted grand parties, the talk and envy of the Southern socialites, but its glory days past, it sat dejected, forgotten. A celebrity past its prime. If she closed her eyes, she could almost hear a melancholy sigh, and she couldn't help but reach out and touch the traditional white wainscoting that lined the walls.

"It's amazing, the front door is unlocked, but this place seems untouched," Camille said as they had wandered into another oversized room, and she approached a grand fireplace with a lavish mantel. A faded portrait of a man with heavy sideburns was displayed above it. He was dressed in a white high-collared shirt with a silk cravat loosely tied at his neck. An open, well-tailored short jacket exposed a textured beige vest underneath. He bore a stern look with an incessant stare.

Based on the clothes and age of the painting, Elizabeth presumed the friendly looking fellow was the plantation's founder, Frederick Lawton.

Danny glanced at the portrait and moved away. "Gives me the creeps. He watches us wherever we go."

Elizabeth assumed the room was a library, as three walls were lined with shelves filled with hardbound books. She freed a book and wiped at the dust before she thumbed through the pages. Despite the dust and slight fading of the covers, they appeared to be in good shape, showing little, if any wear. She guessed that they were more for show than consumption of knowledge. She remembered the old woman's comments to Jackson and reviewed the titles, but found no fairytales or knights in this library.

"I don't get it. What are we looking for?" Danny asked, coming up behind her, but Elizabeth only shrugged in response. She really had no idea what connection this place had to her case, if at all. She might have misinterpreted the old woman's cryptic message and be completely on a goose chase, but what else was she to do. She was at a dead end in the case. A goose chase seemed better than sitting idly by doing nothing.

As they made a complete circle of the ground floor, they found themselves standing once again in the foyer. Elizabeth turned to the red patterned carpet that snaked up the center of the staircase and began her ascent. "Let's go see what's upstairs."

"Nuh-uh, I'm not going up there," Danny protested.

Elizabeth waved her hand. "Fine, stay down there."

She could hear slight footsteps behind her and guessed it was Camille. It didn't take long before Danny was following closely behind them. At the middle landing, Elizabeth turned to the divergent staircases and saw that there was no measurable difference, as at the top a wooden railing lined an open corridor that linked the two sides. She chose left for no particular reason, and neither Danny nor Camille protested as they followed behind.

The hallway of the second floor was awash with light blue walls interrupted by bulky wooden doorframes intermittently spaced along each side. At the end, a large arc-shaped window stood guard at the intersection of another hallway running perpendicular. On full alert with its arching brow, the window allowed the remaining daylight to filter through, reminding Elizabeth that they were on borrowed time, at least as far as their light was concerned.

Elizabeth started with the first door on her left and pushed it open. A waft of musty air struck her. The room smelled of age. Two sets of heavy dark blue curtains were held back by gold ropes, exposing large windows that covered one wall. In the middle of the room, stood a sturdy four-poster bed fully clothed with a fluffy comforter and four large frill covered pillows that were a matching off-white. She assumed that they were once a true white, but time had a say in it. Matching nightstands and a dresser completed the set, and she walked to each and opened the drawers but found them empty. There were outlines on the wall where pictures once hung, but now there were no personal effects, nothing to tell the story of who once occupied the room.

She pulled open a second door that led to a medium-size sitting room with two overstuffed yellow high back chairs that were slanted to face a window, and a small graceful table stood between them with a book resting on top. A sweet floral scent drifted into the space, and Elizabeth turned in a circle trying to find its source.

"Do you smell that?"

"What?" Danny asked from the doorway.

As quickly as the scent came, it dissipated. "Never mind."

Elizabeth lifted the book on the table and caressed the familiar cover. She opened it and looked inside. "Wow, this is a first edition."

Danny and Camille came over to inspect her find, but didn't seem as impressed and moved on. Elizabeth stood there holding the small piece of history in her hand and wondered its worth. *To Kill a Mockingbird* was mandatory reading in school, but it left an impression. She delicately flipped through the pages and stopped on a page that was marked by a folded piece of paper tucked inside. It was an incomplete letter in neat cursive writing addressed to "My love" and consisted of only a few lines that professed heartfelt emotion. Elizabeth hoped that the author found another way to reach the intended recipient, and that it wasn't an unrequited love.

Before neatly tucking the paper back inside, she read an underlined passage on the page that advised it was a sin to kill a mockingbird because they did nothing but make music. She traced her fingers over the words before she closed the book and set it back on the table.

Danny's voice calling for her broke her tranquil moment, and she turned away and moved to a second door that led out of the room. She followed it to an adjoining bathroom where a freestanding claw-foot bathtub sat center stage. Its feet were made of heavy silver, with a majestic pattern that spread up the leg. A delicate porcelain sink stood at its side, with matching silver handles, but the toilet was less dignified. A tacky faded green and white floral patterned shag carpet covered the top seat, embarrassing it, and Elizabeth was tempted to set it free. She could only imagine the bad toupee jokes it endured from its other porcelain roommates. She realized that the house was getting the better of her and moved on through yet another door and found herself in a bedroom. This one seemed more masculine, but the furnishings were uneventful in comparison.

In the few moments that they stood there, the room visibly darkened as the sun started its descent toward the horizon. Danny pulled the chain on a nearby lamp and stared at it when it didn't light. "There's no electricity."

Elizabeth held back a jibe about the brightest bulb in the box, and instead longed for her car, which contained a trunkful of useful equipment, including flashlights. A sudden illumination caused her to turn, and Danny was holding his cell phone using the flashlight feature. Realizing that she, and probably Camille, left their phones in the car, she was glad that she held back her quip because he was looking brighter than the two of them at that moment.

She located another exit leading to a different room, and they carried on, weaving from one room to another, as each room had more than one entrance and exit. One could almost travel the entire second floor without ever having to use the hallway.

Near the end of their journey, they found themselves in the far corner of the second floor from where they started. The room was darker than the others. It only had two small windows where the last graying light seeped in, and brown wood paneling covered the walls. It featured an overbearing fireplace on one side with two matching deep blue chairs cowering in front, and books lining two additional walls; however, it was the fourth wall that caught her attention, where a large framed Confederate flag hung near the entrance. Danny and Camille lingered in the doorway as Elizabeth approached it.

She had momentarily lost sight of the home's origin, but the symbol on the wall was a stark reminder. The earlier sympathy she conjured for the antebellum home was fading, and a feeling of antipathy rose within her. She yanked at the corners of the frame until it separated from the wall, and she released, allowing it to fall. The shattering of the glass made a small echo through the closed room.

"Ooops, it slipped," Elizabeth said as she walked over it.

Camille and Danny offered no comment and finally came into the room as though it was now all clear.

"Shine your light around the room," Elizabeth said, and Danny obliged, slowly working the light across the bookshelves. She noted that these books were not as neatly packed in as the room downstairs. The books were unevenly lined up with some tilting to the side to accommodate the uneven gaps between them. This, she guessed, was the real library. She scanned the titles, most of which she didn't recognize, but found a common theme of pro-segregation and pro-Confederacy ideology. Danny picked up a booklet that was lying on the lip of the bottom shelf.

"The Southern Manifesto." He dusted the cover off on his shirt. Elizabeth gave him a shrug, clearly not as well versed on her Confederate history. "The resolution signed in 1954 by all the US senators and members of the House from the former Confederate states," Danny said with a bit of smugness that he had something over Elizabeth.

Now it rang a bell. The Southern senators and congressmen signed the manifesto in opposition to the Supreme Court's ruling in *Brown v. Board of Education*, the landmark civil rights decision that marked the beginning of the end of segregation.

Danny opened the cover and read a passage as she peaked over his shoulder. "We decry the Supreme Court's encroachments on rights reserved to the states and to the people, contrary to established law and to the Constitution."

That was enough for her. She returned her attention to the room and completed a circle, learning little more than when she entered, except that this seemed to be the only room that offered one exit.

"I don't know what else we can find here in the dark. Maybe we should head out," Camille said with a slight sadness in her tone. Elizabeth knew that she was hoping that they would find something of use, something that told who the old woman was, something that said Jackson Francis was innocent. Instead, they left with nothing more than an extra coat of dust on them.

Reluctantly admitting defeat, Elizabeth nodded and started toward the door, but something caught her eye. "Shine the light over there." There was a protrusion in the wall on the far side of the fireplace that she had not previously noticed.

As they approached, she realized that it was another door, but this one was different. There was no door handle, and it was flush with the wall, blending with the wood paneling and would have gone unnoticed had it not been ajar.

"This was not open before," Danny said, trepidation in his voice. Elizabeth didn't need to see his face to know that he was torn between sticking with the group and running out of the room on his own.

Elizabeth grasped the side of the open door, fully intent on investigating.

"Don't open it!"

"Danny, relax," Elizabeth said. "Why don't you give me the phone and you sit in the chair."

He allowed himself to sink into the chair cushion and extended his arm, offering up the light. Elizabeth reached for it and snagged her finger on the braided bracelet around his wrist, scraping her hand on the metal key woven into it. Danny jumped, he was wound so tight, and she knew that she had to make this quick for his sake.

She pulled open the door and entered before Danny could offer a last-minute protest, and she could feel Camille's warmth behind her as they nearly shared the same space. If she was as freaked as Danny, she was keeping quiet about it. The room was small and offered no windows. A wooden table sat in the middle of the room with six matching wooden chairs neatly tucked in around it, and a small bookshelf rested in the corner with most of the books spilled out into a heap on the floor.

A large map pinned to the wall was the room's only decoration, and with the meager light, Elizabeth couldn't see what it depicted. She moved in for a closer inspection to discover a hand-sketched map on yellowing paper that was frayed on the edges. It contained a series of dotted and solid lines that ran vertically and diagonally across the page, with a few arc shaped lines in between, but there didn't appear to be any order. Interspersed with the lines was a busy collection of squares, circles, and triangles, but there was no recognizable structure or landmass. On the left side of the map were three circles with lines sticking out of their circumferences, resembling crudely drawn suns, much like a child would create.

They formed an arc down the side of the page with dotted lines in between, which she presumed to represent a setting sun.

She remembered Samuels's advice to follow the setting sun and wondered if there was more to his words than a caution of nightfall. She tapped her finger on the top sun and followed its path west to its sunset. As she reached the final sun, she felt an indentation in the wall and pulled back the lower corner where she found a small hole only big enough to fit two fingers. She poked her thumb and index finger inside and pried out a tightly rolled bundle of paper.

"What is it?" Camille asked from over her shoulder, her breath tickling Elizabeth's ear.

"Not sure." Elizabeth attempted to use the light to read the document, but it proved too difficult. She tucked the roll into the waistband of her pants for later review. Using Danny's phone, she took a picture of the map.

Either curiosity got the best of him or he was no longer willing to sit in the dark alone, because Danny stepped a few paces into the confined room. He kept his hands close to his sides, as though he was afraid to touch anything. "I suppose you're going to want to go through that door now," he said with defeat in his voice and jutted his chin to the opposite wall.

Elizabeth and Camille turned to the direction he indicated, and she noticed a narrow wooden door on the far side of the room. She walked over and pulled it open. The others were close behind her. They huddled together in the center of the small room, and Elizabeth methodically trailed the light along the walls.

"Holy shit," Danny breathed out. "There is a fucking arsenal in here." Elizabeth couldn't have said it better.

The walls were lined with what Elizabeth could best describe as military style weapons, enough to supply a brigade. There were scopes, muzzles, and other devices she had no clue what they did, but looked dangerous. A long metal box sat below the weapons and she leaned over to open it. The dust on the cover gave her some assurance that the weapons had been idle for quite some time, possibly forgotten. The box contained a multitude of long, slender cylinders that tapered at one end. "Bullets," she said and continued sifting through to discover coils of wire and in the corner, a single oval object, which she lifted for better inspection.

"I think you should put that back, very gently," Camille whispered, her eyes never leaving the grenade in Elizabeth's hand.

Elizabeth slowly and ever so gently moved back to the metal box. Danny grabbed the cell phone that was still in her other hand and held it out for her as she cautiously set the oval explosive back in its place and closed the lid.

"This is more than enough for your average home defense. What the hell was going on?" Elizabeth asked more to the room than to her friends. She slumped against the far wall to take it all in for a brief moment.

"I don't know, but you think we can get out of here now?" Danny asked as he turned to the door. She knew that this was more than he had signed up for, and he would think twice before asking if he could come along again.

Elizabeth pushed herself off and started to follow, but a slight clicking sound stopped her. "Wait."

Danny heard the sound and froze.

"It's a door," Elizabeth said, and Danny let out an audible breath and looked to the door that stood slightly ajar next to her.

"I must have opened it when I leaned on it," she said, and without waiting for a quorum on what they should do, she opened it the rest of the way and stepped inside.

"You have got to be kidding me," Danny muttered as he stomped toward the new passage. He appeared to resign himself to his fate that they were not leaving until they crawled through every crevice of the godforsaken place and stepped forward with the light, revealing a cramped wooden staircase. He didn't even bother to ask if the plan was to take the stairs.

The staircase was only wide enough to accommodate one person, so Danny stepped back and gestured for Elizabeth and Camille to take the lead. "Ladies first," he said as he handed the cell phone to Elizabeth as she passed. She doubted the act was meant to be gallant. Elizabeth cautiously navigated the small passage, testing each wooden step before placing her full weight upon it, with some stairs protesting louder than others. Camille followed gripping the back of her T-shirt to ensure that she didn't get separated. The atmosphere was stale and heavy, and Elizabeth felt as though they were breathing the same air that had been trapped in the confined space since the 1840s. The stairs wound down a circular path, and she imagined the three of them as a train set, with her as the engine, Camille the middle, and Danny the caboose.

When they reached the bottom, a single door stood between them and their way out. The thought of having to turn around and traverse back up the stairs was more than she thought Danny would be willing to do, and expected him to push his way forward and kick the door in if necessary. Fortunately, a simple turn of the handle and the door easily gave up its hold, and they piled out into another small room. This one was considerably cooler and more refreshing. She saw multiple canned goods and boxed items with expiration dates well past their prime.

"It's a food pantry," Danny said in case she and Camille hadn't figured that out for themselves.

She closed the door to the stairs to make their presence less noticeable, not that she expected the kitchen pantry to have any visitors, but she was being mindful of Samuel's graciousness. Once closed, the door was no longer noticeable, as there was no handle to reopen it. It merely looked like another wall of shelves. She had to admit it was a clever escape route.

Danny pushed open two slatted doors, and they exited into the kitchen. Since she'd made a cursory pass through the room earlier and discovered nothing of note, they didn't linger and instead tried to make their way back to the front door.

Danny took the cell phone from her and assumed the lead, as they snaked through a few rooms continuing the train formation, but with Elizabeth now in the middle and Camille on the end. When the caboose stumbled after running a bit off course and hitting a chair, Elizabeth turned and helped balance her, and they resumed their course with Camille reattaching herself to Elizabeth's shirt for extra security. The return trek seemed to be taking far longer than the inbound one, but Danny refused to admit that navigating the first floor seemed much easier the first time through when they still had daylight.

"You're going the wrong way. We need to go back through that door and turn left," Elizabeth said.

"This coming from a woman who thinks north is down."

Before Elizabeth could respond or Camille could intervene in their bickering, an accusing voice came from behind a bright flashlight. "What are you doing in here?"

They stood frozen like the proverbial deer in headlights; all they needed were antlers.

Elizabeth stepped forward and shielded her eyes from the light. "Do you mind?" She gestured to the flashlight, which was lowered to allow her to approach.

"You shouldn't be here. I could arrest you for trespassing."

Elizabeth smirked at the empty threat. "The caretaker gave us permission to be here." She approached Grace and reached out to lower the light, which was once again in her face.

"What caretaker?"

"Samuel. I ran into him outside earlier, and he said we could look around, as long as we closed the place up tight. What are you doing here?"

Grace wasn't in the mood to entertain questions, and turned to the other two. "Come on, you need to leave."

Elizabeth was visibly incensed at the order. "We have permission to be here."

"Right, the caretaker." With Elizabeth standing within arm's reach, Grace trailed the light down and admired the black workout pants before returning back to her shirt. "What are you wearing? Does your shirt say 'Homie'?"

"Why yes, yes it does." Elizabeth crossed her arms in defiance.

Grace kept her eyes trained on her and showed no emotion when Camille stepped forward and stood shoulder to shoulder with Elizabeth, as though prepared to defend her if necessary. She would have laughed at the absurdity if it weren't for the jealous streak that ripped through her. "Let's go," Grace barked with more force than she intended.

Elizabeth hesitated at the command, and Grace recognized the look and decided to defuse the situation by turning and walking away first. The trio followed, and Grace waited outside the front door and securely closed it behind them, ensuring it was locked.

"How did you get in here?" she asked as Elizabeth walked past.

"It was unlocked," she responded without turning back.

"Unlocked," Grace said to herself. She remembered the "unlocked" boys school in the Raymond Miller case, where the locks were cut and doors pried open. *Seems she's getting better at it.*

Elizabeth continued to Camille's car and pulled open the door but hesitated before entering, and Grace watched every subtle move she made from the slight caressing of her thumb on the door handle to the faint twitch of her foot.

Come on turn around. Look at me.

Without turning back, Elizabeth settled herself into the car and closed the door, keeping her eyes trained ahead, and Grace closed her eyes and inwardly sighed. *Why did it have to be so hard?*

When she drew her eyes back to the car, her breath hitched as a set of beautiful blue eyes were staring back at her. That was all she needed.

CHAPTER EIGHT

Elizabeth sat at the outside café table in the warm air and enjoyed the uptick in the late autumn temperature. With her palm holding up her chin, she poised over an open manila folder that held the pages she appropriated from the secret room. Stealing was too harsh a word in her mind because they were discarded, as best she could tell. She flipped through the six nonstandard sized sheets that measured six inches by three and a half. Each page bore a jagged edge indicative of being torn out of a book, a date book she guessed, because each page contained days of the week printed out with the date next to it. It would seem innocuous enough, but for the fact that it was a date book from 1864.

However, it seemed that the preprinted dates didn't suit its author, as the day and year were crossed out on each page and new dates for April 1865 were written in their place. Writing was scribbled on each page, and it appeared to serve as a journal. The problem was the script was difficult to decipher, in part because of the faded ink, but more to the fact that the words made no sense. She recognized the individual letters, but they were illogical, forming no words, as though it were code. She truly wished that she could piece together the story for no other reason than it was a century-and-a-half-old piece of history. There was one page that she could make out and that was a sketch of a home with a caption below, but it was as nonsensical as the rest of the pages, and if she had to guess, the drawing was of the White Horse Plantation home.

She wanted nothing more than to call Grace and tell her everything from the stash of weapons in the home to the haunting pages in front of her, but she didn't for both professional and personal reasons. Not quite ready to unpack the complexity of their budding relationship, instead she called Rich, who already seemed knee-deep in the case. She thought of meeting him at his office, however she always did that bringing his favorite vice, jelly beans, as payment for his help, and she felt she owed him more and invited him to lunch. She wasn't sure he would accept because she had never seen him outside the gray government office where he worked. She simply associated the county recorder's office with Rich, as if that was the only place he existed, like a child who was surprised to learn that her teacher didn't live at school. However, Rich did accept her invitation, with quite a bit of enthusiasm, and she'd been sitting and waiting ten minutes past their scheduled time to meet.

She smiled when she saw him approach; his freshly combed strands of hair sat neatly across his balding head. He straightened his shirt as he approached, then jammed his hands in his pockets when he saw her.

"Hi, Rich." Elizabeth stood and gave him a warm hug. She could almost feel him blushing at the contact.

"I'm sorry I'm late," he fumbled. "There was an issue in the office. A file was misplaced. It should have been under 'p' for permit, but it was under 'l' for license." He shook his head in disgust at the unforgivable lapse, and Elizabeth nodded along trying to show her appreciation for the gravity of the mishap.

"No problem. Thank you for meeting me."

A waiter approached for their orders and as soon as he left, she pushed the manila folder to his side of the table. She had already described her adventure the day before in detail on the phone, and even sent him photos from her phone of the pages, but it didn't do the document justice.

He gingerly flipped through the pages with a distressed look on his face. "These pages are a small piece of history and deserve better care than being carried around in a folder. They need better protection. You should probably photocopy them and keep the originals in a plastic cover somewhere safe."

Appropriately reprimanded, Elizabeth promised she would do just that as soon as their meeting was over, and he continued to inspect the writing. He spent several minutes carefully scanning each page. Their lunch arrived, but it was ignored. Rich was too absorbed in the papers, and Elizabeth was too absorbed in watching him.

When he finally lifted his head, she breathed out, "Well?"

Much to her disappointment, he wasn't able to decipher any more meaning than she did.

"What is the interest with the papers anyway? I understand that they're intriguing, given the age and all, but what relevance does this have to your client?"

Elizabeth knew that was a fair question because both Danny and Camille asked the same, and she had lain awake at night asking the very thing. Instead of arguing that her gut told her it meant something, she provided the only logical answer that she could. "Samuel—" she started, but was interrupted.

"Samuel?"

"He is the caretaker of the White Horse Plantation. I ran into him before I went into the home," she explained. "He said the walls hold many secrets. At first I thought he was speaking figuratively, but then I found these pages shoved in a crevice of a wall."

He smiled, and she wasn't sure if he was placating her or thinking of ways to have her committed. Nonetheless, he offered to reach out to his old college roommate, a historian with the local Civil War museum, who would have better insight into the context of the writings.

CHAPTER NINE

With a designer coffee warming her hands, Elizabeth leaned against her car parked outside an overpriced coffee house, uncertain whether she should leave another message. At first, she battled with herself on whether to call Grace. What would she say? Would Grace want to hear from her? When she ran into her at the White Horse Plantation, Grace seemed distant and annoyed, and that troubled Elizabeth more than she realized at the time. A quick check-in call would allay her fears. Fear of what, she asked herself repeatedly, but she didn't want to answer her own question. What if Grace found whatever they started to be too much trouble? So she called Grace, not once or twice, but nearly a dozen times since the morning, and each time it went to voice mail. Grace was now avoiding her.

She set the coffee on the top of her car, reached into her coat pocket, and pulled out her phone. She had come to memorize the pattern of rings and Grace's outgoing message and waited impatiently for the beep. She wasn't sure what she would say, but she was going to give her a piece of her mind. "Hi, Grace, it's Elizabeth. Call me back please." *Okay, maybe that was a little mellower than initially planned.*

However, that did little to settle the unrest mounting within her. She needed to see her, but realized that she didn't even know where Grace lived, and now she was angry. Grace knew where she lived. Grace knew her friends. What did Elizabeth know? She knew where Grace worked.

Elizabeth yanked open her car door and brought her engine to a roar. She hastily pulled out of the parking spot, and her forgotten coffee cup tipped over and spilled down her windshield. This pissed her off even more because somehow that was Grace's fault too, as was the speeding ticket she earned on her drive to the police station.

By the time she pulled into the station parking lot, she was nearly boiling over. She slammed her car door and marched to the front entrance and took her place in line. Fortunately for her, and possibly for those in front of her, the line was short because with each passing moment, her temperature gauge rose. When her turn came, she spoke to the desk officer through gritted teeth. "I am here to see Detective Grace Donovan."

"What?" the officer asked, forcing Elizabeth to repeat herself, and she overly articulated each word.

"Is she expecting you?"

"Yes." A lie, she knew, but she was far beyond caring.

After writing down Elizabeth's name, the uniformed officer disappeared through a side door, and she looked around the lobby and spotted the chair where she sat on her first visit to the station. Instead of meeting the rumpled detective that she created in her mind, she met the sleek, beautiful woman who was the epitome of her name. She remembered how uncharacteristically flustered she was at their first meeting, and a crack in Elizabeth's cranky demeanor formed.

When the desk officer returned, Elizabeth's steam began to whither, and she met him with a more cordial demeanor.

"I'm sorry, ma'am, there was an emergency. Detective Donovan went to the hospital."

"Oh my God, where?" she asked, reaching out and grabbing his arm.

"Memorial," he answered as he pulled his arm away.

Elizabeth ran to her car, her mind frantically racing, all prior thoughts abandoned. She chastised herself for her earlier pettiness. *What if Grace was seriously hurt or worse?*

She pulled into the emergency room parking area and ran through the automatic glass doors, dodging an exiting wheelchair.

"Grace Donovan," she barked to the attendant at the front desk.

"What is the last name?" the elderly woman asked in a calm voice.

"D-O-N-O-V-A-N," she spelled out to ensure that there were no additional delays.

"Donovan, G has been admitted to room 426, fourth floor."

"Thank you," Elizabeth yelled behind her, as she was already on her way down the hall before the woman finished her sentence.

As she jabbed at the elevator button in an attempt to make it come faster, she searched the area for the stairs as Plan B. Before she needed to put the alternative plan into action, the elevator doors opened, and she rushed inside.

When the elevator finally reached the fourth floor, she darted out, counting the room numbers as she passed. She reached room 426, pushed open the door, and slid to an abrupt halt on the linoleum, startling the sole occupant, who stared at her more in amusement than fear.

"Uh, sorry," Elizabeth uttered and stuck her head out the door to verify the room number. She turned to face the man in the bed who continued to watch her, and she looked to the white board on the side wall that listed the patient's statistics and the name "Donovan, G" at the top.

"I'm so sorry. I must have the wrong room," she said and bowed in apology, as she began to back out. Just when she thought she made her escape, the door was pushed open, slamming into the back of her, nearly sending her to the ground.

"Are you all right? I didn't expect anyone behind the door."

Elizabeth turned to see the most beautiful eyes she could hope for. They were bluer than she even remembered.

"Grace!" She threw herself at her and held on, afraid to let go.

Grace returned the hug. "Honey, what are you doing here?" she whispered.

Elizabeth pulled back slightly, not ready to let go, and pointed to the name on the board. "I went to the station, and they said you were in the hospital. I thought…" But she couldn't finish the thought.

Grace squeezed her arms in a show of compassion before breaking contact. She guided her to the bed. "Elizabeth, this is my father, George Donovan. He was admitted early this morning with chest pains, but it turned out to be indigestion from all the greasy food that he's been eating, and his diet is going to substantially change." Grace seemed to be talking more for her father's benefit than for Elizabeth's.

Elizabeth did all that she could not to cry with the black, heavy weight that seemed to pin her down lifted, allowing her to breathe. Although the appropriate greeting would have been a hello or handshake, she reached forward and embraced him. "I am so glad you are all right."

He patted her on the back. "There, there, sweetie, I'm going to be just fine," George said.

Elizabeth pulled back to look at him and wiped an errant tear from her eye. There was no mistaking that this man was Grace's father. They shared the same eyes.

"I'm sorry, I didn't mean to intrude," she said, suddenly feeling foolish.

"You don't need to leave. The more the merrier." The large grin on his face told Elizabeth that he meant what he said. "Not a whole lot to do here," he said, pointing to the snow on the television that hung from the ceiling. "Stay and keep us company."

Elizabeth appreciated the offer because she wasn't ready to leave just yet. She was still trying to gain her sea legs after the ordeal.

"So, how do you know my daughter?"

"We worked together," Grace interjected.

"So, you're the stubborn one," he said and beamed at Grace.

Elizabeth cocked her head to the side and eyed both father and daughter, as Grace stared at him. She wasn't sure what she was missing, but she knew it was significant. A warm look passed between them, and Grace gave him a nod before turning to Elizabeth. "I'm glad you came. There are some things we need to talk about. The Francis case, that is."

Elizabeth inhaled a small breath. Although she was beyond happy that her day turned out so well, she was hoping that Grace would want to talk about things of a more personal nature, but that would have to keep for a later day.

"Pop, would you mind if Elizabeth and I went downstairs, so we can talk shop. I'll be back soon."

"You go on ahead. I think I could use a bit of a nap."

Elizabeth barely knew the man, but she knew that she liked him; she liked him a whole lot. She reached down and hugged him good-bye. A handshake just seemed inferior at that point. "Please take care of yourself, Mr. Donovan. I can already tell that you are a very special person."

He returned her hug with equal force and whispered, "Take care of my daughter."

"I will, I promise," she whispered back before letting go.

Grace guided Elizabeth to the cafeteria on the floor below, barely speaking a word on the journey. It seemed that they each had a lot to process.

"So I don't recommend the lasagna. It looks a bit runny," Grace said as they entered.

"Thanks, I'll just stick to Jell-O."

"Jell-O? You're not supposed to eat that on purpose."

"What do you have against Jell-O?"

"It's the stuff you're forced to eat when nothing else goes down, and it's slimy and slithers down your throat." Grace shuddered.

Elizabeth chuckled. This was the conversation she needed.

"Let's get a table," Grace suggested and led her to the corner, with her hand on the small of her back. Elizabeth relished the attention, but it was short-lived. When they reached their table, Grace reverted to their professional relationship and assumed her role as Detective Donovan.

Grace leaned forward with her elbows on the table and asked, "What were you doing at the White Horse Plantation?"

Elizabeth started with the words the woman uttered to Jackson and went through a rundown of how she came to trace the phone number to the plantation. When she reached the part of her asinine occult visit, Grace covered her face, as though she couldn't bear to watch as the story unfolded.

"What about you? What were you doing there?" Elizabeth asked when she finished.

Grace exhaled and steepled her fingers in front of her. "We had no identity match for the woman, so I started asking around, having searches run in old cases, and I got a hit."

Elizabeth leaned forward in interest. "And?"

"Her prints matched an old cold case that was stuck in the backlog, waiting to be entered into our system."

"She was a suspect?"

"No." Grace paused and looked around as though checking if there were any eavesdroppers. "She was the murder victim."

Elizabeth stared at her, waiting for the punch line, but Grace only stared back. "Wait, you can't be serious?"

"Very serious."

"How is someone murdered twice?"

"That's what I'm trying to figure out. She was allegedly stabbed to death and her body found near the side of a service road leading to the plantation. There was scant evidence, and the case went cold immediately."

"So who is she?"

"Don't know. She was a Jane Doe back then too. No family or friends came forward. There isn't really much to go on."

"When was this?"

"May 1963."

"You think she was from the plantation?"

"Can't say. She could've just been dumped there because it was a deserted road."

Elizabeth sat pensively for a moment. She knew it was her turn to share. "In the house, upstairs, there's a room in the far back corner with a secret door."

"A secret door?" Grace asked, clearly skeptical.

"Yes, a secret door. It's on the left side of the fireplace. There's a closet inside that room that is filled with guns."

She had Grace's attention. "What do you mean?"

"I'm telling you, Grace, there was enough for a small army in there."

Grace took out a small notebook from her jacket breast pocket and scribbled notes that looked like nothing more than scratches, and Elizabeth smiled at the small fact that she learned about Grace; she had horrendous penmanship.

When Grace finished, Elizabeth added a final thought. "Oh yeah, and if you see a framed Confederate flag smashed on the ground, it was an accident, kind of."

Grace nodded. "Noted."

Elizabeth toyed with the idea of telling her about the pages she found in the wall, but thought better of it. It wasn't that she wanted to keep something from Grace, but if she revealed the pages, then Grace would be required to demand that she turn them over, and she wasn't ready to do that just yet. She first needed to understand the relevance, if any, that the writings had on her case. If and when she had any information, she would gladly turn over the pages, as well as anything she learned, but for now, for the sake of their fledgling relationship, the pages would remain confidential.

With that decided, Elizabeth moved along the conversation. "So, now what?"

"I secured a court order to dig up her grave."

"I want to come." Elizabeth nearly jumped out of her seat.

Grace smiled. "I assumed you would." She took a moment to study her. "Meet me tomorrow morning at nine outside the front gate of Mason Cemetery on Grand."

CHAPTER TEN

G race stood at the entrance gates of the cemetery checking her watch. It was ten after nine, and she was a little worried. She expected Elizabeth to have been there waiting for her when she arrived or before the cemetery even opened at sunrise. As she pulled out her phone to call, a red Roadster came down the road, a little faster than necessary in Grace's opinion.

"I'm so sorry I'm late," Elizabeth puffed out, grabbing her bag from the back seat as she spoke. "My mom called early this morning saying there was an emergency, so I had to rush over there."

"Everything all right?"

"Depends whether you consider her shoe closet desecrated by a feline an emergency."

"I don't really know what to say to that."

"No worries. Neither did I." Elizabeth stopped in front of her, close enough to touch, but kept her hands to her sides. "Did I miss anything?"

"Nope, they just got started. It's just up the hill."

They followed a path that cut through the heart of the cemetery, and with the morning warming up, Elizabeth pulled off a red scarf draped around her neck and hung it over her bag, while commenting on the brief synopses on the headstones as they passed. Some had much to say and some very little, and for those, she wondered what they did in life to earn the bare minimum at the end.

Grace had walked a few paces before she realized that Elizabeth was no longer with her and turned back. She found her bent over a grave pulling at the weeds that were covering a name.

"What are you doing?"

"It doesn't seem right. We should at least be able to read the guy's name. I don't know what he did, but I guess he deserves at least that."

Grace stooped beside her and began to help. There was a time that she would have shaken her head and kept walking, but that was before she let Elizabeth in. Now she would expect nothing less from her and herself. Once they cleared the gravestone and the name could be read, they continued to the gravesite of the unknown woman, where they found a crew of men operating a small excavator. A sizeable hole had already been dug, and they arrived in time to see them pull back and manually dig the remaining dirt out around the coffin.

Grace flashed her badge when a man in a black suit approached them. She assumed he was cemetery personnel based on his bleak attire and professional mournful expression. Nodding his head, he moved away attempting to keep a respectful distance. Once the crew freed the coffin, a small crane was used to hoist it from the newly excavated hole, and the exhumation was complete. The cemetery man signaled for them to approach, and as they got closer, the smell of the freshly dug dirt permeated the air.

Elizabeth moved closer to Grace, so their arms touched, as they stood over the coffin, and Grace welcomed the contact. As the lid was opened, a waft of stale air hit them causing them both to blink and turn away before peering inside.

"Well, that's a bit anticlimactic," Elizabeth said as she leaned closer.

"Where's the body?" Grace asked the cemetery man.

The coffin's sole contents were several medium sized rocks, which Grace presumed were there to match the weight of a body.

"I-I don't understand," the man stammered.

Grace didn't hold the man responsible. She knew this happened well before his time and likely didn't involve the cemetery at all.

"I need to make a call," Grace said, and she stepped away for some privacy.

Elizabeth was curious how she was going to explain this one to her supervisors. While she waited, she wandered through the nearby rows, continuing her exploration of headstones and the lives they depicted.

When Grace found her, she had a look that Elizabeth couldn't decipher. "You okay?"

She nodded and gestured toward the open coffin. "What are your thoughts on all this?"

"I think we need to know more about what this woman was doing in 1963. Why did she want people to think she was dead, and why did she come back now?"

"Well, she clearly didn't do this alone and that's what bothers me most."

"What do you know about the first case?"

"There really wasn't much, just a cursory police report and a follow-up investigation report that didn't provide many more details. According to the investigation report, the cause of death was blood loss as a result of a single stab wound to the abdomen. If there was a murder weapon and personal effects, they're gone now. The only thing left is a very thin case file with the report and the victim's prints. Just enough to look legit, but not enough to conduct an investigation."

"So now what?"

"I have to finish up here, but I'll walk you back to your car."

Elizabeth felt like she was being dismissed and reacted. "I don't need you to walk me to my car. I know the way."

"I didn't mean to upset you. I just need to get some things done."

Elizabeth took a deep breath to center herself. "I understand." And she did, but it was a reminder that they were still not on the same side. She knew that she should be grateful for all that Grace shared because as much as Grace believed in the system, there was no way of knowing whether the prosecutor would have shared this information during discovery. "Thank you, Grace. I know you didn't have to include me in on this."

Elizabeth put on her brave face to mask the sulking, self-pity that she allowed herself to indulge in on her walk back to the car. It wasn't that Grace couldn't share more details, but it was the feeling of being shut out again.

❖

Elizabeth sat on the floor of her living room, leaning against the couch, head tilted back, with Camille next to her mirroring the position. An empty bottle of red wine rested between them. Danny lay sprawled out on his back at their feet, and an open pizza box rested in the middle of them with only a single slice left to spare.

"So let me get this straight. The woman was murdered not once, but twice." Danny held up his counting fingers as he spoke for emphasis. "And no one knows who she is. What the hell did she do in her past life?"

That seemed a fair question, but Elizabeth could only shrug because any more movement seemed too much effort. She was on her second glass of wine, and since she rarely exceeded a single glass, its intended effect was kicking in. Camille lolled her head to the side to face her. "Can we use this to prove that my brother didn't kill her? It seems obvious this woman had enemies."

Elizabeth closed her eyes and contemplated the question. "I think it helps, but it's not enough. We need to know who this woman was. Maybe if we know her identity, we'll know who wanted her dead."

Camille slapped her hand on her leg, nearly missing, and said with more volume than necessary, "That's it! We need to know who she is."

It was then that Elizabeth noticed the glassy look in her eyes and realized that Camille was a glass of wine or two beyond her limit. With great effort, she pushed herself up to make preparation for her houseguests. No one was going home tonight. Danny hadn't partaken in the wine, relegated to soda by Elizabeth much to his dismay, but she knew that she was in no shape to be driving him home.

She made a brief exit and returned with her arms full of blankets and a pillow and dropped them onto the couch. "Okay, folks, it's getting late. Camille, why don't you take the extra bedroom at the end of the hall, and, Danny, you can have the sofa."

"I'm fine," Camille said, and she leaned her hands against the couch to hoist herself up, but the lower half of her body didn't comply. "Stop moving the couch."

"Hmmm," was Elizabeth's only reply as she helped her stand. Camille leaned heavily on her as she attempted to gain her balance. "Let's find you that bed."

She gave Danny a brief wave and navigated Camille to the back bedroom and helped her sit on the bed. "You think you can handle it?" Elizabeth hadn't realized how much Camille had to drink, but she didn't begrudge her. She had been under tremendous strain with her brother's criminal case and her grandmother's failing health. On the contrary, Camille was a rock.

Camille stretched out on the bed and closed her eyes. "Will you stay with me, just for a little while?" A tear escaped down her cheek.

"Of course." Elizabeth seated herself on the edge and began stroking her soft, ebony hair. "Just sleep," she said, and when Camille's breathing evened out, she slowly pulled her hand back. But before she could make a quiet retreat, Camille captured her hand and held it to her breast.

"Please don't go," she said before pulling Elizabeth's hand to her lips and placing a soft, warm kiss at the base of her palm, which sent a tingle through her body.

How she wished this was Grace. Why couldn't it be? It was so simple. Elizabeth closed her eyes and relished the thought. She returned her eyes to Camille and wondered what it would be like. Would she and Grace ever be together or would there always be a case or other excuse in their way? Another sensuous kiss caressed her hand, and she could feel a warm tongue linger. God, it felt good, the warmth, the intimacy, the want. The problem was it wasn't Grace and nothing less would do.

She extracted her hand. "You should sleep now." She pulled herself up and closed the door behind her without looking back.

CHAPTER ELEVEN

Elizabeth was the first one up, and she quickly showered and dressed before she turned her attention to finding something to eat for her guests. She figured dividing up the leftover slice of pizza wouldn't do. She fumbled through the refrigerator and heard a grumble from the lump on the couch as the blankets twisted and turned in protest to the offending noise.

"What time is it?"

"It's about seven thirty."

Elizabeth continued her ministrations in the kitchen, managing to find eggs and English muffins. It wouldn't make Martha Stewart (or her mother) proud, but it would have to do. Better than sharing a slice of pizza, but judgment on that should be reserved until after the eggs were cooked.

Danny begrudgingly sat up when the smell of food hit him.

"What's for breakfast?"

Elizabeth placed a warm plate in front of him, and she impressed herself with the scrambled eggs; they were neither runny nor crusty. Danny didn't notice as he began to shovel the food into his mouth. Elizabeth swore he swallowed without chewing. In a matter of moments, he handed the empty plate back and stood to head to the bathroom.

"Mind if I take a shower?" he asked as he was already heading down the hallway.

"Sure, and you're welcome by the way," she called after him.

She placed the plate in the sink and heard footsteps approach. "Now what did you forget?" She was surprised to find a rumpled Camille standing at the entrance of the kitchen. She hadn't yet had a chance to mentally unpack what happened the night before. Instead she went to bed with lustful thoughts of Grace.

"Sorry, I thought you were Danny. Morning, how did you sleep?"

"Fine, thanks." Camille fidgeted with a fork that sat on the countertop. "So, do you need any help?"

Elizabeth could feel the thick air between them, but was unsure what to say. "I got it covered." She handed over a plate that matched Danny's, and Camille accepted it without making eye contact and moved to the living room, head bowed.

A few feet in, she abruptly turned and moved back toward the kitchen. "So..." she drew out, staring directly at Elizabeth, causing her to swallow in anticipation of the words to come. "About last night, are we okay?"

"Yes, of course. We're definitely okay," Elizabeth responded with relief. In the brief moments, she had conjured so many different possibilities of how that conversation would play out.

With that, Camille returned to the living room and sat on the couch to enjoy her home cooked meal, and Elizabeth resumed her cleanup duties. It seemed that they both needed a little space to allow the remainder of the tension to drain through them. The brief moment of solitude was broken by the ringing of the phone that sat on a long table just outside the kitchen. Given the time and the fact that no one else other than telemarketers called her at home, she knew it was her mother.

"My mother," she said to Camille as she lifted the receiver and gestured that she was going to take it in her bedroom. She didn't want her to witness the flustering mess that her mother could reduce her to during their conversations.

Grace tucked Elizabeth's red scarf under her arm and straightened her shirt collar before she walked up the path to the front door. She found the scarf on the cemetery path the day before and she looked forward to returning it. She hesitated before knocking and wondered if it was too early, but then delivered three solid knocks. When the door opened, it was unclear who was more shocked to see the person on the other side of the door—Grace or Camille.

An awkward moment passed before Grace spoke. "I just came by to drop this off. Elizabeth left it behind yesterday." She thrust out her hand, and Camille accepted the scarf.

"Elizabeth's in the bedroom. Do you want me to get her?"

"No," Grace snapped. "Just let her know that I came by."

Grace didn't wait for a response and turned and took long, swift strides back to her car. She felt an overwhelming need to escape.

The open, two-story apartment building that once looked to serve as a motel, sat with a fresh coat of paint, which helped its look a bit, but not a lot. The front gate was rusted, the roof tiles in disrepair, and the lawn was on the wrong side of healthy. Nonetheless, the second apartment on the left on the top floor was where Danny called home, and he seemed rather pleased with it, which was all that mattered in Elizabeth's mind. She helped him settle into his new place during his first week of work, offering the first and last month's rent, along with the security deposit.

On this particular bright, crisp morning, she sat in her car snuggled between a decrepit pickup truck and a fire hydrant and waited for Danny, who had run in to make a quick change into fresh clothes. To fill her time, she listened to a debate on a local station between Democratic State Senator John McDermott and Reverend Rick Peterson. The debate jumped in topics from the state's right to self-regulate under the Tenth Amendment to the appointment of Judge Powers for the state Supreme Court. Reverend Peterson advocated for Judge Powers, as well as for the religious liberties law currently on the court's docket.

Elizabeth wanted to yell at the radio as Reverend Peterson used inflammatory language in support of his conservative views, but found comfort in Senator McDermott's rational responses that were based on the law. The senator was better versed on the Constitution, and the reverend began to falter and stumbled over his words. Satisfied that the self-righteous reverend would be on the losing end of the debate, she turned off the radio and returned her attention to Danny's apartment building.

There was still no sign of him. They parted ways with Camille shortly after breakfast, citing her own need to return to her place to shower and change. When the five-minute stop turned into fifteen, she used the alone time to call Grace. She was sorry that she missed her when Grace stopped by. She would have loved to put the real person to her fantasies of last night.

When her voice mail picked up, she waited for the appropriate time to speak. "Hi, Grace, I'm sorry I missed you this morning. Maybe we can get together for lunch or dinner? Okay, well I guess I'll talk to you later. Oh, and thanks for the scarf."

Danny finally made his reappearance wearing dark corduroy pants and a long-sleeve polo. *And that took fifteen minutes?* On the drive into SILC, Danny had no qualms about commandeering her radio, turning it to a hip-hop song that in her opinion was not deemed music, but extensive talking that didn't even rhyme. She shook her head.

"What? You too old for this music?" Danny asked.

"Music? The rhyme doesn't count if they have to mispronounce the word to make it fit."

Using the controls on her steering wheel, she changed the channel to an eighties station, but he balked and turned the knob back. A battle ensued and only blurbs of music could be heard. She resigned herself to the testosterone-induced lyrics and did her best to go to her happy place in her mind for the last five minutes of their drive.

At the clinic, she lingered in the waiting area for a moment admiring the changes. She had to admit, somewhat reluctantly, that her mother knew her stuff. The dowdy and worn office had been transitioned to classy and functional. Light tan walls were accentuated with white crown molding; sleek, but comfortable, leather seats were complemented by a matching couch; and in the corner, a graceful fountain gurgled playfully. *Ah, the fountain.*

She pulled out two wicker baskets that sat under a sturdy table in the center of the room and found a collection of newly purchased toys to suit multiple ages. *Okay, sometimes my mother rocks.*

She continued to admire the changes as she moved through the clinic, including an expanded kitchen to make up for the closet they previously called a kitchen. She turned to see her office door open, and a slight panic rose in her. She had made it a habit of keeping it closed since the work started to keep the dust in her office to a minimum. What would she find or not find in there?

She cautiously approached and moved inside her newly painted and furnished office. Behind a stately glass desk was BD, with a new gray cushion on the seat to accentuate its newly polished black leather, as well as to add comfort. Elizabeth had to smile.

She settled in but not before running her hands over the smooth, cool glass of the desk surface. It certainly beat the scarred wooden desk that had small ruts and holes. She pulled over a short stack of files and began sorting through. She had spent the day before working on non-Francis case matters that she had been neglecting, and today would be more of the same. Although the clinic couldn't afford to bring on a new attorney, she was managing to keep up with the help of the small army of legal interns that she recruited from her day at the law school.

"Oh good, you're here," a familiar voice called from her doorway.

"Morning, Mom." She wasn't surprised to see her because their early morning phone call had originated from the clinic. "The furniture looks great. I can't thank you enough for what you've done for this place. The toys in the waiting area are a really thoughtful touch."

"I know."

Elizabeth chuckled at the answer. Her mother didn't need praises; she knew her worth.

"Elizabeth, I want to introduce you to the contractor responsible for this renovation." She heard the formal tone in her mother's voice and lifted her head. "Frank DeRoso, my daughter, Elizabeth Campbell. She's the attorney who runs this place." There was a slight emphasis on the word "attorney," which worried her. Her mother was selling her to a new prospect.

She forced a smile and stood to greet the man responsible for the new and improved version of SILC. "Nice to meet you, Frank. Thank you so much for all the wonderful work you and your men have done."

"You can't give me all the credit. Your mother was the driving force behind all this." They gripped hands, and she noted he was ruggedly handsome with a kind face and endearing smile, but her mind was fully preoccupied with a particular detective.

"Coming," her mother called out the door to a phantom voice. "You two get acquainted while I see what they need."

Smooth, Mom, real smooth. Elizabeth gestured to her new, never been sat in, leather guest chair, and Frank sat down. "She is an interesting woman," he said.

"That she is, without a doubt."

"So, you run this place. Your mother has told me all about the great work you do here."

"Yup." She smiled and nodded. *Has she given you my dress size, my preference for sleeping in on weekends, and dates in which I am available to possibly...oh, I don't know...get married?* "So, you're a contractor?"

"Yup, that I am."

The conversation picked up and moved to more interesting topics and after they spent a respectable amount of time conversing, he politely excused himself to return to his duties. He wasn't half bad if it was another lifetime and he was a different gender.

She turned her attention back to the files and spent the next few hours preparing case memos and briefs. In the end, she was pleased with her accomplishments and felt once again on track, at least as the legal clinic stood. A grumble from her stomach announced that her eggs and English muffin from the morning had worn off. She checked her phone to see if she had missed any calls. *Nothing from*

Grace. She slipped the phone into the side pocket of her bag and jumped when it began to chime. She pulled it back out.

"Hello," she answered, a little breathier than she would have liked.

"Hi, Elizabeth, it's Rich."

She tried to hide her disappointment at the voice on the other end and went through the polite greeting process. Despite her initial reaction, she was glad that he called, as she planned on reaching out to him in the afternoon, but she would have liked a lunch date from a certain blond detective.

"I'm sorry to say that my friend was unable to find anything of use on the papers you found. He didn't have any better luck deciphering it but guessed it was probably a personal journal. He offered to perform a chemical analysis test to date the paper, check its authenticity."

"Thanks, Rich, I'll keep that in my mind. On another note, what information do you think you can gather on the life and death of Josiah Webb?"

"Who?"

"Josiah Webb was the last family member to live on the White Horse Plantation. He apparently died on the plantation."

"Shouldn't be too hard. I'll see what I can dig up."

After a promise to get the information to her as soon as possible, they spent another minute conversing before Rich was called away, and Elizabeth was free to go in search of food and a possible lunch partner.

CHAPTER TWELVE

When Elizabeth walked into the courtroom, Grace was sitting in the far corner of the front row behind the prosecution table. She was unsure whether her presence was voluntary or not. Pretrial hearings generally didn't involve witnesses; they were meant as a venue to air out any motions or other issues before jury selection and trial. Camille was unable to rearrange her work schedule and was absent.

There were other matters on the court's docket that morning, so Elizabeth approached the court clerk to announce herself and returned to the gallery. During the perfunctory check-in process, Grace never looked her way, but instead busied herself with her phone.

A gentle murmuring of conversations filled the courtroom, as she settled herself in the front row on the opposite side of Grace. After a discreet sideways glance down the row, Elizabeth knew that she was being ignored. When Grace didn't return her call, she was willing to dismiss it as an oversight due to a heavy caseload. She certainly didn't want another episode where she jumped to conclusions because of an unreturned call; however, this was hard to overlook. *She won't even look at me. Now what?* Last she knew, they were on good terms, well, as good as could be expected given their current circumstances. Weary from the yo-yo relationship, she wondered why it had to be so hard.

Consumed with her phone, Grace missed the standing courtroom in response to the arriving judge, and it didn't go unnoticed, by

Elizabeth anyway. *Must be one hell of a text.* Fortunately for her, the Francis case was called first.

After introducing herself, Elizabeth took her seat at counsel's table and trained her eyes on the judge's bench, but she was fully aware that Grace had moved forward and taken a seat behind the prosecutor. A shackled Jackson emerged from a door on her right and was escorted to her side, and she patted his hand in greeting.

"I have a motion here from the defense requesting production of all documents relating to a police investigation of the said victim from 1963." The judge's voice raised in pitch near the end, coming out more as a question.

"Yes, Your Honor. It appears that the victim in this case had been the subject of another investigation in which she was murdered."

"How is that possible?" the judge asked.

"That is what the defense would like to know, which is why we requested any and all documents relating to the 1963 crime and subsequent investigation."

Turning to the prosecution, the judge asked, "Care to enlighten me?"

"Through our investigation of the case, we have learned that the victim may have been involved in an earlier incident, but due to clerical errors, may have been misclassified as a murder," Assistant District Attorney Wilcox answered.

Elizabeth wanted to jump from her seat and yell, "Liar, liar, pants on fire," but restrained herself, not because she didn't believe the statement was appropriate, but as hurt and angry as she felt by Grace's actions, she couldn't do anything to betray her. It was unlikely that she had permission to reveal the 1963 case to the defense, much less bring her along on the gravesite excavation, and as a result, had been very careful to protect Grace's involvement in her attainment of that information. Instead, she alluded to her own research as the source of her knowledge.

"Your Honor," Elizabeth calmly spoke. "Even if the prosecutor's assertions are correct, the fact remains that the identity of the victim is still unknown. Access to the prior investigation might provide insight as to the victim's identity."

"Is this true?" the judge asked ADA Wilcox.

"May I have a moment, Your Honor?" The prosecutor turned behind him and leaned into Grace. Elizabeth couldn't hear the contents of their discussion, but the body language clearly indicated friction. He returned his attention to the judge. "Yes, Your Honor, that is correct."

"Well, that being the case, the court orders that the prosecution turn over any and all information relating to the 1963 crime and any and all information and evidence from the investigation to the defense within forty-eight hours. Is there anything else further on this matter?"

"No, Your Honor," ADA Wilcox said.

"No, thank you, Your Honor," Elizabeth offered in a more conciliatory tone.

The court moved on to more housekeeping matters of the case, including setting a date for jury selection and trial. A defendant was guaranteed a right to trial within sixty days of indictment, and there was only about a month left on the clock. Fearing she needed more time to piece together the unknowns, the trial was set out in six weeks. With all pretrial matters complete, the hearing adjourned, and Elizabeth offered a rushed good-bye to Jackson before gathering her belongings to vacate the table for the next defense team. As she stepped away, she was stopped short by ADA Wilcox cutting in front of her to make his exit, which put her face-to-face with Grace, who stood directly behind him. She made brief eye contact before Grace pulled away and opened the swinging door that separated the gallery from the well, to allow Elizabeth to walk in front of her. She offered a small, appreciative smile, but it missed its mark because Grace never removed her eyes from the floor as she passed.

Hoping to avoid a confrontation, Grace held back and watched Elizabeth walk out of the courtroom. Grace had been well aware of her presence from the moment she entered the court. She had been anticipating her arrival from the time she pulled herself from bed after only a few hours of sleep. She spent the prior day filled with thoughts of her and couldn't shake the sick feeling of seeing a sleepy Camille at her door.

She wasn't convinced that there was anything intimate between them, but a part of her, the jealous little green monster that took up a small space inside her, wasn't ruling it out, given the predatory look on Camille's face. She was only grateful that Camille was absent from the courtroom because even the smallest of touches between them was more than she could witness in her beleaguered state; however, her early morning self-diatribe went beyond jealousy.

It was more of what was fair—fair to Elizabeth. Grace couldn't give her what Camille could, even when Elizabeth reached out and kissed her. Grace shut her down, citing their positions in the case as an obstacle. Patience was what she asked of her, but Elizabeth deserved better, and it was this thought that left her sitting with a heavy heart and unable to look at the one woman who exacerbated and fascinated her like no other.

"Excuse me, Detective Donovan," Elizabeth said, catching Grace's attention as she exited the court, as well as the attention of ADA Wilcox, who was standing on the opposite side of the hall. Grace hesitated a moment before taking a few steps, stopping an arm's length in front of her.

"I'm sorry, Elizabeth, I can't." Grace looked at her before averting her eyes.

"You can't what? Grace, look at me."

With effort, she raised her eyes and stared at the hurt and confused face, knowing she was responsible, but she found no words to say. *Selfish, that's what I am.* Elizabeth stepped closer, as though searching for answers in her eyes. Grace wondered if she saw her mental flagellation, pain, or fear. All three would be correct.

"Detective," ADA Wilcox said, breaking their silent exchange. "May I speak with you please?"

Grace allowed her eyes to linger a moment longer; she was not quite ready to let go.

"Detective," he insisted behind her.

Closing her eyes and taking a deep, stabilizing breath, she turned away from Elizabeth and moved to ADA Wilcox, who was so insistent on having her attention, and she felt, more than saw, Elizabeth walk away.

"No fraternizing with the defense, Detective. Need I remind you the side you work for?" ADA Wilcox said.

After he received the last-minute defense motion the day before, ADA Wilcox had questioned her on how they attained the information, coming short of outright accusing her of treason. Grace neither confirmed nor denied his suspicion and instead allowed him to rant. When he neared the end of his bombastic lecture on duty and service, she simply asked whether it would be grounds for a mistrial if the prosecution failed to turn over exculpatory evidence. That stopped him short before he exclaimed, "Exculpatory, my ass," and stormed away. However, the prior day's encounter served as a stark reminder of the canyon that stood between her and Elizabeth, and why she had to let her walk away.

"Detective, are you even listening to me?"

Grace pulled her eyes back to his but remained silent. Instead, she imagined ways she could squish him, envisioning him with a little cockroach body under her hard sole boot.

"I don't care what fucking team you play for," he snapped, "but keep your hands out of that tart's pants."

Before he could even take his next breath, Grace slammed him against the wall. With her forearm pushed into his chest pinning him, she barked, "Don't ever speak of her that way. I will drop you without any care of the consequences. Understood?" When he met her with only wide-eyed silence, she pushed even harder into his body. "Understood?"

"Understood," he spit out.

She released her hold and only then realized the crowd that had gathered to watch the spectacle. Wilcox straightened his jacket and picked up his briefcase, uttering "fucking dyke" as he stomped away.

Taking in a deep shaky breath, Grace ran her hands through her hair before turning around in search of the bathroom so she could regroup in at least semi-privacy.

❖

"She wouldn't even look at me," Elizabeth said on her fifth round of pacing. She was in no condition to return to her office, so she sought out the comfort and counsel of Michael. After flopping herself into a brightly colored, ergonomic chair that took center stage in his office, she launched herself back up. Michael watched and listened as she moved back and forth from one end of the office to the other, like a human metronome. After a few minutes, she flopped down again, exhausted, and this time stayed down. She sank into the chair and allowed her arms to drop at her side and blew an exasperated breath.

He pulled his chair to her side and grabbed her hand, resting it in his lap. "Tell me what happened, from the beginning."

"She's been pushing me away. She says it's the case, but she wouldn't even look at me," Elizabeth said. She went on to explain the events that led up to her bursting into Grace's father's hospital room, babbling and hugging the man like he was a long lost relative. "Oh God." She covered her face. "He must think I'm a real idiot."

Michael wisely chose to stay quiet.

"We talked after and everything seemed fine, not great, but okay. But this morning, she wouldn't even look at me. What did I do?"

He squeezed her hand. "Honey, you didn't do anything wrong. It is all her. I can go beat her up for you."

She appreciated his attempt at humor, but she couldn't get herself to smile.

"You know what you need?" he asked. "A night out." Elizabeth's only response was a groan. "I'm serious," he said. "You and me, some music and dancing. It will be good for your soul."

"I don't have it in me," she said, but she knew protesting was futile. She was going out that night if he had to drag her there.

"Detective Donovan."

Grace winced at the sound of her name and blew out a breath before turning to face the voice. Her sergeant stood in the doorway of his office and beckoned her to approach. The look on his face indicated that it wasn't for tea and cookies. She moved toward him, avoiding eye contact with the others in the office, but she could hear bits of their murmuring as she passed, none in her support. She was the youngest and only female detective in the unit, and that didn't garner her any sympathy among her colleagues.

"Close the door," came the order when she stepped into the room, and she complied with the request.

Her sergeant, a red-faced man with a thick neck and wavy graying hair that he kept close-cropped, sat behind a cluttered desk, littered with files, papers, and a collection of photographs. In one of them, he was actually smiling, something she had never personally seen.

"Have a seat." Another short command. She had to admit that he was a fair man, but for any detective who stepped out of line, hell was to be paid. Once she was seated, he leveled a stare. "I got a call from the prosecutor's office."

"I thought you might."

"Assaulting a prosecutor? What the hell, Donovan! I should take your badge right now." She was surprised at how willing she was to give it up at that moment. She could work security at the mall, but reality set in. It would never pay for her father's care.

"I apologize, sir. I lost my head. The prick, uh, prosecutor, ran off at the mouth hurling insults. And questioning my ability to investigate the case. I'm a good detective, sir." She held her head high, and he nodded in agreement. She knew that he regarded her as was one of his best, and up until now, she had caused no problems.

He leaned his elbows on his desk and clasped his hands. "The prosecutor's an ass. Everyone knows it. Between you and me, I've had the urge to throw him against the wall a time or two. But you gotta keep your head. He can make things very difficult for you and me. Understand?"

"Yes, sir." Realizing that he was going to let her slide with a warning, she loosened her grip on the chair.

"All right, get out of here."

She stood and exited his office to return to her desk. *What a fucking day, and it's not even half over.*

❖

"I look like a slut," Elizabeth said, eyeing herself critically in her full-length mirror. She was dressed in a black leather skirt that rode up indecently high, a form-fitting, deep purple shirt that barely contained her breasts, which were being thrust forward by a pushup bra, and what she called "fuck me" high heels; all of which were found in her closet, but she would have never dreamed of combining them. Black eye liner and smoky eye shadow accented her eyes, and her hair was pulled back into an artfully tied ponytail, with a few strands wistfully tucked behind her ear.

"Honey, you look hot," Michael responded, commenting on his handiwork. If he left it up to Elizabeth, she would have shown up in jeans.

"How am I supposed to sit down?"

"We aren't going for sitting. Now move it." He picked up her black leather handbag and shoved it at her as he pulled her out the front door.

She treaded carefully, watching for small rocks, nooks and crannies, and other lethal obstacles that could take her down in her two-inch heels as she made her way to Michael's Porsche. She had come to terms with his plans and decided that he was right. She wouldn't sit around waiting for Grace to decide when and if she was ready to start a relationship. She would live her life, and a night out with Michael was a good way to kick off her new lease on her social life.

After several minutes of conversing with herself in her head, Elizabeth looked around at the moving traffic. "So where are we going?"

"It's a new place that opened up a few months ago. Don't worry, they only charge by the hour, and they have a new *cuuummer* special."

"What!" Elizabeth snapped her head to face him. Realizing that she was being played, she slapped his arm.

"Ouch, that hurt," he protested.

"Then I did it right."

She was nervous, and he was trying to keep it light, even if it meant taking a few hits for the team. They had gone out countless times, especially in their college years, but this night was different. This was a turning point, where she wasn't just accompanying him to a club to hang at his side as his best friend. She was going as an eligible woman.

When he slowed his car to turn into the drive, she nervously peered at the sign announcing Wilting Willies. "You think that's the best name for a club? People aren't coming here for wilting willies."

He offered no comeback and instead concentrated on finding a spot that was close enough to the entrance, but far enough to be safe from drunken patrons stumbling out of the club. Like Elizabeth, he was proprietary about his car. Music spilled out of the front door each time it opened, and he moved in rhythm. He was ready to get the party started, and he stepped out and moved around to open Elizabeth's door. She hesitated, staring at the purple neon sign.

"Are you *cuuumming*?" he asked.

She accepted his proffered hand and pulled herself up and straightened her skirt that had managed to hike up nearly to her hips.

"Oh Lord, please don't tell me you're wearing *those* underwear?"

"Don't look at my underwear! And what's wrong with them?"

"They're cotton and floral. Need I say anymore?"

"Shut up." She stormed ahead of him making it three steps before she faltered and stumbled in the gravel.

"Oh Lord, the pay by the hour thing might be the only way you see any action tonight." He gripped her arm and helped her navigate to the front door. A man in ripped jeans and a tight white T-shirt, showing off his muscular build, perched on a stool inside and requested their identification before they could pass. Once proving they were of legal age, they moved into the inner sanctum, and Elizabeth blinked to adjust to the darkened room that was accented with neon lights that streaked across the floor. A long bar ran across the wall closest to the door, and several round tables with stools lined the wooden dance floor that took center stage. The club was fairly full, enough to keep it bustling, but not uncomfortably so. He steered her to a vacant table on the opposite side and pulled out a high stool for her. She could only stare at it.

"You expect me to climb up on that?"

Michael eyed the situation, and he hoisted her up. "Upsy-daisy." She plopped on the seat and hung on to the table as she almost fell off the other side.

He offered to get them some drinks, and she stared off at the dance floor watching the couples do a modern form of a mating dance. They made it seem easy, no hesitation, no tension, no "I can't because our jobs stand between us." By the time Michael returned, she had herself worked up and was almost talking to herself.

"You can let go of the table," he said. "And maybe look a little less pissed off."

She closed her eyes and rolled her shoulders, reminding herself why she came. She was going to have a good time if it killed her, and at the moment, it felt like it just might, if the shoes didn't get her first.

"Hi, do you mind if I share your table?" someone asked from behind her, and she turned to acknowledge an attractive dark haired woman dressed in jeans, T-shirt, and black leather boots. "All the others are full." She gestured with a drink in her hand.

"Please," Michael eagerly responded, and he popped off his seat to pull out the empty stool.

"Thanks. I'm Melissa."

"Hi, Melissa, I'm Michael, and this is Elizabeth," he replied, gesturing to Elizabeth, in case she didn't notice her sitting there.

Elizabeth felt a little like the last pick in the litter of kittens that the owners were desperately trying to give away.

Melissa offered a cordial nod in her direction and glanced at the cleavage spilling out of her shirt. "So, are you newcomers?"

Elizabeth nearly spit out her drink at the question. "Excuse me?"

"Is this your first time coming here?" she asked, speaking slower.

"Oh, uh, yeah, first time here," Elizabeth fumbled out.

The conversation between them stalled, and Michael intervened. "How about you?"

"I have been here a few times, but I don't seem to get out very often with work and all."

"What do you do?" Michael asked.

"I'm a lawyer."

"Really, Elizabeth is too," he said, making no attempt to hide the excitement in his voice. "You are two peas on a pod."

"Peas in a pod," Elizabeth corrected him.

"What?"

"It's 'two peas *in* a pod.'"

"In a pod, on a pod, whatever. I think you two should dance," he blurted.

If Melissa wasn't sitting between them, she would have slapped him upside the head, and he knew it, giving her a Cheshire cat grin.

Melissa turned to her. "You game?"

"Uh, sure." Elizabeth finished her drink, hoping for some liquid courage, then looked down and hesitated. Melissa recognized her predicament.

"Allow me." She offered her arm, and Elizabeth slid down while Melissa helped her balance when her feet hit the floor, putting them at equal height. Once seeing her soundly to the ground, she said, "You look great by the way."

"Thanks, this is Michael's doing," she responded, gesturing to her attire as if it was an apology, but from Melissa's appreciative look, no apologies were needed.

A slow ballad began to play, which sent a sense of relief and panic through Elizabeth; relief that it was a more manageable pace with her shoes, but panic because it meant close contact with her. Melissa sensed her trepidation and lightly placed her hand on her shoulder, allowing a comfortable amount of space to exist between them, and they moved in rhythm.

"So what area of law do you practice?" Melissa asked.

Elizabeth explained her work with the Southern Indigent Legal Center, and the conversation put her at ease. Melissa was attentive, asking several questions about her cases.

"Sounds much more interesting than what I do day in and day out."

"Which is?"

"Corporate transactions."

"Oh." Elizabeth wasn't sure what more to add, as she couldn't envision an area of law that was more of an extreme opposite to what she did.

"No worries. You need not say anymore. The money is good, but the work, well, that's not so exciting."

Elizabeth offered a genuine smile to Melissa's honesty.

"So, Elizabeth, tell me, why is it that your friend Michael felt the need to dress you up and drag you out to a club when you would clearly rather be elsewhere?"

"It's that obvious?"

Melissa moved her head slightly from side to side, as though contemplating her answer. "Yup, pretty obvious."

"It's sort of a long story."

"What's her name?"

Elizabeth stopped and stared directly into her eyes but didn't answer.

"Sorry, I didn't mean to pry. It's just written all over you."

"I'm trying to escape that tonight. How about we talk about something else?"

"So, chocolate or vanilla?"

"Chocolate or vanilla what?"

"Ice cream." Melissa smiled.

"Mint chocolate chip."

"Of course. You are definitely not a chocolate or vanilla kind of gal."

"I will take that as a compliment."

"As you should."

The easy conversation continued for several songs, until Elizabeth had to cry mercy because of her feet, and Melissa gallantly guided her back to the table. They bantered naturally, with Michael coming and going in between dances, and three hours slipped by.

It became clear that Michael had found a new friend when he stopped returning to their table, and as much as she was enjoying Melissa's company, the evening was catching up with her, and she was ready to call it a night. Elizabeth scanned the crowd for her ride.

Michael made his way back, and it was then that Elizabeth realized the drunken state he was in. "How many drinks did he have?"

"Probably a drink or two beyond merry."

It seemed Elizabeth would be their designated driver, since she'd only had the single drink when she arrived.

"There you are," Michael slurred as he stumbled to her, touching the tip of her nose. "Isn't she a cutie? So you two going to get it on?"

"All righty, I think it's time for us to go." She kicked off her shoes and hopped down to wrap an arm around his waist.

As she attempted to reach for her shoes, Melissa stepped in. "I got this." She grabbed Elizabeth's purse and shoes and followed behind. When Michael began steering her off course, Melissa moved to his other side, and with her free arm helped Elizabeth navigate.

It took several minutes to reach the car, as Michael continually stopped to spout out random facts, Elizabeth's least favorite being, "I can see your boobies," as he stared down her shirt, which led to a one-sided discussion about her underwear. She could hear Melissa chuckling through his monologue.

When they reached the car, Michael provided Melissa with lots of fun Elizabeth facts, including her propensity to dance naked in the mirror after every shower. At that tidbit, Elizabeth let go of her hold and allowed him to fall into the passenger side of the car. "Oooops." She patted him down searching for the keys and felt a bulge in his pocket. "These better be your keys," she said as she reached inside.

After she unlocked the door, Melissa helped guide him inside, and Elizabeth shut the door behind him. They both watched him for a moment as his head lolled to the side and his eyes closed.

"You going to be okay with him?" Melissa asked as she handed over Elizabeth's belongings.

"Yeah, I'll just leave him to sleep in the car."

Melissa reached into her back pocket, pulled out a small leather billfold, and removed her business card. "You have a pen?"

Melissa wrote a number on the back of the card. "Here's my cell. Call if you ever want to hang out, have lunch, or just talk. No strings attached."

Elizabeth accepted the card and squeezed her hand. "Thank you, Melissa, for everything." She placed a soft kiss on her cheek before turning to move to the driver's side. As much as she enjoyed Melissa's company, she wouldn't call.

CHAPTER THIRTEEN

Making as much noise as possible, Elizabeth clanked around the kitchen, and when that didn't work, she began dropping things on the floor, which only resulted in Michael turning to find a more comfortable position. Despite her promise to leave him in the car, she half carried, half dragged him into the house the night before and dropped him on her couch, where he remained comfortably tucked under a blanket, obnoxiously snoring. She thought about the prior evening and Melissa, a beautiful, sexy, attentive, and best yet, available woman who clearly showed interest, and yet, it wasn't enough.

Since she was unable to take it out on the person that really angered her, Michael became her surrogate. With a pot in one hand and a metal spoon in the other, she stood over him and began to beat them together above his head, causing him to bolt up straight.

"Oh sorry, did I wake you?"

Michael dropped back down and threw his arm over his eyes. "You're evil."

"Time to get up. It's after eight."

"Go away and leave me here to die in peace."

Elizabeth's ringing cell phone cut off her reply. She looked at the caller ID before answering. "Hi, Amy, what's up?"

"You better get down here. The clinic has been broken into."

"Did you call the police?"

"They're on their way."

"What's missing?"

"Nothing that I can tell so far, but it's a mess."

"All right, I'll be there soon."

Elizabeth's earlier mission to torture Michael all but forgotten, she gave him a quick rundown of the conversation, while gathering her things to head out the door.

She made it to work in forty minutes and pushed open the front door of the clinic to find it just as Amy described—a mess. The chairs were tipped over, drawers opened and the contents pulled out and sprawled across the floor, and supply cabinets were stripped completely bare. Rosa, Danny, and others were up-righting the furniture and making piles of the paperwork and files that were thrown about. Amy stood in the corner with two police officers who were diligently taking notes, and Elizabeth approached them.

"Hi, I'm Elizabeth Campbell, the supervising—" Before she could finish, Elizabeth's mother made her entrance with her usual flair, and all heads turned in her direction.

"What's going on here?" she demanded, and everyone stood still hoping to avoid her wrath. She paid them no attention, her sights set on the police officers.

"Uh, never mind, you can talk to her," Elizabeth said sympathetically as she and Amy backed up to give her wide berth. "So what's happening?" she asked Amy.

"Someone pried open the front door and basically trashed the place."

"Anything missing?"

"I don't think so. The police think it was someone looking for money or drugs."

SILC was located in the seedier part of town, so the assessment seemed logical. "They sure were thorough. No drawer or cabinet left unturned."

From what Elizabeth could garner from the conversation between her mother and the police, which wasn't difficult to overhear given her mother's state, SILC's alarm system was only a few days away from being installed, waiting on the rewiring of the new kitchen, which proved fortuitous for the burglar. Unfortunately for the police officers, her mother found their patrolling of the neighborhood lacking, and if Elizabeth heard correctly, they were grounded.

She felt pity for the officers, but not enough to intervene as self-preservation kicked in, and she moved into her own office to assess the damage. Her office looked like a snow globe that had been turned upside down and shaken, and she moved to BD, which was resting on its side, and up-righted the chair, soothing apologies for its mistreatment. She had to give her mom credit though; the new seat cushion remained firmly in place.

She spent the next hour cleaning and reorganizing her office, as the rest of the staff and construction workers did the same under her mother's command. She had no doubt that SILC would be back in business by lunch. She was placing her files in alphabetical order in her filing cabinet when a knock on her partially opened door drew her attention.

"Come in," she said without turning.

After placing the last file in the cabinet, Elizabeth finally turned to acknowledge her guest. Rich stuck his head through, followed by the rest of his body, and assessed the state of her office.

"Oh hi, Rich, sorry. I thought you were one of the workers."

"What happened?" he asked as he started picking up loose pens and pencils that were strewn on the floor near the door.

She offered what little information she knew and relieved him of the writing utensils in his hands and redeposited them into the cup on her desk. "Have a seat." She wasn't expecting him, but his visit was a welcome reprieve.

Rich dropped a thick manila folder on her desk as he sat. "This is the information I pulled on the Lawton Plantation, also known as the White Horse Plantation because of the stables it kept in its heyday. It's basically been maintained by the same family since it was built in 1840 by Frederick Lawton."

Elizabeth nodded at the information she already knew and reached for the folder, which appeared to contain a series of property transfer deeds and tax records. She thought it best not to ask how he obtained some of the documents.

"There isn't a lot there about the early years. But what I pieced together, the property survived after the Civil War through sharecropping and continued in that existence until the 1950s, when it fell into arrears with its property taxes, and the government sought to seize it."

"So the government took over the property?"

"No, just as the property was going on the auction block, the recently widowed Josiah Webb paid the back taxes and interest and moved to the plantation."

"So, why did he wait and let it fall into arrears?"

"Looks like he was broke. He didn't seem to have any type of profession, at least nothing I could see in the records, but his wife had some family money, which he inherited when she passed away." Rich took the folder from her hands and flipped through the documents. "Here's her death certificate."

After reading the typewritten page, she looked at him. "She died of unknown causes. How does she die of an unknown cause?"

"Now look at the date that the property taxes were paid on the plantation."

"About a month after her death. So we think there might be some foul play in his wife's death? Why did he care so much about the property? It would seem like such a burden."

"I asked myself the same question, so I did some more digging."

Elizabeth could only smile. Rich was worth his weight in gold.

"It seems Mr. Josiah Webb had a history of skirmishes with the law when he was younger. He was a vocal segregationist and many of his arrests related to his *cause*." He emphasized the last word by making quotation marks with his fingers. "There seemed to be concern about possible activities that were taking place on the property."

"How do you know?"

"There were three more property liens filed by the government during the five-year period prior to Webb's death, but each time Webb managed to catch up on his taxes."

"What's unusual about that? You said the government nearly auctioned the property off at one point. I'm guessing he ran out of his wife's money, so he was struggling to keep up with the taxes."

"Yeah, but that was after years of nonpayment of taxes. The other three times occurred in a short period of time immediately after Webb defaulted on the taxes, like they were just waiting for the opportunity to seize the property."

"And if the government gained control of the property, no search warrant was needed," Elizabeth finished. She wasn't surprised at the government's interest in the home given the Confederate flag and weapons she found, but guessed law enforcement was dealing in suppositions on Webb's activities, which wouldn't be enough to gain a warrant, and they were trying to find creative ways to access the property.

"From there, it seems Webb came into another source of money because thereafter he kept up with the property taxes."

"What was the source of income?"

"Nothing he was willing to report because there is nothing documented."

"So what became of these suspicious activities?"

"Nothing, from what I can tell. In September 1963, Josiah Webb died in a horseback riding accident on the plantation. The last page in the folder is his death certificate."

She turned to the document and studied it. "This doesn't make sense. Josiah Webb didn't keep any horses on that property. According to Samuel, he was allergic and hated them."

He stared at her for a moment. "Oh right, the caretaker."

"With Webb's death, who owns the property now?"

"Bounty Ministries," he answered. "It's a religious nonprofit founded by Webb about six months before he died. He transferred the title of the property to this foundation. Claimed it was a religious retreat."

"He was looking for the tax breaks to keep the government off his back."

"That would be my guess."

"What do we know about this foundation?"

"I thought you'd never ask." Rich was in his element. "After Webb's death, control of Bounty Ministries passed to Jefferson Webb."

"Webb's son?"

"Exactly, and it continued to exist as a religious organization with a small but consistent following, nothing notable, until about five years ago, when Jefferson died and Reverend Rick Peterson took the helm. He turned the fledgling organization into a televangelical church that broadcasts on some off-brand cable channel, and it's following has grown."

"I know of him." Elizabeth remembered the debate she heard on the radio. "He's an ass. What's his relationship to Webb?"

"He's Webb's grandson. Appears he not only gave the church a new look, but also changed his name from Webb to Peterson, his mother's maiden name, probably for better ratings. And according to their website, they're looking to break ground for construction on a new site for its flagship mega church."

"Where's the money coming from?"

"Donations. It's one of those pay to pray churches."

Before Elizabeth could offer a response, Rosa rapped on the open door and walked in with a small stack of papers in her hand. "I'm sorry to bother you, but this came in over the fax, and it looked important."

Elizabeth accepted the papers and thumbed through them. "Oh, this is timely. It's from the DA's office. It's the police report and investigative notes on the 1963 murder." She looked up to further elaborate, when she realized that her words were falling on deaf ears. Rich's eyes were locked onto Rosa and his mouth hung slightly ajar, which she would have found inappropriate if Rosa wasn't returning the gaze. She stared between them for a moment before realizing that they were probably waiting for a proper introduction. "Oh sorry, uh, Rich Porter, this is Rosa Sanchez."

Rich stood, nearly knocking over his chair, and thrust out his hand. Rosa gingerly accepted with a small giggle. "So, have you been working here long?" Rich asked, flustered, still holding her hand.

Feeling like a voyeur, Elizabeth looked away to give them some semblance of privacy and realized that the best course of action was to vacate the room. She excused herself, but it didn't matter because she no longer existed. She closed the door behind her, then nearly ran into Danny who was carrying a small table with a stack of books precariously balanced on top. "Uh, that's not going to end well."

"What?" He turned, and as if on cue, stumbled over a box resting on the floor and the books were sent flying across the room.

"Never mind." She walked on in search of a bit of peace to review the faxed documents. She ducked her head into a few rooms but found every space bustling, and finally settled in a supply closet. She strategically left the door partially open to allow for enough reading light, but still provide privacy.

Engrossed in her reading, she didn't notice Camille poking her head through the open slot and jumped at the sound of her voice. "If you're going to play hide-and-seek, you might let others know; otherwise you'll be sitting here all day."

"Damn, I knew I was doing something wrong."

"So why are you in here?" Camille asked. "What's wrong with your office?"

"It's was occupied," she said as she stood.

Camille followed her to her office, and Elizabeth handed over the faxed documents. "This is the police and investigation reports from the 1963 murder. There isn't much there."

Camille nearly snatched it from her hands and read the pages. When she reached the end, her shoulders sank. "This is it?"

"Seems so."

"So now what?"

"Let's see if there is anyone who still remembers the case."

CHAPTER FOURTEEN

I know, I know." Elizabeth argued with her voice-automated navigation system that urged her to turn around because she passed the address. After completing a U-turn, she pulled into the asphalt driveway and assessed her options for parking, which were to squeeze in between parked cars near the entrance or park in the far corner with multiple open spaces under a tree. Corner it was.

Several elderly people sat on wooden benches that lined the walkway, and she could hear snippets of their conversations as she passed. The group consensus of the women on the first bench was that Mrs. Jensen couldn't possibly be only seventy-five. Two men on the second bench argued about who cheated during the prior evening's game of pinochle. However, it was the third bench that caught her attention. Apparently, the woman in room 3B was seen sneaking out of 3F in the middle of the night, all the while having not-so-secret relations with the man in 2A, but 3F was seen two nights ago cozying up to the woman in 1G, who was purportedly sleeping with 2A. She had to slow her pace to catch the last of it because she didn't want to miss out. *Wow, who knew Crestview Assisted Living could be so much fun.*

After crossing the comfortable, well-furnished lobby, she was greeted by a perky twenty-something woman behind a counter. The room had the feel of a hotel rather than a retirement home.

"Hi, I'm here to see Jack Rourke. He's expecting me." She called the retired detective after finally tracking down the sole surviving member of the investigation team from the 1963 murder case, and she was not only pleased to learn that he remembered the case, but was willing to talk about it.

"Yes, he mentioned that he was expecting a visitor. He's in the game room. Go down the hallway, and it's the first door on the right," the woman said with a great deal of enthusiasm.

"Okey dokey," Elizabeth responded, which caused her to smile to herself. The woman was rubbing off.

She followed the woman's directions and stood in the entryway of a large room with multiple tables on one side, a pool table in the middle, and a collection of small couches and stuffed chairs around a widescreen television on the other side. The room was half full with residents dispersed throughout the tables and couches, and in between, there was a raucous game of pool underway between two men. Unsure which of the men was the retired detective, she asked a group of women at the closest table, and without lifting her head from the set of cards in her hand, a woman pointed in the direction of the shouting in the middle of the room.

Elizabeth approached a man holding a pool stick at his side heckling his mate, who was bent over preparing for a shot. "Hi, I'm Elizabeth Campbell. I am looking for Jack Rourke."

"That would be me," the man replied, as he used his pool stick to prod his friend in the backside.

"Knock it off, Jack," the friend grumbled as he turned to face his opponent. "Elizabeth!" Recognition crossed the man's face as he stared at her with a wide smile.

"Mr. Donovan?"

"It's George, remember? We're on a hugging basis." He tossed the stick on the table and reached out to wrap his arms around her.

She couldn't help but allow him to engulf her, and she returned the hug. She really liked him and could see much of Grace in him when she wasn't being Detective Donovan.

"So you live here?"

"Home sweet home. What brings you here?"

"Well, I actually came to speak with Mr. Rourke."

"Who? Oh, him." He pointed to his friend. "He's no mister. He's just Jack."

"He's right. Call me Jack," he said, inserting himself into the conversation. "So what's the interest in that old case?"

"Is there someplace else we can talk that's a bit more private?" Elizabeth asked.

"Oh sure, follow me."

Elizabeth and George followed Jack down the hall to an elevator that took them to the second floor. She wasn't sure how appropriate it would be for George to be part of the conversation, given that he was Grace's father, but he seemed so happy to see her that she didn't have the heart to exclude him. After exiting the elevator, they made a left and abruptly stopped in front of room 2A. She hesitated for a moment, remembering the bench conversation about the love connections, and if she remembered correctly, 2A prominently stood in the middle of it. She chuckled.

"What's so funny?" Jack asked.

"Oh, it's nothing," Elizabeth answered.

"Come on in." He opened the door and gestured for her to walk in front of him. She took in the room, which consisted of a kitchenette in one corner, a small sitting area with a television next to a window, and a double bed in the middle. She couldn't help but look at the bed and think again of the legend of room 2A.

"Thank you for agreeing to meet me, Jack."

"Of course. So what can I do you for?" He motioned her to the couch and sat next to her.

She pulled out the file of the first murder investigation and handed it to him. "I'm currently working on a case in which my client is accused of murdering this woman."

"You mean they finally solved this case fifty-some years later?"

"Nooo, I mean that my client is accused of killing this woman last month."

"I don't understand."

"I don't either, which is why I'm here."

Elizabeth studied the reports and there were several glaring issues that she thought should have raised red flags from the beginning. The police report consisted of two pages and the facts, which were sparse, consisted mainly of noting the victim's physical appearance and clothing. There was little information about the murder weapon or the injuries sustained. However, what was even stranger was the fact that the police report was dated more than a week after the murder and there were no names anywhere on it. It didn't specify who the responding officers were, who the coroner was, or even who authored the report. The only two names contained in the entire file were on the subsequent investigation report—Detectives John Stalworth and Jack Rourke. Based on her research, John Stalworth passed away more than ten years ago, and this left her with Jack, the only known remaining member of the investigation team.

"The police report," she tapped the file for emphasis, "says that this woman was stabbed to death in 1963 and her body was found in a ditch off the side of a road near the old White Horse Plantation."

"Yes, I remember. She was a young woman, probably about twenty. We never learned her name."

"You remember it?" Elizabeth was afraid that time might have compromised his memory.

"Yes. As a detective, there are certain cases that stick with you. I was a new detective. That was my first homicide case. She was so young, but it was the fact that we didn't know who she was that really got to me. She was clean-cut, well dressed, someone that you think people would notice if she went missing, yet no one came forward to identify her."

"So, you saw her, her body that is?"

"Well, no." Jack rubbed his chin. "That's what I remember from the initial report. My partner Stalworth and I were assigned to the case about two weeks later. The autopsy was already done. The body was buried."

"Was that normal?"

"No." He paused and looked as though he was going to say something else, but changed his mind. Elizabeth stared at him and waited to see if he had anything more to add, and when Jack didn't say anymore, she said, "I read the investigation report, but there is so little there. It looks like the case was closed only a few weeks after the murder. Why?"

"Wasn't my call. I was the low man on the totem pole. My captain wanted us to move on to other cases. There were no leads. Hell, we didn't even know who she was. The case was stale and new cases came in. This one got shelved."

"Is there anything you can tell me about the case?"

He opened the file and began reading the report. Elizabeth looked up to George, who had been silently sitting across from them during the conversation, and gave him a smile.

"How is Grace?" she asked.

He looked concerned. "Why are you asking me? I thought you two…you know."

"We're not on speaking terms. Your daughter is the detective on my case."

"Oh my, that can make things complicated."

"I'll say."

"This is all of it?" Jack asked, oblivious to their conversation.

"Yes," Elizabeth answered.

"I knew I was green, but I didn't realize I was that green. This case wasn't meant to be solved." Jack rubbed his chin again, a trait that she was beginning to associate with him.

"What do you mean?"

"Stalworth, he was the senior detective and I was new to the unit, so I followed his lead. It was his plan that we split up. He sent me out to the scene where the body was found to look around for anything that was overlooked, and he interviewed the people that lived in the nearby home and the teenagers that found the body."

"There is no indication in the report that anyone was interviewed."

"I see that." A look of hurt washed across Jack's face. "When no new evidence came in, I wanted to go the morgue to see her myself, but Stalworth told me that she was already buried. I asked about the family, what if they came, how would they identify her? He said if they were coming, they would have been there by now, and we had her prints for identification if it came to that."

Elizabeth surmised that the fingerprints were meant to be a substitution for the nonexistent body in case the family did show up.

Jack trailed his finger over John Stalworth's signature on the bottom of the report. "He was a legend in our unit. I didn't think to question him." He released a deep sigh. "Then, it wasn't long before a new case came in and then another." He closed the file and returned it to her. "I'm sorry."

His apology seemed deeper than not being able to provide more information to Elizabeth, but for letting the woman down.

"Thank you for taking the time to talk to me," Elizabeth said as she packed the file in her bag, but he didn't seem to hear her. He was staring off scratching his chin.

"You said that your client is accused of murdering this woman a month ago?"

"Yes. The 1963 case was in the cold case unit, and somehow Grace, Detective Donovan, matched the prints of the current victim to the old case. She had the body exhumed, and well, there was no body. The casket was empty."

"Has anyone looked at the mortuary records to see who buried the body?" George asked. Elizabeth hadn't thought of that.

"Let's go check this out," Jack said as he slapped his knee and pushed himself up.

"What do you mean?" she asked.

"I mean, let's go back to where she was supposedly buried and get to the bottom of this."

"But I think we will need a court order to see the mortuary records, assuming they still exist."

"Order smorder. We don't need no stinkin' order."

Elizabeth really liked this guy.

Jack rose and donned a brown fedora, and George followed behind. Elizabeth shook her head. *This should be interesting.*

When they stepped out of the elevator, a group of women were huddled around a small table in the lobby, and Jack tipped his hat to them as they passed, and the women giggled.

Jack stopped by the reception desk and advised the perky woman that they were going for a drive. He clearly wasn't looking for her permission, and she seemed to know better than to argue with him.

As they walked to the parking lot, it dawned on Elizabeth that her car was a two-seater and there were three of them. It was unlikely she was going to cram one of them in behind her seat, and one of them was sure as hell not driving her Roadster, so she could squeeze in the back. "Um, gentlemen, it seems we may have an issue."

"What is that, young lady?" Jack asked.

"My car only seats two."

"Oh, no need to worry. I have my car."

"Really? You drive?"

Jack pulled the keys from his front pocket. "Of course I do. It's a big hit with the ladies."

He guided them to a light brown Cadillac that Elizabeth guessed was about as old as she was. He opened the passenger door for her, which squeaked in protest, and she hesitated before she stepped in. It took effort to pull the seat belt across her body and additional effort to locate the buckle shoved below the seat cushion. Clearly, seat belt use was optional in Jack's car.

The engine knocked and sputtered as they pulled out of the parking lot, and Jack asked, "Where to?"

She pointed out the directions to the cemetery and hung on to the door handle. Jack seemed to pay little attention to speed limits or stop signs. Now she knew how the passengers felt in her car. As they approached a light, she tried to calmly advise, "There's a red light."

He didn't seem to hear her, or if he did, he chose to ignore her.

"Red light," she said with more force.

"What's that?" he asked as they sailed through the intersection, and she could hear a few screeches behind them.

"Never mind."

Elizabeth tried to steady her breathing as they pulled into the cemetery lot. She really had to reconsider her own driving habits. She tried to push open the door, but it stuck.

"Oh, allow me." Jack came to her side and yanked open the door. "Madame." He offered his hand to help her step out, and she could see why he was so popular with the ladies.

She walked between Jack and George up a bricked walkway, and she felt like linking their arms and singing lyrics from "We're

Off to See the Wizard." She couldn't decide who was the Tin Man and who was the Scarecrow. She realized that Toto was also missing when a squirrel scampered by. *That will have to do.*

When they reached the office for the cemetery, she turned to them. "It might be better if you let me do the talking."

"As you wish." Jack held the door open for her, and she entered a small room. An elderly woman sat behind a desk, and Elizabeth approached her while Jack and George held back. She explained her need to look at the records for the burial of the unidentified woman.

"You mean the grave that they just dug up," the woman said, annoyed.

"Yes."

"I can't show you that. That's confidential."

"Well, the woman is dead. I don't think she'll mind."

The woman was clearly not amused.

"Excuse me, ma'am." Jack stepped forward and removed his hat and held it to his chest. "I'm Jack Rourke." He extended his hand to the woman, and she reached out to accept it. When he had her hand in his, he bent to kiss it. "It is a true pleasure to meet you."

Elizabeth stepped back and watched, certain Jack wouldn't be able to melt the woman.

"I'm sorry that we disturbed you," Jack said, charm dripping from him.

"Oh no, you're no bother," the woman responded, practically batting her eyes.

Okay, I'm wrong. Jack is the master.

"You see, I was the detective that worked on the poor woman's case. It never felt right that she was buried without a name. My friends and I are trying to make this right, and we had this thought that if we could possibly see the burial records, we might be able to learn something about this woman that could help us put a name on her grave. It only seems right. No one should die alone and without a name."

He was good.

"Of course." The woman's demeanor completely softened. "Let me see what we have. The records are in the other room. I had to pull them from storage when the grave was exhumed."

The woman disappeared behind a side door, and Jack turned to George. "And that is how it is done."

Before George could respond, the woman returned with a file in hand. "Here it is."

Jack stepped forward. "Please allow me." He pulled out the woman's chair as she sat, and she giggled, reminding Elizabeth of the women in the lobby.

She opened the file and handed over the documents to Jack. He remained quiet for several moments as he reviewed the pages, and Elizabeth resisted the urge to step forward and read them with him, in case it offended the woman.

When he finally looked up, Elizabeth asked, "Well?"

"I'm not sure what to make of it. Everything is signed off by Captain Norm Caldwell."

"Who's Norm Caldwell?"

"He was in charge of the homicide unit."

"So you think he knew the grave was empty?"

"Looking at these papers, I don't see how he couldn't have known. Before the casket was sealed, he signed off verifying the identity of the woman."

"Yes, that is procedure," the woman said. "The mortuary must have someone identify the remains before the casket is closed to ensure that there is no mix-up with the bodies."

Jack returned the papers to the woman. "Thank you for allowing me to look at these. I appreciate your time."

The look on the woman's face indicated that she was hoping to spend more time with him, and Jack didn't disappoint. "I don't suppose that you would do me the honor of having dinner with me one evening?"

"Of course," the woman nearly spit out. "I would love that."

Jack took down the woman's number and kissed her hand once again before returning his hat to his head. "Until then."

If Elizabeth had never witnessed swooning before, she had now.

Once they returned to the car, Elizabeth turned to Jack. "So what do you think?"

He rubbed at his chin. "Not sure. Let's think this through." He started the car, and Elizabeth's heart accelerated before he put the car in gear.

She kept her eyes trained on the floor and used the conversation to distract her. It seemed to make the car ride easier.

"So we know that at minimum Stalworth, Captain Caldwell, and probably someone at the mortuary knew the woman was alive and helped cover it up. Why?" Elizabeth asked.

"Very good question. Why would they want people to think she was dead?"

"Witness protection," George blurted out.

It seemed the only reasonable explanation to Elizabeth. "That would explain why you were pressured to shelve the case. Your captain knew she was really alive and didn't want anyone else to know."

Jack stared straight ahead. "It's just hard to believe. Stalworth and Caldwell, they were good men."

"They probably had a good reason," Elizabeth said. "What do you think that she knew? I assume that she had information they wanted, and they were protecting her. If someone had already tried to kill her, then what better way to protect her than to let the world think she was dead."

"And why did she come back?" Jack added.

Elizabeth knew that whatever the information, it would lead back to the White Horse Plantation. She was going to have to do some serious research into Josiah Webb. When the car engine stopped, Elizabeth was surprised to find that they were already at Crestview Assisted Living.

As she came to expect, Jack was at her door assisting her out. "Why don't you come inside? Maybe if we put our heads together, we can figure this out." He offered her his arm and she accepted, and they strolled to the front door. She was the envy of all the ladies at Crestview.

As they passed through the lobby, they were stopped. "Where have you been? I was worried sick."

Elizabeth turned to find Grace approaching them.

"Oh hi, Gracie. I didn't know you were coming by today," George said.

She doubted that Grace heard her father because her eyes continued to bore through Elizabeth.

"Where did you take my father?"

"Technically, I didn't take him anywhere. He drove." She pointed to Jack.

Grace wasn't buying it, as her stare never wavered.

"Grace, relax. I'm fine. We just went for a little outing," George said.

Grace turned to her father. "I didn't know where you were." Her voice sounded weak, and Elizabeth felt remorse. She knew how important her father was to her, and she should have never taken him along.

"Grace, I'm sorry." Elizabeth's apology went unacknowledged as Grace turned and walked away. Elizabeth debated whether she should follow her, but stayed put. When Grace was no longer in sight, she turned to George. "I'm sorry."

"I'll go talk to her. She'll be fine."

She watched George walk down the hall after Grace, then turned to Jack, who remained quiet through the entire exchange. "Thank you. I really appreciate all your help."

He tipped his hat at her. "It was my pleasure, young lady. I forgot how much I loved my work. Retirement has its perks, but I must say that it felt good to get out there and do something useful."

Grace walked into her father's room and sat in her usual seat next to his recliner. She was staring at the television, which would have seemed normal had it been turned on.

She didn't hear her father come in until he spoke. "Gracie, I'm sorry that I upset you. I just went for a little adventure with Jack and Elizabeth."

"*Adventure*. I know all about Elizabeth's adventures. Where did you go?"

"The cemetery where you dug up the grave. Jack was a detective on the case. When she told him about this case, it was his suggestion to go. I tagged along." She sensed that he was trying to offer a defense for Elizabeth. Part of her was angry, but another part was happy to see that her father seemed fond of her. How her world with her father had changed in such a short time. It was not long ago she was avoiding conversations about her personal life, and now her father was going on adventures with—*my what? What was Elizabeth?*

She realized that she allowed herself to go off track and pulled her thoughts back to the case. "What did you learn?" She knew why Elizabeth came to Crestview. It was the same reason she came—Jack Rourke. Grace recognized the name of the detective on the 1963 investigation report. She had talked with Jack several times during her visits with her father. He was very interested in her work, and she knew that he missed it and relived his days through Grace.

"The lady at the front office let Jack look at the burial records."

Grace looked at him, momentarily forgetting the question she asked, but her mind quickly caught up. "Anything interesting?" She had asked to see the records the day the grave was dug up, but was told that she would need a court order, something ADA Wilcox was reluctant to do, claiming it was a waste of time, and chastised her for not staying focused on the current case. However, thanks to Jack and Elizabeth, a court order wasn't needed because her father told her all that they learned, as well as their witness protection theory, which Grace had to acknowledge seemed plausible. This concerned her. She was happy that pieces of what once seemed an impossible puzzle were coming together, but she was afraid where they might lead or, more specifically, where they might lead Elizabeth. How could she protect her?

"Hold up there. I can't walk as fast as I used to."

Elizabeth turned to see Jack speed walking to catch up to her in the parking lot.

"I got to thinking," he said once he reached her. "Why did she come back? If she went into hiding, why come back now?"

Elizabeth had been thinking the same thing, but her mind felt a little muddled after her encounter with Grace, so she was happy to talk it out. It helped focus her. "Before she died, she wrote a note in lipstick on her purse. It was hastily written and most of it was smeared by the police handling of the purse." He looked aghast at the comment, but said nothing and allowed her to continue. "I finally figured out that she wrote the phone number to an abandoned plantation, the White Horse Plantation, at least it used to be the phone number. It was near this property that her body was found in 1963."

"She lived there," Jack said.

"I was thinking the same thing. Why else would she give out a phone number that no longer exists? What I can't figure out is what she wanted us to know about that place."

"Who lives there now?"

She explained what she knew about Josiah Webb and the multiple tax liens on the property. "Before Webb died, he transferred the property to some religious organization, but it seems pretty much abandoned, but it's his death that doesn't add up."

"What do you mean?"

"The reports of Webb's death indicate that he died on the plantation in a horseback riding accident, but a caretaker that oversees the property said that Webb hated horses and that he didn't keep any horses on the property."

"Maybe we should talk to this caretaker and find out who else lived on this property."

"We?"

"Slow down. There is a utility road coming up on the right," Jack said, holding a map while balancing the old investigation report on his lap.

"I don't see anything," Elizabeth said as she slowed her car.

"You passed it."

"Where?" She put her car in reverse.

"Stop! Right there," he said, pointing to a small opening between a collection of overgrown bushes.

She turned into the gap and took it slow as her car bounced on a rugged dirt road, and she tried not to flinch when branches scraped against the side of her Roadster. A few yards in, the space opened, offering a wider road to navigate.

"It was just up ahead here, somewhere on the right. That's where she was found." He motioned his head toward a ditch that ran parallel to the road.

She stopped the car and looked around, but there was little to see. Only bushes and trees that flanked the side of the road. "You said earlier that it was some teenagers who found the body."

"Yes, they were probably looking for a quiet place, if you know what I mean." He raised his gray scraggly eyebrows in rapid succession for emphasis.

"How do we know this woman was here? Do we know if this woman was really attacked? None of the witnesses were interviewed."

"When I came out here during the investigation, I found dried blood on the leaves on the ground. A good amount of it. Something happened." Jack strained his neck to look outside the car as if he was still expecting the blood to be there. "There was something else." His voice trailed off.

"What?"

"I almost forgot. I found a locket on a gold chain." He rubbed his chin. "It had a picture of a young man, an African-American man."

"You think it belonged to her?"

"I found it in the leaves with the blood, so I assumed so."

"So, where did the locket go? It's not in the report."

"I gave it to Stalworth to log into evidence," Jack answered. She wondered what else never made it into evidence.

Elizabeth drove on, hoping to find where the road led and soon found the answer, as it came to an abrupt stop at the edge of the

White Horse Plantation. She recognized it because she could see in the distance the broken-down barn that Samuel had warned her to stay clear of.

"Let's go see if we can find the caretaker," Jack said as he opened the door, not waiting for a reply or for her to put the car in park for that matter. He began to walk through a narrow path, and Elizabeth caught up after locking her car, which made her chuckle. What were the odds of someone finding her car and breaking in?

When she reached him, Jack was stopped in front of a small opening off to the side of the trail that was surrounded by crudely constructed wooden posts that attempted to function as a fence, but most of the pieces were missing. The few that remained standing appeared to barely be doing that.

"It looks like an old cemetery," she said as she moved closer for a better look. Her real clue was the solitary wooden cross that served as a grave marker with a collection of rocks piled at its base. What she assumed were remnants of other crosses were now splinters of wood scattered over the area. The packed dirt was hard and cracked from the lack of care or concern.

"Probably an old slave cemetery."

There was a stillness that surrounded it, as though even the critters that inhabited the area were paying their respects. Part of her wanted to enter for closer inspection, but she didn't want to disturb the sacred space and instead offered a silent prayer for the poor souls, hoping they found greater joy in their next life. She moved on toward the main property and Jack followed.

When she approached the barn, Jack called out, "Hold up." He was panting when he reached her, and she felt guilty. She hadn't taken him into consideration when she set her pace.

"Sorry about that." She gestured toward the barn. "Samuel said it's unstable." She laughed. "Get it?"

Jack stared at her with a confused look.

"The barn is un-stable. It's a pun."

"What?"

"Stable, barn...oh, never mind."

Jack moved past her, clearly ready to let it go. She directed him to the former slave quarters and called out Samuel's name, which went unanswered.

"This place is a cross between fascinating and eerie," Jack said, and he looked toward the main house. "You went inside there?" He didn't wait for her to answer and walked to it.

She called out Samuel's name a few more times as they approached the house and scanned the property looking for him. Jack tried the door handle, but it didn't open. "Looks like it's locked."

Elizabeth walked up the steps and tried the handle. "I think it sticks." She squeezed the latch and handle and pushed, and it gave way. The inside of the house looked undisturbed from her last visit, and she didn't want to drag Jack all the way around the first floor because she sensed that he was tiring out but was too proud to say anything. Instead, she wanted to save his energy for the stairs and the walk back to the car.

She took the stairs slowly and waited at the top for Jack. He was puffing, and she searched for a chair for him, but he refused. She skipped the maze of rooms and took the main hallway that wrapped around the top floor to the office with the secret room. "Careful," she said as she walked over the broken frame on the floor, while the glass crunched beneath her shoes. He paid little attention to it and seated himself in one of the wingback chairs as she walked around the room. The room still carried the same oppressive feeling, even in the daylight.

The secret door was no longer open, and she assumed Grace came back and closed it. She ran her hand along the wall where the door should have been and pushed with no success. "How does this thing open?" She began fiddling with parts of the mantel near the wall, convinced that there was a secret lever that would open the door.

After several minutes, she plopped down into the chair next to Jack and sighed. Between them stood a small table with a lamp and black rotary telephone, and she began to run her hands underneath the edges of the table.

"What are you doing?" he asked.

"Looking for a button that will open the door."

"I see."

"Don't look at me that way. There is a door right there. I just need to figure out how to open it."

"What do you and the barn have in common?"

"I am not unstable. There is a door right there." She actually thought his joke was funny, but wasn't going to admit it. She opened a set of doors below the tabletop and found a concealed vintage tape recorder. She dropped to her knees for a better view. It had only one silver reel and no tape. *Interesting.* She lifted the phone off the table to search underneath and found a business card. She had to pry it up with her fingernails, as it had solidified to the table.

"What's that?"

"It's an old business card for State Senator Robert Powers." The back of the card was stained brown from its long-term contact with the table, but the handwritten lettering "EJF 3/17" was still legible. She was about to ask Jack's take on the card when she noticed him starting to nod off and realized that he had overextended himself, or she had overextended him. "How about we head back?"

In answer to her question, Jack began lifting himself off the chair. She helped him stand, and they walked arm-in-arm at a leisurely pace through the hall and down the stairs. She pulled the front door tightly closed and looked across the property where they would need to walk to get to her car. She realized that it would be too much for Jack.

"You know what, why don't you wait right here, and I'll go run back to the car and pick you up in the driveway."

Jack didn't protest and began to lower himself to sit on the front step, and she helped guide him down.

Elizabeth began heading back in the direction from which they came. When she reached the small cemetery, she nearly ran into Samuel, who stepped out onto the path. "You scared me. I didn't think you were here."

"I was wondering whose car that was."

"I hope you don't mind that I came by."

"You are always welcome," he said with a warm smile. "I enjoy the company. I spend too much time talking to myself 'round here."

She watched as Samuel straightened some of the wooden posts that surrounded the cemetery.

"Samuel, when we last met, you told me that the walls hold many secrets. Did you know what I'd find?"

He continued his task without looking at her. "All these ol' places hold secrets. Too many lives lost not to," he said while kicking the dead foliage around the post he had just erected, forming a small pile, as though he was trying to keep it a respectable distance from those at final rest. She guessed it was his way of paying his final respects to those who unwillingly gave their lives to the land and were now a part of it.

"But what about the pages I found in the wall?" she asked.

"I couldn't rightly tell you. I don't really go inside there much. I prefer it out here."

Samuel's responses seemed to be more riddles than answers. "But—"

"I'm afraid I'll have to be heading home. Olivia's expecting me," Samuel said, looking up at the last of the sun that struggled to remain and cutting off any further exploration of the issue.

"Wait, just one more thing. How many children did Josiah Webb have?"

Samuel scratched his head. "Two—a boy and a girl. I really must get going now."

"But wait." She held out her hand, as if to hold him in place. "His daughter, where is she now?"

"That is a very good question. You be careful, now." He tipped his hat and turned away, unwilling to be kept from his preordained schedule. She watched him disappear through the path that led to her car.

A cracking sound behind her caused her to turn sharply. As the sound of footsteps grew louder, so did the sound of panting.

"Jack, what are you doing? I told you I'd come get you."

"You were taking too long, and I just needed to catch my breath."

He was a stubborn one.

"Who were you talking to?" he asked.

"You just missed Samuel."

He only offered a "humph" in response as he passed her and continued toward her car. She began to follow when she stumbled over a small post protruding from the ground that had been exposed by Samuel's raking.

Jack returned to her. "You all right there?"

"I'm fine. I just kicked a broken post that—" She looked at the protrusion, which would have seemed innocuous if it was made of wood like the other posts, but it was metal. She kicked at the remaining leaves and dirt that obscured it. "This isn't a post. It's a handle." She knelt down, the cool earth seeping into her knees, and began wiping at the dirt. When the silky dirt surface turned hard, she swept more frantically, until she touched metal ridges. A hatch made of the same rust colored corrugated iron sheets used to patch the slave quarters was exposed. She stood and pulled on the metal handle that tripped her up. The door was heavier than expected, and she released her hold once she had it halfway open, allowing gravity to take it the rest of the way, and leaves and debris fluttered when it slammed to the ground.

She dropped back to her knees and peered over the side of the cement hole. She guessed it was twenty feet deep. A braided rope two inches in diameter was tied to the door and hung down, caressing one side of the concrete wall. Several knots trailed down the length of the rope to assist in climbing.

Jack bent over for a better view. "Looks like a box."

"A box?" Elizabeth asked.

"It's where the slaves were kept in punishment. It was unbearably hot in the summer and just as unbearably cold in the winter."

A fury swelled within her and she snatched the rope.

"What are you doing?"

"I'm going down."

"Hold on there. This isn't safe. You don't know if that rope will hold."

His protests were futile because she was already on her way down before he finished his sentence. Using the knots as a foothold, she slowly descended into the concrete pit. Her tight grip on the coarse rope burned her hands, but she refused to loosen her hold out of fear of falling. When her next step down met ground, she released the rope and blew on her palms to lessen the stinging sensation. The air was moist and musty and carried a stench of decaying leaves. The concrete floor was covered in several inches of soft mud mixed with the dead foliage that she assumed seeped through the covering with the rainwater.

"What do you see?" Jack called down, and she looked up at the light and saw him peering down.

She turned in a circle, and it reminded her of a crude concrete crypt. It was nothing more than a gray box, just as Jack described it. She stretched her arms out to her sides, and it was wide enough in both directions so that she couldn't touch both walls at the same time. She assumed this was strategic, so that its inhabitants couldn't scale the walls and climb out. Without the assistance of the rope, there was no escaping the box.

She ran her hand over the cool concrete and felt several ridges in the wall. She looked closer and found several more on all sides. They were human claw marks, scratches deeply embedded by those desperately detained. She traced the marks with her fingers, and a chill started at her fingertips and radiated through her. She shuddered and pulled her hand back as though it was burned. She closed her eyes and tried to swallow, but her throat locked and a wave of panic ripped through her. She had to escape. Spots formed in her eyes as the walls closed in. She looked up for the light and it seemed to narrow, and she could no longer find Jack. She frantically grabbed around for the rope, but couldn't find it.

"Jack! Jack!" She thrashed her arms about the space in another desperate attempt to find the rope.

"What's wrong?"

She looked up again and his face came into view. "Where's the rope?"

"It's right here." He wiggled the rope side to side, and she saw its serpentine movement and stepped forward and urgently grasped at it. Her foot caught on something buried in the mud and she bent to free herself and pulled at a cloth item that wrapped itself around her shoe. She was about to throw the material back to the ground when she felt an irrational sense of sympathy for it being trapped at the bottom of the box, and she shoved as much of it that would fit in her front pocket and began to climb. Her muscles burned as she lifted one hand over the other hefting herself up. The footholds helped keep her from sliding back down, but it was pure arm strength and sheer will that was going to get her out of the concrete crypt. She didn't look down and continued pulling her weight up, until she reached the end of the rope. She felt hands grab at her, and Jack was on his knees doing what he could to tug her out. She grasped at the metal door, hoisted herself up, and rolled out onto the ground. She lay motionless on her back staring at the darkening sky.

Jack hovered over her. "Are you hurt?"

She shook her head, unable to find her voice. She needed a few moments to gather herself, and he seemed to recognize that and sat back giving her the space she needed. Her skin was on full alert and covered in goose bumps and she shivered.

"Let's get out of here," she said as she stood and lifted the metal hatch and let it slam closed, sealing the box once again, before she started toward the car.

"A little help here?" Jack called behind her.

She turned and saw him still on his knees, struggling to push himself up.

"I'm so sorry." She moved to him and grabbed him under the arms and helped pull. Her muscles shook at the exertion, and she was afraid she might drop him. When he finally got his feet under him and stood, she stepped back and her knees wobbled. She offered him her arm and guided him back to the car, but she wasn't sure who was in better shape, and it felt as though the car was parked on the other side of the state.

When they finally sat in the soft leather seats, she paid no mind to the dirt that they both tracked into the car. At that point, it seemed trivial. She pulled the seat belt across her chest, desperate to get to the main road and out of the suffocating canopy of trees that blocked the sky and served as a reminder of where she just was. When she tried to fasten the belt, the material that dangled out of her pocket blocked her way, and she pulled it out.

"What's that?" Jack asked.

"Found it on the bottom of the box."

She opened it up and turned it around. It was a woman's sweater. Its true color was no longer discernible, as it was encrusted with years' worth of mud.

"How do you suppose that got down there?" he asked.

She shuddered at the thought.

Chapter Fifteen

Elizabeth held up the slightly damp sweater for a closer inspection. She had left it spread out on the kitchen counter overnight to dry, and she could now at least tell its original color, a light pink. Pinned to the left side of the sweater was a white plastic name tag displaying the name MARGARET in all capital letters. Although the sweater offered little to tell of its original owner, the contents of the pocket were more revealing. There was a folded, soggy paper that was now a dry, brown, crispy paper with a few holes at the creases and smeared black ink, but there was enough left behind to reveal its true nature. It was a flyer for a rally in support of the Freedom Riders.

Elizabeth knew of the Freedom Rider movements that began in 1961 in response to the US Supreme Court's ruling in *Boynton v. Virginia*. In *Boynton*, the Court held that segregation of interstate transportation facilities was unconstitutional. Brave African-American and white men and women tested the Southern states that refused to relinquish their segregation laws and rode in public buses together and were met with hostility and violence. She caressed the edges of the page that symbolized a small piece of history.

She needed to know more about Margaret and why her sweater was at the bottom of the box.

❖

A pigeon pranced around the base of the park bench, pecking at the particles on the ground. It slowly inched its way closer to Grace, who sat on the end, and the bird began turning in circles in a mating dance. "Thanks for the ego boost, buddy, but you're barking up the wrong tree." She peeled off her suit jacket, as the late morning temperature climbed. It felt more like summer than late fall.

In the playground, a group of children climbed apparatuses, as their worried mothers scampered behind them trying to save them from injury. A wave of sadness traveled through her that seemed to be twofold. She thought of her own childhood, growing up without a mother. Her father did an admirable job playing both roles, but there were times that she would have loved the smothering love of an overprotective mother. When she was young, her childhood scrapes and bruises, of which there were many, were greeted with a quick drying of her tears, a pat on the back for bravery, and a caution to be more careful next time. It was the only way he knew, which set the tone for how she handled her adult scrapes and bruises.

Her other sense of sadness was not from the past, but what was to be, or better said, not to be—motherhood. She loved children. She loved their simplicity and honesty. They said what they meant. It wasn't always rational or pretty, but it was honest. It wasn't only her job, but her life choices that made it seem improbable. Her longest relationship was six months—three months of continuous sex, followed by two months of attempting to define the relationship, and finally one month of breaking apart.

She drew in a ragged breath as her thoughts turned to Elizabeth, as they frequently did. She had analyzed well into the night the anger that she took out on Elizabeth the day before, and she knew it was deeper than the fear for her father's safety. It was anger at what she desperately wanted, but couldn't have. Although her mind came to terms with her decision, her heart was still struggling with it.

The pigeon, which had given up its romantic interest in her when it found a pile of crumbs, fluttered at the arrival of a visitor, but refused to abandon its stash. Grace turned away from the children and looked to Casey, her longest relationship.

"Casey, thank you for meeting me."

Casey sat next to her, leaned in, and brushed a kiss across her lips for old times' sake. Grace tried to muster an interest, but what once was, was no longer. Casey pulled back slightly and placed her hand on her thigh. "I'm glad you called."

It wasn't that Casey was irrational, irresponsible, or unpredictable that ended the relationship. It was that they were too much alike. Casey was a prosecutor with the organized crime unit, which was how they met. Once the novelty of the sex began to wear and they settled into the day-to-day of a relationship, there was little that sparked her interest, a contrast to a particular nonprofit attorney who was irrational, irresponsible, and unpredictable and set every fiber of her being ablaze, and they'd barely kissed. She chastised herself for allowing her mind to go there once again.

"Are you there?" Casey asked, and Grace hadn't realized how long she had allowed her mind to wander.

"Sorry, I haven't had much sleep. I was hoping to discuss a case with you." Although she attempted to mask it, she saw the disappointment in Casey's face at Grace's purpose of their meeting. Grace didn't mean to lead her on, but given her contentious relationship with ADA Wilcox, she felt it best to discuss the Francis case outside of the DA's office.

Casey straightened her shoulders and sat back slightly, giving Grace more room, but kept a proprietary hand on her leg. "Okay, how can I help?"

"Let's say there was an ongoing investigation by local police into an organized crime syndicate, and there is an attempted murder of what turns out to be an ideal witness for the police in this investigation. The suspects believe that this witness was killed, so the police perpetuate their belief by conducting a cursory murder investigation and then shelving it as a cold case to protect the witness."

"We're talking about witness protection."

"Yes. How does it work?"

"How long ago are we talking about?"

"Nineteen sixty-three."

Casey raised her eyebrows but said nothing. "Well, the witness protection program wasn't founded until 1971, and then it was only federal. So, *if* this occurred as you say, then it was definitely off the books. Whoever arranged this did so on his own."

"What would happen with the witness if, let's say the case never goes to trial?"

She shrugged. "The witness just disappears on her own I guess, assumes a new identity. Not too hard to do in the sixties, before technology."

It wasn't lost on Grace that she used the feminine pronoun. "You know what case I'm talking about, don't you?"

"Perhaps. I know you're working on the case with ADA Dickhead. I check in on you from time to time. I've picked up the phone more times than I'll admit to call you, just to talk, but, well, you know." She paused and looked toward the playground. "How about we go out for drinks, just to catch up?"

Grace winced at the offer, then tried to mask it, but it was too late.

"Ouch, not the reaction I'm used to getting."

"Sorry, It's just…well, things are complicated, and it's probably not a good idea."

"I don't suppose this has anything to do with you slamming Dickhead up against the wall outside the court. News travels."

Grace scrunched her nose. "You heard about that, huh?"

"Oh, don't worry, you're a local hero."

Grace smiled, relieved that there were more in her corner than she realized. Grace looked back toward the playing children, and an awkward moment passed. She was now ready to end the conversation, having obtained the information she needed, but didn't know how to tactfully extract herself.

Casey gave her a wistful look and then patted her on the knee. "It's okay, Grace, I get it. We can still be friends. I'll look around in the old case files in my unit and see if there is anything from sixty-three that might look like it belongs to your case." She pushed herself up and walked back the way she came without turning.

❖

Elizabeth slouched in the booth of a diner with Danny opposite her. He was deeply contemplating the menu. Her head was still swimming from the day before, in part from her exploits with Jack, but also her brief encounter with Grace, which still weighed heavily on her. She needed to talk out all the information she had learned to help her focus, so she called Camille and asked her to meet for lunch at a diner near Camille's work and brought Danny along.

Camille approached and slid in next to her. "So what's going on?" she asked as her greeting.

"Can't decide on the deluxe burger with fries or the roast beef with coleslaw," Danny answered.

"I think she meant something a little more substantive than that."

When the waitress arrived for their orders, Camille selected a salad without looking at the menu, but Elizabeth wasn't hungry, so she opted to stick with her coffee.

"In that case, I'll have the deluxe burger with fries, and she will have the roast beef with coleslaw," Danny said, pointing at Elizabeth.

"Danny, I'm not hungry."

"Then more to share," Danny said as though the problem was solved and handed the menu to the waitress.

"So back to my original question," Camille said. "What's going on?"

"It seems the report of the woman's death, her first death that is, was greatly exaggerated."

Elizabeth explained her visit with Jack Rourke, and Camille gripped her arm when she told them about the witness protection program and held on tightly through the remainder of the story.

"I think this woman could be Josiah Webb's daughter."

"Are you sure?" Camille asked, excitement evident in her voice.

"From everything we know, she was killed at the plantation."

"How do you know?" Danny asked.

"Her body was found just outside the plantation, and she directed us to the plantation with her message. So, it only makes sense that her death, or purported death, occurred on the plantation. When I went back there—"

"You went back to the plantation?" Camille interrupted.

"I went back with Jack, so we could talk with Samuel, and he said that Webb had a daughter. And I think it was Webb who killed her."

She looked at them both and they were staring back, hanging on her every word. "Jack said that the woman had a locket with a picture of an African-American man. Given what we know of Webb's history, Webb and his daughter didn't see eye to eye on race relations. Perhaps Webb learned of his daughter's relationship, and he lashed out against her. Maybe he didn't mean to hurt her; maybe he acted in the heat of passion."

"If Webb was responsible, then it would explain why no one came forward to report her missing," Camille added. "As long as he thought she remained unidentified, Webb wouldn't endure police scrutiny, something he could have done without."

"Exactly, and as long as Webb thought she was dead, she was safe from him. The arsenal we found was enough to start a small revolution. I'm guessing he was up to something and whatever information his daughter amassed over the years living on the plantation would have been very interesting to law enforcement."

"Witness protection," Danny blurted out, as if he was just catching on, which caused the waitress, who had just approached their table, to jump.

Elizabeth offered an apologetic smile, and they waited in awkward silence until the waitress left before they resumed their conversation.

"I'm confused," Danny said as he shoved several fries into his mouth. "If she was giving up all this information, then why wasn't this Webb guy arrested?"

"Because he died a few months later. With Webb's death, the information was probably no longer of use. Their suspect was deceased. Case closed. What I don't know was whether Webb's death was at the hands of one of his own people, who thought he had become a liability, or overzealous law enforcement, who decided to forego the judicial system."

"Why did she come back?" Camille asked, staring at her salad that remained untouched. That was the question that haunted Elizabeth.

"I need to see the purse," she offered in response. "The woman went through an effort to give away a nearly empty purse. Maybe the lipstick message that she scrawled on it was its only value, but I can't overlook the possibility that there is more to it." Although Elizabeth had ample photographs of the purse and its meager contents provided by the prosecution, she needed to see it herself. "I'm heading to the DA's office to deliver a request for production of the purse."

Camille wiped away a tear that escaped down her check and Elizabeth squeezed her hand, and even Danny stopped eating for a brief moment and reached across to put his hand on top of theirs in a show of solidarity. No words were needed.

Chapter Sixteen

Elizabeth sat in the hard plastic chair in the lobby of the police station, impatiently waiting. She had come to know it well over the last few months and didn't bother to look around or people watch. Instead, she stared at the beige linoleum squares on the floor and unconsciously tapped her foot in rhythm to her bouncing knee. She was too tired to pace.

She personally delivered her request for production of the purse to the district attorney's office the day before and had the pleasure of meeting ADA Wilcox, who was equally pleased to see her. After a terse conversation that included Elizabeth's threat to follow up her request with a motion to compel filed with the court, Wilcox capitulated and arrangements were made for Elizabeth to stop by the police department the next morning to view the purse, which was currently stored in an evidence locker.

She had been waiting nearly an hour, no doubt a power play, and she considered going to the front desk to harass them, but frankly, the moment of quiet was welcomed. She leaned back and closed her eyes and allowed her mind to wander where it pleased. In a light sleep, she dreamed of Grace calling out to her.

"Elizabeth."

Her eyes snapped opened. It wasn't a dream. Grace was standing a few feet in front of her.

"Are you ready or should I come back when you're done napping?"

She rubbed at her eyes. "What are you doing here?"

"I work here." Elizabeth stared at her waiting for a better answer. "You asked to see the purse."

"Oh, right." She expected a uniformed officer associated with the evidence room to meet her, and she wondered if Grace's presence was her doing or the prosecutor's. She rose and dutifully followed behind her, and she couldn't help but smile. They were playing out a very similar scene to when they first met, but this time she kept her eyes trained on Grace's backside instead of finding interest in the offices that they passed. Grace wore black slacks with a white form-fitting turtleneck, and she realized that she had never seen Grace in anything but pants. She allowed her thoughts to wander to the feel of her smooth long legs under her hands, but it didn't take long for her mind to circle back around to their present state, in which they weren't speaking to each other for reasons Elizabeth didn't understand.

She debated breaking the ice and offering another apology for taking her father to the cemetery. It would at least be a start; however, before she could find the right words, she was cut off by ringing coming from Grace's pocket. Grace yanked out her phone and barked, "Donovan." Elizabeth smiled, that was familiar, but her smile faded as Donovan's mood softened. *Who was she talking to?*

She could garner very little from the half of the conversation that she could hear because most of the talking seemed to come from the other end, but it was clearly a friendly chat.

"Thanks for calling me." Grace hung up the phone and continued leading her through the corridor.

Elizabeth warred with herself. Should she say something or pretend as though she didn't notice the conversation? She would pretend that she didn't notice. That was the best approach. It wasn't her business anyway.

"So who was that?" She couldn't help herself.

"Work call," Grace answered without breaking stride.

Work, right.

Before Elizabeth could explore further, they entered a small room where a man sat behind a glass window. Grace pulled out her identification, and the man buzzed them through a side door. Once inside, Elizabeth found herself in a small windowless room with a metal table taking center stage. The white purse was on the table, and Elizabeth approached it, thoughts of Grace's telephone call pushed aside.

"Don't touch it," Grace said, and Elizabeth cocked an eyebrow in her direction. She could see remnants of black powder where it had been dusted for prints. "Ah hell, who am I kidding? Half the precinct has probably touched the damn thing."

Elizabeth lifted the purse and inspected the lipstick. It was one thing to see photographs, but to hold it in her hands was a whole other experience. This was the last thing this poor woman touched. What was this woman trying to tell them? She held it up and slowly turned it around, side to side, and top to bottom. As the photographs showed, most of the lettering was smeared, and she couldn't decipher anything additional.

She ran her fingers across the metal clasp and followed the loop of the small white handle. It was hard to believe that the woman died for this thing. She pulled apart the clasp and it made a faint clicking sound as it opened. She peered inside. A dark lining covered the inside, and as she rotated it around, the contents slightly clanked together. She pulled out the brush and turned it in her hands, inspecting the fine craftsmanship of the back and handle that depicted a quaint scene of a majestic home with two proud pillars surrounded by trees and a wavy stream trailing down the handle with flowers on each side. It almost looked like a Monet painting carved into silver. The photographs of it didn't do it justice. It was much more beautiful in person.

She set it on the table, then closely inspected the matching compact mirror that had a carving that resembled the brush. On the backside, there was a field of flowers with trees surrounding it, and the front had the wavy stream cutting through trees that led to a cross in the middle. She opened it. The inside was bare. She closed it and placed it next to the brush. Last, she held the lipstick tube and twisted it between her fingers. On one side, the wavy stream ran down the length of the tube, with a small row of homes flanking its side, and the rest covered in a field of flowers. She removed the cover and confirmed that the shade matched the writing on the purse before setting it next to its companions.

With the contents emptied, she put her hand inside and ran it around the lining. She could feel the smooth cool material under her fingers. "There has to be something more. Why was she so desperate to pass this off?" She really didn't expect Grace to answer, as she still believed it was a simple robbery gone wrong. "Do you have a flashlight?" Elizabeth asked.

"Why?"

"Because I thought about checking out some crawl spaces when I'm done here and forgot my flashlight." Given the places they had found themselves in recently, she realized that Grace might take her seriously and followed it up for clarification. "I want to inspect the inside lining."

She could see Grace debating with herself before she turned to leave the room. Just as she exited, she popped her head back in. "Don't steal anything while I'm gone."

"You got me. Destruction of evidence was my defense plan."

While Grace was gone, Elizabeth inspected the inside of the bag, feeling for any anomalies inside to no avail, then she held it as close to her face as she could. "Go any closer and your head will get stuck inside."

Elizabeth couldn't help but smile at Grace's attempt at humor and accepted the flashlight she held out. As she dutifully inspected every inch of the inside, her hope of finding a secret message deflated. There was nothing.

"Didn't find anything, did ya?"

"You already knew," Elizabeth said.

"Inspected it myself."

"So why didn't you say something?"

"Because you had to look for yourself."

Grace knew her. She handed back the flashlight and reached for the silver pieces to repack them.

"Just leave it as it is. The evidence guy is going to want to inspect it before he puts it away. I'll show you out."

They walked back in silence, but Grace stayed at her side, instead of taking the lead as she had on the trek in. When they reached the door, Grace held it open, and Elizabeth walked past her, but stopped in the doorway and turned to her. "Whatever I did, Grace, to make you so upset with me, I'm sorry. But at some point when this is done, you'll have to talk to me."

Elizabeth didn't wait for a response and continued walking out of the station, and Grace watched her go. "Please be safe, Elizabeth," she whispered before closing the door. The call from Casey did little to ease her mind. There were no records in the prosecutor's office of an investigation into the White Horse Plantation or the woman's murder. Despite what Elizabeth thought of her, she didn't believe it was an open and shut case. A dead woman returning to be killed a second time was anything but ordinary, and why she wouldn't let up on finding out why she came back.

The reception area of SILC was quiet, but Elizabeth saw her mother's car parked out front, so she knew that was a false sense of security. She was sure there was chaos going on somewhere in the office, but she wasn't in the mood to deal and walked to her office trying to avoid contact with any other human. A large marble counter stood in front of her door, which she assumed would be part of the kitchen, but for now was blocking her entrance. She weighed her options—find help to have it moved or crawl over. She hiked up her skirt and jumped on top, but the counter was slicker than she expected, and she slid off the other side and landed on the floor in her office.

"I'm good," she said to the ceiling as she lay on her back.

"That was fun to watch."

Elizabeth sat up and turned to her unexpected guest, who was seated by her desk. "Jack, I didn't know you were here. Otherwise, I would have made sure my foot got caught and I was left dangling for a better show."

"Now that I might pay to see."

"How did you get in here?" She couldn't imagine him hoisting himself over the counter.

"That wasn't here when I got here, and I think your staff sort of forgot about me."

"I'm so sorry."

"Don't be. I feel safer in here. There is a woman out there who scares me."

"You and me both. So, what brings you to my side of town? I thought you had enough of me."

"I haven't been able to get this case off my mind and thought maybe I could be of some help." She couldn't help but notice the eagerness in his voice. She guessed that Crestview Assisted Living could get a little boring for someone like Jack, who still craved adventure.

"All right, what do you think of this?" She pulled a large Ziploc bag from her messenger bag, followed by a smaller plastic bag. Opening the larger plastic bag, she said, "This is what I found at the bottom of the box." She unfolded the sweater and laid it across her desk. "In the pocket, I found this." She removed the flyer and set it next to the sweater.

Jack studied them closely, as a detective would. "It's possible that it belongs to Webb's daughter."

"I thought that too, but…"

"But what?"

"What if it's not? What if it's someone else's?"

Jack rubbed his chin, staring at the flyer and sweater in consternation. "All right, what do you suggest?"

"Let's go to the library and see what we can find in the local newspaper archives about this Freedom Riders rally."

Jack slapped his knees in what she had come to know as his "I'm game" gesture and pushed himself up. "We only have one problem."

"What's that?"

"How do we get out?" He pointed to the counter blocking the doorway.

Realizing that she was going to need help, she approached the counter and hoisted herself over, and much like the first time, landed on the floor on the other side, just in time for her mother to witness.

"Honestly, Elizabeth, would you stop playing around. What are you doing climbing on the furniture, and in a skirt?"

"Oh, I don't know, it just seemed like so much fun, I couldn't resist. Never mind the fact that there is no other way in or out of my office."

❖

"Jack, will you please sit back? You're blocking the screen."

He huffed but complied with Elizabeth's demand. "How are you supposed to read these things? The print is so small."

Elizabeth rewound the film and stopped on the article that she needed after her second attempt. The dial on the microfilm reader was touchy, but she was getting the hang of it, after nearly three hours of scanning archived newspapers articles. The *Southern Register* had been defunct since the mid 1980s, but luckily, the library had preserved the paper's history through microfilm. Starting their search in 1961 and now concluding 1967, they had amassed a large printout of articles, which Elizabeth laid out in chronological order across the table.

The first headline article covered the disappearance of two prominent Freedom Rider protestors who were responsible for organizing the well-attended rally that took place in the town's public bus station. The two rally organizers, Jeffrey Small and Peter Christianson, were last seen leaving in Jeffrey's white '57 Plymouth Fury after declaring the June 1962 rally a success to fellow protestors. A description of the car followed, including its gold stripes down the side and shark fins on the back. Pictures of the two young white men, which she guessed to be school photos given their formal nature, took center stage.

In the same paper, but buried way in the back, was a two-line article that told of a missing young African-American woman that read more like a classified ad for a lost dog. There was no description or photo or any additional information as to the nature of the disappearance. There was just a name—Margaret Williams, a local waitress, which explained the name tag on the sweater. Elizabeth was incensed.

The remainder of the articles spread across the table detailed the discovery of the young men's bodies near a ravine on the outskirts of town, each with a bullet wound to the back of their heads, execution style. The Plymouth Fury was not found.

The murders would have been forgotten, at least by the local police, if it weren't for the persistent protests for justice by the Freedom Riders. According to the news articles, a break in the case came in 1966 when a local farmhand named Tobias Stokes was charged with the deaths. The African-American man was accused, tried, and convicted based on a single eyewitness, who claimed he saw Stokes the night of the rally with the victims. Apparently, that single witness was given more weight than the family and friends of Stokes, who all testified that he was out of town that night, visiting his ailing mother. After the two-day trial and two-hour jury deliberation, he was found guilty and sentenced to death.

There was no additional mention of Margaret Williams.

CHAPTER SEVENTEEN

Elizabeth walked to SILC with the phone to her ear, trying to catch up on her voice messages. She had spent the better part of the morning in mediation on behalf of a client seeking child support for her two children.

Just as she approached the penis man on the wall, a firm hand gripped her arm and yanked her into a recessed doorway of a vacant shop.

"Give me your bag."

"You can't be serious," Elizabeth said in irritation, as she turned to face a man dressed in black wearing a ski mask. The man snatched her bag off her shoulder, and she held on to the strap, but the gun pointed into her side told her to take this robbery more seriously, and she let go.

He dug into her bag and started dumping out the contents, including her wallet. "Where are the papers?" he asked.

"I don't know what you're looking for."

It was clearly not the answer he wanted, and he slammed her back, causing her head to hit the wall. She closed her eyes in an attempt to squash the nausea that erupted from the pain, and when she opened them, the gun was pointed into her chest.

"I'm not playing games with you."

Elizabeth stayed quiet and looked down at his hand holding the gun, while his other hand nervously twitched at his side. "If you only tell me what you are looking for, I can help you." She could hear the tremor in her own voice.

A door slam, followed by laughter and a pair of voices, caused the man to turn his head, and she took the opportunity to push him backward giving her some space to swing her fist. She connected with the side of his head, and he turned to her and slammed the butt of the gun against her face. Stunned by the pain that radiated from the point of impact at the side of her jaw and traveled across her head, she stumbled forward and made eye contact with two men who stood next to a car halfway down the block. She opened her mouth, but no words came out.

The man grabbed her by the hair and started to pull her back into the doorway before he realized the two men were jogging toward them, and they began shouting. He released his hold of her and took off running in the opposite direction. Elizabeth remained motionless, and when the men reached her, they spoke, but it took her several moments before she could register any of their words. Instead of answering them, she bent to retrieve her bag and began to shove the items back in. The men took over her task and tried to convince her to sit, but she insisted on continuing to SILC. The men walked her to the clinic and relayed the events to Amy, who rushed to her side and tried to help lead her to a chair in the lobby, but Elizabeth insisted on going into her office.

Before she reached her office door, Danny and her mother joined Amy and guided her to the guest chair in front of her desk. She tried to convince them that she was not seriously hurt, only stunned, but their continued pampering proved they weren't persuaded. Elizabeth closed her eyes, and their voices seemed to fade, and she found her headache subsided to a more tolerable level. It was a set of warm hands touching the sides of her face that pulled her back, and she opened her eyes to find Camille standing over her. She wore a serious look and continued running her hands through Elizabeth's hair and down her neck.

"Where does it hurt?" Camille asked.

"I'm fine. I just have a headache and my jaw aches."

Camille looked unconvinced, and in the attempt to get the attention off of her, Elizabeth asked, "How did you know?"

"Danny called me." Camille continued running her hands across her shoulders and down her arms. "Are you hurt anywhere else?"

"No, I'm fine, really."

Camille pulled out a small pen flashlight from a bag at her feet and shined it in her eyes, which Elizabeth found extremely annoying.

"We really should take her in and have her looked at," Camille said to her mother, who was hovering over.

Before she could protest again, Amy entered, and Elizabeth had to blink at the sight of Grace who entered behind her. Grace dropped to her knees in front of her and caressed her face, and she leaned into the touch.

"Elizabeth, honey, are you all right?" Grace's voice shook as she spoke.

A tear slipped down Elizabeth's face, and Grace used her thumb to wipe at it. Elizabeth leaned forward and allowed Grace to fully wrap her arms around her.

"I've got you," Grace whispered in her ear.

Elizabeth released her pent emotions, not only from the attack, but the hurt and frustration that she held at bay since the day Grace rejected her in court. Tears began to fall, and she pressed her face into Grace's shoulder. "Baby, I'm so sorry," Grace said as she stroked her hair.

When Elizabeth brought her head back up, Grace cradled her face and leaned in and softly kissed her lips. Elizabeth deepened the kiss, and she could taste her salty tears on her own lips. Elizabeth buried her head in her neck and allowed herself to be engulfed by Grace's arms. "Honey, we need to get you to a hospital, just to make sure everything is okay, please."

Elizabeth nodded into her shoulder, and Grace slowly stood, gently pulling Elizabeth up with her. Camille backed up to give them space, and it was only then that Elizabeth became aware of the others in the room. Grace wrapped her arm around her and guided her toward the front door. Her mother reached out and touched her cheek as she passed, and they made brief eye contact. If her mother was surprised by their show of affection, she didn't show it. Her eyes were only filled with concern for her well-being. Grace walked her to the passenger side of her car, which was double-parked outside the clinic, and the others followed, making plans on who would ride with whom.

❖

Elizabeth stared in her bathroom mirror and took stock of the different shades of purple and blue across the side of her face. She then turned her attention to her plaid flannel pajamas that she hastily grabbed on her walk into the bathroom and shook her head, which sent a wave of pain and nausea through her, and she had to close her eyes until it passed. She had spent the entire afternoon and most of the evening in the emergency room, where she had a medical exam, CAT scan, and a police interview, which Grace insisted upon. She was diagnosed with a concussion, but everything was still in its proper place and nothing was broken. She was released with the promise that she would have someone stay with her overnight in case of any unforeseen complications. She had several volunteers, including her mother, Amy, Danny, and Camille, but when Grace spoke up, assigning herself to the job, the others capitulated without argument, even her mother.

Her time in the bathroom to wash up and change was the longest period that she had been separated from Grace since the ordeal began. Even now, Grace was sitting outside the door waiting. That thought turned her attention back to her reflection in the mirror. *Why did I grab these pajamas?* She could hear Michael laughing at her in her head. Resigned to her fate, she opened the door, and as expected, Grace was there to guide her to bed. After she was safely tucked under the covers, Grace sat next to her and stroked her cheek. Her eyes fluttered closed and her breathing shallowed. The pain medication was kicking in.

Elizabeth shifted her position, and a pain shot through the side of her head, causing her eyes to dart open. It took her a moment to recognize her surroundings, but the warm body pressed against her back and the arm draped over her stomach was unfamiliar. She slowly turned and found Grace fast asleep on top of the covers still dressed in her clothes. Elizabeth extracted herself and pulled an extra blanket from her closet and covered her before she snuggled back in, resting her head next to Grace.

CHAPTER EIGHTEEN

E lizabeth woke and stretched out but felt only empty space. She opened her eyes to verify that Grace was gone. She wondered if she had imagined her presence, but was relieved when Grace walked in with a coffee cup in her hand.

"You're awake." Grace set the cup down next to her bedside. "Rumor has it that this is a necessity in the morning."

Elizabeth wondered which of her friends betrayed her and revealed her addiction to coffee.

"Your friend Michael called."

Michael, of course it was him.

"He had heard about yesterday and left a couple of messages. He sounded really worried, so I picked up his call on your home phone. I hope you don't mind."

Elizabeth cradled the cup of coffee. "Not at all. Thank you."

Grace sat on the edge of the bed, and Elizabeth scooted over to give her more space. She couldn't help but admire her. Even in rumpled clothing and with her hair slightly askew, Grace was beautiful.

"How are you feeling?" Grace asked.

"A lot better than yesterday."

"You need to take it easy today. Promise me."

Elizabeth swallowed hard at the look on Grace's face. It was more than concern. It was despair. "Grace, are you okay?"

Grace looked down at her hands and shook her head. "I was so scared when Amy called me. You could've been more seriously hurt or..." Her voice trailed off.

Elizabeth set down the coffee and turned Grace's face toward her. "I'm sorry." Elizabeth understood the feeling, as it was not long ago that she rushed to the hospital thinking Grace was hurt.

"I tried to let you go, Elizabeth. I thought it was the best thing for both of us, but I just can't."

Elizabeth leaned forward and kissed her. Grace pushed Elizabeth back against her pillow, never breaking contact, and Elizabeth opened her mouth slightly, allowing Grace's tongue to slip in. Elizabeth ran her hand up Grace's leg, which forced a groan from her throat, before Grace pulled back. "We can't, not yet. It's not that I don't want to. God, do I want to." Grace stood and began pacing. "You need to heal and—"

"The case," Elizabeth finished for her.

Grace nodded and looked to her, clearly expecting a rebuke, but none came. Elizabeth wanted nothing more than to feel Grace's skin on her naked body, and she shivered at the thought, but knowing that Grace wanted it too made it easier. Grace wanted her.

"Why are you smiling?" Grace asked with suspicion.

"I can wait."

Grace sat at her desk twisting a pencil in her hand, staring at her computer. She had reluctantly left Elizabeth that morning in the care of Michael, who arrived shortly after their talk. She found it hard to relinquish Elizabeth's care, even if it was to her best friend. She couldn't shake the thought that she could have lost her, and Elizabeth would have never known how she felt.

The next best thing she could think to do was work on the godforsaken case. At this point, she didn't care if it resulted in a conviction. She just wanted it over. She had no way of knowing for certain if Elizabeth's attack was related, but given that the attacker passed over her wallet and demanded papers, she had a hard time believing that it was a random act of violence.

The problem was that she had no idea what the attacker was looking for, and apparently, neither did Elizabeth. With no new information on the current murder case, Grace turned her attention to the 1963 case. She began investigating Josiah Webb after her visit to the White Horse Plantation and found that he was a very unlikeable man with a sordid past. She had every reason to believe Elizabeth's theory that the woman was Webb's daughter, but what did she know then that nearly got her killed? Better yet, what did she know now that did get her killed?

CHAPTER NINETEEN

Elizabeth sat at her desk thumbing through papers. It felt like it had been weeks since the attack, but it had only been two days. She had spent the day before curled on her couch with a parade of visitors, each bringing food. It seemed a babysitting schedule had been created, and by the evening, she craved solitude. Her mother had been one of her caretakers, and Elizabeth waited on edge for her mother to mention the intimate scene that she had witnessed between her and Grace, but she never brought it up. Elizabeth wasn't sure if she was in denial or waiting until Elizabeth was in better shape before she pounced on the subject. Either way, Elizabeth decided she would let her mother take the lead on broaching the subject.

Elizabeth turned her thoughts to Grace, something she had done frequently over the last twenty-four hours. She hadn't seen her since she left her house the day before, but she had checked in several times. Their conversations were warm, and it was clear Grace was full of concern, but there were no personal discussions like in her bedroom.

"You really shouldn't be here," Amy said, causing Elizabeth to look up. She hadn't heard her come in.

"I can't sit around my house another day. I'll go stir-crazy."

Amy took the seat across from her. "You really scared us."

"I know and I'm sorry."

"Don't be sorry, just be careful. Whoever it was is still out there."

"I know. I'll be careful."

"You better," Amy said in a motherly tone and rose to head back out the door.

"Amy." Elizabeth called her back. "Thank you for calling Grace."

"She would've never forgiven me if I hadn't."

"Who wouldn't forgive you?" Rich asked from the doorway. "Wow, look at that bruise."

Elizabeth didn't answer the question and instead motioned him to come in. Amy continued out of the office, and he took her vacant seat.

"I just came by to see how you're doing. Rosa told me what happened."

Rosa, huh. She had wondered how those two were faring, and she was happy to learn that there was something there.

"So did he get the papers?"

Elizabeth stared at him.

"Rosa said he wanted the papers," he clarified.

"What papers?" she asked.

"I assume it's the papers that you found hidden at the plantation that you showed me. What other papers are there?"

Elizabeth had completely forgotten about them and dismissed them when they couldn't be translated.

"You still have them?" he asked.

"I don't know. The clinic was broken into and everything was thrown around and…Oh my God, that's what he was looking for in the clinic." She stood up. "Help me out here." She began tipping BD on its side, and Rich helped her lower the chair to the ground. She unfastened the seat cushion from underneath that her mom had installed and pulled it off. Below the cushion and on top of BD's worn, cracked leather seat, sat a manila folder. It seemed her mom's seat cushion offered more than comfort, but also a great hiding place for documents. She had Rich to thank for the documents being safe. She only hid them because of his insistence that she take better care of them and when she found them moved by the workers after they did some repairs in her office, she found them a more secure place. She looked at Rich. "It's all here." She spread the pages across her desk. Although she had no greater insight as to their meaning, she had a new appreciation for them.

"What's the name and address of your friend that works for that museum? I think I want to pay him a visit. He might not be able to read it, but maybe he can give us something to work with."

After passing over the information, Rich became distracted by Rosa, who made her entrance to see if Elizabeth needed anything. She never did that, so Elizabeth knew it was a ploy to get Rich's attention. As quickly as Rich entered, he left with Rosa close at his side, which made Elizabeth smile.

She continued to entertain a string of visitors in her office, making it impossible to get any real work done, not that she really could have. Her mind was fully distracted by the revelation that the pages she found at the plantation were the cause of the clinic break-in and her attack. She knew that somehow these would provide the missing link, if only she could understand them. She debated going to meet Rich's friend alone, but knew that this would upset Grace. She had to admit to herself that she was still shaken knowing that whoever wanted these papers was still out there. So she called Grace and sat waiting for her, enjoying the brief moment of silence, which proved to be short-lived.

"So what's with the papers?" Danny asked as he walked in and scooped a handful of Skittles from the bowl on her desk.

"Help yourself."

He shoved them in his mouth. "Than—" Before Danny could finish the word, a Skittle flew out of his overpacked mouth and hit her on the forehead and plopped on her desk.

"Danny, that is just gross."

Unfazed, Danny picked up the errant Skittle and popped it back in his mouth.

Elizabeth had to turn and look out the window at the row of trash cans in the alley, which she found more appealing than watching him chew. She turned back around when the lip-smacking quieted down. "The papers that the guy was looking for—"

"How are you feeling today?" Camille interrupted as she entered and took the seat next to him.

That was a question Elizabeth wouldn't mind not hearing again for a while. After assuring her that she was doing much better, she pulled out the papers. "This is what the guy was looking for." They both took a turn reviewing the pages and debated what some of the words meant, but neither could provide any additional insight. It didn't take long before Danny lost interest and went back to his task of helping Amy file documents.

"I'm going with Grace to meet one of Rich's friends, who may be able to help," Elizabeth said to Camille once Danny left.

Camille approached her and leaned against the side of her desk so their legs were touching. "You can't go with her," she said sharply, surprising Elizabeth. "She is trying to help convict my brother. You can't trust her."

A tap on her door drew their attention, and Elizabeth offered a tight smile at Grace, who stood in the doorway. Elizabeth wasn't sure if she heard Camille's comment. She motioned her in, and Grace looked between them before she sat in the guest chair.

"Are these the papers?" she asked.

Elizabeth scooped them up and handed them to her, and Grace leaned back and closely reviewed them. She held them up to the light and turned them around, leaving no inch uninspected.

"Where did you get these?"

"From the plantation, in that secret room. They were hidden in the wall."

"Why didn't you tell me about them earlier?" Grace's voice was curt.

"I didn't know that they were relevant, and you can't read the writing." She knew it wasn't really an excuse, and Grace had every right to be mad.

"You tampered with what could be important evidence."

"I didn't tamper with anything. I didn't do anything to them."

"The jury won't know that."

"Isn't that what you're hoping for?" Camille interjected.

Grace didn't respond to her and instead stood up and looked at Elizabeth. "I'm parked outside. Come out when you're ready." She picked up the empty manila folder on Elizabeth's desk and placed the pages inside.

"I'm going with you," Camille said.

"No, you're not," Grace responded as she walked out.

Grace left the clinic without making eye contact with anyone and yanked open her car door. She sat seething in the driver's seat with the manila folder resting in her lap. She wasn't sure what upset her more—the close proximity of Elizabeth and Camille or the fact that Elizabeth withheld the papers that she found from her.

When Elizabeth opened the door and sat, Grace didn't look at her and instead started the engine. She waited until Elizabeth was seat belted and then pulled out.

"Grace—"

"I don't want to talk right now. Can we just ride in silence?"

The silence lasted less than a minute.

"Grace, I'm sorry I didn't tell you about the papers before. I know I should've, but I don't know... It's just so complicated." Elizabeth let out a frustrated squeak, which Grace found endearing, but wouldn't admit it.

"I shared what I knew with you, Elizabeth."

"Grace, I'm sorry."

"What's the address?" Elizabeth looked at her, confused, and Grace clarified, speaking slowly. "The address where we're going."

She could tell that this annoyed her, but instead of bantering back, Elizabeth pulled out a slip of paper from her bag and read it off. The remainder of the drive was in silence.

When they pulled into the museum parking lot, Grace opened her door and began walking ahead. She could hear Elizabeth's heels clicking on the ground as she tried to catch up. She hesitated at the front door and held it open, allowing Elizabeth to pass in front of her. Elizabeth approached a woman sitting at an information desk and asked to speak to Dr. Bob Beadle. Grace looked at her sideways wondering if she had just made the name up.

"Do you have an appointment?" the woman asked.

"No," Grace answered and pulled out her badge.

As the woman dialed Dr. Beadle, Grace stepped away to observe some of the artifacts. There were Confederate uniforms and weapons lining a wall in glass cases. She was conscious that

Elizabeth was lingering close by. As upset as she was, she wasn't going to let her out of her sight. The sound of footsteps on the tile floor drew her attention to a middle-aged man quickly approaching. He had a round face and small, closely set eyes. His name definitely fit.

"I'm Dr. Beadle. How may I help you?"

To Grace's surprise, Elizabeth stayed quiet and looked to Grace to answer his question. "Is there somewhere we can talk?"

He escorted them off to a side room with several photographs lining the walls with a row of benches going down the middle. He sat on the middle bench, and she sat next to him. Elizabeth sat next to her but gave her some space.

"I need you to look at some documents and tell me what you can about them." She pulled out the pages and handed them over. He took them, and she noted a slight tremor in his hand as he read them. After flipping through each page, he looked at her.

"I'm sorry, I can't read these. If you want to leave them with me perhaps I can spend some more time with them and even test their authenticity."

Grace looked to Elizabeth to get her thoughts, and she noted that Elizabeth was staring at the man's hand that was twitching.

"Elizabeth, are you—"

"It was you!" Elizabeth stood and squared off with him.

"I don't know what you're talking about." The man stood and tried to put some space between Elizabeth and himself.

She pointed to the side of his face near his ear, where a slight bruise showed. "That's where I hit you."

Grace stood, grabbed him by the front collar of his shirt, and threw him to the ground. She dug her knee into his chest as he cried for mercy. "Please, I don't know what you're talking about."

Grace looked to her. "Are you sure?"

"Yes," Elizabeth croaked out, but she didn't need to hear the answer. The look in Elizabeth's eyes, a mix of anger and fear, told her all she needed to know.

Grace roughly pulled him up and twisted his arm behind his back and cuffed him. She began reciting the *Miranda* rights as she marched him to the door. Elizabeth picked up the folder and the scattered papers that fell from his hand during the scuffle and caught up to her.

Grace pushed him into the back seat of her car and called for police backup to transfer him into custody. She didn't want him riding in the same car as Elizabeth. When the black and white police car drove off with him securely seated in the back, Grace went in search of Elizabeth and found her sitting on the front steps of the museum.

"Are you okay?" she asked as she sat next to her.

Elizabeth leaned into her, and she put her arm tightly around Elizabeth's shoulder. She was slightly conscious that some might see her but knew that Elizabeth needed her at that moment. She kissed the side of her head and held on until Elizabeth was ready.

When Elizabeth pulled away, she looked at Grace and tapped the folder on her lap. "He knows exactly what these papers are and what they say."

Grace agreed. He knew the significance of the documents, which is why he was so desperate for them.

Elizabeth sat in the chair next to Grace's desk, waiting for Grace, who was called into her sergeant's office. She had been gone for over fifteen minutes, and she was feeling anxious for her return. When she saw her reemerge, she knew something was wrong by the look on Grace's face.

"What's wrong?"

"You will have to go with Detective Martinez. He will take your statement."

"But why? I want to stay with you."

"I'm sorry, but I can't. You're defending the Francis case, and given that I am the lead detective on that case, my sergeant doesn't believe that I should be involved in this investigation."

Elizabeth could tell that Grace was shaken, and she didn't want to make it any harder on her, so she went with the other detective without another word. She followed the bulky man to a small room, and they sat on opposite sides of a table. She explained the attack again in detail and how she recognized the man as her attacker. It was the twitch in his hand that drew her attention. It was distinctive. The detective looked skeptical, but she knew the moment she saw the nervous twitching and then the voice. The bruising on the side of his face only helped confirm the identity.

"So what's next?" she asked after he finished taking notes.

"Well, I'll send this to the DA's office, but without a positive facial identification, any half decent defense attorney will produce a dozen witnesses placing him on the other side of town when the attack occurred. You should know how that works."

Chapter Twenty

E lizabeth nervously paced next to her car. "Where is he?"
"Relax. It's only three thirty. He's probably a little lost.
This place is not that easy to find," Jack said in her earpiece.

After putting some distance between herself and the arrest
of Bob Beadle, she knew that Detective Martinez's assessment of
the case was true. Beadle would likely walk based on the current
evidence, Elizabeth's identification of his nervous twitch, even
though she was certain beyond any doubt. Although initially upset
to learn that he posted bail only twenty-four hours after his arrest,
she began to see it as an opportunity to not only strengthen the case
against him, but to learn more information about the cryptic pages
that he so desperately wanted.

With the help of Jack, they devised a plan to meet Beadle at the
White Horse Plantation to discuss a possible trade of the documents
in exchange for information. She knew Beadle would be wary of
any contact with her, but she also banked on the fact that he was
desperate for the documents. He hung up on her on the first call as
soon as she introduced herself. On the second call, she blurted out,
"There are more pages," before he could hang up and that hooked
him. It was a lie of course, but he didn't know that. It was also a
lie that she could give him the original documents because she no
longer had them. Grace confiscated them. All she had to work with
were copies.

When Beadle stayed on the line the second time to listen to her
plan, she advised him that she found the documents at the White

Horse Plantation and told him that she would personally show him where he could find more. It seemed too much for him to pass up, and he accepted her offer with the caveat that she came alone, another lie. He warned that if he sensed any foul play, he would not only fail to show, but report her to the police for harassing him, a chance she was willing to take.

Compliments of Jack, Elizabeth was wired and the entire conversation would be recorded. It seemed Jack had saved some of his toys from his detective days. As Jack sat in his car covertly parked in the tangle of trees and brush off the entrance drive, Danny was hiding in the house. His sole purpose was to act as her protector. Elizabeth didn't want to bring him, but he refused to be left behind once he overheard Elizabeth on the phone with Jack, and he threatened to tell her mother if he couldn't come.

She seriously contemplated calling Grace. In fact, she spent most of the night debating with herself. By morning, she decided that she wouldn't tell her because she knew Grace would never approve and would probably go so far as showing up at the plantation to stop her. This seemed to be her only shot at understanding not only the document, but unraveling what the hell happened that caused a woman to be killed twice.

"There's a car coming up the drive," Jack said in her car.

Elizabeth turned her attention to the driveway and took a deep, stabilizing breath. "Showtime."

A white, newer model, midsize sedan approached and stopped several yards from her car. It seemed he was assessing the situation before he came any closer. Elizabeth never took her eyes off the car, and after several moments, it came closer and parked. Several more moments passed before Beadle opened the car door and exited, and he stood close to his car and turned in a circle surveying the property.

She remained quiet, not wanting to spook him, and let him advance toward her at his own pace. When he finally approached he asked, "You alone?"

Hearing his voice made her shiver. Memories of their encounter on the street near the clinic flooded back, and she swallowed hard before she spoke. "Yes. I have nothing to gain by bringing anyone else into this. All I ever wanted is to know what these documents mean. My client's life depends on it."

"All right, show me the documents."

She turned and walked toward the entrance of the home, and she waited for him to follow. He continually scanned the area while he walked. She pushed open the door and led him to the front room and sat on the couch. She had no idea where Danny was hiding but hoped he was close by.

Beadle stood in the middle of the room, taking it all in. "My God, look at this place. You could almost feel its history."

The awe of the home had worn off for her, and she continued to stare at him, watching his every move. His twitch was absent, which she took as a good sign.

"Where are the documents?" he asked.

"Nope, you first. I want to know what this document is and why it's so important to you." She pulled out copies of the pages and set them on the table in front of her.

He watched her carefully, as though he was weighing his options. "Why would I tell you that now?"

"Because if you don't, you will never see the original documents, and I will never show you what else this home hides."

He continued to stare at her as he chewed the inside of his mouth. "All right, fine." He approached her, and she tried not flinch when he came around the table and sat next to her. He lifted the pages and held them up for a better view. "These are pages from a diary. It's written in code."

"I gathered that much. Whose diary is this?"

He looked at her for a moment before answering, as though he was still undecided. "John Wilkes Booth."

"*The* John Wilkes Booth? As in the man who shot President Lincoln?"

"Yes. He was killed twelve days after the assassination of Lincoln at a farm in Virginia where he was hiding. A red appointment book that Booth used as a diary was recovered. It was alleged that his last entry was on April 14, 1865, the day he assassinated Lincoln, but there had always been speculation that there was more. In the book, there were pages that had been torn out. The consensus was that Booth tore them out, possibly to use for other purposes like jotting down notes, but there were others that believed the pages were deliberately removed by someone else after his death."

"Is that what you believe?" Elizabeth asked.

"This is what I know. These pages prove it." He pointed to the handwritten dates on top of the entries. "There are five separate entries written between April fifteenth and April twenty-fifth, the day before he died."

Elizabeth took the pages from his hand and held them up close to see for herself. "What is he saying? Why is he writing in code?"

"He knew his fate. He was a hunted animal with nowhere to run. It was only a matter of time before he was caught and killed. I believe he feared his diary would fall into the wrong hands."

"So he wrote in code?"

"Exactly."

"How do you know what it says?" she asked, turning the pages sideways, trying to make some sense of the letters.

"I have seen it before. It's a common coding practice of the time. Each letter stands for a different letter of the alphabet."

"So what does it say?"

"No, first you show me the original pages and the other things you say are here."

"No."

"Excuse me?" he said.

"I'm not giving any of it to you until you tell me everything I want to know. Once I get the information I need, you can have it all and do as you like with it. You can claim full discovery."

"Why should I trust you?"

"I don't think you have a choice."

He shook his head. "Not good enough."

"Then I guess we're at a standoff. You'll never find the documents on your own." She started for the door, hoping to call his bluff.

"All right, all right. I'll tell you what I know."

She turned and sat back on the couch.

"The Knights of the Golden Circle. They are one of the best secret organizations that ever existed in US history and one of the least known."

"Booth was a member?" she asked.

"That's what this proves. It had long been debated whether the KGC was involved in the assassination."

"What do you know about the KGC?"

"The KGC grew out of several Southern organizations that believed in nullification, the concept put forward by South Carolina Senator and Vice President John C. Calhoun."

"Nullification, the concept that the state should have the right to nullify a federal law if the state believed it was unconstitutional. But that theory was struck down by all federal courts, including the Supreme Court."

"Exactly, but that didn't mean the idea died. It only fueled the subversive groups. Nullification became an important ideal as the battle for the preservation of slavery heated. When it became clear that the South could no longer expand its slave territory, it began to look outside the United States. Two Southern senators formed the Order of the Lone Star to sponsor a filibuster expedition to free Cuba from Spain's rule and make it a new slave state. From this idea, the KGC was born, founded in 1854 by George Washington Lafayette Bickley. Some say the KGC spawned from the Order of the Lone Star, and others believe it grew up alongside it and expanded upon its ideas. Either way, it was formed to create a slave empire. Bickley had this grand idea of invading Mexico, South America, and the Caribbean Islands. Along with the Southern states, this newly conquered territory would create a golden circle of a slave empire in the Western Hemisphere."

"How come this isn't in the history books?" Elizabeth asked with skepticism.

"Needless to say, Bickley's plan failed. He began to assemble a military in Texas, but there was insufficient funding for the weapons, militia, and supplies to invade Mexico. At that point in 1860, the Southern states began to secede from the Union, and Bickley shifted the efforts of the KGC to stand behind the newly formed Confederate government. As he saw it, slavery as a whole was at stake. There are varying accounts of the KGC's involvement in the war, from surreptitiously infiltrating the North and obtaining valuable intel to providing battle troops that helped capture Union forts in the South. There has also been speculation that the KGC was behind the first assassination attempt against Lincoln in 1861."

"So what became of the KGC?"

"That depends on who you talk to."

"What do you think?" Elizabeth asked, trying to cut through the long history lesson.

"In 1863, Bickley was captured by Union troops when he entered Northern territory. He was held as an enemy spy for the remainder of the war. This weakened the KGC and their efforts."

Elizabeth sighed. She had enough of the backstory and wanted to fast-forward to something more relevant to current events and gestured her hand, urging him to move along.

"When the South lost the war, several of the KGC fled to Mexico, refusing to live under Union control. The rest went underground. The castles began to disintegrate or merge with other groups."

"Castles?" Elizabeth perked up. First knights and now castles. Webb's daughter was not ranting about a fairytale.

"Oh, right, I skipped that bit. The KGC was organized as a hierarchal structure with three branches, called degrees, which consisted of rank-and-file military, commercial, and governing— the governing degree being the most secretive. The organization, particularly the top degree, was full of rituals and secret codes. Often these codes were left behind for others as a means of communication and could be left as written notes or even carved on signposts or trees. This was particularly useful during the war where covert intel could be passed along right under the noses of the Union army."

Elizabeth was beyond frustrated. It was clear that if asked the time, Beadle could only answer the question after first explaining how to build the watch, but she knew she had to rein in her impatience because only he could give her the information she needed, and she could not afford to cross him at this point. Instead, she tried to tactfully steer him along. "And the castles?"

"The KGC existed in several Southern states, and each KGC territory had a castle or headquarters. There was usually a person who oversaw the castle who was referred to as a captain."

"What became of the KGC?"

"It's generally believed that the organization eventually collapsed or became absorbed into other groups. It's likely that its structure became the basis for other white supremacist societies, including the KKK."

"What if it isn't gone? What if it was just dormant?"

"Why?" he asked with suspicion.

"Just speculating." She was not about to reveal the woman's warning to Jackson to beware of the knights. *And what was it Jackson said...the purse was the key to the castle.*

"Some would like to believe that the KGC planned for a second revival. There were millions of dollars of gold that went missing near the end of the war. Confederate President Jefferson Davis ordered the gold to be loaded on a train and moved from the Confederate capital in Richmond to the deeper south to ensure the Union didn't get it. Somewhere along the line, the gold went missing. Legend has it that the KGC was behind this. They took the gold and hid it with the belief that when the time was right, they'd have sufficient funds to rise again."

Elizabeth had grown up hearing about the legend of the Confederate gold and the gold hunters that spent a lifetime tracking clues that were purportedly left behind. She gave little stock to it. She figured if it existed, it would have been found by now. However, there was something that Webb's daughter wanted others to know.

"So what do Booth's pages say?" She had almost forgotten that was why she met with Beadle in the first place.

He took the pages from her hand and began reading. "His code work is identical to that of the KGC. I've studied any known samples of it since grad school. Although the KGC had many different coding systems, some very intricate using symbols, pictures, and letters, with only some relevant and others merely decoys, this is a basic code, which leads me to believe Booth was merely rank-and-file military. It's just a matter of rearranging the alphabet."

"That's great and all, but maybe if you could just skip to the end and tell me what it says."

"Booth confirmed that the assassination was a KGC act, which not only proves that they were still in operation after the war, but were still operating at a high enough level that they could pull off such a feat. As the days went on after the assassination, he became disillusioned by the group, believing they abandoned him. He gave names of some of the higher members, something a KGC member is sworn to never do. Booth believed that his death would not be at the hands of the military, but the KGC."

"These names that he gave, was one of them Frederick Lawton?"

Beadle looked at the papers again and flipped to the last page. "Yes," he said with surprise in his voice. "How did you know?"

"Frederick Lawton built this plantation."

"You think he was responsible for Booth's death…to shut him up? It would explain how these missing pages ended up here." He clearly wasn't expecting her to answer because he continued. "The orders from Washington, DC, were to take Booth alive, and it seemed feasible considering Booth was trapped inside a barn surrounded by the Union army. Instead, a lone soldier, Boston Corbett, fired a shot through the boards of the barn, fatally wounding Booth." Beadle was so excited that his body vibrated. "Corbett claimed that it was a sudden sense of rage at the sight of the man that caused him to fire, but what if that wasn't it…" His voice trailed off, and he seemed to forget she was there.

When he mentally returned, he looked at her. "You must show me the rest."

Although Elizabeth had obtained all the information she needed regarding the papers, there was one thing more. "You knew what these pages were when Rich sent them to you."

"Of course I did. Do you have any idea what an historic find this is? With these missing pages from Booth's diary, I'll be the most celebrated historian in modern history."

"I didn't understand the importance of the documents before, but now I get it," she said, placating him. "Breaking into my legal clinic and attacking me on the street, it was for the greater good. You needed these pages."

"Exactly!" He nearly jumped from his seat. "I didn't want to hurt you. I just needed these pages."

She hadn't expected that it would be so easy to elicit a confession from him, all of which was being recorded.

"Dr. Beadle, I want to show you something. I think you will find it quite exciting." She rose and led him around the first floor, weaving in and out of rooms. At first he seemed taken by the antebellum mansion, but he began to grow annoyed when she didn't seem to be leading him anywhere.

"Do you know where you are going?"

"Sorry, it's just that this place is so big. I just need to get my bearings." The problem was she hadn't planned it out very well with Danny, and she had no idea where he was hiding. She continued circling around the first floor, until he roughly grabbed her arm and pulled a gun from his coat pocket.

"Enough with the games." His twitch was back.

"I think it's just through here." She pointed to a doorway, and he pushed her toward it. She went into the kitchen and walked the circumference of the room with him right behind her, prodding her in the back with the gun a few times. She was running out of options. As she passed the pantry, the door flung open hitting Beadle, and the gun skittered across the floor. She dove for the gun as Danny pounced on Beadle. It seemed Beadle was no match for a teenager, and Danny had him easily pinned.

"Where are the handcuffs?" she asked.

"In my coat pocket," Danny replied.

She reached in his pocket and retrieved the cuffs, which were another one of Jack's mementos from his police days, and she snapped one side around Beadle's wrist and inserted the other through a loop in a metal fireplace door. It seemed that she was getting good with these things. Once he was securely held, she turned to Danny. "The pantry? You hid in the pantry?"

"I figured he wouldn't find me there."

"Well, neither would I!"

Before she could continue her rant, Jack came huffing and puffing into the room at a pace that she was sure he was unaccustomed to. "Are you all right?"

"We're fine," she answered for the two of them.

"What are you doing in the kitchen? Why not subdue him in the front room where you were sitting?" Jack asked.

"Where's the fun in that?" she said as she handed Jack the gun and headed to her car to call Detective Martinez.

Elizabeth sat staring at Detective Martinez's well organized desk, with every piece of paper neatly stacked and the pens and pencils perfectly aligned in order of height. She resisted the urge to move one of the pencils out of place to see how long it would take for him to notice. She had been waiting for the detective's return for nearly an hour. Danny sat at her side, but he was distracted by his phone. Jack stood in the corner conversing with other detectives, reminiscing about the good old days. He was in his element.

To say that Detective Martinez was annoyed that Elizabeth took matters regarding Beadle into her own hands would be an understatement. He was downright livid, but he had to begrudgingly agree that the recording was damning evidence and perfectly legal in the state, which only required one party in the conversation to give consent. After taking statements from Elizabeth, Jack, and Danny, he disappeared to oversee the processing and questioning of Beadle, and they were instructed to wait for his return.

She could see Grace's desk on the opposite side of the room and wanted to walk to it and explore, but the other detectives in the room spoiled that idea. Instead, she sat and waited. *To hell with it.* She began flicking the pencils on the desk, scattering them.

"What the hell do you think you're doing?" Elizabeth heard from the doorway and looked up, surprised by the reprimand for her pencil rebellion, before she realized it was Grace. She approached and stood towering above Elizabeth, with her hands on her hips. "Will you come with me please." It wasn't a question.

Elizabeth followed her out into the hallway, trying to formulate an explanation. When they reached a relatively isolated corner, Grace turned and leveled an angry stare. "How do you think I felt when I learned that you lured Beadle to a secluded area, unprotected, so you could what…get a confession?"

"Jack and Danny were with me."

"Oh well, then that makes it much better. You had an old man who can't walk a block without getting winded and a teenager who finds himself handcuffed in a woman's bathroom. Why do you keep doing these things?"

"Grace, I wanted to tell you, but I knew you wouldn't approve."

"Damn straight. You're reckless, and you not only put your life in danger, but Jack's and Danny's as well. What am I supposed to do with you?"

"Do with me?" For some reason, that comment struck a nerve, but she took a calming breath. "Grace, I know you don't understand, but it had to be done. There was no other way."

Grace ran her hands through her hair. "Elizabeth, I—" Grace stopped as a pair of police officers passed by in the hall.

Elizabeth reached out and touched her arm. "Grace, I'm sorry."

Grace pulled back and diverted her eyes, scanning the hallway for any other visitors. "Not here. I have to go." Without allowing Elizabeth an opportunity to say another word, she turned and walked down the hall, and Elizabeth watched her until she turned the corner. Her heart sank. Although her scheme achieved what she hoped, she wasn't so sure it was worth it.

Elizabeth rolled the bowling ball down the alley and watched it veer to the side—another gutter ball. If it was possible to obtain a negative score in bowling, Elizabeth would discover it. Danny and Raymond were in a dead heat for first place. It seemed Raymond was a natural. As Elizabeth retook her seat, Danny consoled her. "Look on the bright side, if they gave points for how many pins you could knock down in the lane next to us, you'd be winning."

Elizabeth offered a weak smile. Her heart wasn't in the game, it was with Grace. She had left a lengthy message on Grace's phone that could be characterized as rambling, but there was so much going through her mind, and she wanted to get it out. Grace had yet to return the call, and she resisted the urge to call again, knowing that she needed to give her space. It was Danny's idea for a bowling night, and Elizabeth thought it would be a good distraction. She extended the invitation to Raymond because she hadn't been able to spend much time with him. When she picked him up and swapped out her two-seater for her mother's car, she and her mom touched on a variety of discussion topics, including the nearly completed construction of the clinic and Elizabeth's desperate need for a haircut, but the subject of Grace didn't come up, for which she was grateful.

"Your turn again," Danny called to Elizabeth, who looked at the scoreboard to see that he had bowled a split.

She pushed herself up and searched through the line of bowling balls trying to find hers. She hefted the ball in both hands and threw it down the lane, and it bounced before it veered to the side and found its way once again into the gutter.

"You bowl like a girl."

"Is that a bad thing?" Elizabeth couldn't hold back her smile as she turned to Grace, who was standing back, shaking her head in mock disgust.

"Let me show you how this works." Grace picked up a ball from the ball return, and in one fluid motion, her arm moved forward and released the ball. Elizabeth watched as it sailed into the pins and knocked them all down.

"Hey, that's not fair. You can't bowl for Elizabeth," Danny protested.

Grace looked at the scoreboard. "I don't think you have anything to worry about." She turned to Elizabeth. "Seriously, you haven't knocked down one pin?"

"Sure I did. It just wasn't in my lane." Elizabeth moved to a pair of seats that was set off from the rest, and Grace joined her. "How did you know we were here?"

"I'm a detective." She smiled and relented. "I asked Jack."

Elizabeth invited Jack to join, but wasn't surprised that the long day had been enough for him.

"I got your message. I didn't understand most of what you said, but I got the gist." Grace leaned forward and rested her elbows on her knees, grasping her hands in front of her. "I was very upset when I heard what you did. You scare me with your impulsiveness."

"I'm sorry, Grace. It was never my intention to upset you. I just didn't know what else to do. There is something going on...there's something that we're supposed to figure out. Webb's daughter wasn't crazy."

"I know. I listened to the recording. Where do we start?"

"There is something more to that purse," Elizabeth said.

"We've both been through it. What's left of the writing doesn't make sense. There is no secret message hidden inside. I've had it poked, prodded, and x-rayed. There's nothing there."

"It doesn't make sense, unless..."

"What?"

"We've been so focused on the purse. What about the things inside it?"

"All right, tomorrow we'll take another look." Grace held out her hand, and Elizabeth laced her fingers in between.

"Elizabeth, you're up," Danny called again. She reluctantly released Grace's hand and approached the ball return.

"Oh, this isn't going to be good," Grace said as she watched her wind up.

CHAPTER TWENTY-ONE

Elizabeth sat in her office with her door closed. She would have locked it if it had one. The activity in the clinic was in full force, and she had no desire to be a part of it. She was exhausted even though she slept soundly, even sleeping past her alarm clock. The case, the attack, the conversation with her mother that had yet to happen, and most of all, her erratic relationship with Grace was wearing her down. The evening before, they separated in the parking lot of the bowling alley, and Grace offered a soft chaste kiss at their parting, a complete one-eighty from where they were in the afternoon. She took a breath and pushed the thought aside. There was only one of the issues that she could address—the case, but that too proved to have its challenges.

Her original plan of meeting Grace to take a second look at the purse was foiled, at least temporarily. ADA Wilcox was not going to make it easy for her. He denied her request for a second review of the purse, claiming that he had already complied with her first request, so she was forced to file a motion with the court compelling the government to comply. It took little effort to draft and file, and she had no doubt that the judge would grant her motion. It was only a matter of the delay.

To occupy herself, she did her own research on the Knights of the Golden Circle, and Beadle's rendition seemed accurate by many of the sources she found. The KGC was ensconced in secrecy, mainly operating in the shadows, and had some influence in Southern politics, but its degree of influence seemed to be up to debate. Its clandestine practices included a ritual of hand signals to fellow members, maps that offered more wrong clues than right, and messages written in code, as the Booth papers proved. If Beadle's interpretation of the Booth papers was correct, the White Horse Plantation was a KGC castle, which would have made Frederick Lawton, the patriarch of the plantation, the captain of that KGC territory. None of that would seem unusual given the time period, but based on her research, the KGC dissipated after the Civil War.

The question that nagged at her was, what if it didn't disappear? What if it was simply dormant, until someone such as Josiah Webb decided to resurrect it? This would explain Webb's desire to save the plantation, even if it meant killing his wife to obtain it. It also explained the arsenal she found there. Beyond that, it provided insight as to what kind of activity Webb was involved in that drew the attention of the authorities. Given that the KGC was notorious for its secretive nature, the authorities probably could gain very little from the outside. However, with Webb's daughter, they found an inroad, that was until Webb died. With his death, the authorities might have assumed that the subversive activities that he initiated died as well. That seemed reasonable given that fifty years had passed with no activity.

Elizabeth would be content to leave it at that, except for the fact that Webb's daughter came back. She was trying to convey a message, a message that led her to a former KGC castle, and it was clearly a message that someone didn't want her to deliver. Who was the intended recipient? It surely wasn't meant to be Jackson. He was just in the wrong place at the wrong time.

There was also Margaret Williams and the Freedom Riders. What was their connection to this?

Elizabeth pulled out the photographs of the lipstick writing on the purse and spread them across her desk. Other than the words "call WHITE DEMON" and "horse plant," of which she was reasonably certain she had extracted their meanings, the only other discernible words were "for" and "Power." "For" was too generic to be of any use, but "Power" was a possibility. She studied the writing closely, and the two things that she noted were that the "P" on "Power" was capitalized and the end of the word was smudged. Staring at the word struck a memory, and she dug through the file for the old business card she found on her second visit to the plantation with Jack. She placed it next to the photo. Senator Robert Powers.

She steepled her hands and stared pensively over the documents. There was something that tickled the edge of her brain, and she couldn't reach it.

"Wait a minute," she said to the empty room and turned to her computer and began typing. She opened a few articles and scanned their content. "Oh, Jesus Christ."

Elizabeth approached Professor Dixon's office and consulted her schedule for office hours on the board next to her door before knocking. She had already checked the professor's office hours on her class website before she came, but she wanted to be sure.

"Come in," the professor's voice carried through the door.

When she entered, she found two students occupying the guest chairs opposite Professor Dixon.

"I apologize. I'll come back." Elizabeth began to back out.

"No need to leave, Ms. Campbell. We're nearly finished." The professor beckoned her with a come-hither hand gesture and a smile.

Elizabeth stepped back inside but lingered near the back of her spacious office and explored an expansive bookcase in an attempt to give the students, who seemed to be having difficulty understanding the latest writing assignment, some privacy. She skipped over the usual legal treatises on constitutional law and trailed her finger along the professor's extensive collection of legal and historical books on the suffrage movement, with memorabilia interspersed between the volumes. There were buttons and ribbons advocating a woman's right to vote, their blemishes from age a testament to their authenticity, and a single framed paper that contained a handbill claiming that "a woman's vote is an irresponsible vote" and warning of the danger it posed to the sanctity of the home.

Next to the blasphemous words was a vintage cylinder-shaped music box. Atop the brass base was a carousel of white porcelain horses with four women riders. They wore ankle length dresses and fashionable hats with small brims upon their heads, and each held a sign with a slogan appropriate for the suffrage movement. Engraved into the base were twenty-eight words that were seventy years in the making. "The right of citizens of the United States to vote shall not be denied or abridged by the United States or by any State on account of sex."

Surrounding the words of the Nineteenth Amendment of the Constitution was the image of a metal gate, resembling a drawbridge gate, with an arrow shaped triangle in the center, painted green, white, and purple. Elizabeth recognized the symbol as that of the suffrage movement from her women's studies class in college. The gate represented the women imprisoned during the Civil Rights movement, and the painted triangle a symbol of the Holloway Prison in England, where the first suffragists were detained. The symbol spread to the United States, and green, white, and purple became the colors of the suffragist flag.

Elizabeth wondered what song the music box played and looked to its side and saw the windup key was missing. Just as well. Best not be tempted.

"That is my most cherished piece of the collection," Professor Dixon said, startling Elizabeth. She turned and was surprised to find that the students were gone. "I'd turn it on, but I lost the key. It plays the 'Suffrage March Song.' Do you know it?"

She shook her head. "I'm afraid not."

Elizabeth stepped forward and took a vacant seat previously occupied by one of the students.

"So, to what do I owe the pleasure?"

"I was hoping I could ask you some questions about the state Supreme Court or more specifically, the current nominee for the open seat on the court, Davis Powers."

Elizabeth remembered the class discussion the last time she was there about the governor's nominee and thought Professor Dixon might be able to provide some insight on the controversial figure that had walked the fringes of the white supremacist society. Through her internet search, she learned that Davis Powers's father, State Senator Robert Powers, also appeared to share a similar view based on his voting record and public stance on several Civil Rights matters.

If Elizabeth put the pieces together correctly, then it wasn't a coincidence that the return of Webb's daughter coincided with the controversial appointment of Davis Powers. But what was the message she was trying to convey? It was well known that the man was divisive, and his past had been litigated in the state legislature for the last two months. However from everything Elizabeth read, it was rehashing old facts regarding a man who spent a lifetime defending segregation and supremacist ideologies, but perhaps Webb's daughter had something different, something yet unknown, something worth killing her for.

"What would you like to know?" Professor Dixon asked, leaning back in her chair.

"If Davis Powers is not confirmed, then what impact would that have on the Defense and Rezoning Act?" Elizabeth reviewed some of the more contentious cases pending on the court's docket, but it was DARA that garnered most of her attention. The appropriations bill on its face seemed innocuous, but upon closer review appeared more like a hodgepodge of ideas crammed into a spending bill. It combined a defense spending proposal, greatly increasing the state's military force to a level previously unseen, with an eminent domain clause, allowing the state to seize large sections of private land to increase public highways, and also allotted for the rezoning of business districts to heavy industrial parks.

"The court is evenly split without a seventh member, so it's likely that the ruling of the lower court would stand," Professor Dixon explained.

Elizabeth learned that the lower appellate court declared the act unconstitutional because it passed in a special session called by the governor, who cited the need for the emergency assembly after the state was underprepared to handle a riot a few weeks earlier. Passage only required a quorum to be present for the vote, and a majority of that quorum to vote in favor of the bill. The contentious issue was whether the governor's motive for calling a special session was altruistic or political in nature, as several senators, who were vocal challengers of the bill, were notably absent. They were members of a highly publicized convoy to an international summer conference on environmental measures, and were unable to return in time for the emergency session.

"And the lower court declared that the act was in violation of the state constitution on procedural error grounds because the bill was brought up in an emergency session," Elizabeth said, looking for confirmation.

"Yes. Residents affected by the eminent domain and rezoning clauses brought suit against the state. One of the issues raised was whether they had adequate representation in the state legislature because the senators in their districts were not present for the vote."

"So without Davis Powers the act would be dead basically."

"Yes. It's unlikely that the US Supreme Court will grant certiorari and review the case because of the Tenth Amendment. Powers not solely designated to the federal government nor specifically prohibited to the states by the US Constitution are reserved to the states, including state police powers to protect the welfare, safety, and health of the state's citizens. Thus, the fate of DARA rests in the hands of the state Supreme Court," Professor Dixon said in the tone she used when speaking to her students.

"Who are some of the biggest opponents of Davis Powers and DARA?"

Professor Dixon looked thoughtful for a moment. "You would probably start with State Senator McDermott. He is the most vocal opponent."

Hearing the senator's name, Elizabeth remembered the program she heard on the radio, in which the senator was in a heated debate with Reverend Rick Peterson, the current owner of the White Horse Plantation. She found it funny that everything seemed to always tie back to the plantation in some manner.

CHAPTER TWENTY-TWO

Elizabeth stood in the small room with the metal table, waiting for Grace to return. She had received the court's ruling on her motion that morning and wasted no time reaching out to ADA Wilcox, demanding an opportunity to see the purse again. The prosecutor made no effort to hide his disdain for her and advised that the purse could be viewed precisely at noon, and she was limited to thirty minutes with it before he hung up on her. She smiled at the empty threat because she knew damn well that Grace would pay no mind to ADA Wilcox's orders.

"What are you smiling about?" Grace asked as she reentered followed by a uniformed officer carrying a cardboard box. The officer lifted the lid and removed the purse and placed it squarely in the middle of the table.

"Let me know if you need anything else," he said before he exited, closing the door behind him.

Grace opened the purse and removed the three items, and they both stood staring at them. Elizabeth moved first and picked up the mirror and opened it, and Grace followed and picked up the brush. Elizabeth again admired the carvings of the scenery on the outside before she opened it and again inspected the inside. She tried to lodge her fingernail behind the mirror to see if it would come loose to no avail. She watched as Grace inspected the brush, trying to lift the padding beneath the bristles, but it was securely connected. They traded off items, but there was nothing to be found. Grace reached for the lipstick tube. She opened it and lifted the lipstick out of the container, closely inspecting the inside. She then handed it to Elizabeth, who did the same.

"There's nothing here. There are no inscriptions and no secret compartments," Grace said.

"Damn." Elizabeth set down the lipstick and watched it roll across the table until it was stopped by the brush. "Oh my God, wait a sec."

Elizabeth moved the three items around on the table like puzzle pieces. After trying a few different ways, she arranged them in a line, with the brush on the left side with its bristles facing down, the lipstick tube in the center, and the compact mirror on the right. "It's a map."

Grace looked hard, and Elizabeth pointed it out. "Start with the brush. See here on the face of it, there is a house, and then there is what I first thought was a river going from the house down the handle. But it's not a river, it's a path. You see here on the lipstick tube. If you put it longways against the handle, the path continues across the lipstick tube. And now here." She pointed to the compact mirror. "The path lines up with the front side of the mirror and ends here at the cross."

"I see it, but this doesn't tell us where it is."

"But it does. Look at the house. The pillars in the front, it's the White Horse Plantation."

Grace looked uncertain, and Elizabeth continued. "Now move down to the lipstick tube and see this row of homes. These are the slave quarters. From there, we move to the cross. There is an old slave graveyard in the back of the property, and there's a single cross that still stands."

"Okay," Grace breathed out. "It's a little surreal, but I see it."

"I think we need to look at the cross."

"I knew you would say that."

"Grace, you don't have to come. I can get the others to go with me."

Grace's only answer was a glare.

"Okay then, I guess we're going back to the plantation." Elizabeth removed her phone and took a picture of the three items that formed a silver map before she dropped them in the purse.

❖

Grace carefully navigated the tree tunnel and pulled into the circular drive. To Grace's amusement, Elizabeth sat quietly looking around in curiosity, as though she had never seen the place before. Elizabeth suggested that they drive separately to avoid being seen leaving the police station together, but Grace was uneasy about Elizabeth driving alone to the plantation, even though Grace would be meeting her. Elizabeth's last adventure at the plantation with Beadle still sat heavily with her. Instead, Grace offered to pick her up at her home.

Exiting the car, Grace looked to the two-story antebellum mansion before turning to the expansive property. She couldn't help but find it mind-boggling that the property remained as it did, untouched by the outside world.

"She is amazing isn't she?" Elizabeth asked as she moved beside her.

"She?"

"That's what Samuel calls her and it kind of stuck."

Grace smiled at her, unsure of what to think of her friend Samuel. She moved closer to the home, but stopped short of the front steps and reached out to touch one of the columns. "I guess you've gotten to know this place pretty well."

"Yeah, but I still get a chill every time I come here." Elizabeth looked up to the second floor. "Did you remove the arsenal hidden upstairs?"

"No, I haven't been back since the last time I found you here. It would be a little hard to explain how I suddenly came up with a stash of weapons that I found hidden in a secret room in a forgotten mansion." Elizabeth turned to her with a look she couldn't decipher. "What?"

"Then who closed the door?"

"What are you talking about?"

"When I came back here with Jack, we went up to Webb's office on the second floor, but the door to the secret room was closed. I couldn't figure out how to open it. I assumed you had come back and closed it."

"Maybe it closed on its own." At least Grace was hoping so because otherwise it meant someone else was here. "How did you get in the room in the first place?"

"The door was open just a bit. I didn't even notice it at first."

Grace debated with herself before she walked up the steps and approached the front door.

"What are you doing?" Elizabeth asked.

"I need to see this room. I need to know if the weapons have been removed." Grace squeezed the door handle and pushed, but it didn't budge. "Damn, it's locked."

"No, it's not. It just sticks."

Grace was sure that she was going to pull out some burglar tool to pry her way in, but instead Elizabeth grabbed the handle and pushed, and the door gave way. Elizabeth walked in first and barely acknowledged the first floor and headed up the stairway.

However, Grace took it slow and admired the piece of history as she walked through it.

"Come on," Elizabeth said as Grace fell behind. She was already at the top of the stairs while Grace still stood in the entry of the living room.

"All right, all right. Pushy aren't ya." Grace moved up the stairs and joined her, allowing Elizabeth to lead.

Elizabeth stopped in front of a room. "The only thing of note that I found here was a book with a half-written love letter inside." Grace followed behind as Elizabeth led her to an adjoining sitting room. Elizabeth pointed to a small table. "There."

Grace lifted the book using the bottom of her shirt, but internally chuckled because she figured Elizabeth's prints were probably all over it. "*To Kill a Mockingbird*." She opened to the page with the slip of paper and read the words that were passionate and aching at the same time. A sigh slipped from her before she checked herself and carefully tucked the paper back in for safekeeping. She looked to Elizabeth, who had been watching her, and she felt exposed.

"Show me the secret room."

Grace followed behind Elizabeth around the hallway to a dark paneled room with a frame on the floor near the entrance surrounded by scattered glass. "The flag I take it."

"Yup," Elizabeth said as she walked over it, and Grace did the same. "Here's where the door should be." Elizabeth ran her hand along the paneling next to the ornate fireplace. Grace couldn't help herself, and she started feeling along the mantel looking for a secret lever. Maybe she had seen too many movies, but it seemed anything was possible in this place.

"I've looked all over, and I can't figure out how it opens." Elizabeth walked over to the bookshelves and began removing them.

"Maybe it has a secret pass code. Abracadabra." Grace waved her hands in front of the wall.

"Are you done yet?"

"Considering I'm talking nonsense to a wall, yes, I think I'm done."

Elizabeth replaced the book in her hand and headed for the door. Grace started behind her but was stopped by a faint clicking sound. "Elizabeth, hold up." She turned and saw the door slightly ajar.

"What did you do?" Elizabeth asked.

"I didn't do anything. It just opened."

Elizabeth walked into the small room and pulled out her cell phone for light. She peeled back the corner of a map on the wall. "This is where I found the pages from Booth's diary. And in here is where the weapons are." She moved to a wall opposite the secret door and opened the narrow wooden door.

Grace moved into the small space with her and took stock of the weapons lined against the wall. "This is a serious collection. It looks like it's still here though."

Elizabeth bent and extracted a long metal box and slowly opened it. Grace knelt beside her. "Looks like bullets."

Elizabeth continued to stare inside the box.

"What's wrong?" Grace asked.

"The grenade is missing."

"The grenade?"

"Yes, there was a grenade in here."

"Are you sure?"

"Yes, I'm sure. I held it in my hand."

"You held a grenade?"

"Well, I didn't know it was a grenade at the time. It was dark in here."

"Oh, even better."

Elizabeth closed the box and slid it back against the wall.

"Who else knew about the weapons?" Grace asked.

"Danny and Camille were with me when I found them, and then there was Jack, but we couldn't get into the room."

"Are you sure you didn't tell anyone else?"

"Yes, I'm sure. It's possible that members of Webb's..." Elizabeth hesitated as though trying to formulate the correct word, "organization are still around and knew about the stockpile."

She should have confiscated the weapons when Elizabeth first told her about them.

"Are you all right?" Elizabeth asked.

"Let's get out of here," Grace said and headed out of the secret room. "Leave the door open," she said as Elizabeth was about to close the door to the room.

Grace waited for Elizabeth in the hallway and walked silently at her side as they exited the home. A part of her wished she hadn't asked to see the room because with that knowledge came a responsibility—a responsibility to report the cache of weapons, and more importantly, the missing one. This would lead to an inquiry as to how she came to learn of the weapons, and that is what concerned her.

She pulled the front door tightly closed and began walking down the path to a row of smaller wooden structures. She hadn't realized her pace until Elizabeth jogged to catch up and touched her arm. "Grace, honey, slow down."

"I have to report the weapons."

"And they'll want to know how you found them," Elizabeth finished.

Grace turned away and looked out over the land. She needed a moment to herself, and Elizabeth seemed to recognize that and walked to a set of steps that led to the first wooden shack and sat. Elizabeth's long, graceful fingers played with a nail protruding from a stair. Her light brown hair caressed her face, accenting her deep blue eyes, and perfectly fell around her slender shoulders. Grace couldn't help but watch her. There was no doubt that she was a beautiful woman. There was also no doubt that Grace would never be so foolish as to try to walk away again, the consequences be what they may when her boss and ADA Wilcox learned of their relationship.

"What are you smiling about?" Elizabeth asked, carefully watching her.

Grace wasn't prepared to answer that question, so a diversion tactic was in order. "So what are these buildings?"

Elizabeth stood and faced the shack. "These were the slave quarters. On the map, they were the row of small homes on the lipstick tube."

Grace still couldn't get over the fact that the woman had a map engraved into her silver pieces. A piece of paper would have sufficed for most people. She was even more amazed at how Elizabeth put it together. She had stared at the contents of the purse both in person and in photos, and she never saw it. Elizabeth was remarkable both inside and out.

"What?" Elizabeth asked as she caught Grace staring.

"So the cross would be down this way," she said, pointing down the path.

"Follow me."

Grace gladly did so, watching Elizabeth walk as she went, and she didn't notice much else until they reached a small opening in a wooded area that was surrounded by a handful of posts, most of which were no longer standing. A single cross stood near the middle with a mound of rocks piled in front.

Elizabeth pulled at her sleeve before she entered the small cemetery and directed her a few feet away. "Jack and I found this the last time we were here." She bent and pulled on a metal handle, and Grace took over and opened the hatch door. "Jack said the slaves were put in here for punishment. I found a woman's sweater at the bottom."

Grace peered over the side. "You went down there? Jesus, Elizabeth, that was reckless and dangerous. What if the rope broke?" She took a breath in an attempt to calm herself. She didn't want to start an argument, but she didn't know how to get through to Elizabeth. "Please, Elizabeth, can you try to be a little more careful?" She didn't know how to convey what Elizabeth had come to mean to her without sounding foolish or needy, so she left it at that.

Elizabeth moved closer and looked her in the eyes. "Yes." She stroked Grace's cheek before she turned back to the cemetery.

Grace touched the side of her face and swore she could still feel the warmth of Elizabeth's hand. Suddenly feeling silly for her schoolgirl behavior, she caught up to Elizabeth, who was standing near the cross.

Grace kicked at a few shards of wood that were spread around the ground. "I wonder why this cross is still standing?" She looked to Elizabeth who remained silent, staring at the cross. She couldn't read the look on her face and Grace moved to her. "What is it?" When she didn't answer, Grace's concern grew, and she reached out and caressed her arm. "Elizabeth, what's wrong?"

"It says Samuel Harris on the cross."

Grace looked at the name carved into the wood in block letters. Below it were the dates 1938–1963.

"It's Samuel," Elizabeth said barely over a whisper. A tear escaped down her cheek. "He was here. I spoke to him. He let me in and led me." She nearly stuttered the words. "That's how I found the room and Booth's papers." Grace couldn't even pretend to understand, but didn't doubt that Samuel was real, at least for Elizabeth, and that was enough for her.

"She wanted us to find his grave," Elizabeth continued, never taking her eyes off the cross. "I never gave much thought as to why this cross was still standing when the others were in pieces. She must have added it."

Grace couldn't help but feel that there was more to it than just the grave and couldn't believe she was about to say it. "I think we need to dig these rocks up and see if there is something else buried here." That should have been Elizabeth's line.

Elizabeth looked wary. It was clear that disturbing Samuel's grave didn't sit well with her, but she didn't protest. Grace began moving the rocks, setting them in a neat pile to the side. She tried to show as much respect as she could in the process. When she neared the bottom, a corner of a wooden box protruded. Grace began hastily removing the rocks, not caring where they landed, and uncovered the box. Elizabeth knelt at her side and reached for it, but Grace pulled her arm back before she touched the box. "No, wait. Give me your scarf." She motioned to the red scarf hanging around Elizabeth's neck, a scarf she now knew well.

With the scarf acting as a barrier between her hands and the box, she lifted it out. It was the size of a toolbox with two rusted metal latches that blemished the wood below. They stepped out of the cemetery and returned to the step that Elizabeth previously occupied, neither saying a word.

Grace cradled the box in her lap and struggled to lift the latches. Using the scarf, she removed a corroded brass disk that consisted of two concentric circles that were secured together by a central pin in the middle. The larger circle was about two and a half inches in diameter and could fit in the palm of her hand. The inner circle was about an inch smaller in diameter and could turn around the central pin. Engraved on the circumference of both circles were the letters of the alphabet. In the center of the smaller circle, the letters CSA were written in script. Grace turned the inner circle, and each letter lined up with a different letter of the outer circle. "Looks like a decoding device, a fancier version than the one you'd find in a cereal box." She turned it over to find the inscription "F. Labarre Richmond VA" on the backside.

She set the device on the step next to her and extracted a cracked black book that was bent to accommodate the box's size. Thick yellowing pages filled the inside. She pulled open the book where a small silver key was wedged near the binding and left a distinct imprint of the key on the pages. It had an oval shaped head with a series of numbers imprinted on one side, but was otherwise nondescript.

"Any idea where this goes?" Grace asked. Elizabeth leaned in for a better view, and she could feel her hair tickle the side of her face and inhaled its soft, sweet fragrance.

"No. What's in the book?" Elizabeth asked.

What book? Oh, right, the book. Grace used the scarf to thumb through the pages, and though the ink was faded, she could see that it was filled with neatly printed letters in random order that formed nothing more than nonsensical words. "This is just gibberish."

"No, it's encrypted," Elizabeth said and pointed to the brass disk.

"Of course it is." Grace knew she shouldn't be surprised with WHITE DEMON a phone number, the Booth pages in KGC code, and a map engraved into silver pieces. Why would these pages be in simple English? She turned to the back of the book where several folded pages were tucked inside. As she opened them, they cracked in disapproval at the disturbance. She was pleased to find that the typewritten pages were legible and even better, in English. "This I can read."

With her interest piqued, Grace nearly tore the top paper trying to turn the page with the scarf. "Damn it. I have some gloves in the car. Let's wait on this." Elizabeth didn't protest, which concerned her some because she knew that patience was not her strong suit.

Grace picked up the box to redeposit the book and heard something slide across the wooden surface. "There is something else in here." She pulled out an oval locket on a broken silver chain. She fumbled with the locket, trying to pry it open with the scarf, and it popped out of her hands and landed in the dirt at the base of the stairs. Elizabeth jumped to retrieve it, and before Grace could issue a warning, she used the bottom of her shirt to pick it up. *She's learning.*

The thinner material of the shirt allowed Elizabeth's fingers to be more nimble, and she popped open the locket and held it between them. The picture inside was small, and time and the elements had been unkind, making it difficult to decipher, at least Grace thought so.

"It's Samuel."

"How can you be sure? You can barely see him."

Elizabeth didn't answer her and instead looked over to the cemetery. "Her name was Olivia. Samuel spoke of her every time we met. He was her lover. I think Webb killed him, maybe because he found out about them. She confronted her father and threatened to expose him, and he killed her, or so he thought. He probably didn't have time to bury her like Samuel before she was found." Her voice sounded hollow.

She put a protective arm around Elizabeth and pulled her close, kissing the top of her head. Remaining in Grace's embrace, she stared at the locket that now rested across her knee. "Jack said he found this locket when he inspected the crime scene." She gestured her head in the direction past the cemetery. "He gave it to his partner Stalworth to log into evidence, but it never made it there. Now we know it's because he gave it back to her." She looked down again at the locket. "This proves that she came back. Maybe she killed her father in revenge and stole these things."

❖

Grace walked Elizabeth up to her front door. It almost felt like they were returning from a date, if traipsing through a haunted antebellum estate and digging up a grave could be considered a date. They spent over an hour sitting in Grace's car outside the plantation reviewing the contents of the box, specifically the folded pages in the black book, which appeared to contain a series of intelligence information collected from 1960 to 1963 on at least two dozen people. "Confidential—S. Powers Only" was typed in the top right corner of each page.

When they reached Elizabeth's porch, they found Danny and Camille waiting, and Grace tried to conceal her annoyance. She knew that she wouldn't be able to spend the evening with Elizabeth, but she was hoping for just a bit more time with her.

"What brings you guys here?" Elizabeth asked as she dug for her key in her bag.

"I texted you this afternoon and said we were coming by," Danny answered. He gave Grace a "what's up" head nod, and she offered one in return. Camille ignored her presence, which was fine by Grace.

"Sorry, I guess I was distracted and never checked my phone." Elizabeth opened her front door and flipped on her light, and Camille and Danny entered, clearly no invitation needed.

Grace hesitated in the doorway, her hands sunk into her front pockets, while Danny and Camille made themselves comfortable on the couch, and Elizabeth busied herself in turning on the lights and starting the fireplace. Grace watched Camille, who was in turn watching Elizabeth, and that didn't sit well with her.

Elizabeth finally noticed Grace still perched against the doorframe and approached. "Are you coming in?"

"No, I need to get going." She glanced over Elizabeth's shoulder at the duo who had taken up residence. "I just need to get that sweater." On the drive back, Elizabeth explained her research connected with the discovery of the sweater, including the newspaper articles on the disappearance of Margaret Williams and the murder trial of the two Freedom Rider protestors.

"I'll be right back." Elizabeth disappeared down the hall, and Grace was left staring at the two interlopers. Not willing to carry on idle chitchat, she stepped back out onto the porch to wait.

Elizabeth reemerged and handed over a large Ziploc bag with a smaller one on top. "Here is the sweater and this is the flyer that was in the pocket," she said, tapping the smaller bag. She looked back to the house. "Sorry, I didn't know they were coming."

Grace offered a tight smile. "Just let me know if you come up with anything."

"I'll walk you to your car."

Grace reached behind Elizabeth and closed the door in an attempt to get some privacy from the others. She pulled Elizabeth close and ducked her head, placing a firm kiss on her lips. Elizabeth moaned in approval. Grace savored her for a moment, feeling her body molded to hers and basking in her warm skin.

When Grace finally pulled back, she placed another soft kiss on her forehead. "Good night." Grace was effectively marking her territory. *To hell with Camille.*

Elizabeth watched her leave and touched her mouth. "Damn, that woman can kiss." When Grace drove off, she turned back to the house momentarily forgetting about her houseguests.

"What's with you?" Danny asked.

"What?"

"You're all red."

Elizabeth dismissed his question and asked the question that had been in the back of her mind since she got home. "What are you guys doing here?"

"We just came to check on you. We were getting a little worried," Camille answered.

"You didn't come into the clinic today," Danny added.

Elizabeth pulled her phone from her bag hanging by the door and approached the couch. Camille scooted Danny over so that she could sit next to her. Elizabeth searched her phone for photos she had taken of the items in the box. Grace had taken them to book into evidence, but allowed Elizabeth to take photos. She began the tale as to how she and Grace found the wooden box.

"So when Olivia told Jackson—"

Camille interrupted her. "Olivia? I thought we didn't know her name."

Samuel was always in a hurry to get back to his Olivia. Now she knew why. They had been separated too long. Elizabeth only then realized that in each of her meetings with Samuel, she was alone. No one else had seen him. She remembered their first encounter outside the slave quarters just after her ethereal experience inside. What was it that happened while she sat on the floor of that wooden shack? This led her to wonder if Samuel's presence had something to do with why the White Horse Plantation remained untouched; he was its protector.

"Elizabeth?" Camille asked, a little concerned.

"Sorry." Elizabeth took a breath and refocused. "Samuel mentioned her when we met. Olivia was Webb's daughter, his forbidden love."

"But you said the dude's dead," Danny said.

Elizabeth flinched at Danny's insensitive use of slang for a man with whom she had felt a strong connection, even though they only met a few times, but she opted not to reprimand him. He didn't know any better.

"Samuel is dead. Webb killed him and buried him in the graveyard behind the plantation. That's what I think turned Olivia against her father. After her father died, she went back and put up a cross for him and buried these items at his grave probably for safekeeping." She held out her phone.

"Is that a key?" Danny asked.

"Yes, along with her locket with Samuel's picture, and this device that is some kind of decoder and likely goes with this black book." She swiped the screen to the different pictures as she spoke. "See, the book's in code. Shoved in the back of the book were several pages with confidential information on dozens of people, like they were being monitored. I think it was essentially a hit list."

"What do you mean?"

"I recognized two names. They were organizers of a Freedom Riders protest, who went missing shortly after. They were later found murdered."

"You think that Webb was behind it?"

"It would explain the cache of weapons, but I don't think he was working alone. There was information that wouldn't have been easily known, especially before the age of the internet. There was someone on the inside that had access to that intel and was feeding it to Webb."

"Who?"

"My guess would be State Senator Robert Powers. The top of the intel reports say 'S. Powers,' and I found the senator's business card in Webb's office. What I know of the senator, they shared an ideology."

"He was doing the senator's bidding," Camille said.

"It would explain how Webb suddenly came into money."

"Why not just pass on this information instead of a purse? Wouldn't that have saved a lot of trouble?" Danny asked.

"Yes, if she had it with her." Elizabeth spoke slowly, afraid she was going to lose Danny. "I think she stole it from her father and buried it. She didn't know what else to do with it at the time. She may not have had the opportunity to go back and get it. After all, she was supposed to be dead."

"It still seems so far-fetched. The map engraved into her hairbrush?" Danny asked.

Elizabeth had to admit it was eccentric, but she felt the need to defend Olivia because Samuel would want her to. "I think it was a learned habit. She grew up under KGC reign. From everything I read about the organization, it was all about secrecy, codes, and maps. Maybe she feared it would fall into the wrong hands and didn't want to make it so easy."

"Well, that's for sure."

"This leaves us with the question," Camille finally spoke. "What does she want us to do with this information now?" Camille cradled Elizabeth's hand that held the phone and moved her thumb along the screen, caressing Elizabeth's palm in the process.

Not wanting to read too much into the intimate act, Elizabeth held the phone out to Camille. "I don't know what any of it means right now. Grace will look into the documents and see what she can come up with." With the sound of Grace's name, Camille visibly flinched, and for a moment, Elizabeth considered defending her, but realized that Camille would never see past the fact that Grace was the detective on her brother's case.

"So what do we do?" Danny asked.

CHAPTER TWENTY-THREE

Grace dragged herself up the steps of the police station and walked through the sliding doors, mindlessly waving at the deputy working the front desk as she passed. From the time she left Elizabeth on her front step the night before until now, she had gone over countless ways she would explain to her sergeant about the weapons at the White Horse Plantation, and in particular, how she knew there was a missing grenade. She had even entertained the thought of not saying anything at all, but her conscience wouldn't allow that, not when she believed that someone was out there with the missing weapon.

She passed her desk, not stopping to boot up her computer, and walked to her sergeant's office. He was leaning in his chair as though expecting her. "Donovan, have a seat."

She complied and sat, holding up her head and squaring her shoulders.

"Something you need to say, Donovan?"

"Yes, sir." She started from the beginning and explained how she discovered the White Horse Plantation and finally ended with how she came to discover the wooden box buried at Samuel's gravesite. She left no detail out, including her partnership with Elizabeth in several of her endeavors. She needed to come clean. She was no longer going to hide her relationship, even if it meant her job. Her sergeant remained motionless, leaning back in his chair, hands clasped in his lap. His stare never wavered. She figured he was giving her a chance to launch her defense before he brought down the gavel. She finished her story with the discovery of the cache of weapons and specifically the missing one.

"I know."

"Sir?"

"Ms. Campbell is here."

"She's here?" Grace hadn't seen her on the way in, but then again, she barely took her eyes off the floor her entire walk in.

"She's sitting with Detective Martinez. She told a slightly different tale. She took full responsibility for traipsing through the home. She claimed the plantation's caretaker gave her permission, but it seems that the said caretaker is dead. Not sure what the evidence code says about permission given by a ghost haunting an estate." He said it with a straight face, and Grace didn't know how to take any of it, and she remained silent.

"Martinez is driving Ms. Campbell out there, so she can show him where it is. I think you should go too. Having another female along on the ride would be a good idea."

Grace stood and moved to the door, but he stopped her. "Grace, what you do and who you do it with on your own time is none of my business." He smiled at her—that was a first.

She turned and scanned the room and found Elizabeth sitting in the corner near Detective Martinez's desk. They made eye contact, but Grace couldn't get herself to smile. She wasn't angry, far from it. She was just stunned by the sudden change of events.

"All right, let's go," Detective Martinez said as he approached her, and he motioned Elizabeth to the door.

Elizabeth stood and waited for Grace. "Detective Donovan, nice to see you."

"Ms. Campbell," Grace replied in the most formal tone she could muster.

Finishing her paperwork from the evidence she logged in from the White Horse Plantation, which included the contents of the wooden box, the sweater, and an arsenal of weapons, Grace ignored her ringing phone. When the caller persisted, she finally answered.

"What the hell do you think you're doing?"

She didn't need an introduction to know who the caller was. "How may I help you, counselor?" She wasn't overly surprised by ADA Wilcox's call; in fact she was expecting it. On the drive to the plantation earlier that morning, she called Casey requesting her assistance in obtaining the warrants needed to confiscate the weapons and to dig up Samuel's grave. She figured this fell into her jurisdiction of organized crime. Just over an hour after their conversation, Casey had a signed warrant for the weapons and delivered it personally to the plantation.

"So this is Elizabeth Campbell," Casey said as she approached Grace, who was standing outside the plantation home with Elizabeth and Detective Martinez. She handed over the warrant to Grace and openly assessed Elizabeth, who seemed undaunted.

Grace squirmed. There was too much happening too fast. First her sergeant and now her past and present were colliding.

Elizabeth stepped forward and extended her hand in greeting. "Yes, I'm Elizabeth." They exchanged pleasantries before Casey turned to Grace. "It will take a bit longer to get the warrant to dig up the grave. That requires more of an explanation." She looked back and glanced at Elizabeth, who started for the front door of the home with Martinez following behind. "I hope it works for you. I really do."

"Who gave you permission to search a plantation?" The terse tone of the prosecutor brought Grace back to the present conversation.

"The court that signed the order," Grace responded in an upbeat tone. She was actually annoyed, but she refused to let him know it. "What is it that you're afraid we'll find?"

"I'm not sure what side you're working for, Detective, but I'm putting a stop to this," ADA Wilcox growled.

"Truth, that's my side. Now, if we're done here—"

Wilcox hung up before she could finish her statement, and she knew she had just burned a bridge.

CHAPTER TWENTY-FOUR

A ll right, just follow my lead in here," Elizabeth said to Jack as they approached the glass door to an office adjacent to the church that housed Bounty Ministries. On a whim and at a loss for where else to turn in the case, she decided to pay a visit to Reverend Rick Peterson, better known as Reverend Rick to his followers. Before coming, she listened to a recording of his weekly program that openly espoused racist, homophobic, xenophobic, and misogynistic rhetoric. He cited diversity as one of America's greatest downfalls. She knew it wouldn't be an easy task getting the opportunity to speak with the man and figured she would have to get through his assistant, so she brought Jack as her backup, given his recent success in getting the burial records at the cemetery.

Elizabeth dressed for the occasion, wearing a yellow dress with a hem that fell well below her knees and a high button-up collar, leftover attire mandated by her mother for a family wedding. Michael had banished it to the farthest corner of her closet, and she had to admit that there was little that was flattering about the dress, but it was conservative and just the image she was hoping to portray during her visit with the self-righteous reverend.

"May I help you?" a woman asked from the front desk as they entered the traditionally appointed office. She was wearing a dress that rivaled Elizabeth's, and she was convinced that they would be kindred spirits.

"Hi, I'm Elizabeth Campbell and this is Jack Rourke. We were hoping to speak with Reverend Peterson."

"You don't have an appointment," she said in a flat tone.

"True, but we won't take much of his time. We just need to discuss some business about the White Horse Plantation."

"You don't have an appointment."

"I understand, but I'm sure he will be very interested—"

"You don't have an appointment," the woman interrupted.

"I know I don't have an appointment," Elizabeth said, exasperated. *Okay, maybe we're not kindred spirits.* "But I would just like a word with him."

"You don't—"

"I know, have an appointment." She turned to Jack. "A little help here. Do your Jack Rourke thing."

"Oh no, she is way out of my league. She's got that Stepford thing going on."

"If you don't leave, I'm going to call the police," the woman said with a bit more inflection to her voice.

"That won't be necessary."

Elizabeth turned to see Grace standing behind them. She didn't hear the door open.

Grace approached the desk and pulled out her badge. "I'm Detective Grace Donovan. These two"—she gestured to Elizabeth and Jack—"are with me. I need to speak with Reverend Peterson on police business. Please let him know that if he chooses not to speak with me here, then I can get a warrant and bring him down to the station, nice and public. I'm sure that would be a big boost for his ratings."

"One moment please," the woman droned and exited through the door near her desk.

"Ah, I miss the power of the badge," Jack said.

"What are you two misfits doing?" Although the question might have been meant for the two of them, her eyes never left Elizabeth.

"The same thing you are, trying to get some information on the plantation. He and his so-called ministry are the current owners of the plantation with its cache of weapons."

"A phone call or even a text along the lines of 'Hey, Grace, Jack and I were thinking of heading up to Bounty Ministries to have a chat with Reverend Rick. Wanna come?' would have been nice."

Elizabeth pulled out her cell phone from her bag and began typing. Moments later, Grace's phone pinged, and she rolled her eyes before she pulled it out and read the text. *Hey, Grace, you're really hot when you act all detective-like. Wanna come?*

Before Grace could offer a reaction, the woman returned. "Follow me." She turned back to the door expecting them to follow, and Jack gallantly gestured to allow them to walk in front of him.

Elizabeth walked first and Grace caught up. "What are you wearing?" She eyed the dress up and down.

"What? This doesn't suit your tastes?"

"I think I like you in the 'Homie' T-shirt better."

"With or without a bra?"

Grace walked into the doorframe, and Jack chuckled as he passed her. "She's a spitfire."

At the woman's instruction, Elizabeth stepped through the entryway of the first interior office with Jack following behind and Grace bringing up the rear.

A man she presumed to be Reverend Rick stood from behind the desk. "How may I help you?" He gestured to a couch, and Grace and Jack sat, but Elizabeth continued to stand. The reverend took a seat opposite them.

Grace pulled out her badge and introduced herself and offered no introductions for Elizabeth and Jack, which she figured was just as well. Grace was leading this show.

"As I am sure you are aware, we secured a warrant to remove a stockpile of weapons from the White Horse Plantation after receiving a tip as to their existence. We removed dozens of firearms, none of which were legal," Grace said, her eyes boring through the reverend.

"I know nothing about those weapons. I, through Bounty Ministries, own the plantation, but I have only been there a few times, and I assure you, I never stayed very long. The place has been abandoned for more than fifty years and is uninhabitable. If there were weapons, they were hidden there long before I came to possess the property." Reverend Rick spoke with ease and confidence, as a well-seasoned orator would.

Grace assessed him for a minute before pulling out a small notebook from her coat pocket. While Reverend Rick's attention was drawn to Grace's note taking, Elizabeth casually stepped closer to the bookshelf for a better view of its contents. The neatly lined books were intermingled with photographs and collectibles, including a small glass case with a revolver inside. She knew nothing about guns, but assumed it was a relic based on its display. She found it ironic that there were no religious themed books, art, or trinkets for such a religious man, but there was a gun. *Long live the Second Amendment.*

"How did your church come into possession of the property?" Grace asked.

"I'm sure you know, Detective. The property was owned by my grandfather, who founded Bounty Ministries. The church, as well as the property, has since passed to me."

"What's your relationship with Powers?" Grace asked, swiftly changing topics, and the reverend's comfort level seemed to diminish.

"Who?"

"Judge Davis Powers and his father, the late Senator Powers."

"I assure you, I do not know what you are talking about."

During the course of the questioning, Elizabeth had migrated from the bookshelf to the glossy wooden desk for a perusal. There seemed nothing out of the ordinary, but for a neat stack of papers that rested near the edge closest to her. It wasn't the paperwork that got her attention, but the paperweight on top. She lifted the brass disk that resembled the one they found in the box at Samuel's grave. It was in much better shape and didn't contain the same lettering on the back, but its resemblance was unmistakable. She held it up for Grace to see.

"Excuse me, do you mind not touching my things." He removed the disk from her hand.

"Interesting souvenir," Elizabeth said as she watched him set it back on the stack of papers.

"Unlike the other one, this is only a replica."

Grace seemed to ignore their exchange, and Elizabeth backed away toward the couch and offered no reply.

"What are your intentions with the property?" Grace asked, resuming her questioning.

Reverend Rick perched against his desk. "I'm selling it. I have no need for it."

"It's been in your family for over a hundred and seventy years. You're going to sell it just like that?"

"It's a relic and an eyesore. I'm building a flagship church for Bounty Ministries. It will be three times the size of our current church."

"And you need the funding."

"Yes. I'm trading in a dilapidated plantation of the past for a vision of the future." His eyes lit up as he spoke.

"So you can hold larger audiences who can listen to you spew your hate?" Elizabeth spoke up. She knew she should have stayed quiet, but the man repulsed her. She nearly snarled at him.

He turned on her. "I speak the word of God. It is only hate to the ears of sinners."

Grace stepped forward just as Elizabeth started to approach him and grasped her arm, guiding her to the door.

"Thank you for your time, Reverend Peterson. I will reach out if I have any more questions."

"You can call me Reverend Rick."

Elizabeth turned her head toward him as Grace was ushering her out. "Do you spell that with a D?" Grace gave a firmer nudge to hasten her departure.

Jack threw back his head and laughed. "I get it." He continued chuckling until they reached his car parked on the street. Elizabeth gave him a hug and thanked him for coming, while Grace stood back and remained silent.

Once Jack drove off, Grace turned to her. "How did Reverend Rick know about the brass disk that we found at the grave? The contents of the box were not listed in the warrant because they were already in evidence."

"Damn, that means we have a leak. The question is—is it on my side or yours?"

Chapter Twenty-Five

Grace shielded her eyes from the morning sun as she approached the workmen standing around the makeshift cemetery. She received a message from Casey shortly after leaving Elizabeth at Reverend Rick's office that the warrant was signed.

"What are you guys waiting for?"

"We weren't sure which one to dig up?" one of the workers said.

"What are you talking about? There's only one..." Grace stopped and stared at the second mound lying parallel to Samuel's grave. *Oh shit.* "Dig them both up."

Grace rested her head on her desk. It had been an endless day, or was it even still the same day? She looked at the clock to see that it was 12:35 a.m. A second forensic team was brought in after the discovery of the second grave. The scene was meticulously scoured, and whoever buried the second body left no identifying evidence, just a recently deceased body buried less than twelve hours before discovery. It was in good shape and identification was easy, aside from the driver's license in the pocket, the face was recognizable— Reverend Rick Peterson.

There had been talk of political enemies who despised his teachings, but Grace doubted it, not after what she and Elizabeth uncovered. It wasn't only the placement of the body next to Samuel's grave that told her this murder went much deeper, it was the manner of death. The reverend was killed by a single gunshot to the back of the head, execution style. However, this wasn't the concerning part. It was the fact that Samuel was killed the same way. His remains had been preserved by the dry, hard soil, and his manner of death was discernible, including the bullet that was extracted from the back of his skull—a bullet that matched the bullet removed from Reverend Rick. They were killed by the same Smith & Wesson Model 36 circa 1950s revolver, but she didn't need the medical examiner or forensic expert to tell her the make and model of the weapon. The gun was left behind in Reverend Rick's shallow grave. She inspected it at the scene and found that the gun had jammed after firing, likely due to age and lack of proper care.

She also knew that she had seen the gun once before. As Elizabeth had overtly snooped through Reverend Rick's office, she had surreptitiously inspected the contents and noted the gun in the glass case on the shelf. She searched the reverend's office after leaving the scene and confirmed the glass case was now empty.

Elizabeth pulled her robe tighter around her as she peered through the side window next to her front door. She was startled awake by the 2:00 a.m. knocking. She reasonably assumed it would be friend not foe, as a burglar wouldn't likely be so courteous as to announce his visit prior to entering, but given the events she experienced recently, she couldn't be too careful.

She twisted the locks and reached out, pulling Grace inside. "Honey, what are you doing out so late? Are you all right?"

"I couldn't sleep." Grace walked to the couch and allowed her body to drop.

Elizabeth curled up against her and began stroking her hair, pulling errant strands from her face. "Honey, what's going on?"

Grace explained the discovery of Reverend Rick buried alongside Samuel. "Forensics says it was the same gun that killed them both. It seems he was killed less than twelve hours after our meeting."

Even though she didn't like the man, she felt some remorse for him because no one should die in such a violent manner. "I'm sure he acquired a lot of enemies, but this isn't about his church and ideology. I think someone didn't want that property sold."

"I'm leaning toward that possibility. The report came back on the items found in the wooden box." Elizabeth intertwined her fingers with Grace's, prompting Grace to bring Elizabeth's hand to her lips for a gentle kiss before she continued. "As suspected, the reports were intel gathered on politicians, civil rights leaders, and activists located throughout the state. Several of them disappeared or were found murdered. Only two of the cases went to trial."

"The two young men who were the organizers of the Freedom Riders protest."

"Uh-huh," Grace said, lolling her head to the side to face her, Elizabeth's hand firmly nestled in hers.

Elizabeth recalled the news articles she read on the trial. "Tobias Stokes was convicted of their murders based on a single witness, who claimed he had seen Stokes with the Freedom Rider protestors the night of the rally. He was sentenced to death."

Grace nodded. "I pulled the case file. They both died from a single gunshot wound to the back of the head, with the same kind of Smith & Wesson. The weapon was never recovered."

"Stokes was just another victim." Elizabeth slumped back and closed her eyes. "One gun, four murders. Reverend Rick probably inherited the gun. Little did he know, he would be the last of its legacy."

"There's more. The silver key that was in the book went to a safe deposit box."

Elizabeth sat up. "What did you find in it?"

"Nothing. In March 1963, it was cleaned out in one of the largest bank robberies in state history. Over ten million dollars in cash and gold were stolen and never seen again. It was double the amount of cash and assets the bank normally kept at that time, but several national nonprofits and the federal government transferred funds in anticipation of the Equal Justice Fund."

"Yeah, I remember that program. It was launched to eradicate poverty and the disparity in social programs and education in the African-American communities. I'm guessing it's not a coincidence that the bank was robbed at that time," Elizabeth said.

Grace used her free hand to rub at her eyes. "No. There were only a handful of people who knew about the deposits, and the money was set to be dispersed throughout the state starting the next day. The FBI and state police thought it was an inside job, but the investigation led nowhere. The money never surfaced, and they believed it was laundered within twenty-four hours through an offshore account." Grace's voice grew raspy at the end.

"But?" She knew there had to be more to Grace's story.

"But, in the reports found at Samuel's grave, there was intel on the Equal Justice Fund, including details on funding from the national nonprofit organizations. During the robbery, one of the guards was shot and killed. Although testing hasn't been done, some of the weapons confiscated at the plantation are the same caliber."

"And the safe deposit box?" Elizabeth asked.

"It was the only box that was robbed. It belonged to none other than—"

"Senator Powers."

"Nope, but close. His son, Davis Powers. When he was interviewed by the police, he claimed there was only insurance paperwork inside and nothing of value to anyone else."

"I'm sure, you know how those twenty-somethings get bogged down in insurance paperwork. The senator didn't want his name on the safe deposit box. That might be how Webb got the confidential intel reports." Elizabeth rested her head against the back of the couch and stared at the ceiling. "Maybe Webb planned to go rogue, tired of being the rank-and-file military of this new KGC. He was vying for a place at the top of the pyramid. He wanted to be captain." The circle of murder suspects for Webb was widening. Elizabeth turned to Grace. "The robbery, it was March seventeenth?" She didn't wait for an answer and continued. "I found Senator Powers's business card in Webb's room. On the back 'EJF 3/17' was written—Equal Justice Fund, March seventeen."

Grace dropped her head back and closed her eyes, and Elizabeth figured she was too tired to offer a response, but Elizabeth's brain was blazing with all the new information and her mind turned to Samuel. "Will they be able to identify Samuel?"

Grace turned to her and tightened her grip on Elizabeth's hand that still rested in her lap. "It's not likely. There's nothing to compare it to. There are no records of him," she said apologetically.

"Thank you, Grace, for trying."

Grace gave her a weak smile, and Elizabeth could see the effort made to keep her eyes open. She went in search of a pillow and blanket, and when she returned, she found Grace sound asleep. She guided her head down onto the pillow and pulled up her feet and removed her boots. She carefully covered her, tucking in the edges, and placed a kiss on her forehead before she turned out the lights.

CHAPTER TWENTY-SIX

G race sat outside in the waiting area as the clerk furiously typed notes from the words being pumped into her ears through her headset. She didn't have an appointment, so she expected to wait. It was an impromptu visit to Judge Powers. When she woke up that morning on Elizabeth's couch, she realized that she slept, she actually slept, not just a restless version of it. She felt good. She felt even better when she saw Elizabeth in the kitchen fussing over a pan of eggs that were being beat within an inch of their lives. "Whatever they did, they're sorry," Grace joked. She removed another skillet from the flame that had very crisp pieces of sausage.

"Sorry, breakfast is not my forte. Well, actually, cooking in general is not my forte."

Grace didn't care. Food was the furthest thing from her mind at the moment. What occupied the forefront of her brain was Elizabeth standing in pajamas, pajamas that were see through in the kitchen light, and there was no bra to hide the breasts that stood at attention with two very pink nipples that poked at the material.

Grace limited herself to voyeurism and kept her hands to herself. She did what she could through breakfast to keep her eyes trained on her eggs, but she couldn't help but let her eyes drift up from time to time, just for a little peek.

When the topic turned to the case, she extracted herself from the table and carried her dishes to the kitchen. She needed some distance from the perfect breasts to be able to focus on that conversation.

Given that there seemed to be a connection between Webb and Powers, both father and son, she had a strong hunch that Judge Davis Powers was somehow intertwined with whatever was going on. Elizabeth believed that it was his sudden rise to fame in the media as a result of his nomination to the Supreme Court that brought Olivia back, but the question still nagged at her—why?

"I'm sorry, but the judge is still on the bench. It's going to be another thirty minutes," the clerk said, breaking Grace from her thoughts.

"Not a problem. I'll wait."

The thirty minutes turned into an hour and thirty, but Grace waited it out. The judge continued his duties as an appellate judge, and she reviewed the court calendar before she came to ensure that he would be in town and not soliciting votes at the state capitol.

"He is ready to see you now." The woman stood from behind her desk and led Grace to an oversized dark mahogany door. The woman opened the door but didn't step into the room and instead moved to the side to allow Grace to pass.

Grace walked into the spacious room that had furnishings that matched the door. A white haired man bordering on obese sat behind a desk that would seem too large for the average person, but was appropriate for him. He reviewed paperwork in front of him and said nothing as she approached. "I'm Detective Grace Donovan. Thank you for taking the time to see me, Your Honor."

The man remained silent and continued reading. Grace was adept enough to know that it was a power play, so she decided to wait him out, and she continued to stand and watch him in silence.

When it seemed enough time had passed for him, he lifted his head and acknowledged her. "What can I do for you, Detective?" He didn't invite her to sit down.

"I have some questions about a pending murder investigation."

"Yes," he replied, making no effort to hide his impatience.

Grace pulled out a folder from the bag resting on her shoulder and extracted several photos of the intel reports. "May I?" She gestured with the photos in her hand, requesting to approach.

He waved his hand to her, and she moved closer, and when she stood opposite him at the desk, he snatched the photos from her.

"These documents belonged to your father." It wasn't meant to be a question.

He sorted through them before tossing them on the desk and glaring at her. "I don't recognize these."

"It's intelligence information gathered on multiple people that opposed your father. Several people listed in these reports disappeared or were found murdered."

"Detective, these have nothing to do with me. Now, if you don't mind—"

"They were stolen from your safe deposit box in March 1963." She knew she was stretching that one because she couldn't prove it, but she was looking for his reaction.

"What are you implying?"

She took note that he didn't deny it. "I'm just asking questions, sir. Only two of the murders from that list went to trial. You defended Tobias Stokes, the man accused of the murders." She hadn't really thought to look at the players involved in the Stokes trial until after her conversation with Elizabeth, when it became apparent that Stokes was convicted of a murder that he didn't commit. Quick research by Casey into the DA's records confirmed that Davis Powers, a newly minted attorney, was appointed defense counsel.

"I wouldn't remember that. I was a defense attorney back then, and the court assigned countless indigent cases to me."

"I would think you'd remember this one. Tobias Stokes was African-American, and from what I could see, your only African-American client in your illustrious defense attorney career. The rest of your clients seemed to be of a very different demographic."

"Look, Detective, I don't know what you're getting at, but as I'm sure you're aware, Mr. Stokes was convicted of those murders by a jury of his peers."

So he does remember. "Jury of his peers? An all-white jury, with a white prosecutor, white judge, and white defense attorney." She couldn't help but think back to the book Elizabeth showed her at the White Horse Plantation, *To Kill a Mockingbird.* "But you, sir, were no Atticus Finch."

He scrunched up his face, the analogy clearly lost on him. "Detective, I think your implications are bordering on slander. You keep this up, and the rest of your career will be spent directing traffic."

She didn't acknowledge his threat and continued. "Well, sir—"

"That's Your Honor to you," he said.

"I apologize, Your Honor." She knew better. She was only doing it to goad him. "Let's look at this from a different perspective. An intelligence report compiled by your father on his political enemies was in your safe deposit box, until stolen in one of the largest bank robberies in state history. The intel reports even contained information about the bank and its assets. A bank where you conveniently kept your safe deposit box, allowing you a slight advantage in attaining knowledge of the inside working of the bank, but I digress."

She noted the tight grasp of his intertwined fingers that rested on the desk, but he made no effort to stop her, and she continued. "Some may consider it a conflict of interest if the murder victims were listed on your father's report, a report in which most of the people disappeared or were murdered, a report that was once in your possession. It also can't be ignored that a defense attorney, reputed for defending white supremacists, takes on the defense of Stokes. Pretty good way to make sure that those two murder cases got closed with no fingers pointing toward your father."

"You can't prove any of this and nobody cares about some dead ni—" He stopped himself short of saying the word and pushed back his chair. Grace was afraid that the force would send the chair flying backward, but it managed to stay on all four wheels. He visibly calmed himself and looked directly at her. "I don't need to speak with you."

"No, Your Honor, you don't, but given that you are up for confirmation, a very contested confirmation, it may not bode well that you are refusing to cooperate in a murder investigation."

He slammed his fist on the desk. "This is blackmail."

"No, Your Honor, it's just the facts."

She could hear him breathing through his nostrils as his chest rose in rhythm. He never broke eye contact. "A fifty-year-old murder trial has no connection to the investigation of an old woman killed in a knife attack, in which the suspect was caught red-handed," he said through gritted teeth.

"I never mentioned that the murder investigation involved an old woman."

"Nice try, Detective, but I looked you up while you were sitting outside. I know what case you're working on."

Nice recovery. "Actually, Your Honor," she made it a point to emphasize the title, "I'm investigating the murder of Reverend Rick Peterson. He was killed with the same gun as the Freedom Riders protestors. The gun was found at the scene at the White Horse Plantation, a plantation I believe you once frequented."

"Why would you assume that?"

"Well, your father, Senator Powers, seemed to have, shall we say, a working relationship with Josiah Webb, who owned the plantation. They shared an ideology and vision, until he decided to turn on your father and steal the intel reports." She made the last part up, but she was on a fishing expedition.

Judge Powers didn't answer, but instead stared at her with a look of ill intent. "Detective, I think we're done here."

"Just a bit more." He made no effort to invoke his Fifth Amendment rights, so she carried on. "There was another body buried next to Peterson—Samuel Harris, the caretaker of the plantation. He was killed with the same gun." She agreed with Elizabeth that given the fact that Reverend Peterson had possession of the gun, it was probably passed down the family line, along with the property. This made Webb a likely murder suspect of the Freedom Rider protestors and Samuel, but as she laid out her case to the judge, she was even more convinced of his complicity. "Webb didn't like his daughter seeing Samuel, did he?" That question was for Elizabeth.

"Olivia was a disgrace to her family with that ni—black boy," he spewed out with hate before he checked himself. She clearly struck a nerve and wondered if he had some unrequited feelings for her back in the day, making Olivia's relationship with Samuel a double slap. Grace was also heartened to have confirmed Elizabeth's theory of Olivia's identity, as well as her purported first death and Samuel's murder.

However, as she assessed the judge, she doubted he carried out Peterson's murder. It wasn't just his age and physical condition that made it improbable, but the murder weapon used. The judge wouldn't have used a gun that could be tied to the Freedom Rider protestors, or Samuel for that matter. That was careless, and he didn't strike her as careless.

Grace had run out of questions, at least ones that she thought he might answer. "Thank you, Your Honor, for your time. I'll see myself out." She turned without waiting for a reply, not that she was expecting one, and walked out of the office, the reception area, and the courthouse as fast as she could. She couldn't seem to get far enough away from the man.

CHAPTER TWENTY-SEVEN

Elizabeth slapped her hand on the bedside table in a feeble attempt to grab her ringing cell phone, but only succeeded in knocking it to the ground. When the ringing stopped, she settled back into her pillow, the phone forgotten until it rang again.

"Uggh!" She reached down and began searching the floor to no avail and leaned over the side of the bed for a better view, which proved to be a mistake because the rest of her body followed. She lay on the ground with one leg caught in the twisted sheet, and her phone rang for a third time.

"What?" Whoever had the nerve to call this early didn't deserve manners. She heard Grace's soft laugh on the other end.

"Catch you at a bad time?"

"Just a bit tied up at the moment." She kicked her foot trying to free it, but the sheet refused to release its possessive grip.

"What are you doing?"

"I fell out of bed trying to reach the phone, and I'm lying on the floor. My foot is stuck in the sheet."

Grace remained silent.

"Grace, are you still there?"

"I'm here. I'm just trying to picture it, and it looks pretty good. What are you wearing because I'm picturing you in the little pajama set you had on the other morning."

Elizabeth found herself aroused by the low timbre of Grace's voice. "Grace, if you keep talking like this, I'm going to have to pleasure myself, and you'll have stay on the phone and listen."

"Oh Jesus, I'll call you back."

The line went silent, and Elizabeth tossed the phone on the floor and used both hands to pull her foot free. She plopped on the bed and waited for Grace to call. Just as she started to drift off again, the phone rang and this time, she took more care in locating it.

"Are you available to talk?" Grace asked.

"You mean am I still touching myself? Wait, just one more sec, almost there." She took a couple of deep breaths into the phone for show.

"You're killing me."

Elizabeth didn't hold back her giggle. "Now that we got the phone sex out of the way, what else do you want to do?"

"I don't know."

"You called me, remember?" Elizabeth loved that she had her so flustered.

"Right, um...give me a minute."

"Was that your zipper?"

"No, that was not my zipper. I'm sitting at my desk going through my notes."

"If you say so."

"Will you stay on track please?"

"You started it."

"I'll have to remember that next time."

"Next time?"

"Never mind. Please try to focus." She could hear Grace take a fortifying breath. "I got the forensics report back on the sweater you found."

"And?"

"There was dried blood and two sets of hair follicles. There was enough of a viable sample to run them through the database."

"You found a match?"

"No, not exactly. A partial match, someone related to both samples."

❖

Elizabeth walked down the hall to the fourth-story apartment. She adjusted her blazer and hiked her bag higher on her shoulder to delay having to knock on the door. She continued to process the information Grace gave her that morning, as it fumbled about in her head. She raised her fist and gave a gentle knock, trying not to disturb any of the other neighbors since it was still early. When the door opened, she was met by Camille's surprised look.

"Is everything okay? It's Jackson isn't it? What happened?" she asked in rapid succession as she pulled Elizabeth inside.

"No, Jackson is fine. I'm sorry to bother you so early, but I had some questions, and I couldn't wait."

"Of course, sit down." Camille guided her to the couch, and she took a seat next to Elizabeth, but perched on the edge still in full alert. She looked about the modest living room that was warmly furnished. Mrs. Francis entered the room dressed in a robe. Elizabeth assured her that Jackson was fine in response to her startled look at her presence.

Mrs. Francis took a seat in a light brown recliner that she guessed was her usual seat in the room based on the personal items and medication bottles on the table beside it. She tightened the tie around her robe, as though bracing herself.

"On one of my visits to the plantation," Elizabeth said, "I found a woman's sweater."

"Plantation?" Mrs. Francis asked.

Elizabeth realized that Camille had been withholding information about the developments in the case from her, probably due to her health concerns. This made Elizabeth more uneasy, and she looked to Camille for silent permission to bring her up to date before she enlightened Mrs. Francis on all that they had discovered. Mrs. Francis sat motionless absorbing every detail.

"So Jackson is okay?" Camille asked again.

"Yes. I'm here because a forensic lab ran tests and found a partial match of the DNA found on the sweater."

"To who?" Camille barked.

"To Jackson. His DNA was entered into the system once he was arrested."

Mrs. Francis looked confused. "They have his DNA?"

"Yes, a state can collect DNA from anyone that has been arrested to input into a national database to determine if it matches any other unsolved crimes."

"Oh." Mrs. Francis nodded.

Camille bolted up. "That's ridiculous. This is that detective's doing. My brother had nothing to do with any of this. He's never been to the plantation."

Elizabeth stood and stroked Camille's arm in an attempt to calm her. "I know. The DNA was only a partial match. It means that it's likely he's related to whoever owned that sweater."

Camille stared at her and her mouth dropped open, but no words came out. Elizabeth knelt in front of Mrs. Francis, who had her head bowed. "Mrs. Francis, it's your sweater. You're Margaret."

She lifted her head, her eyes filled with tears, and ineffectively wiped at them. Elizabeth always referred to her as Mrs. Francis, and she'd had to look through her old case files to confirm Mrs. Francis's first name on a health care proxy that she had once drafted for her.

"Yes, but I don't understand what this has to do with Jackson." She sniffled as she spoke.

"You went to the Freedom Riders rally."

"Yes." She cleared her throat as her voice began to falter. "There were two young men. They came into the restaurant where I was working and handed out flyers and told us about the rally that evening. I had never participated in anything of the sort before, but they were so inspirational. They spoke with passion. I felt compelled to go. I had stayed quiet in the corner too long."

That simple statement went right to Elizabeth's heart. "What happened?"

"The rally was like nothing I had seen before. It was people, black and white, holding hands and singing. I stepped in with them, and a woman I didn't know took hold of my hand and held it. That was the first time a white person ever touched me like that."

Elizabeth only then realized that she was holding Mrs. Francis's hand, and she gave it a soft squeeze.

"When the rally was finished, it was late," Mrs. Francis continued. "I was going to walk home, but the two young men offered to drive me. When we were only about a quarter-mile from my home, a car came out of the dark and forced us off the road. Another car then appeared. The men, there were three of them, yanked us from our car. They threw me in the back seat of one of their cars." If she had to guess, Elizabeth would peg Judge Powers, Webb, and possibly Webb's son as the three. "I never saw the other young men again."

Elizabeth couldn't decide whether to tell her that the other men were murdered, but Mrs. Francis ended her debate.

"I read in the newspaper that those men were killed." She stared off and her voice took on a vacant sound, as though she was no longer feeling the words. "They drove around, and I tried to open the door and escape, but the man in the passenger seat jumped into the back and began beating me. I remember the metallic taste of blood as it poured from my mouth and nose." She ran her tongue around the inside of her mouth as though the taste was still present. "When they stopped, we were on a small side road surrounded by woods. They dragged me out and they…" She squeezed her eyes shut, but a tear managed to escape despite her efforts. "They were animals."

Elizabeth reached for a tissue on the side table and placed it into her hand. Mrs. Francis dabbed at her eyes and balled the tissue into the palm of her hand. "When they finished with me, they dragged me to a small opening in the trees. There was a hole and they told me to climb in. They then took away the rope, my only way out, and closed the door on top. I was sure that they left me there to die. It felt like I was in there for weeks, but it was two days."

"How did you get out?"

"She came."

"Olivia?"

"Yes. She opened the door and threw down the rope. She nearly had to lift me out because I was so weak. She gave me food and water and hid me in a barn on the property until nightfall. She then helped me escape. I walked for about three hours I'd say, until someone found me wandering the road."

"Did you go to the police?"

"No."

"Why not?"

"Honey." She stroked Elizabeth's cheek with her soft, creased hand. "You have to understand, it was 1962. I was black. They were white. There was no police, judge, or jury that would believe me. I survived. That was as much as a black girl could hope for."

Elizabeth felt an overwhelming urge to cry, and Mrs. Francis reached down and wrapped her arms around her in comfort. She felt silly that she was the one being comforted, but her warmth and strength felt good. Sitting back on her heels, she took a deep breath and looked up to Mrs. Francis. "The DNA from the sweater..." Elizabeth faltered for a moment and collected herself. "There were two sets of DNA collected from the sweater. Jackson was a partial match for both."

Mrs. Francis nodded. "My Frank knew I was pregnant, but he understood. He married me anyway. He raised Robert as his own."

Elizabeth heard Camille sniffle but kept her focus on Mrs. Francis. "Olivia was the woman that was killed in the alley. The purse, it wasn't by chance that she gave it to Jackson. She was trying to get it to you. She found you, but she knew she wouldn't make it."

Mrs. Francis scrubbed her face. "This is because of me? Jackson is in trouble because of me?"

"Mrs. Francis, this isn't your doing, but do you know why she was trying to reach you?"

Instead of answering, Mrs. Francis pushed herself up, and Elizabeth stood to help her. She watched her walk from the room, and Elizabeth looked to Camille, the rims of her eyes were red, her grandmother's story taking its toll. Mrs. Francis returned holding a medium-sized white plastic storage bin. She ignored Elizabeth's request for assistance and plopped down in her chair, setting the box in her lap.

She removed the lid and began riffling through a collection of photos, children's artwork, handmade cards, and other mementos from Jackson's and Camille's childhood. She pulled out a black box and caressed the top. "She gave this to me when I left. She said it would be important someday. I honestly don't know why I kept it."

Elizabeth gingerly accepted the box, but she hesitated to open it. Camille had no reservations and took it from her hands and unceremoniously lifted the lid. Elizabeth leaned into her for a better view. Inside was a tape reel. Camille dumped it out into her hand. The black magnetic tape was still tightly wound around the spool.

Elizabeth remembered the vintage tape recorder hidden in Webb's room and figured this is where Olivia got it.

"Do you know what's on this tape?" Elizabeth asked Mrs. Francis.

She shrugged in response. "I wanted to burn it, erase it all from my life, but something about the look on Olivia's face when she gave it to me made me keep it."

"We need to turn this over to Detective Donovan."

"Why? So she can say my brother knew this woman all along? No." Camille crossed her arms.

"You take it and do what you need to do," Mrs. Francis said, overriding Camille.

CHAPTER TWENTY-EIGHT

A ll rise," the bailiff commanded as the judge entered the courtroom.

Elizabeth and Jackson rose in unison. ADA Wilcox barely lifted himself from his chair, apparently, fully standing was too much effort. The judge eyed him before he took his seat but said nothing.

"It seems we are back here again, on yet another defense motion requesting access to evidence in the possession of the prosecution. Why can't the two of you just get along?"

"I apologize, Your Honor, but the prosecution is denying the defense access to important evidence—" The judge waved at Elizabeth, cutting her off, and gestured for her to take a seat.

He looked down at the papers in front of him, which Elizabeth presumed to be her motion. "Let's see if I have this straight. The defense located a book on an abandoned property, and the defense found this by using a...let's see here." He adjusted his glasses and flipped the page. "A map carved into a silver brush, compact mirror, and lipstick tube, which were found in the victim's purse. Am I with you so far?"

"Yes, Your Honor," Elizabeth replied.

"The defense also discovered a tape reel that was given to the defendant's grandmother more than fifty years ago, but the relevance was only recently known after determining the victim's identity. How am I doing?"

"You are correct, Your Honor."

"The defense turned over all of this to the lead detective on the case, which is how it came into the possession of the prosecution. Is this correct?" he asked, looking at the prosecutor.

"Yes, Your Honor," ADA Wilcox said begrudgingly.

"And now, the prosecution is denying the defense access to the very evidence that it was instrumental in discovering. Mr. Wilcox, are you looking to lose this case on appeal because from where I am sitting, you're trampling on the Fifth Amendment."

"Your Honor, the defense requests are frivolous. There is no indication that this evidence has any relevance to the current case."

The judge's only response to the prosecutor was to lower his glasses on his nose and level a glare. "Counsel's motion is granted, as well as any other future motion filed by the defense in relation to the production of evidence, any evidence, whether the prosecution deems it relevant or not. Mr. Wilcox, have I made myself clear?"

"Yes, Your Honor," ADA Wilcox responded without making eye contact.

Elizabeth wanted to stick her tongue out at the prosecutor, but knew that wasn't proper courtroom decorum and simply stood when the judge rose to depart.

"Bitch," ADA Wilcox whispered harshly, as she passed to make her exit.

She stopped, turned, and smiled. "Yep, and it feels damn good."

Elizabeth sat in the middle of her living room floor with papers spread about her in every direction. Within two hours of her court hearing, the prosecution courier delivered to her office copies of the pages from the book and the intel reports. It was probably a first in the history of ADA Wilcox's career, but she was glad to see that he took the judge's admonishment to heart. Receiving a copy of the tape reel was going to take more time due to concern over erosion of the magnetic tape, as it hadn't been stored properly. It wasn't simply a matter of making a copy. Restoration of the tape would be required before a copy could be made, so she contented herself with copies of the documents for the time being.

With Grace's research and her conversation with Judge Powers, Elizabeth was reasonably certain that she ascertained what she needed from the intel reports, so she concentrated on the cryptic journal. She first attempted to decipher the text at her office, but multiple interruptions made the task futile. Interpreting the text would take patience and concentration, and she opted to bring it home because she had neither at the clinic. The soft glow of the fireplace warmed her back, and she nursed a glass of red wine that was nestled between her crossed legs. She was in her second hour of deciphering, or better said, attempted deciphering. Several letters on the first two pages were circled, and when she spelled those out, they read "BROWNS OPINION." Beyond that, there was no rhyme or reason to the letters.

Feeling weary, she closed her eyes, but she could still see the letters. A knock at her door startled her, and she nearly toppled her wine glass standing up. She looked through the side window before she pulled the door open, and Grace stepped inside. She wondered if this was going to become a habit; she hoped so anyway.

Grace looked at the fireplace and the papers spread out on the floor in front.

"Did I interrupt…" Grace seemed to have forgotten her own question as she stared unabashedly at Elizabeth's attire.

Elizabeth looked down, and as fate would have it, she was dressed in her "Homie" T-shirt, which came down to her thighs, just enough to cover her floral cotton underwear. "I can put on the yellow dress if you prefer."

Grace stepped toward her and cupped her breast before ducking her head to capture Elizabeth's mouth. The kiss was urgent and consuming. Without breaking contact, Grace moved her hand under the shirt and massaged her breast and caressed her nipple with her thumb. Elizabeth gasped at the sensation, and she felt paralyzed by the delicious currents that ran through her. Grace was completely in the lead.

When Grace's mouth moved lower, trailing warm, languorous kisses down her neck, she breathed out, "Grace, if you're going to pull back…oh God." She interrupted herself when Grace's mouth reached her collarbone. "We have to stop now. We're passing the point of no return."

Grace lifted her head, her lips slightly parted, with a want in her eyes beyond anything that Elizabeth had previously seen. Grace stepped back and drew her eyes down Elizabeth, and she had never felt so vulnerable. Grace turned her back, and she swallowed hard and squeezed her eyes tight, not willing to watch her walk out. This was even harder than before. No matter their previous discussions and plans to wait, she couldn't see this as anything but a rejection.

She opened her eyes, startled by the grip on her hand and soft tug that followed. She noted Grace's jacket and gun holster were now hanging over the chair, next to her boots. She offered no resistance when Grace led her down the hallway and to the bedroom. Standing next to the bed, Grace spoke no words as she gripped the hem of Elizabeth's shirt and lifted it over her head, leaving Elizabeth in her underwear.

Grace ran her fingers down Elizabeth's chest toward her stomach as her eyes trailed after them. Elizabeth's skin trembled in their wake.

Elizabeth yanked on Grace's form-fitting T-shirt that was tucked into her slacks, and Grace smiled before she lifted her arms to allow it to be removed. Elizabeth ducked both hands inside her bra, kneading her breasts, before she moved her hands to the back to undo the clasp and free them. Elizabeth's hands continued down until she reached the belt. She unbuckled it and undid her pants. She tugged on them, getting them to the top of her thighs, and knelt to slide them down her legs. Grace stepped out of them. Elizabeth slid her palms up her legs and stopped at the navy blue silk underwear, much more sensuous than her own. She moved her hands to her hips and offered a wet kiss on her stomach just above the underwear line and slowly lowered her mouth, sucking as she went. As she slid off her underwear, she used her tongue to taste. Grace hissed and gripped Elizabeth's shoulders. "I need…"

"What, baby, what do you need?" Elizabeth asked as she pushed Grace back until she sat on the bed.

CHAPTER TWENTY-NINE

Elizabeth linked her fingers with Grace as they walked toward the clinic. Grace stopped to admire the painted penis on the wall. "Nice artwork."

"It's growing on me."

"I hope not too much," Grace said with raised eyebrows, which earned her a playful slap.

When they approached the clinic, Elizabeth reluctantly released her hold of Grace's hand to allow her to open the door, and she passed in front.

"Morning, Amy," Elizabeth chirped.

"Morning, ladies." Amy offered a broad smile and a wink.

She felt Grace's hand rest on the small of her back, which turned to a slight tickle as soon as they passed the lobby, causing Elizabeth to giggle. Once in her office, Grace wrapped both arms around her and ducked her head for a kiss.

"You taste good," Grace moaned next to her ear and allowed her hands to wander down Elizabeth's body in exploration.

"Don't mind me."

Elizabeth pulled back like she was bitten and whipped her head to the side to see her mother sitting in the guest chair. "Mom, what are you doing here?" Elizabeth self-consciously straightened her shirt and walked to the other side of the desk.

"Pleasure to see you, Mrs. Campbell," Grace said cordially, holding her ground.

Elizabeth's mother didn't acknowledge the greeting and instead took aim at the elephant in the room. "Tell me, Detective, what are your intentions with my daughter?"

"Jesus, Mom," Elizabeth said. She knew this talk was coming, but not in front of Grace.

Grace's eye contact never wavered. "Ma'am, your daughter is the most impulsive, irrational, and reckless person that I have ever met, and I've completely fallen in love with her."

Elizabeth's mother allowed a moment of silence to pass as she assessed Grace, then stood and turned to Elizabeth. "Finally, someone who understands you." She patted Grace's arm as she exited. "Welcome to the family."

Elizabeth sank into BD. "Did that just happen?" Just like that, the conversation that had yet to happen with her mother was over in a matter of moments, and her mother left smiling.

"You underestimate my charms," Grace said as she moved to the other side of the desk and leaned over her chair, putting both hands on the armrests. As she leaned in for a kiss, Elizabeth asked, "You love me?"

Grace pulled back and leaned against the desk. "Yes, Elizabeth, I am hopelessly in love with you. You're either going to break my heart or make me the happiest woman alive."

Elizabeth stood and inserted herself between Grace's legs. "I like the latter." She stroked Grace's cheek with her thumb. "I love you, Grace."

"Elizabeth, here is the file you were looking for," Danny said as he walked in and casually dropped a file on the desk. "Oh, hey, Grace," he said in acknowledgment with his customary head nod, as if their positioning was nothing out of the ordinary.

Grace smirked and pushed herself up. "I guess I should let you get to work. I'll pick you up at three."

Elizabeth squeezed her hand and nodded, and Grace strolled out softly whistling with her hands in her front pockets.

"So what's at three?"

She turned to Danny, who had taken up station in the guest chair. "We're going to meet a cryptologist."

"Cool, will there be mummies and stuff?"

"No, Danny. A cryptologist deciphers codes. Grace gave him a copy of the book we found at Samuel's grave. Hopefully, he can figure it out because I sure as hell can't."

Danny seemed to lose interest in the conversation once he realized that there were no tombs or pharaohs involved and wandered off.

Elizabeth pulled out the cryptic pages and made the futile effort of reviewing them once more. Whatever secrets it held, it was something Olivia thought to be relevant to come forward now, risking her life. She sat contemplating Olivia's intentions and was unaware of Camille's presence, until she tapped her hand.

"Earth to Elizabeth."

"Sorry, I didn't even hear you come in." Camille was sitting in the chair opposite her.

"I could tell. Where were you?"

"I was just looking at the pages from the book and wondering why Olivia thought they're relevant now."

"And?"

"And nothing. I've got absolutely nothing." Elizabeth leaned back and noticed Camille's work clothes. "What brings you to these parts?"

"I just got off the night shift, and well, I just couldn't get my mind off of this," she said, pointing to the pages. "So I thought I'd stop by."

"Olivia was trying to get a message to your grandmother, something to do with this book and probably the tape reel. What I don't understand is why she gave the purse to Jackson? Why not see your grandmother?"

"Maybe she couldn't. Maybe she was afraid that she'd be seen if she went to the apartment."

"So she was waiting, hoping that one of you would..." Elizabeth looked at Camille's hospital scrubs. "Jackson said that he went to the store because you were running late from work, and your grandmother didn't want to wait. Olivia was looking for you, but she got Jackson instead."

Camille bowed her head and remained silent.

"Camille?"

"Yes," she said barely over a whisper.

"Camille, tell me what happened." Elizabeth felt betrayed, but she realized that it was Jackson who was really betrayed. Camille kept her head bowed and didn't answer. "Camille, talk to me."

She lifted her head and tears were running down her cheeks. "It isn't what you think."

"Tell me." Elizabeth was doing what she could to contain her anger.

Camille inhaled a shaky breath and looked down at her clasped hands. "She called our apartment the day before. I was the only one home. She rambled on about the knights coming back. I wanted to hang up on her, but she said she had information on my grandfather, my real grandfather. I listened because I've known for a while that there was something in our family history that was amiss." She looked at Elizabeth. "When I was in nursing school, we studied blood types and we traced our own family history. My grandfather was type B and my grandmother type O. My father was A. I never said anything to my grandmother." She looked back down, clearly, eye contact was too difficult for the next part. "I agreed to meet. Told her I'd meet her by the alley at four. It was on the way to the store, and I had to pick up my grandmother's prescriptions, so it was a good cover. I didn't want my grandmother or Jackson to know. I told her I would have a yellow canvas bag, that's how she'd know it was me. My grandmother always made us take that bag. She didn't like the plastic store bags. You know, the environment."

Camille stopped as if she could go no further, so Elizabeth carried on. "You were late from work."

"There was an emergency. I couldn't leave," she said in her defense.

"So Jackson went instead with the yellow bag."

She nodded. "Will you tell Jackson?"

"I'm leaving that up to you."

Grace cradled Elizabeth's hand in her lap as she stared off at the bare gray wall in the waiting area of the industrial building that had been converted to a cryptology lab. Elizabeth had remained silent since explaining Camille's involvement in Jackson's meeting with Olivia. This gave Grace even more reason to dislike the woman, but she opted to remain mute on the subject for Elizabeth's sake. She was hurt enough by Camille's deceit, and any sharp words from Grace would only compound that.

"Detective Donovan, sorry to keep you waiting."

Grace stood to acknowledge a man approaching in a button-down checkered shirt and khaki pants, sporting a ponytail that reached past his shoulders.

"Thank you for taking the time to meet, Dr. Miles." She introduced Elizabeth.

Grace contacted the professor at the local university after doing her due diligence in online research for experts in cryptology. She provided limited information as to the suspected origins of the book and instead wanted to hear his interpretation.

"Let's go to the lab."

He kept a quick pace, and Grace kept up with long strides and followed him through a nondescript door and down an equally nondescript hallway. She could hear Elizabeth's footsteps behind her. When he came to a sudden halt, Grace had to pull up short to not collide into him, but it was too late for Elizabeth, who walked into her.

Elizabeth shrugged. "You liked it and you know it."

Grace did what she could to keep her professional demeanor and entered the lab maintaining more of a cushion between her and the professor. The lab was wall-to-wall monitors, keyboards, and other electronic devices. Wires and cords seemed to extend in every direction. There were a few students dispersed through the room absorbed in their own projects.

The professor stopped at a station in the middle of the room and began shuffling through papers next to an oversized computer monitor. "Okay, this is what I've done so far."

Grace and Elizabeth huddled around to get a better view.

"This device is a Confederate cipher disk." He held up a picture of the brass disk with the two concentric circles. "The letters CSA on the front mean Confederate States of America. If it's the real deal, there will be a stamp on the back 'F. Labarre Richmond VA,' which is the maker's mark. There are only three original Confederate cipher disks known to exist today." Grace recalled the very inscription on the back of the disk, but opted not to say anything. It would only be a distraction. The professor continued. "During the Civil War, messages were coded in case they were intercepted. The recipient of the message would use this device to decipher it."

"How does it work?" Grace asked.

"Both the sender and the recipient of the message must agree in advance on the key. The most common would be to select a letter on the inner circle and line it up with the letter A on the outer circle. For example, if S was lined up with A, the letter S would be deciphered as the letter A and T for the letter B, and so on. The letter S would be the key."

"Seems simple."

"The coding could get more complex, in that words could be written backward or the first and last letter of each word reversed. It was a time-consuming effort, but nowadays, the computer does the work in a fraction of the time."

"So what do you have on our text?"

"Well, I input it all into the computer, but it doesn't follow a single key."

"What does that mean?"

"It means that each letter in the text has a different key." He looked at Grace and Elizabeth who stared blankly back. "Okay, it's like this. If I line up S on the inner circle of the cipher with the A on the outer circle, then that will decode the first letter. However, the second letter in the text will have a different key. It will not be S to A, but a completely different letter matched with A and so on. I've run multiple scenarios through the computer program, but without the master key, it's an endless set of possibilities. We need the master key."

"There were letters that were circled in the text. Could those letters be the key?" Elizabeth spoke up for the first time.

"Yes, I thought that too. I ran the letters BROWNS OPINION into the scenario, including multiple variations and mixed them around, but it didn't match. I still got nonsense."

"So what? This can't be deciphered?"

"We need the master key."

Elizabeth moved to a nearby chair to sit and cradled her head in her hands. Grace sat beside her and mirrored her position, while the professor began typing into the computer. The room remained quiet, but for the clicking sound of fingers on keys.

"Wait a minute." Elizabeth popped up. "What if the master key is a known document?"

"What are you thinking?" Grace asked.

"*Brown versus Board of Education*, the Supreme Court decision that ended segregation. That would have been on Webb's mind."

"Browns opinion." The professor began furiously typing. "I can download that decision and have it run against the text. It's going to take an hour at least."

Grace leaned back and stretched out her legs. "We'll wait."

Two and half hours, two cups of coffee, and a bathroom visit later, the professor declared defeat. "It's just not matching. The computer has run the decision through, starting at every letter from the very top of the title page to the last letter of the opinion. I've run it backward and forward, but nothing is working. I'm not saying it isn't the master key, but if it is, I just don't know how to make it work."

Grace slumped at the enormous letdown and turned to Elizabeth, who sat hunched over with her hands clasped. She could see her fingers turning white from the tight grip. With a forced smile, Grace thanked the professor for his efforts, and he promised to keep at it.

On the drive back, Grace tried to make conversation, but Elizabeth remained unusually quiet, only answering when necessary and contributing nothing to the discussion. How she missed her bantering.

"It's not *Brown versus Board of Education*," Elizabeth blurted out, causing Grace to jerk the wheel, and the driver in the next lane to blare the horn.

"Jesus, Elizabeth, you scared me. A little less animation when I'm driving please."

"Webb didn't write that book," Elizabeth said with excitement, ignoring Grace's advisement to keep it down. "That book goes way back, like the Booth papers. It couldn't be the *Brown* decision. That was from 1954." She looked at Grace with the spark back in her eyes before she pulled out her phone and began typing. "Professor Miles said the coding method was popular in the Civil War and there was the cipher disk."

"And?" She knew this was going to be good.

"We're looking at the wrong decision." Elizabeth continued to work her phone, and Grace pulled over to give Elizabeth her full attention. "*Brown versus Board of Education* overturned *Plessy versus Ferguson. Plessy* was decided in the late 1800s, which upheld segregation, declaring that the concept 'separate but equal' was not in violation of the Equal Protection Clause of the Fourteenth Amendment. That is more in line with the thinking of the author of that text."

"But why would the circled letters say 'Browns Opinion'?"

"Because…" Elizabeth held out her phone to Grace, and she could see the written Supreme Court decision on the screen. "The majority opinion in *Plessy* was written by Justice Brown."

CHAPTER THIRTY

Elizabeth stared out her office window and watched the rain beat down, finding the melody it played on the lids of the trash cans entrancing. There was plenty to do, but she lacked the mindset to do it. By the time she came up with the idea of *Plessy v. Ferguson*, Professor Miles had already left the lab, and when Grace finally spoke to him that morning, he informed her that he had classes, and it would have to wait until the afternoon. To wait— to delay an action until a later time or until another event occurs, Elizabeth looked it up. One of the many useless tasks she engaged in while she waited. She even offered to help the workers put in the new flooring in the kitchen, but they simply stared at the stapler in her hand.

She restlessly shuffled a copy of the Booth pages that were resting on her lap; she had spent part of her morning deciphering them. After the tutorial on decoding from the professor, she decided to take a shot at it and found the pages easy to crack in comparison to the journal. The letter K was the key, and she got it on the first try, figuring it was the most obvious letter from a member of the KGC. The code remained consistent throughout, making its translation easy, but she learned nothing new from what Beadle told her.

Unable to sit in the chair any longer, she decided to head across the street to pick up a salad for lunch. She wasn't hungry, but it was something to do. She donned her raincoat and ignored Amy's advice of taking an umbrella as she walked out the door. Ten minutes later, she returned with a white plastic bag tucked under coat. It was about the only thing dry, and she ducked past Amy's empty desk trying to avoid her admonishment.

She peeled off her coat as she entered her office and jumped at the sound of Grace's voice. "You're soaking wet. Let me guess, you fell in the toilet?"

Elizabeth offered no response and instead wrapped her arms around her and kissed her before taking her seat. If Grace was annoyed by her now shared wet condition, she didn't mention it.

"Tell me you have some good news."

Grace took a seat and slid a folder across the desk. "It was the *Plessy* decision. It took him less than thirty minutes to crack it once he input it."

Elizabeth opened the folder and read the title out loud, "The second secession." She trailed her finger down the pages mumbling a few words and became immersed in the history of the document. There was no author attributed to the work, but considering that the *Plessy* decision was issued in 1896, plus the bits of information she gathered from her computer research as she read, the author was likely an early decedent of Frederick Lawton.

It seemed to ramble at first on societal order, nothing that surprised her at that point, but it began to focus on what she could best describe as a road map aimed at obtaining secession through pure segregation of the races in the post-Civil War era. It started with the call for silencing those that opposed them, citing the assassinations of two early civil rights leaders as an exemplar to be emulated–George W. Ashburn and John Prentiss Matthews.

From the document and her research, she learned that Ashburn, a vocal opponent of white supremacy, was assassinated in Georgia in 1868. More than twenty members of the newly formed KKK were arrested in connection with his murder, many of whom were prominent residents of the state and were being represented in the criminal trial by a former Confederate general and the former Confederate vice president. However, Ashburn's murder trial became a pawn in the passage of the Fourteenth Amendment, which was hanging in the balance. Georgia agreed to the ratification of the amendment in exchange for the dismissal of the criminal charges.

The second name bore an equally troubling tale. Matthews organized the Independent Party in Mississippi, which challenged the controlling local white supremacist Democratic Party. He was assassinated in 1883 while attempting to vote in defiance of the local Democratic Party directive, which forbade anyone to vote in favor of the Independent Party. Despite Matthews's public execution at the polling place, an all-white jury found the defendant, Ras Wheeler, not guilty, and Wheeler went on to have a successful political career in the state.

After memorializing the assassinations of these two men, there was a list of names, and although she couldn't find the other names in her computer search, she assumed that they all met similar fates. She couldn't help but draw a parallel to the intel reports that were found in back of the book and suspected that Webb was attempting to emulate his predecessor's vision. During this document's time, the loss of slavery and secession was fresh on the author's mind. For Webb, it was the loss of segregation, but they were both trying to hold on to an era that they were losing.

The document continued to lay out several steps in furtherance of its agenda, focusing on more specific plans for segregating the state's population through legislation and force. There was a detailed plan for redistricting, gerrymandering at its best, to weaken the legislative power of minority groups, as well as a less detailed plan on creating physical barriers that would separate the races. There was also a call for a state run militia, but its details were vague.

Elizabeth took a sip from the coffee cup in her hand and then stared at it, wondering how it got there. She looked around her office and realized that she was alone and nearly two hours had passed. She debated stepping out of her office in search of Grace, but didn't want to lose her train of thought and returned to her computer. She found several details of the document troubling, not because of its racist history, but because she feared history might be repeating itself.

Grace returned with a sandwich and placed it next to her. "Your mom says it's your favorite. You need to eat. You've been at this for hours."

"My mom, huh?"

"Yup, we've had some bonding time while inspecting the new kitchen. Learned a few fun facts. Did you really have an invisible friend?"

"I was four, and I used to talk to my stuffed bunny, Pebbles," Elizabeth said with indignation.

"Did Pebbles answer back?"

She waded up a piece of paper and tossed it at Grace. "Do you mind if we get back to this?" she asked, gesturing to the document.

"What do you have?"

As Elizabeth went through what she learned, it was clear that Grace was already familiar with the document, but she was able to provide more insight as to the historical context from her computer research. "Grace, this reads just like the plan that was created with last year's redistricting legislation and the governor's appropriation act, DARA, that is sitting at the Supreme Court. If the court upholds DARA, we will soon have the largest state run military in US history, which the state might need to counter the protests once the government implements the second half of the bill—the eminent domain clause. Under the guise of improving infrastructure, the bill proposes to claim large areas of land to build highways. Combine that with the current rezoning of industrial areas, and we have physical barriers that separate counties, and in some cases cities. I'm sure if we draw it out on a map, we'll find that race and socio-economics were primary considerations in delineating these boundaries."

"And Davis Powers's confirmation will decide the fate of DARA."

"Yes, and Olivia knew this."

Grace stood and began to pace. "Even if we went public, there's nothing illegal about any of this, so far anyway. There's just not enough concrete evidence to link Powers to any wrongdoing in the Freedom Riders case. We'd never be able to prove that the intel reports came from his safe deposit box. It would be dismissed as speculation."

"That's why Olivia wanted Mrs. Francis to go public with the recording. I'm sure that reel came from the hidden tape recorder in Webb's office. I'm guessing there's an incriminating conversation on it that Davis Powers would prefer not go public."

"The recording is still undergoing restoration. It's going to take a week before it's ready."

"We don't have a week. The state senate is set to vote on Powers's confirmation next Tuesday, and you know as soon as he's on the bench, the conservative block will push for a ruling on DARA." Elizabeth slouched and scrubbed at her face. "This can't be happening."

Grace sat in the chair in defeat.

"Wait a minute," Elizabeth said. "Senator McDermott— Professor Dixon said he's Powers's greatest opposition. What if he shares this information with his fellow legislators, particularly those on the fence about the judge?"

"That could put the senator in danger if word got out to the wrong people. He could end up like Reverend Peterson. And we have to remember that we have an informant amongst us."

Elizabeth had lost sight of that detail, but her money was on ADA Wilcox. "Understood, but I think it should be Senator McDermott's choice."

❖

Grace and Elizabeth sat in the conference room opposite Senator McDermott, and the table between them was strewn with photos and documents. After her conversation with Elizabeth, Grace called the senator's office and explained the urgency of the meeting. McDermott agreed to the spontaneous meeting with the caveat that it occurred after hours at his district office. After learning the purpose of the meeting, he was uncomfortable with it taking place in his office at the capitol, and Grace seconded that thought.

They had spent the first hour of their meeting laying out the evidence against Judge Powers, including the sordid history of the White Horse Plantation. The senator listened with rapt attention, only asking a handful of clarifying questions. Now, Grace and Elizabeth sat in silence, which they had done for the last half hour, exchanging only questioning glances, as McDermott carefully studied the documents in front of him. She couldn't read his body language and had no idea whether he was willing to accept the wild tale that they unfolded before him.

The senator finally lifted his head and removed his glasses. "This is incredible. I've never cared for the governor or his people, but I would have never guessed that they were this nefarious. If I wasn't so repulsed, I'd say this was genius. I never put it together, and I've studied DARA backward and forward."

"I don't think anyone else would either, until it was too late anyway," Grace replied.

"So you can't go public because there is nothing here on Judge Powers that could be proven." As a former Civil Rights lawyer, the senator seemed to understand Grace's predicament. "If we go public with this idea that DARA is part of a larger master plan to implement a modern form of segregation, at best we'll be labeled crazy conspiracy theorist and at worst sued, and we'd be lucky to find night janitorial jobs. So what do you propose?"

"We don't go public. We go private," Elizabeth said with a devious smile. She explained the restoration of the tape reel and that she believed it would be damning evidence against Judge Powers. "But it won't happen by Tuesday when the senate is set to vote on Powers's nomination."

Senator McDermott nodded. "So you want me to take this behind closed doors to some of my fellow legislators. Let them know what they're really voting for." He picked up some of the documents again for inspection. "This could work. Even some of the senators on the other side of the aisle wouldn't want to be caught voting the wrong way if this hits the fan. We're in election season."

CHAPTER THIRTY-ONE

Grace sat outside the office of yet another state senator. Jack was at her side, softly snoring. She didn't blame him. The schedule they had been keeping was wearing her out. She couldn't imagine the toll it was taking on an octogenarian. It had been three days since she and Elizabeth had the meeting with Senator McDermott, and that was the last time she saw her. They had spoken several times, but once the senator committed to their plan, Grace decided to play personal bodyguard to ensure his safety until the state senate voted on Judge Powers's confirmation. Given that the protection service was off the books, she was spread thin, and Jack volunteered to assist. She didn't believe he was truly up to the task, and she certainly wasn't going to trust him with a gun, but he was an extra body that could stay awake while she got some sleep. She also appreciated his company and learned he had a quick wit and a sense of humor. She saw why he and Elizabeth got along so well.

Since engaging Senator McDermott, he had attended multiple meetings with members in the senate, but it was unclear whether he had influenced them, as he was met with skepticism and noncommittal responses. It seemed that the senator was more willing to accept the backstory of Judge Powers and DARA than his colleagues. Tomorrow was the confirmation vote for Judge Powers, and they were on their last stop of their covert tour. When the senator emerged through the door, he offered her a shrug, which she took to mean things didn't seem to go so well. As he gave some last-minute instructions to an aide at his side, she gently shook Jack, who jerked his body to full alert, embarrassed that he fell asleep on the job.

"Time to hit the road." It was nearly five in the evening, and they would spend one more night ordering in at the hotel room that they shared with the senator. She was looking forward to a hot shower and a little private time for a conversation with Elizabeth. After going through the highlights of their days, their discussions evolved to intimate pillow talk, which helped fill the empty spot that took up residence in her chest over the last few days. After months of the tug-of-war that her mind and heart played, to not hold back and tell Elizabeth all that was going through her, from her deep emotions to her sexual desires, was in and of itself an unbelievable feeling, but for it to be returned was indescribable.

"I got to use the john."

That was a buzzkill. Grace turned to Jack. "All right, I'll walk with the senator to the car and pull up around the front and pick you up."

"Sounds like a plan."

She watched Jack head down the hall and then turned to the senator, who signaled that he was ready to go. She walked beside him as Senator McDermott discussed the lack of concern a number of his colleagues showed for the revelations about Judge Powers.

"If this doesn't matter, then what does?" he asked.

It wasn't a question that could be answered, so she stayed silent and held open one of the double doors that led out of the capitol. "The only thing I know is that when the vote comes tomorrow, we will have done everything that we could."

"I just hope it's enough."

"Gun!"

A single pop echoed through the air.

"Oh my God, this can't be happening," Elizabeth said in a continual chant.

Her mother weaved through the pedestrians and moving cars in the parking lot, trying to get to an open spot before it was taken. Elizabeth was in no condition to make the hour-long drive to the hospital. This seemed even worse than the last time she rushed to the emergency room. This time, she had confirmation that Grace was shot. She had to be all right.

A knock on her front door had alerted Elizabeth that something was wrong. She hadn't turned on her television or listened to the news on the drive home. At first, she hoped that Grace had found a way to surprise her, but when she opened the door to find her mother standing on the other side, she nearly crumpled. Somehow she knew. She could count on one hand the number of times her mother had come to visit Elizabeth's home, and never unannounced.

"Is it Grace?" If it was her father or Raymond, her mother would be calling from the hospital.

"There was a shooting at the capitol."

"Oh God, no."

Elizabeth turned on the television, but the news coming from the scene was sketchy, and she remained glued to her spot a foot away from the screen with the remote still clutched in her hand, hoping someone, anyone, would tell her that Grace was fine, but that didn't happen. A reporter broke the detail that Senator McDermott was believed to be the intended target, but a detective standing near him was struck by the bullet instead.

Elizabeth pushed open the car door just as her mother pulled into the parking spot and ran to the front door. The hospital was in full bloom with activity in all corners of the waiting room, but Elizabeth kept her eyes trained on the man behind the desk. "Grace Donovan, where is she?"

The man spoke the letters as he typed them into the computer to ensure that he had spelled them correctly. "Donovan, yes, she's in the ER. What is your relationship?"

"I'm her girlfriend."

"Okay, ma'am, you will have to wait here."

"To hell with that, where is she?"

"Ma'am, if you can just have a seat—"

"I need to see her now."

"Ma'am, please…"

"Sir," Elizabeth's mother said as she stepped up to the counter and gave him the look—the look that could make grown men crawl into a ball and weep. "I don't think you understand," she clearly articulated. "My husband, Charles Campbell, is the founding partner of Campbell, Roberts, Addelstein, and Krass, the firm that just won the largest judgment against this very hospital for negligence and cost the jobs of at least a dozen people." She smoothly slid a business card across the counter, which Elizabeth assumed belonged to her father. "I do not seriously think that you want to leave his daughter sitting in the waiting room when her girlfriend is in the ER." She made a show of reading the man's name badge. "Do you understand me, William?"

William visibly swallowed. "Well…ma'am, I just need to, um, call, um my supervisor."

"If you say so." Elizabeth's mother pulled out her phone and started dialing.

"Okay, ma'am, I'll buzz you through those doors," he said, pointing to a set of double doors. "The nurses' station will be on the left."

"Thank you," Elizabeth's mother said as she replaced her phone in her purse and linked arms with Elizabeth, walking her to the door.

"Mom, I had no idea there was such a lawsuit."

"There wasn't, but William didn't know that." She loved her mother.

Once at the nurses' station, she allowed her mother to do the talking because she seemed to have lost her voice from fear of what they might tell her.

"Elizabeth, fancy meeting you here."

She turned to see Jack casually strolling toward her.

"Jack," she croaked out. "Where's Grace?" She desperately grasped at him, as if trying to feel if he was real.

"Right over there." He pointed to Grace leaning against the wall, talking to a uniformed officer.

She launched herself across the room and leaped at Grace, who managed to catch her, and she held on tight, afraid to let go. In the warmth of her embrace, she allowed herself to fully unravel and openly cried. Grace stroked her back and offered soothing words until Elizabeth pushed herself back. "God damn it, Grace. You scared the hell out of me. They said you were shot!"

It was then that she noticed the bloody shirt and bandage wrapped around Grace's arm, and her emotion catapulted back to fear. "Oh my God, Grace, you're hurt."

"It's nothing, just a couple of stitches. The bullet grazed me."

Elizabeth began to fuss with Grace's shirt and wiped at the dried blood until Grace stilled her hands with her own. "Honey, I'm fine. I promise." Keeping a hold of her, she guided Elizabeth to a set of plastic chairs that provided some privacy from the bustle around them, and Grace wrapped her good arm around her shoulders. Elizabeth tucked inside, a position in which they remained, until the uniformed officer gingerly approached them.

"I'm sorry to disturb you, Detective Donovan, but the doctor wanted me to let you know that the senator would be ready to leave shortly."

Grace nodded and the officer slipped back into the crowd. Knowing Grace still had a job to do, Elizabeth took a fortifying breath, wiped at her eyes, and pulled herself up straight. She needed to be strong, and focusing on the case helped. She would wait until she got home to fall apart again, and with her newfound resolve, began peppering Grace with questions.

Grace described how she dove at Senator McDermott when she heard the word "gun" yelled from the crowd. That warning, as brief as it was, allowed her to move the senator from the crosshairs of the kill shot, causing the bullet to skim past Grace as they fell to the ground.

"My phone shattered when I hit the ground or I would have called you. I meant to call as soon as I got here, but things got a little chaotic," Grace offered in apology, and Elizabeth squeezed her hand in acceptance.

"What about your father?"

"Jack said he called him."

Elizabeth was relieved that George Donovan wasn't sitting around fretting about whether Grace was seriously injured or worse.

"With the confusion that followed the aftermath of the shooting, no one was able to get a description of the shooter, other than an individual wearing a gray hooded sweatshirt who had been hiding in a set of bushes. No one could even say for certain if the shooter was male or female. The gun was discarded at the scene, stolen from an off-duty officer's vehicle this morning."

"So this person is still out there."

"I had to let my sergeant and Detective Martinez know where I'd be in case something came up," Grace said in response to the unasked question that sat heavily between them—who knew Grace was going to be there?

Senator McDermott approached them, looking ragged, but alive. Although he wasn't hit, the doctors conducted an exam to ensure that he wasn't injured in the fall, and fortunately, he only suffered moderate bruising on his hip where he landed.

Elizabeth pushed herself up and hugged Grace fiercely before she walked out the double doors. Her mother appeared at her side and wrapped an arm around her before guiding her to the car. She was thankful because she had no idea where they parked. Her mother, her rock.

CHAPTER THIRTY-TWO

Elizabeth stomped around the clinic looking for something to take out her frustration on. She knew the state senate was in the process of voting on Judge Powers's confirmation, but she was completely in the dark. It seemed that the breaking story of a car chase through three counties took precedence over a state Supreme Court nomination. Every local news channel and website dedicated itself to aerial coverage of the driver, carelessly whipping through the roadways with a platoon of police following closely behind. She couldn't call Grace because she didn't have a working phone. As she passed a hammer resting on the kitchen counter, she snatched it up and eyed a small nail in a cabinet door that could use one more good hit. She lifted the hammer above her head, but before she could bring it down, Amy grabbed it from her.

"I don't think so. Why don't you go play in the street or something? That's less dangerous than messing with your mother's kitchen."

"Whose side are you on?"

"Your mother's of course. Need you ask?"

Elizabeth returned to her office and clicked on her computer in hopes that the idiotic driver was apprehended and the rest of the world could resume, but no such luck.

"There you are," Danny said as he took a seat. "Jack's been trying to get a hold of you. Said he left you a couple of messages and finally called me."

She began riffling through her bag that rested near her feet and then turned to her desk and did the same. "Damn it! Where did I leave my phone?" She tried to mentally trace its last known location and resigned herself that she left it at home, which wasn't a surprise, given her current mental state. "What did he say?"

"He said that he was going to the plantation, and he wanted us to meet him there. He said there's something we need to see."

"The plantation? What in God's name for? Between us and the police, what stone hasn't been unturned?"

"Don't know." Danny shrugged. "Something about the woods, I think. I just know he said it was important."

She turned to her computer and searched for an aerial map of the plantation, wondering if they literally missed the forest through the trees in their explorations of the property. After scanning the map, she looked to Danny. "I don't see anything out of the ordinary, but then again, I don't even know what I'm looking for." She grabbed her bag and didn't bother to shut down her computer. "All right, let's go." She kept a brisk pace through the clinic, stopping at Amy's vacant desk to scribble a note, before continuing to her car, leaving Danny to keep up.

"Should I call Camille and have her meet us there?" he said breathlessly as he settled into the passenger seat.

"No." She never told Danny about Camille's betrayal and didn't feel like explaining now. "But call Jack and let him know we're on our way and get some more info out of him," she said.

Danny complied and pulled out his phone from his jacket pocket. "He's not picking up. I got his voice mail."

Elizabeth listened as Danny left a message with instructions to call him back immediately. She couldn't imagine what Jack could have learned about the plantation during his time at the capitol, but assumed it involved Judge Powers. During the course of their drive, Jack never returned the call, and as they approached the road to the plantation, Danny hit redial on his phone. "I'll try him again. His phone skills are underwhelming, and who knows if he even knows how to listen to a message or if he even knows he has one."

She couldn't argue that one.

"Oh hey, Jack, where are you? What?" Danny covered his other ear. "We're at the plantation. Where are you?" He turned to Elizabeth. "He says he's about fifteen minutes away." She guessed more like ten given his penchant for ignoring lights.

"Ask him what we're doing here?"

"Elizabeth wants to know what we're doing at the plantation." Danny stuck his finger in his ear. "Say that again. You're breaking up." He looked at his phone before he stuck it in his pocket. "We lost the signal."

She would just have to wait a bit longer to learn the big mystery. She drove through the now familiar stretch of trees that formed a canopy above and pulled up next to the white horse statue in the center of the drive.

"I'm going to look around while we're waiting for Jack," she said, pushing open her car door. She glanced over the open fields before heading toward the wooded area beyond the stable. She heard Danny jog to catch up, but he stayed behind her, as she ducked her head into the dilapidated structure that Samuel had warned her to stay clear of. As he described, she could see a large pile of broken wood below a gaping hole where the ceiling used to be.

"Elizabeth, look over here."

She turned and scanned the property. "Danny, where'd you go?"

"Over here."

She followed the sound of his voice around the corner of the stable and was startled when Danny grabbed her arm and snapped a cuff around her wrist. "What the hell!" She ineffectively tried to pull away, as Danny encased the other half of the cuff around his wrist.

She could only stare at him as he smirked. "Funny isn't it. This is how it all started." He held up their joined hands. "I swiped them from Jack after Beadle was arrested."

"Very amusing, Danny," she said nonchalantly, but alarm bells were screaming in her head. "Where's the key?"

"That's exactly what I asked, remember? Then you dragged me to the clinic. I have to admit, the handcuffs were an unexpected turn of events. I thought you were just going to talk me into not hurting you, like a normal person, and then I would show you that I really didn't have a weapon. You would take pity on me when I told you I was hungry and take me under your wing. Well, it worked in the end, better than I expected."

A wave of vertigo passed over Elizabeth at the realization that in a matter of seconds, her world had been turned upside down and shaken, and she desperately turned toward the house, searching.

"Oh, silly you, he's not coming. Jack didn't really call. He doesn't even have my cell phone number, and I don't have his. Fooled ya."

Elizabeth couldn't even swallow, much less speak, and began pulling away, towing Danny with her in the direction of the car.

"Stop." She ignored him and kept moving, which took all her effort. "I said stop!" He yanked her back, causing her to lose her balance and fall to her knees. Her free hand scraped on a rock, and she clutched it.

"Stand up." He pulled on her cuff, digging it into her wrist, and the pain of it forced her to comply. She tried to conceal the rock behind her back as she stood, and he shook his head. "Seriously, you don't think I know you by now. Drop the rock."

They were in a standoff as she glared back at him. He pulled out his other hand that had been tucked in his pocket. "Check and mate." He gripped a green oval in his palm. *The missing grenade.* He put his hand in front of her, and she could see his index finger firmly stuck in the ring. "Grenade beats rock."

She released the rock. "What do you want?" she croaked out.

"You're going to help me figure out the map."

"What are you talking about? What map?"

"Webb's secret room, the map on the wall." Danny jerked on her cuffed hand, as he reached into his pocket and pulled out his phone. His thumb glided across the screen, as he navigated it and then held out the phone to Elizabeth. She could see the photo she had taken of the hand drawn map that hid the Booth papers.

"You can't be serious."

"Deadly," he said, caressing his thumb across the grenade for show.

She never gave much thought to the map and wasn't even convinced it was a map. "Assuming you're right, what do you expect to find with a hundred-and-fifty-year-old map? Some long lost Confederate gold?" Her voice rose as she spoke. "Seriously? This is all about some silly legend?" At this point, she was yelling and flailing their joined hands.

"Well, the Confederate gold would be a bonus," he replied in an even tone, unfazed by her tantrum.

She took in a sharp breath and mentally scolded herself when it hit her. "How could I be so dense? The money from the bank robbery is still here. It was assumed that they laundered it through some offshore account right after, but what better way for Webb to turn the tables and gain the respect and power he thought he deserved than by hiding the money instead. Then Senator Powers and the others in the group would be at his mercy. That explains why they didn't want the property sold." She was talking more to herself at this point. She looked at Danny. "I take it that Reverend Rick didn't put much stock in the theory that the money was on this property."

"He should have listened."

"Danny, you didn't." He refused to make eye contact. "Oh, Danny, no. Olivia, did you kill her too?" His silence and continued refusal to look at her answered her loud and clear.

"Oh God, why? What…who?" She wasn't even sure what she was trying to ask at that point. "I need to sit down." She turned to a fallen tree a few yards away, and Danny capitulated, allowing her to lead. She sank down onto the log and cradled her head in her hands. The murders made more sense in retrospect. They were hasty, with no common theme, indicating inexperience and improvisation. The knife and gun were weapons of convenience. She understood the killing of Reverend Rick; he had gone rogue and had become a liability, much like Webb, but Olivia, how did they know about her? "How did you know Olivia came back?"

"There were two people that stood between Powers and the nomination."

"Margaret and Olivia." Margaret, she was easy to find, even Olivia did that. "He raped Margaret." Danny nodded in confirmation. "But she couldn't identify him."

"No, but Olivia could. It was only a matter of time after the nomination was announced that she would come back looking for her. And she had the tape."

She knew that tape would be damning and figured Mrs. Francis was only spared because they believed Olivia had possession of it. "So you were staking out, waiting for her to come back?"

"They've advanced since the sixties and are a bit more high-tech."

"You tapped her phone. Is that how you knew Mrs. Francis was coming to my office that morning?"

"Leave nothing to chance. Now, I've given you enough. Let's go." He stood, pulling her up, and she didn't resist. She had momentarily forgotten the threat he posed, as her mind still filtered through the pieces of the story.

"Danny...that's not even your name is it?"

"Guess what? I'm not eighteen either."

"Who's behind this?" What she had learned about the KGC from Beadle and what she had gathered from Webb's experience with the group was that there was a hierarchy, and she knew Danny wasn't the pinnacle of that. The fact that he killed Olivia in daylight just off a major street, killed Reverend Rick with a gun that was easily traced back to the plantation, and better yet, handcuffed himself to her using a grenade as his weapon of choice, which would kill them both, proved that he wasn't the brains of the operation. He was the rank-and-file military, much like the role Webb filled, and like Webb, he was going to get himself killed. The question was whether he was going to take Elizabeth with him.

"Is this the part where I'm supposed to confess everything and give you all the names?" he asked.

As far as the confessing part, Danny pretty much did that already. He filled in all the missing pieces, except for the names. How many more of them were there? Who was the person pulling the strings? What was he called? *The captain, that was the title. Who was he?*

He shoved the phone back at her, forcing her to take it. "All right, do your thing. Figure this out."

"Have you considered using a metal detector? There is likely to be gold or silver as part of this stash."

"You think I'm that stupid?"

Elizabeth decided to take the Fifth on that question out of deference for her own well-being.

"They've scanned every inch of this property by the best metal detectors at least twice," he said.

They. Always the pronoun, never the name. "I hate to state the obvious, but...if it hasn't been found by now, then it isn't here."

"Oh no, it's here."

"How can you be so sure?"

"After the robbery, Webb brought the money here, and when he refused to turn it over, he was surveilled. He never left the property with the money. You can't just walk out with ten million dollars without being noticed."

Elizabeth wasn't sure what to think. If Danny's version was to be believed, then the money was still on the property, but after fifty years of searching, it was nowhere to be found. "What makes you think that this map has anything to do with the missing money?"

"Because that is a KGC map of the Confederate gold. Webb found the gold." In answer to her questioning look, he continued, "Webb wasn't so bright. He sold several coins when he needed money."

So it wasn't the payments from the KGC that got his property out of hock, but the Confederate gold that she swore didn't exist.

"Wherever the rest of that gold is, that's where we'll find the money," Danny said emphatically.

She was going to have to take his word for it because she didn't know what to think, as well as the fact that he held the grenade. Continuing to dispute it seemed futile and dangerous, but she did have one question. "If you are so sure *this* map leads to the money, then why don't you have the money?"

Danny kicked at some leaves. "Because I can't read it, and I can't go back without the money."

That was another tidbit of information that she filed away. Danny wasn't in their good graces. She assumed it had a lot to do with the work she and Grace did in campaigning against Judge Powers's nomination. If she learned anything from the fates of Booth and Webb, the rank and file of the KGC could become expendable quickly. She returned her eyes to the phone and began assessing the map. She didn't give a damn about helping Danny or finding the money, but it seemed that this was the only way she was getting out of the situation alive.

The map didn't appear to be anything more than a series of lines, figures, and shapes of squares, triangles, and circles of various sizes. They looked haphazardly drawn and didn't resemble any structure or landmark on the property that she could see. Solid lines were going in various directions across the page and some in the shape of an arc, and there appeared to be no logical order. There were small triangles, circles, and parallel lines clustered together throughout, while several medium sized circles had v-shaped carets on their circumference. As she stared at it, she did note a pattern—the circles with the carets appeared only at one end of each of the solid lines. On the left side of the page were the three crudely drawn suns with dotted lines connecting them, depicting the path of a setting sun, the same path her fingers followed to find the Booth papers.

Danny leaned in for a view of the screen. "Well?"

She shuddered as his breath tickled her ear. "You...they," she fumbled out, "have been studying this map for how long? And you expect me to crack it in five minutes?"

"You're the one who pieced together the damn map in the purse."

"*That* was a map, *this* is a bunch of nonsense." Just as the words came out of her mouth it hit her. "Wait, it isn't supposed to make sense. Just like the book we found at Samuel's grave. You need the key to decipher the code. Like the book, the map is useless without its key."

"So, the next obvious question is where's the key?"

Elizabeth closed her eyes in an attempt to clear the clutter in her head and momentarily erase Danny from her view. Webb had already deciphered the map, so the key was on the property. The question was whether Webb kept it because he no longer needed it once he found the gold. She opened her eyes and stared at the map. He did keep the key. *Just remember to follow the setting sun.* Those were Samuel's words. The Booth papers were with the map for a reason.

"I think the key is in the Booth papers, but I don't have the copy of the papers with me. If you had only warned me that you were going to kidnap me using handcuffs and a grenade, I would have come better prepared."

"You have a picture of it on your phone."

"Yes, but, hating to state the obvious…"

Danny stuck his free hand in his pocket and pulled out her phone.

She snatched it. Messing with her phone was going too far. "Really? What else did you steal?"

He stuck his hand in his pocket again and pulled out a crumpled paper. "This." It was the note that she left on Amy's desk when they left the clinic. As he crunched it into a ball in his fist, so went her last hope that anyone would learn where she was.

Grace walked through the front door of the clinic, endorphins still pumping through her veins. The last several days had been exhausting and endless, but today was a good day, better than that, a great day. Powers's nomination was defeated by twelve votes, a larger margin than either she or Senator McDermott had hoped for, even in their most optimistic scenario, a likely backlash effect from the assassination attempt. Those on the fence voted in solidarity with their colleague, and a ripple effect formed once the "no" votes started. She hoped that some of those votes were not just for self-preservation of their careers if the Powers scandal broke open, but that some of the senators actually cared. There was no better way to end this day than to spend it with the woman who made it possible. Using Jack's phone, she had called Elizabeth before she left the state capitol to break the news, but it went directly to voice mail. Now she wanted nothing more than to hold her and whisper in her ear luscious words that she would make true later that night. It made her tingle at the thought.

She stopped at Amy's desk to acknowledge her and ask for permission to pass through, not that she expected Amy to deny her access, but the look on Amy's face set off an alarm. "What's wrong?"

"I...I'm not sure. This came in the mail." She handed over a paper, and Grace nearly snatched it. It was a letter from the Social Security Office advising SILC that there was an error in their payroll records because there was no match between the name Daniel Johnson and the provided Social Security number.

She felt relief. She thought there was a problem with Elizabeth and not an employee issue. "Does Danny know? He's a kid and probably gave you the wrong number."

"Danny's the one who opened it. I found it sticking out in his trash. And now he's not here and neither is Elizabeth. I don't know where they went. They've been gone for more than two hours with no word."

The hair on the back of her neck stood up. She knew in that moment it was Danny, and she chastised herself for not seeing it earlier—his sudden arrival at the outset of the case and his involvement in every aspect. She failed Elizabeth. *Oh dear God, I should have been here protecting her.* "We have to find them. Call her." Her voice shook, and she didn't even attempt to hide her fear.

"I've called her and Danny, many times. It just keeps going to voice mail."

"Call her again."

Amy complied and after a few moments shook her head. "It's her voice mail again."

"Fuck!"

"I tried calling you, but I couldn't reach you either."

Grace pounded her fist on the doorjamb as she passed it, heading for Elizabeth's office. She paid no attention to the pain that radiated through her hand at the impact.

"Oh, Grace, is Elizabeth with you?" Elizabeth's mother asked as she approached her and clutched her arm.

"No." Grace wanted to cry. Any semblance of hope that she was clinging to that this was all a misunderstanding unraveled the minute she saw Beatrice Campbell's face.

She walked into Elizabeth's office and sat in BD. Elizabeth's mother and Amy sat in the chairs opposite her, looking at her for a plan of action. Elizabeth was missing and she had to find her.

"Did she say anything about what she was doing today?" Grace asked.

"No. She was just pacing around, waiting for the results of the judicial nomination, and then she was just gone. No one saw her or Danny leave," Amy said, her hands tightly gripped in the prayer position at her chest.

Grace noticed Elizabeth's computer light and moved the mouse, and the screen lit up. "She left her computer on." She zoomed out the map on the screen and realized that she was looking at the White Horse Plantation. "They went to the plantation."

Elizabeth enlarged the picture of a Booth page on her phone, which depicted a drawing of the White Horse Plantation. She could see the white horse statue in the center of the drive, the antebellum home in its prime, and the surrounding plantation in full bloom. Below the picture, Elizabeth studied the caption still in code, but she was now in a better position to decipher its meaning. She had already discovered that K was the letter to be matched with A from her earlier review of the document. Drawing in the dirt with a stick, she reorganized the alphabet putting K as the new A. "Danny, type these letters in your phone." After reading off the decoded letters, she took his phone to read the message. "Where the sun meets the steed, then follow KGC." She repeated it aloud a few times, before returning to the map and pointing to the corner of it. "See the setting sun, here. It stops next to this picture." The small drawing next to the last sun consisted of two congruent circles side by side with two triangles on top of each circle. "We start here."

Danny huffed and threw up his arms, taking Elizabeth's arm with him, and she eyed the grenade in his hand, concerned by his movement. "Where the hell is that supposed to be? I don't see any circles or triangles around here."

"Relax will you. Put your phone on top of mine, so I can see the two together." She squinted, as she studied them. "See here, the bottom left corner on the map, the circle and triangles are next to the setting sun, which would be the west, and on the Booth drawing in that same corner, there is the white horse statue that is in the driveway, which is also in the west." She pointed in the direction as she spoke. "There's the steed."

Danny stared at her with a blank look.

"A steed is a horse, Danny, or whatever the hell your name is."

"All right then, let's go."

"Hold up. First things first. Put that grenade back in your pocket. The last thing we need is for you to drop it."

"Nice try."

"We are handcuffed together. Where do you think I'm going to go?" He shook his head. "Not a negotiation. You want my help, that goes back in your pocket."

He finally conceded and redeposited the explosive into his jacket and pulled out his hand in a show that it was empty.

"Oh and, Danny." She waited until he turned to her, cocked her arm back, and delivered a blow across his face with her closed fist, causing him to stumble, and she teetered with him. "That was for shooting Grace." Blood began streaming down his nose, and he made no effort to proclaim his innocence. She figured it had to be him, given the stolen gun from an off-duty officer, another idiotic move, which seemed to be his signature.

She wanted to raise the topic earlier, when they addressed Reverend Rick and Olivia, but she feared her own temper in combination with the grenade in his hand. She knew it was still a risk with the grenade only slightly more secure, but she couldn't resist. It felt good.

She glared at him, daring him to fight back, and he wiped his nose on his sleeve and began walking in the direction of the home.

They remained silent, until they stood at the front of the white horse statue.

"Now what?" he asked in a subdued tone.

"Look for any writings, drawings, or anomalies. It won't be obvious."

They each searched the statue starting from its head and slowly worked their way around, feeling with their hands as they went.

"There's nothing. I think you're wrong. It's not the statue."

She looked at the map again and looked below the horse. "Look under the horse," she chuckled. She pointed to the two circles on the map and then to the prominent testicles.

He ducked his head. "I don't see anything."

"Use your hand."

"I'm not touching it."

"Oh Jesus, it's not real." She nudged him to the side and knelt down. "Take this." She handed him her phone and used her free hand to caress the horse's private parts. *This is a new low. I'm feeling a horse's scrotum.* "I feel something." She scrunched herself below the horse for a better view. *Somebody clearly had a sense of humor.* "It's one of the markings from the map." She pulled herself out and gestured for Danny's phone. "It's this marking," she said, pointing to a circle with the v caret surrounding the circumference.

"But there are a couple of those. How do we know which one?"

"There was an arrow pointing straight ahead, so it's this one on top of the map." She tapped it. "See? It's in a direct line with the circles and triangles symbol."

They carried on searching trees, rocks, and structures, looking for any extraneous marks or drawing.

"This could be anywhere," Danny finally said in exasperation, after they walked a straight path for several minutes.

"Give me back my phone." After Danny complied, she compared the two maps. "These maps depict the same area, so it would be here on the Booth drawing." She pointed to the drawing near the edge of an open field, where it met the tree line. "It should be up ahead." The fields were now overgrown and looked nothing like the Booth rendition, but she could still tell where the field's edge used to be in comparison to the forest.

Danny didn't argue with her and allowed her to lead. Once at the tree line, they meticulously scanned the tree trunks.

"It's here," Danny said with excitement.

Below the circle symbol carved in the tree, there was a single triangle with several lines sticking out from the three sides of the shape. She consulted the map, and there was one triangle that resembled it, which was back in the direction that they just traveled.

"So now we go back?" Danny said incredulously, taking out his irritation on her.

"This is your idea. I'm happy to call it a day."

In response, Danny took several long strides in the direction from which they came, pulling her along.

"Hold up." Over the door of a wooden shed, she spotted an artistically carved triangle with a sun in its middle and its rays extending beyond the boundaries of the triangle. "There's the triangle with the lines extending out." Etched into the bottom of one of the doors, they found the next symbol, a square with a triangle on top, resembling a crude drawing of a house. Following their same method, they located the symbol carved on a small rock wall that separated the driveway from an overgrown grass area that was approximately twenty-five yards from where they started at the horse statue, and they were again instructed to turn back and return in the direction they just came from.

After two more locations, they found themselves standing in the same vicinity of the second symbol on their journey and stopped to analyze the map and Booth drawing. They were going nowhere, except back and forth over the same area. Elizabeth focused her attention again on the caption below the Booth drawing. *Where the sun meets the steed, then follow KGC.* She looked back at the map and traced her finger over the path they walked and realized that there was a method to the madness. It was the letter "K", which explained why they backtracked part of the way, just as the letter would require if written. The circles with the v carets were basically roundabouts in which they would return back the same direction.

Once she figured that out, it became easier to navigate the remainder of the clues, and she was able to skip several of the points as they traced the letters "G" and "C" across the property, only having to retrace their steps once because one of the clues seemed to no longer exist. As they closed in on their final symbol of a circle below a solid line that resembled an exclamation point, which she found fitting, Elizabeth could see the yellow police tape surrounding two pits in the slave cemetery. However, the symbol wasn't the cemetery. If it was to be lined up with the base of the K and G, then it was just short of it. She knew that there was only one thing of note in that area—the box.

She brought Danny over to it and attempted to lift the cover. "A little help here."

With their synchronized movement, the cover fell to the ground, and Danny peered inside.

"I can tell you from personal experience that there is nothing inside. It's all cement, even the bottom."

"Maybe it's beneath the cement."

Shaking her head at the implausibility, Elizabeth explained that she found Margaret's sweater at the bottom of the hole, and according to Mrs. Francis, her abduction occurred about a year before the bank heist. If Webb had buried the money at the bottom, then the sweater wouldn't have still been down there. "If there really was Confederate gold, that is where he probably found it and then moved it somewhere else. Wherever you find the Confederate gold, you will find the bank money."

"Why should I believe you?" Danny asked, making no attempt to hide his distress.

"You've been part of this from the beginning. I told you about the sweater when I found it. You've seen it yourself."

A string of expletives flew from his mouth, and without warning, he dropped to the ground, bringing Elizabeth down with him. He leaned over the side of the hole. She nervously eyed his jacket. "Can you please be a little less erratic? You do have a grenade in your pocket."

He seemed to ignore her as he studied the inside of the hole. After several moments, he pushed himself back up, more expletives spilling from his mouth, and began to pound his hands on his head. "I need that damn money." His unraveling concerned her deeply. Before, she thought she had him under control, but now she was chained to a desperate, cornered animal. She guessed the money was going to be his only savior.

In a frenzy, he whipped around facing the home, on heightened alert. "What was that?"

She tried to keep her voice calm in hopes of settling him. "I didn't hear anything," and just as she said it, she saw several figures emerging out of the tree tunnel. Even from the distance, she recognized one of them. As if she sensed her, Grace began heading in their direction with her long strides, a gun at the ready in one hand, while several uniformed officers fanned out on both sides.

Danny ducked behind Elizabeth and grabbed her around the waist, pulling them both back and chanting "fuck" in the process. "They're not getting me, not unless they get you first." He had pulled the grenade back out, and it was now snuggled into her chest. "Take it." She fumbled trying to grab it with her hand joined to his and snagged her finger through his braided rope bracelet in her haste. She felt the metal key woven into the bracelet cutting into the inside of her wrist, but didn't lessen her grip. Danny kept his finger in the metal ring. "One wrong step or you drop it, the ring gets pulled."

Now she was the one chanting "fuck."

When Grace and the other officers were at the edge of the slave quarters, he shouted, "Stop right there or she dies."

She could hear one of the officers yell "grenade," and Grace froze along with the other officers.

"This is how this is going to work," Danny shouted. "All of you are going back the way you came, get in your cars, and leave. No helicopters, no more backup. If you fuck with me, I pull this ring and Elizabeth dies."

Grace's stare never wavered, but she could see her fist opening and closing as he spoke. She holstered her gun and raised her hands in a gesture of submission. The other officers followed suit, and the group began backing away, but Grace refused to turn her back, until she was no longer in sight.

With the group no longer in view, Danny began pushing her toward the forest. "Danny, we can't keep walking like this." She gestured toward the grenade they continued to jointly hold. "One of us is going to drop it." He took it with his free hand, and she yanked her hand away. With her finger still caught in the bracelet, the bracelet snapped, and she winced at the pain, but it was quickly forgotten as he was again off, forcing Elizabeth to keep up with his near running pace. She doubted he knew where he was going. It seemed his only plan was to go in the opposite direction of the police.

After several minutes of dodging trees and underbrush, Danny came to a sudden halt, causing her to stumble and fall to her knees. He tilted and bobbled the grenade slightly, and she closed her eyes in anticipation. When nothing happened, she opened her eyes again and saw another set of hands cradling below Danny's, prepared to swoop in if he lost his grip on the grenade. She followed her eyes up to the figure standing in front of them.

"You're gonna drop that, son."

She exhaled. "Samuel." She wasn't sure if she was hallucinating from her near-death experience, or she was already dead and Samuel came to take her.

"I told you guys to back off," Danny snapped. Either she and Danny were having the same delusion or Samuel was in fact standing in front of them.

"I don't wanna hurt you, son. I'm just here to help," Samuel said in his smooth, soothing voice.

"I'm not your son. Get out of my way."

Samuel stepped back and motioned for Elizabeth to stand. "You need to let her go."

"Fuck you."

Samuel was unfazed. "The police, they're everywhere out there. Your only hope is to head out in that direction." He pointed deeper into the trees. "There's a stream 'bout two hundred yards in. Follow it up and bear east when you get to the top of the ridge.

They won't follow you there." Danny stared at him intently, clearly contemplating this option. "But I assure you, you won't make it with her attached to you like that. She's just gonna slow you down."

Danny shifted from foot to foot and furtively looked around. The sound of distant voices echoed through the trees, causing him to jerk, and Samuel placed his hand under the grenade, in the ready again, in case Danny lost his hold. In an unexpected move, Danny switched the grenade into his handcuffed hand, jammed his other hand into his pant pocket, and roughly pushed a key into Elizabeth's palm. Her hands were sweaty, and she fumbled with it, trying to undo the lock.

While she struggled, Danny never looked away from Samuel. "You know where the money is."

Samuel simply nodded.

"Where?"

"Under the wishing stair."

Any reply Danny had was cutoff when the tight metal cuff released its hold and she was free. Danny ran in the direction Samuel suggested. She saw the ditch, but Danny didn't.

"Get down," Samuel yelled to her, and she dove for the ground to avoid flying rocks and debris.

Panic ripped through Grace as the echo of an explosion filled the air. She ran toward the center of the eruption, stumbling on the uneven ground, but refusing to give up her hastened pace. The reverberation of a scream pierced her ears, and only when it stopped, did she realize the sound tore from her own throat. She ran past the cemetery and darted through the trees, searching. Her foot caught on an exposed root, sending her to the ground, but she sprang up and carried on without care for her own well-being. *Where is she?* "Elizabeth!"

She stopped and turned in a circle, frantically scanning the area for any signs of life. She cursed her panting breath and pounding heart, as it drowned out any subtle sounds the forest offered.

"Elizabeth!" *God, please answer me.* Movement on her left drew her attention and she ran again, nearly diving to the ground when she saw her. She crawled the final distance to Elizabeth's prone body. "Baby, I'm here."

She cradled her. Bloody cuts covered Elizabeth's arms. Her eyes opened, and she stared back, stunned and lost. "I've got you. You're going to be okay," Grace whispered as she rocked her.

"Sssamuel," Elizabeth lisped out.

Several of the officers soon caught up and hovered over. "Get an ambulance."

Elizabeth pushed herself up and looked toward the epicenter before turning away and burying her head into Grace's shoulder to avoid the grisly scene.

Grace stood at the edge of the forest line, impatiently barking out orders to the officers processing the scene. Danny's body was now concealed by a blue tarp, awaiting the arrival of the coroner. She was glad he was dead. She would have killed him herself, had she had the opportunity. She stood on the line between the forest and the plantation property so that she could keep an eye on Elizabeth, who was sitting on the steps of one of the slave quarters, the same step they both occupied after discovering the items at Samuel's grave. Elizabeth repeated his name several times after she found her. She watched as paramedics finished cleaning the cuts on Elizabeth's arms. She should have been more seriously injured. Grace couldn't explain any of it, but she believed in Samuel and knew she could never repay the debt she owed him.

Elizabeth patiently sat as the paramedics attended to her cuts. She tried to assure them that she was fine, nothing that a good shower couldn't take care of, but they weren't persuaded and continued to tend to her. She suspected that Grace had something to do with their attentiveness. She toyed with Danny's broken rope bracelet that rested across her knee, and she couldn't remember how she came to possess it. The archaic metal key that was woven into the bracelet left an imprint on the inside of her wrist when their hands jointly held the grenade. The whole event was surreal. She missed so many clues about him because she just wasn't looking, but in hindsight it all made sense. The only unanswered question was who was pulling the strings?

From the corner of her eye, she saw Grace continuing to stand guard at the edge of the property and a sense of giddiness filled her. She knew that she should probably be feeling shock at Danny's betrayal or remorse at his death, but she couldn't help her feelings. It was over. A huge weight that had been oppressing her for the last two months had been lifted. The case could finally be put to rest, and there were no more impediments that stood between them.

As the paramedics packed up, Grace headed over. She didn't want her to be alone, and Elizabeth smiled at her as she approached. How could she be smiling? Grace was still in turmoil over the ordeal, knowing that there was a very different way this day could have ended, but she wouldn't delve too deeply into that thought; she just couldn't. Her throat locked as she attempted to swallow.

She took the seat next to her and turned to Elizabeth. "Marry me?" The question came out without forethought, an uncharacteristic trait for Grace, but there was no regret.

"What?"

"I know what I feel, and I'm not wasting another day. I nearly lost you."

Elizabeth looked at her with an expression that seemed to be a cross between confusion and shock. "Wow, I..." She turned her eyes to the open plantation field before returning them to Grace, and a smile crept over her face. "Yes."

Grace leaned in and kissed her, gently at first, mindful of her injuries, but the sense of urgency ruled reason, and it deepened to a passionate, sensual kiss. She didn't give a damn who watched.

When they finally parted, Elizabeth looked back with carnal eyes. "My only condition is that you do that every day," she breathed out.

Grace felt much lighter, and a bit wetter.

"Excuse me, Detective Donovan."

She turned to the asshole that broke the moment. "What!"

"The, um, uh, coroner is here." The officer stumbled away.

Realizing the poor timing of her proposal, she took a breath to center herself. "We should be finished up soon, but there are a couple of questions," Grace said in the form of an apology. She hated shifting gears, but she was desperate to get it over with, so they could get the hell out of there and carry out the rest of what she planned in private.

"What was Danny's motive?" Elizabeth asked for her. She explained what she learned from Danny and her adventure with the KGC map and Booth drawing, which led them back and forth across the plantation. "In the end, there was neither the bank money nor the gold."

"It's probably long gone by now."

"No, just before Danny...you know, Samuel said it was under the wishing stair."

Grace gave a questioning look, unsure if Elizabeth was suffering from delayed trauma. "What wishing star?"

"Wishing stair," Elizabeth corrected her, patting the step between them. "I met Samuel for the first time right here, while I stood on this step. When it squeaked, he told me that a squeaking stair is a lucky stair, and I had to make a wish. This is the wishing stair."

Grace cocked her head. "Did you make a wish?"

"I did," Elizabeth said, smiling. "And it just came true."

Grace leaned in for a kiss before returning to business. "So you're telling me the money is underneath this slave quarters?"

"Yes. See all the corrugated iron sheets surrounding the structure? They served not only to protect the integrity of the dilapidated home, but shielded its discovery from a metal detector."

Grace felt a rise of adrenaline, and a small shiver traveled through her. "This is incredible."

"I know, isn't it," Elizabeth said, caressing the stair.

"Not the money." Elizabeth looked at her in confusion. "I just asked you to marry me, and you said yes."

Another kiss was in order, and they took their time and no one dared to intervene.

CHAPTER THIRTY-THREE

Elizabeth stood at the back of the line of students outside Professor Dixon's office door, waiting for the usual throng to dissipate. She used the time to reflect on the last few days. True to Samuel's word, the bank heist money was found beneath the slave quarters, every dime, although the hype of the KGC gold was overplayed. There was only a few thousand dollars of the legendary gold recovered. But what pleased Elizabeth the most was having the case against Jackson dismissed, much to the dismay of ADA Wilcox, who in his usual form, insisted that all the events were irrelevant to the prosecution. Fortunately, his supervisor didn't agree. However, for the Francis family, she knew that this was only the beginning. They would need time for healing and forgiveness.

There was only one matter left unsettled. Two days after Danny's death, the tape had finally been restored. There were no surprises. It was a surreptitious recording of a conversation between Webb and a young Davis Powers, who was doing the bidding of his father. They discussed the most recent name entries in the intel report, the manner in which they were to disappear, and preliminary plans for the bank heist that would fund the group's ambitious agenda moving forward. It was expected that it would spread from Southern state to Southern state, until the South once again had restored segregation. It was a ludicrous plan.

At that moment, Judge Powers was being questioned by the FBI, and although damning, it was unclear whether the tape alone would be enough to indict, given the passage of time and legal evidentiary hurdles. However, it was certain that Judge Powers's career would be over, and Elizabeth would take her victories where she could.

As the last student filed out of the office, Professor Dixon turned her attention to Elizabeth standing in the doorway. "Ms. Campbell, pleasure to see you again. Perhaps you should enroll in my course."

She offered a polite smile and sat in the seat she previously occupied on her last visit. "I apologize for disturbing you, Professor, but I just had a few more questions about DARA." She had scoured the bill a second time after the restoration of the tape, looking for any missed clues that might link the judge to the authorship of the bill.

"I'm not sure what more I can tell you, but I will do my best," the professor said as she started to assemble a collection of student papers that were scattered on the desk.

"The bill has a lengthy introduction that reads more like a preemptive legal defense, as though its authors knew that it would be subject to court scrutiny. I researched the two senators who authored the bill, and they're no legal scholars. They aren't even lawyers. They had help."

Professor Dixon leaned forward, resting her chin on her clasped hands. Elizabeth had her interest.

"When I came to speak to your class," Elizabeth continued as she pulled a folded paper from her coat pocket. "One of the topics discussed was on the evolution of the interpretation of the Constitution. You asked which approach was appropriate in interpreting the Constitution—strict or loose construction.

"Yes, I throw that question out to my class every year."

"It wasn't really the question that you asked, but what you said at the beginning of that discussion that had me thinking." She opened the paper in her hand and read, "The Founding Fathers gave us a Constitution of checks and balances because they realized the inescapable lesson of history that no man or group of men can be safely entrusted with unlimited power."

"Yes," the professor said patiently, waiting for Elizabeth's question.

"But there was more to that passage." Elizabeth returned her eyes to the page and continued reading. "Though there has been no constitutional amendment or act of Congress, the Supreme Court can exercise their naked judicial power and substitute their personal political and social ideals for the established law of the land. We decry the Supreme Court's encroachments on rights reserved to the states and to the people, contrary to established law and to the Constitution."

"So, what is your question?" The professor was no longer smiling.

What was my question? "I guess my question is whether Danny ever really had a choice?"

Professor Dixon jolted backward, as though she was physically assaulted. As with Danny, the professor's sudden interest and appearance in Elizabeth's life was not by chance. "Those words you used in class were part of the larger passage from the Southern Manifesto. That passage, in its entirety, appeared in the preamble of the bill, as a preemptive argument as to why the courts didn't have jurisdiction under the Tenth Amendment to review the constructs of the bill." Elizabeth held up the paper that was the first page of the bill. "And, Professor, next time, cite the work that you quote."

Elizabeth only recognized the passage because she remembered Danny reading it in Webb's library at the plantation. It wasn't a coincidence that he pulled out the Southern Manifesto from the bookshelf. It was a document he knew well.

She pulled out Danny's rainbow colored bracelet and twisted it in her fingers. Danny's true identity couldn't be ascertained, despite Grace's diligent efforts. All unidentified calls on his phone were to a throwaway cell phone, and there was nothing personal in his apartment to shed any clues. "You put your doctrine in front of your son," Elizabeth said as she laid the bracelet across the papers that Professor Dixon neatly stacked, with the metal key that Danny managed to weave into it facing up. Although they couldn't ascertain Danny's identity, they did learn that Professor Dixon had a son, her only child.

"I don't know what you're talking about," Professor Dixon said, her warm and open demeanor replaced with cool aloofness.

Elizabeth rubbed her thumb across the inside of her wrist where the key cut into her. "That was Danny's bracelet." She probably wouldn't have noticed the design on the head of the key, as it had been worn down with age, except that its imprint was cut into her skin and it still showed, a checkered pattern with a triangle in the middle—the symbol of the suffragist movement. Elizabeth tapped the bracelet before standing and moving to the bookshelf behind her. She turned the music box to its side to expose the small hole, where the turnkey was missing. "Your missing key."

His mother essentially set him up to die, yet Danny carried a memento of her with him. She guessed all he ever really wanted was her acceptance.

"My son," she nearly snarled. "He was a disappointment. He never did anything right. He even thought he was gay," she spat. Danny didn't lie to Elizabeth about that part.

No remorse, even in his death. He never stood a chance. "He was your son, not just one of your soldiers, Captain." Elizabeth emphasized the last word.

Professor Dixon smirked. "I don't know what you're talking about."

Grace stepped into the room with two officers. She guessed Grace had heard enough. "Elena Dixon, you have the right to remain silent..."

"I know my rights. I teach them every day," she said as one of the officers resumed administering the *Miranda* rights, while escorting her out of the room.

Once alone, Grace pulled Elizabeth close and removed the microphone hidden in the breast pocket of her jacket. "Nice work."

"There isn't enough there to hold her accountable for any of it."

"Probably not, but she's been exposed."

"It won't stop them. We don't know who or how many there really are. There will be another to take her place, and then another."

"One fight at a time."

Elizabeth leaned in and kissed her, savoring the woman she was going to marry. For once, they had nowhere to be, and she was going to relish the moment...until the phone in her pocket vibrated.

Grace pulled back, and Elizabeth yanked out the phone. "A text from my mom."

"She texts too?"

"Uh-huh, and look, she sent a picture of a wedding dress." She handed the phone to Grace.

Grace turned it around in different directions, trying to gain a new, and hopefully better, perspective of the picture. She looked distressed. "Well, um, I'm sure it will look fine on you, honey."

"Oh no, it's not for me," Elizabeth said, making no attempt to hide her smirk. "It's for you."

"Oh hell no! We're eloping."

About the Author

A. Rose Mathieu has been a practicing attorney in California for more than twenty years and finds her most rewarding work to be working with underserved populations. By challenging laws and bringing suits for those with too small of a voice, she has changed legislation for the better. She has always enjoyed writing as an outlet, particularly crafting mysteries with comic relief. Her first try at writing began in fifth grade with a short story that won her the top award in the state. To fulfill her mother's dream of seeing her write, A. Rose picked up the pen again and began to write novels incorporating her expertise in the field of law.

A. Rose Mathieu is on Facebook at https://www.facebook.com/arose.mathieu and Goodreads at https://www.goodreads.com/user/show/65518293-a-rose-mathieu

Books Available from Bold Strokes Books

Captive by Donna K. Ford. To escape a human trafficking ring, Greyson Cooper and Olivia Danner become players in a game of deceit and violence. Will their love stand a chance? (978-1-63555-215-7)

Crossing the Line by CF Frizzell. The Mob discovers a nemesis within its ranks, and in the ultimate retaliation, draws Stick McLaughlin from anonymity by threatening everything she holds dear. (978-1-63555-161-7)

Love's Verdict by Carsen Taite. Attorneys Landon Holt and Carly Pachett want the exact same thing: the only open partnership spot at their prestigious criminal defense firm. But will they compromise their careers for love? (978-1-63555-042-9)

Precipice of Doubt by Mardi Alexander & Laurie Eichler. Can Cole Jameson resist her attraction to her boss, veterinarian Jodi Bowman, or will she risk a workplace romance and her heart? (978-1-63555-128-0)

Savage Horizons by CJ Birch. Captain Jordan Kellow's feelings for Lt. Ali Ash have her past and future colliding, setting in motion a series of events that strands her crew in an unknown galaxy thousands of light years from home. (978-1-63555-250-8)

Secrets of the Last Castle by A. Rose Mathieu. When Elizabeth Campbell represents a young man accused of murdering an elderly woman, her investigation leads to an abandoned plantation that reveals many dark Southern secrets. (978-1-63555-240-9)

Take Your Time by VK Powell. A neurotic parrot brings police officer Grace Booker and temporary veterinarian Dr. Dani Wingate together in the tiny town of Pine Cone, but their unexpected attraction keeps the sparks flying. (978-1-63555-130-3)

The Last Seduction by Ronica Black. When you allow true love to elude you once and you desperately regret it, are you brave enough to grab it when it comes around again? (978-1-63555-211-9)

The Shape of You by Georgia Beers. Rebecca McCall doesn't play it safe, but when sexy Spencer Thompson joins her workout class, their non-stop sparring forces her to face her ultimate challenge—a chance at love. (978-1-63555-217-1)

Exposed by MJ Williamz. The closet is no place to live if you want to find true love. (978-1-62639-989-1)

Force of Fire: Toujours a Vous by Ali Vali. Immortals Kendal and Piper welcome their new child and celebrate the defeat of an old enemy, but another ancient evil is about to awaken deep in the jungles of Costa Rica. (978-1-63555-047-4)

Holding Their Place by Kelly A. Wacker. Together Dr. Helen Connery and ambulance driver Julia March discover that goodness, love, and passion can be found in the most unlikely and even dangerous places during WWI. (978-1-63555-338-3)

Landing Zone by Erin Dutton. Can a career veteran finally discover a love stronger than even her pride? (978-1-63555-199-0)

Love at Last Call by M. Ullrich. Is balancing business, friendship, and love more than any willing woman can handle? (978-1-63555-197-6)

Pleasure Cruise by Yolanda Wallace. Spencer Collins and Amy Donovan have few things in common, but a Caribbean cruise offers both women an unexpected chance to face one of their greatest fears: falling in love. (978-1-63555-219-5)

Running Off Radar by MB Austin. Maji's plans to win Rose back are interrupted when work intrudes and duty calls her to help a SEAL team stop a Russian mobster from harvesting gold from the bottom of Sitka Sound. (978-1-63555-152-5)

Shadow of the Phoenix by Rebecca Harwell. In the final battle for the fate of Storm's Quarry, even Nadya's and Shay's powers may not be enough. (978-1-63555-181-5)

Take a Chance by D. Jackson Leigh. There's hardly a woman within fifty miles of Pine Cone that veterinarian Trip Beaumont can't charm, except for the irritating new cop, Jamie Grant, who keeps leaving parking tickets on her truck. (978-1-63555-118-1)

The Outcasts by Alexa Black. Spacebus driver Sue Jones is running from her past. When she crash-lands on a faraway world, the Outcast Kara might be her chance for redemption. (978-1-63555-242-3)

Alias by Cari Hunter. A car crash leaves a woman with no memory and no identity. Together with Detective Bronwen Pryce, she fights to uncover a truth that might just kill them both. (978-1-63555-221-8)

Death in Time by Robyn Nyx. Working in the past is hell on your future. (978-1-63555-053-5)

Hers to Protect by Nicole Disney. High school sweethearts Kaia and Adrienne will have to see past their differences and survive the vengeance of a brutal gang if they want to be together. (978-1-63555-229-4)

Of Echoes Born by 'Nathan Burgoine. A collection of queer fantasy short stories set in Canada from Lambda Literary Award finalist 'Nathan Burgoine. (978-1-63555-096-2)

Perfect Little Worlds by Clifford Mae Henderson. Lucy can't hold the secret any longer. Twenty-six years ago, her sister did the unthinkable. (978-1-63555-164-8)

Room Service by Fiona Riley. Interior designer Olivia likes stability, but when work brings footloose Savannah into her world and into a new city every month, Olivia must decide if what makes her comfortable is what makes her happy. (978-1-63555-120-4)

Sparks Like Ours by Melissa Brayden. Professional surfers Gia Malone and Elle Britton can't deny their chemistry on and off the beach. But only one can win... (978-1-63555-016-0)

Take My Hand by Missouri Vaun. River Hemsworth arrives in Georgia intent on escaping quickly, but when she crashes her Mercedes into the Clip 'n Curl, sexy Clay Cahill ends up rescuing more than her car. (978-1-63555-104-4)

The Last Time I Saw Her by Kathleen Knowles. Lane Hudson only has twelve days to win back Alison's heart. That is if she can gather the courage to try. (978-1-63555-067-2)

Wayworn Lovers by Gun Brooke. Will agoraphobic composer Giselle Bonnaire and Tierney Edwards, a wandering soul who can't remain in one place for long, trust in the passionate love destiny hands them? (978-1-62639-995-2)

Breakthrough by Kris Bryant. Falling for a sexy ranger is one thing, but is the possibility of love worth giving up the career Kennedy Wells has always dreamed of? (978-1-63555-179-2)

Certain Requirements by Elinor Zimmerman. Phoenix has always kept her love of kinky submission strictly behind the bedroom door and inside the bounds of romantic relationships, until she meets Kris Andersen. (978-1-63555-195-2)

Dark Euphoria by Ronica Black. When a high-profile case drops in Detective Maria Diaz's lap, she forges ahead only to discover this case, and her main suspect, aren't like any other. (978-1-63555-141-9)

Fore Play by Julie Cannon. Executive Leigh Marshall falls hard for Peyton Broader, her golf pro...and an ex-con. Will she risk sabotaging her career for love? (978-1-63555-102-0)

Love Came Calling by CA Popovich. Can a romantic looking for a long-term, committed relationship and a jaded cynic too busy for love conquer life's struggles and find their way to what matters most? (978-1-63555-205-8)

Outside the Law by Carsen Taite. Former sweethearts Tanner Cohen and Sydney Braswell must work together on a federal task force to see justice served, but will they choose to embrace their second chance at love? (978-1-63555-039-9)

The Princess Deception by Nell Stark. When journalist Missy Duke realizes Prince Sebastian is really his twin sister Viola in disguise, she plays along, but when sparks flare between them, will the double deception doom their fairy-tale romance? (978-1-62639-979-2)

The Smell of Rain by Cameron MacElvee. Reyha Arslan, a wise and elegant woman with a tragic past, shows Chrys that there's still beauty to embrace and reason to hope despite the world's cruelty. (978-1-63555-166-2)

The Talebearer by Sheri Lewis Wohl. Liz's visions show her the faces of the lost and the killers who took their lives. As one by one, the murdered are found, a stranger works to stop Liz before the serial killer is brought to justice. (978-1-635550-126-6)

White Wings Weeping by Lesley Davis. The world is full of discord and hatred, but how much of it is just human nature when an evil with sinister intent is invading people's hearts? (978-1-63555-191-4)

A Call Away by KC Richardson. Can a businesswoman from a big city find the answers she's looking for, and possibly love, on a small-town farm? (978-1-63555-025-2)

Berlin Hungers by Justine Saracen. Can the love between an RAF woman and the wife of a Luftwaffe pilot, former enemies, survive in besieged Berlin during the aftermath of World War II? (978-1-63555-116-7)

Blend by Georgia Beers. Lindsay and Piper are like night and day. Working together won't be easy, but not falling in love might prove the hardest job of all. (978-1-63555-189-1)

Hunger for You by Jenny Frame. Principe of an ancient vampire clan Byron Debrek must save her one true love from falling into the hands of her enemies and into the middle of a vampire war. (978-1-63555-168-6)

Mercy by Michelle Larkin. FBI Special Agent Mercy Parker and psychic ex-profiler Piper Vasey learn to love again as they race to stop a man with supernatural gifts who's bent on annihilating humankind. (978-1-63555-202-7)

Pride and Porters by Charlotte Greene. Will pride and prejudice prevent these modern-day lovers from living happily ever after? (978-1-63555-158-7)

Rocks and Stars by Sam Ledel. Kyle's struggle to own who she is and what she really wants may end up landing her on the bench and without the woman of her dreams. (978-1-63555-156-3)

The Boss of Her: Office Romance Novellas by Julie Cannon, Aurora Rey, and M. Ullrich. Going to work never felt so good. Three office romance novellas from talented writers Julie Cannon, Aurora Rey, and M. Ullrich. (978-1-63555-145-7)

The Deep End by Ellie Hart. When family ties become entangled in murder and deception, it's time to find a way out... (978-1-63555-288-1)